RETRIBUTION

RETRIBUTION

KOA KĀNE HAWAIIAN MYSTERY

ROBERT McCAW

OCEANVIEW PUBLISHING

SARASOTA, FLORIDA

ISBN 978-1-60809-556-8

Published in the United States of America by Oceanview Publishing

Sarasota, Florida

www.oceanviewpub.com

10 9 8 7 6 5 4 3 2 1

PRINTED IN THE UNITED STATES OF AMERICA

*To my many friends in Hawaiʻi, who have so generously
shared their love of the geography, culture, and language
of the Island and its people with me.*

ACKNOWLEDGEMENTS

Special thanks must also go to Makela Bruno-Kidani, who has tirelessly reviewed my use of the Hawaiian language, correcting my many mistakes. Where the Hawaiian words and phrases are accurate, she deserves the credit. Any errors are entirely of my doing.

This book would not have been launched without the amazing support of my agent, Mel Parker of Mel Parker Books, LLC. His faith in my work and his tireless efforts made the publication of this story possible.

Many kudos as well to Fauzia Burke and Michelle Fitzgerald at FSB Associates who've introduced my books to so many readers.

I would also be remiss if I failed to acknowledge Pat and Bob Gussin, owners of Oceanview Publishing, who have devoted their phenomenal energies to supporting and publishing my work and that of many other aspiring mystery and thriller writers.

RETRIBUTION

CHAPTER ONE

ABOARD THE FREIGHTER *Bimi*, a bearded figure with brown skin and brutal features stared westward toward Mecca in a brief prayer. The decrepit Philippine freighter plowed down the back of a wave only to rise in a sickening corkscrew motion as it struggled up the face of the next wall of roiling water. Strong northeast winds howled around the bridge and drove heavy seas, tossing them about beneath threatening skies. Lightning crackled, thunder sounded, and driving rain pelted him. The vessel shuddered as if on the verge of coming apart.

The man hated the sea and could only hope to leave the wretched ship before it met its match and sank. He had no fear of death, but he did not want to die—couldn't die—before completing his mission. Having waited years to avenge the killing of his brother, he carried his brother's rifle, and Allah had blessed him with the means to use it. The ship lurched again, and only his dread of divine retribution kept him from calling out profanity.

Near nightfall, the winds abated, and the seas calmed. Gulls trailed the vessel, signaling the proximity of the islands to the west. They were close to the point where he would leave the freighter. *Alhamdulillah*—Praise Be To Allah.

Long after midnight, standing at the rail under a pitch-black sky, he felt the freighter's engines fade to an idle. The vessel slowed. He listened. A minute later, he heard a boat approaching in the distance. The sound grew louder, but its source remained obscured until, as if from nowhere, a dull black speedboat sidled alongside the *Bimi*. Even close up, the little craft remained nearly invisible in the darkness.

The *Bimi*'s crew, steering clear of him as they had throughout the voyage, hauled a rope ladder from a deck storage locker, secured one end to anchor points on the deck, and lowered it over the side. The crew then carried his two cases—one which held his meager personal possessions and the other, long and flat, his precious weapon—down the ladder to the boat.

The captain stepped onto the wing of the bridge and signaled. It was time. No one wished him well when he went over the side. The crew was happy to see him go, and the feeling was mutual. Too close to his objective to be thrown off by a misstep, he concentrated on the rough ropes and narrow footholds of the well-worn ladder as he lowered himself to sea level and stepped into the speedboat.

The man at the vessel's helm held a gun on him until the bearded man recited the code word. Only then did the small craft pull away from the *Bimi*, turn west, and race across the ocean toward the Big Island of Hawai'i.

CHAPTER TWO

HILO DETECTIVE MAKANUI Kaʻuhane stopped under the shade of a giant banyan tree to catch her breath after a ten-kilometer run. She ran a hand through her black hair. Day after tomorrow, she'd bike twenty miles up and down the Hawaiʻi Belt Road. Then, after a day of rest, she'd take to the ocean for a mile-long swim in Hilo Bay. She was training for her twelfth Big Island World Championship Ironman. With another month of hard training, she expected to finish once again among the top ten women, maybe even among the top five.

It was still early—before 8:00 a.m.—when her cell rang. The number on the screen told her the call came from the Honolulu Police Department. Her old boss might want to recruit her back to the Honolulu force, but more likely it was bad news. Apprehension rippled through her. Answering, she heard the deep, imposing voice of her onetime commander, head of the HPD anti-terror squad. "Makanui?" he asked.

"Yeah, Brad. It's been a long time, maybe three years, since we last spoke. You still trying to drag me back to your anti-terror fiefdom?"

"No. You know I'd love that, but that's not why I'm calling. I'm afraid I've got bad news."

"Somebody die?" she asked.

"No. It's Angelo Reyes. He escaped from prison last week."

Not just bad, but terrible news. Makanui pictured Reyes. Short and wiry, his unruly facial hair only partially covered two nasty knife scars, and his cold black eyes telegraphed utter contempt for human life. She'd never forget those eyes. Reyes had been responsible for several terrorist bombings on Oʻahu, resulting in more than a dozen deaths. As a member of the HPD anti-terror unit, Makanui had tracked him for over a year before she and the HPD SWAT team raided his hideout and took him into custody. Unfortunately, during the raid, they'd also accidentally killed his girlfriend.

Reyes declined counsel and represented himself at trial, turning the proceedings into a circus. He showed no remorse, threatening to kill the prosecutor, the judge, and half-a-dozen politicians.

Above and beyond his contempt for the judicial system, he'd displayed particular vitriol toward Makanui, whom he blamed for the "murder" of his girlfriend. After the judge sentenced him to life in prison, he'd turned toward the courtroom audience, pointed a finger at Makanui, and screamed, "I will kill you." In that moment, she'd seen barefaced evil, and it had left its mark on her psyche. She'd not the slightest doubt that he would make good on the threat if ever given a chance.

"How'd he escape?" she asked.

"The prison wardens are still trying to figure that out," Brad responded.

"And they have no idea where he is?"

"You got it. We've got units on alert, and we're checking his old associates and haunts. But as you know from your days tracking him down, he's a slippery bastard."

"Any reason to think he's coming after me?" she asked.

"Only what he said in the courtroom at his sentencing."

"Thanks for the heads-up," she responded before they disconnected.

At police headquarters later that morning, Makanui headed down the hall to share the bad news with her boss, Chief Detective Koa Kāne. In his office, Koa listened intently as Makanui explained the situation.

"How likely is he to carry out his threat against you?" he asked.

"Hard to say. Reyes would have killed me in the courtroom if he could. Five years in prison might have dimmed his anger, but I wouldn't count on it."

"Does he know you're here on the Big Island?"

"Don't know for sure, but it wouldn't be hard for him to find me."

"Does he have friends or relatives here?"

"Not sure, but I'll check."

"Right." Koa got up and moved to the window, looking out over a picturesque Hilo Bay. "We'll put out an APB, alert the TSA and airport patrols. We'll also assign a police officer to work with you," Koa said.

"I'm fine with the APB and airport surveillance, but I don't want a babysitter. It'll cramp my style, and I won't get any work done."

"You sure?"

"Yeah, I'm sure."

"You have camera surveillance around your home?"

"Cameras, motion detectors, lights. The whole works."

"Be careful. Damn careful."

"I will."

CHAPTER THREE

THE BEARDED MAN from the *Bimi* sat alone in the dilapidated barn that served as his temporary home and workshop. A Dragunov sniper rifle lay before him on a long wooden workbench. Once his brother's weapon, it was now his most treasured possession. With a fevered glow in his eyes, he stroked the barrel of the Russian rifle with the delicacy one might use to caress a lover.

After several moments, he disassembled the Dragunov, cleaning and oiling each part before reassembling it. Then, reattaching the scope, he sighted the weapon at a paper target that hung on the wall at the far end of the barn. He braced the gun against his shoulder, nestled the stock against his cheek, and put his eye to the scope. He became one with the weapon as though it were an extension of his body. The telescopic sight magnified the crude drawing of a female body he had scrawled on the paper target, but in his mind's eye, he saw a real flesh and blood woman with crosshairs centered on her heart.

She was an infidel. She had tricked and killed his brother, bringing devastation down upon him and his comrades. Because of her, he spent two years in a tiny cell isolated from everything he'd ever known. Alone, beaten, and starved, his hatred had festered until it exploded into a boiling thirst for revenge that nothing could quench.

He inhaled, let his breath out slowly, and gently squeezed the trigger until he heard the click of the firing pin in the Dragunov's empty chamber. Soon, he thought, he would feel the kick of the weapon as it sent revenge hurdling toward the object of his wrath. He smiled, short on mirth and long on grim determination.

CHAPTER FOUR

THE ALLEY WAS dark, illuminated only where the headlights and spotlights from police cars converged, lighting the area around a body. Called to the scene by the first responding officer, Koa pulled up behind one of the patrol cars and got out. He took in the surroundings. An overflowing trash bin stood to one side of the alley door of a run-down bar. Busted crates and bales of crushed cardboard boxes rested haphazardly against the opposite wall, probably from the nearby grocer. Trash lay scattered across the asphalt, and shards of shattered glass glinted in the artificial light. A grim scene on a dark night. It wasn't the first crime Koa had investigated in what Hilo police called "crime alley," and it didn't look much different than the last time he'd examined a body there.

Moving into the lighted area, he saw blood pooled beneath the body, which lay facedown with its head turned sideways. Approaching closer, he had an uncanny sense that he knew the victim. Kneeling, he pointed his Maglite at the man's face. Johnnie Nihoa, a small-time local Hawaiian thief. Koa had no doubt the man was dead but still confirmed the obvious by checking for a pulse with his gloved finger.

Koa had a history with Nihoa, having arrested the man more than once and seen him all too often in the jailhouse drunk tank. Koa had twice taken the young man aside, urging him to get his life together. Yet, both times, he'd sensed he was too late. Drugs, bad friends, and the indignities of life without family on the lowest rung of Hawaiian society had already shaped Nihoa's fate. Given the body before him on the dirty payment, he'd never forget Nihoa's last words to him: "No worry, *māka'i*. I no scared die."

Now, still in his twenties, Nihoa lay dead in a dirty back alley without anyone to mourn his passing. No one except Koa, who saw the young man as a metaphor for all the lost Hawaiian youth ill-served by their parents, schools, community, state, and country. Sure, they'd made bad choices, but the odds had been stacked sky-high against them from the moment of birth. In Nihoa's case, a drug-addled, unmarried mother along with extreme poverty made for a tough start in life.

Death was an unwelcome companion on Koa's lifelong journey. As a youngster, his father died in a horrible sugar mill accident. He found his closest childhood friend hanging from a forest tree, unable to bear the despair of being molested. At eighteen, Koa had gotten into a fight and accidentally killed his father's nemesis, escaping jail only by covering up the death as a suicide. Riddled by remorse and shame, he volunteered for the Army where in the Special Forces, he saw more death. Maybe worst of all, Jerry, his closest Army buddy, died in his arms from a sniper bullet meant for Koa during their deployment to the disastrous U.S. intervention in Somalia.

Long ago, he'd realized that death had propelled him in many ways, not the least of which was his career in the police force and his rise from a junior detective to the detective bureau chief. Death powered his guilt but also heightened his empathy. His culpability in the death of his father's tormenter informed his whole investigative approach, and his close encounters with death made him a more compassionate and perceptive officer. Having fooled the system, he was determined to avoid being outsmarted the way he'd deceived the cops who'd investigated his crime. When viewing a crime scene, he tried to think like the perpetrator. Paranoia made him look for things others didn't see and enhanced his awareness of what might be missing.

The Nihoa types he encountered on the job motivated Koa to teach canoeing to disadvantaged youth, participate in anti-drug programs, talk civics in high school classrooms, and reach out to Hawaiian kids in the lockup. Yet, all too often, his efforts failed to overcome the tragedies of their lives. Too many ended up in jail or dead from drugs or suicide. A few, like Nihoa, died a violent death, but nobody deserved that end. Koa would not let Nihoa pass unmourned, nor would he let his killer or killers escape responsibility.

As was his habit at a crime scene, Koa let his eyes scan the corpse, absorbing every detail, no matter how gruesome. He called it listening to the dead, trying to envision their last moments. It sometimes yielded important clues and always empowered Koa's empathy for the victims.

Kneeling next to Nihoa's body, Koa noted sores and bug bites covering the deceased's legs above his heavily worn sandals and below his basketball shorts. Needle tracks on his arms evidenced his drug use. A blood-splattered Sex Pistols tee shirt suggested Nihoa had been into punk music. A gold neck chain, almost certainly imitation, stretched across the back of his neck below a crest of unruly black hair.

While Koa examined the body, Georgina Pau joined him, trailed by her crime scene techs. Grandmotherly in appearance with more energy than most teenagers, she prided herself on being the best CSI technician in the state. She and Koa had worked countless felony cases together and shared enormous mutual respect. They exchanged greetings.

"Young," Georgina remarked as she knelt to view the body more closely. "Way too young to die like this."

"Yeah," Koa acknowledged.

"You ID him?"

"Johnnie Nihoa. A local kid with a long rap sheet."

Despite the blood, Koa couldn't tell what had killed Nihoa. He waited while Ronnie Woo, the police photographer, recorded the scene. When he finished, Koa and Georgina slowly turned the body, revealing multiple bloody stab wounds. Koa counted the injuries. The left arm, abdomen, chest, two vicious cuts to the neck, and a bone-deep slash from the left ear to the corner of the deceased's mouth.

"Nasty knife wounds," Georgina said. "Looks like our perp went wild."

"Looks that way," Koa responded. This was no ordinary drunken, back-alley knife fight. This killing had been personal and brutal, filled with hatred and rage. Nihoa, Koa thought, had died at the hands of an emotionally enraged killer.

Koa would wait for definitive word from the autopsy, but a quick look at Nihoa's hands revealed no injuries or broken nails. No defensive wounds. Nihoa, it appeared, had not put up a fight. Maybe he'd been drunk or high, which would square with what Koa knew about the young man's habits. Koa looked again at Nihoa's hands. Surprisingly, they were dirty but not covered with blood. Nihoa hadn't reached for his neck or his belly to staunch the flow of blood. In Koa's experience, nearly everyone fought back or tried to protect themselves. Nihoa, he speculated, must have been near comatose. He made a note to have the coroner run a tox screen.

Although blood had soaked the left pocket of Nihoa's shorts, Koa could see something protruding. He carefully fished out a small scrap of paper. There was writing on it, but he couldn't make it out, and he slipped it into an evidence bag.

A search of the victim's other pants pocket yielded four coins and a torn, fake leather wallet with two fifty-dollar bills, a five, and a single. One hundred dollars amounted to a fortune for a street urchin like Nihoa, who slept in a shelter on the best of occasions. So where, Koa wondered, had Nihoa gotten the money?

Koa found no car keys, driver's license, or credit cards but guessed that Nihoa had never owned a car or qualified for credit. Nihoa hadn't been a good robbery prospect, and despite the hundred dollars in his pocket, nothing about the scene suggested a theft gone awry. Instead, it looked more like an execution.

What, he wondered, had Nihoa done to bring on this level of violence? Had Nihoa angered his killer? About what? Or was this a brutal killing intended to send a message? If so, what message? And to whom? In working a crime scene, Koa let the questions pile up, becoming a road map for the investigation to follow.

After again mentally inventorying Nihoa's wounds, Koa let his Maglite play back and forth across the surrounding asphalt in an expanding pattern until the beam illuminated the base of the wall along the back of the bar building. A black object caught his eye. Moving closer, he saw an open ballistic switchblade with a black handle and a five-inch blade covered in blood. While it could have belonged to either Nihoa or his killer, it was most likely the murder weapon. If not, the blood on the knife meant Nihoa had wounded his adversary, and considering the scene, that seemed unlikely. The extent of Nihoa's injuries did not suggest a weakened or injured opponent. Koa asked Ronnie to photograph the knife before Georgina placed it in an evidence bag.

Turning to the local cop who'd been first to arrive on the scene, Koa asked, "Who found the body?"

"Moses, the Surfboard bartender." The policewoman pointed to the back door of the bar. "He was bringing the trash out to the bin. Saw the body and called 911. Want me to get him?"

Koa thought for a moment before deciding to approach the bartender inside the bar. At this first interview, he wanted the barkeep's initial, unrefreshed impressions of the crime scene.

Cigarette and cigar smoke filled the dimly lit interior of the Surfboard in open violation of Hawai'i's requirement for smoke-free businesses. The owner likely kept his license only by paying off inspectors. Typical Hilo petty corruption. There was also scant evidence that health inspectors had ever visited the honky-tonk. The place was grimy. The ancient surfboard that hung over the bar looked like it would sink in the first decent wave.

Koa didn't recognize the big *haole* behind the bar but saw the man stiffen when he flashed his credentials and guessed he'd found Moses. The man's reaction didn't surprise Koa. He was used to being an unwelcome visitor. The sparse crowd of twenty low-life patrons took their cue from the bartender, and the volume of conversation faded until Koa heard little more than background music from the jukebox. Some discordant tune he didn't recognize.

Koa sat down at the bar and studied the hulking man, who endeavored to ignore him for a time before finally asking for Koa's order. Built more like a bouncer than a bartender, Koa pegged him at six-two, maybe 260 pounds. "Moses?" Koa asked.

The man nodded.

"You report the body in the alley?" Koa asked.

"*Yep,*" the bartender affirmed with a smirk.

"Tell me what happened."

"Nothin' happened. I was takin' the trash out to the bin, jus' like always, an' that Nihoa dude, he was swimming in his own blood. So, I did the 911 thing."

"Anyone else around when you took the trash out?"

"Ain't nobody I seen in the alley."

"You recognized Nihoa?"

"*Yep*. He hangs in 'ere."

"Tonight?"

"*Yep*."

"He with anyone?" Koa asked.

"I weren't payin' no attention to 'is social life."

Koa sensed an evasiveness behind the snarky answer and added a touch of impatience to his follow-up. "I asked you if he was with anyone."

The bartender sighed. "Nihoa, he were with a big Hawaiian fellow, a fellow with a scar on 'is face. On his right cheek."

"This scarface have a name?" Koa asked.

"I dunno. He used to come in 'ere years ago, but I nevah seen 'im in maybe four or five years. Heard he did some time inside."

"But you don't remember his name?" Koa asked skeptically.

"Nope."

"Describe him?"

"Hawaiian. Big. Over six feet and broad-shouldered. Black hair."

"Clothing?"

Moses shrugged. "Like everybody else in here. Nothin' unusual caught my eye."

"Did they leave together, Nihoa and this big Hawaiian?"

"*Yep*. Pretty much."

"Pretty much?" Koa asked. "What does that mean?"

"The big Hawaiian, he paid for the drinks before going out after Nihoa."

CHAPTER FIVE

THE BEARDED MAN pulled the hood of his sweatshirt up over his head to ward off the chilly air at four thousand feet above sea level on the southeast side of Hawaiʻi's Big Island. A light mist floated like a phantom across the broken lava, but the sky above remained clear at this elevation. He knelt on the ground and removed the drone from its case. After checking its batteries and the radio link with its joystick controller, he placed the little craft on a patch of smooth, black *pāhoehoe* lava. Settling into a comfortable squat, he commanded the miniature UAV to lift off. Soundlessly, it climbed to an altitude of 150 feet. Painted light blue, it became invisible against the early morning sky. He sent it westward over a forested area to its preprogrammed observation point.

As it flew its course, the man adjusted the drone's camera, zooming in to focus on a white A-frame cottage with dark green trim around the front door and windows on either side. Lights shone through the front windows, and a dark blue SUV with a blue bubble light atop sat in the driveway. The man checked his watch—6:20 a.m. He had ten minutes to wait if his target maintained her usual schedule. The drone hovered. He waited. Minutes ticked away. Then at 6:30, the front door opened, and she stepped out.

The rage he had sublimated while he steered the drone exploded within him, and he saw nothing but blood red. An image of his brother's face appeared in the red haze, overpowering his thoughts. It flickered and was gone. It was like that every time he thought about the woman. Hatred welled up within him as it had every day for the last week when he'd flown the drone and watched her emerge from her house. He had waited years to find this enemy and would soon be rid of her.

CHAPTER SIX

KOA TURNED TO Piki, still after five years his most junior detective, to locate Johnnie Nihoa's next of kin. Piki remained, in Koa's view, a work in progress. Though impetuous and quick to jump to conclusions, his eagerness to learn, tenacity, and zeal for justice made him a valuable addition to Koa's team. He was boyish in appearance with a friendly, round face and had given up his trademark crew cut in favor of a shaggy dark-haired look at the request of his most recent girlfriend. His age placed him at the cutting edge of the electronics generation. With hacker-level computer skills, he believed that there was nothing that could not be learned from the internet if one knew where and how to look.

It had taken Piki a while to come up with her location, but Koa had eventually learned where to find Rene Nihoa, Johnnie Nihoa's mother. Notification of next of kin was perhaps the most distressing duty for any cop, and Koa anticipated this one would be worse than most. He and Piki drove southeast on Route 130 to the coast at Kalapana, where lava blocked the highway.

Beginning in 1983, *Pele*, the Hawaiian goddess of fire, vented her fury at Puʻu ʻŌʻō in a rain forest on the northern edge of Hawaiʻi Volcanoes National Park. The eruption continued for 35 years, at times creating spectacular lava fountains surging more than 1500 feet high. By April 2018, when she abandoned Puʻu ʻŌʻō, *Pele* had pumped out two-thirds of a cubic *mile* of lava. That outpouring buried the Royal Gardens community, destroyed many historic sites, and covered more than eight and a half miles of coastal highway, some of it to a depth of 35 feet.

They parked not far from the shore, got out of their vehicle, and looked west over an extensive *pāhoehoe* lava flow from the Puʻu ʻŌʻō eruption. The sooty-colored lava, unadorned by a single tree, looked deceptively smooth until you got close and saw the dips, cracks, and crevices left when the superheated magma cooled. Tents, campers, and discarded shipping containers—the ragtag dwellings of down-and-out squatters—dotted the gray-black expanse.

What a horrible place to live, Koa thought. No electricity. No plumbing. No water. No cooling when the harsh midday sun poured unbearable heat down on the unforgiving black rock.

"Which one?" Koa asked.

"It's an abandoned camper shell, off the back of some broken-down pickup. A white one," Piki said as he scanned. "There." He pointed to a white fiberglass shell two hundred yards up the barren ebony-colored slope.

They felt the heat through the soles of their shoes as they picked their way across the lava, avoiding crevices large enough to swallow a man. When they finally reached the camper, they found a woman sitting with her back against the fiberglass shell under a makeshift canvas shade. Rene Nihoa had been a teenager when she gave birth to Johnnie Nihoa and was now in her late thirties or early forties, but this woman looked emaciated and much older with unkempt white hair and soiled clothing.

"Mrs. Nihoa?" Koa asked.

She looked up with glazed, bloodshot eyes. Koa recognized the signs. She was high on something, probably meth. "Who . . . who wants . . . wants to know?" the woman responded unenthusiastically.

"I'm Koa Kāne, Hawai'i County Police. This—" Koa gestured toward Piki—"is Detective Piki."

She held up a bony hand, as though shielding herself from the devil, and stuttered, "You . . . you no going evict . . . evict me?"

"No, ma'am," Koa responded. "We're here about Johnnie Nihoa. Is he your son?"

She nodded. "*Manawa lō'ihi* I no see 'im."

"You haven't seen him in a long time?"

"No, I nevah see 'im."

"I'm afraid I have some bad news." Koa didn't want to shock the woman, so he paused, hoping to let her prepare herself for the worst. "I'm afraid Johnnie is dead."

"Oh. *Manawa lō'ihi* I no see 'im," she repeated.

She didn't ask where or how her son died. Nor did she inquire about viewing him or making burial arrangements. She didn't respond when he asked if she needed anything or wanted them to contact anyone. Instead, she simply dropped her chin to her chest. Koa couldn't tell whether she was in denial or simply retreating into the drug-induced haze she inhabited.

Koa wasn't sure she remembered having a son or understood that Johnnie was dead. To Koa, her reaction rivaled in sadness Johnnie's violent death. Both were such a waste of life, differing only because her plight was self-inflicted. He told Piki to have a social worker visit but had no illusions.

CHAPTER SEVEN

WHEN GEORGINA PUT the fingerprints from the knife found in the alley behind the Surfboard into the state's computerized database, the results shocked her. At first, she thought there had to be some mistake before checking and double-checking the results. Then Georgina compared the prints herself. She wasn't an expert, but the two sets of prints appeared to be the same, and she could quickly identify a dozen identical points. There was no mistake. The fingerprints on the knife belonged to Koa's brother Ikaika.

She tried to wrap her head around this alarming discovery. Ikaika, Koa's younger brother, had been a career criminal in and out of jail for nearly a third of his life. While jailed, he suffered a life-threatening medical problem. He survived and got his life in order, holding down a steady job. He even found a soulmate in a young Hawaiian woman. So far as Georgina knew, he'd been a changed man for the past two years.

The knife with Ikaika's fingerprints and Nihoa's blood was damning evidence. It could send Ikaika to jail for the rest of his life. Koa, who tried to help his brother at every turn and risked everything to save him, would be devastated.

Thinking of Koa triggered alarm bells. Department protocol required Georgina to tell Chief Lannua who would take Koa off the case. No police officer, not even the Chief of Detectives, could investigate the criminal conduct of a family member. She picked up the phone to call the chief's assistant but quickly returned the handset to its cradle.

The chief would expect her to come directly to him without telling Koa, but she couldn't blindside him. No matter what the policy said, she needed to give Koa a heads-up. If she lost her job for warning him, so be it. After all the years and crimes they'd worked together, they'd developed a strong relationship. He recommended her for promotion and supported her requests for more people and better technology. She owed him.

Unsure how he'd react, she called his cell and set up a meeting out of the office. He pressed her for an explanation, but she resisted. "It's serious, but I want to tell you face-to-face somewhere off-premises."

*   *   *

Koa found her request peculiar but trusted Georgina and agreed to meet. She set the time and place—near the statue of Kamehameha the Great in the Wailoa River State Park at 9:00 a.m. The park owed its existence to a double tragedy. The area along the Hilo waterfront had been home to Shinmachi, a Japanese immigrant community dating back to 1913. Tsunamis wrought destruction on that community twice. In 1946, waves thirty-five to fifty feet high, triggered by an Aleutian Islands earthquake, washed over the area. Then, in 1960, after the residents rebuilt, the most powerful earthquake ever recorded sent a massive tsunami racing across the Pacific from Chile. It destroyed Shinmachi and left sixty-one people dead. Hilo residents responded with Project Kaiko'o, turning the area into the Wailoa River State Park with memorials for Shinmachi, Hawai'i's Korean and Vietnam War dead, and King Kamehameha the Great. It didn't occur to Georgina that it would be an eerily prophetic place to deliver the message she carried.

Georgina was waiting in her bright red Mini Cooper, two-door hardtop near the statue of Kamehameha the Great when Koa arrived. The triangular "crime-scene-tech-on-board" sticker on the back of her car made Koa smile. They got out of their vehicles and walked to the left of the giant statue of the man who first united the Hawaiian Islands into one kingdom, finally stopping at the edge of Wailoa Pond.

They had worked dozens of cases together, frequently sharing the macabre jokes that softened the edges of the worst crime scenes. Georgina was the consummate pro, and her meticulous work had been instrumental in solving any number of cases. As their eyes met, Koa was surprised to see the stress lines written across her face. Something was wrong, and she was struggling to control her emotions.

"Okay, Georgina, what is it that you couldn't tell me in the office?"

"I . . ." She started to speak but couldn't find the words.

A dozen thoughts flashed through his mind. Maybe she had a medical or financial problem, a death in the family, or an offer of a better job in Honolulu or on the mainland.

"Please, Georgina, take your time and tell me what's bothering you."

"It's about the knife you found at the Nihoa crime scene."

He felt a momentary surge of relief that her concerns were professional, not personal, but the respite was fleeting. Then, without knowing where it came from, Koa felt an unexpected sense of dread. "What about the knife?"

"I ran the prints. Almost a full left-hand set. They belong to your brother, Ikaika."

Koa felt her words viscerally as sharp as the knife in question. "That's not possible. There's been some mistake."

"There's no mistake, Koa. I ran the prints twice and then verified the match with my own eyes. The points of comparison are numerous, and they match perfectly."

Koa remembered the bartender's words: "He were with a big Hawaiian fellow, a fellow with a scar on 'is face." Ikaika was a big Hawaiian. Six-five and a heavily muscled 250 pounds with a scar on his left cheek from a wound received in a teenage knife fight twenty years ago.

Koa tried to make sense of it. Ikaika had been a troubled child, a violent teen, and an adult criminal. He'd spent a third of his life behind bars. After decades of believing that his brother was innately bad, Koa had learned that two slow-growing brain tumors explained Ikaika's inability to control his behavior. Their removal had given Ikaika a new life and brought untold joy to their mother, who had always believed in her tempestuous youngest son.

Emerged from surgery a changed man, Ikaika had become more introspective and exercised greater self-control. Koa had fought hard and risked his career to free his brother from prison, and the two brothers rediscovered each other like two long-lost relatives suddenly reunited. After resenting Nālani's role as Koa's significant other, Ikaika honored her, and they even became friends.

Now steadily employed, Ikaika enjoyed a committed relationship with Maria, a lovely young Hawaiian woman from Maui. After repeatedly distancing himself from his family in his earlier years, he and Maria were now welcome additions at every event. Just the thought that Ikaika could have reverted to his criminal ways set Koa's head spinning.

Ikaika and Maria had only just dined with Koa and Nālani at the Hilo Bay Cafe. Ikaika and Maria had shared their excitement over their planned camping trip to the summit of Mauna Loa, the largest volcano on the surface of the planet, rising over ten miles from its base beneath the sea and covering more than 2,000 square miles.

Believed by native Hawaiians to be of religious significance, ancient holy men made pilgrimages to Mauna Loa's summit to place offerings at the edge of Moku'āweoweo, the massive caldera atop the volcano. Miles long and a mile and a half wide, it was no wonder that Moku'āweoweo inspired spiritual beliefs even without the volcanic eruptions that created half the Big Island.

Archibald Menzies, the famed Scottish naturalist and the first *haole* to climb the *'āinapō* trail to the summit, is supposed to have said it was "the most persevering and hazardous struggle that can possibly be conceived." Ikaika and Maria planned to take the more modern route along the Mauna Loa trail, but it would still be an arduous climb through an alpine stone desert above 10,000 feet. One could easily get lost trying to follow the *ahu*—stone cairns—in the fog, rain, or snow that could blanket the mountain at any time of year.

Ikaika had been to Moku'āweoweo several times, but Maria had never climbed to the summit, and he was eager to show her the magnificent sight. It had been a lighthearted evening with no hint of trouble. Koa had been a cop long enough to know that life served up the strangest incongruities, but he could not fathom that Ikaika had regressed to his old criminal self and, still worse, become a killer.

"Who else knows about this?" Koa asked, refocusing on Georgina.

"No one. I wanted you to know before I report my findings to the chief. You know he's going to take you off the investigation."

She was right. There was no way Chief Lannua would let Koa investigate a case involving his brother. Yet, Koa doubted that Ikaika could have committed the murder and wasn't going to stand idly by and let some other detective railroad Ikaika.

"Can you give me twenty-four hours?" Koa asked.

Georgina paused and then slowly shook her head. "I can't do that. There's a time stamp on the print comparison report. The chief will have my ass if I don't tell him today."

Again, Koa knew she was right. To make matters worse, the chief had never liked Ikaika. He disliked anything that, in his view, reflected poorly on the department. He would be all over the investigation as soon as he heard the news. On his warpath, he'd find fault with any irregularity. "Six hours?" Koa asked, knowing that he was pushing his relationship with Georgina.

She considered his plea for several moments. "Okay, but not a minute more."

"Thanks. I owe you . . . a big one."

"And this stays just between us?" she responded.

"Of course."

CHAPTER EIGHT

GEORGINA'S NEWS CAME as a devastating blow to Koa. Two years back, his brother's recovery and release from jail marked one of his happiest moments. His mother, Māpuana, who always believed in and supported Ikaika, had been deliriously joyful. He could only guess at the pain Georgina's news would inflict on their mother. It might even be the death of her. Then he thought of Maria. He didn't know her well, but he and Nālani liked her and recognized how good she was for Ikaika. The news would pain her, too, and likely end her relationship with his brother.

Returning to his SUV, Koa knew he had a limited window of time before Chief Lannua took him off the case. He listed the priorities in his head—re-interview the bartender, get Ikaika's story, create a timeline, arrange counsel for Ikaika, and a dozen other steps. As always, he prioritized what he needed to do.

Re-interviewing the bartender and getting together with Ikaika before the chief sidelined him topped his list. If he acted fast, he would have one last chance to squeeze information from Moses, preferably at home away from the Surfboard. Then he could warn Ikaika. He could tackle the other items later after the chief took him off the case.

First getting Moses's address from the duty sergeant, Koa headed for the man's home near the rural community of Mountain View, a tiny town twenty miles south of Hilo. Once the home of the ʻOlaʻa Sugar Company and a supposedly haunted wild-west-style theater, it subsequently became known for its coffee mills and floral farms. He found Moses's weathered house at the end of a gravel road, parked, and knocked several times. When Moses finally opened the door, he appeared in boxers and a tank tee and was none too pleased to see Koa.

"Aww shit. Can't you let a man sleep?"

"Sorry, Moses. Need to ask you some questions."

Moses stood, filling the doorway.

"You going to stand there in your skivvies or invite me in?" Koa asked.

The big man hesitated before stepping back. Koa entered a large rectangular great room with two overstuffed armchairs and a 75-inch TV. Beer cans littered the floor, and shabby furniture sat randomly scattered around the room. Moses tossed a beer can aside and sank into one of the chairs. Not wanting to become infested with the bugs he imagined inhabited the chairs, Koa stood against the wall beside the entrance. Reaching into his pocket, he activated the recording app on his phone. Hawaiʻi was a so-called "one-party consent" state, so Koa was under no obligation to inform Moses that he was recording their conversation.

"Okay, Moses. Tell me about the man with Nihoa last night."

"Shit, do we gotta do this again?"

"Unless you want me to haul your ass down to the station," Koa responded.

"Jesus. I already told ya, he was a big Hawaiian with a scar on ʼis face."

"Describe the scar."

"I dunno. It was a mark on ʼis cheek." Moses drew a line down his right cheek with his first finger.

Koa felt a jolt of excitement. "This scar was on his right cheek?"

Moses rubbed the stubble on his chin, obviously trying to recall. After a moment, he said, "Musta bin 'is right cheek, 'cause he were sitting over by the jukebox with 'is back to me. So yeah, it was 'is right cheek."

Koa had what he wanted but felt compelled to lock in the man's recollection. "So, when you were behind the bar, looking across the bar at his back, you saw the scar on his right cheek."

"That's what I said."

Koa next turned to the timing. "So, the Hawaiian, he was sitting with Nihoa?"

"Yeah."

"How long were they sitting in the bar?"

"I dunno. More than an hour. For sure. Could be an hour and a half. Somethin' like that."

Koa realized that Moses's estimate of time could be vital but also knew that passage of time was difficult for most witnesses to judge and thus often unreliable. "How do you figure that?"

"The big Hawaiian, he was buying, an' they had four rounds. Had to be more than an hour. Probably a good deal longer."

"You carried the beers to the table?"

"What'd ya think. They didn't git up an' walk by theirselves."

Koa ignored the sarcasm. "And when you carried the beers to the table, you got a good look at the scar on the big Hawaiian's right cheek."

"Yeah, couldn't miss it."

"What was happening between the two of them?" Koa asked.

Moses looked confused. "What'd ya mean?"

"Were they talking, arguing? What were they doing?" Koa pressed.

"Drinking. They was drinking. Four rounds, like I said."

"Who left first?"

"Nihoa. He went out the back door."

"And the Hawaiian?"

"He followed after settling up."

"Cash or credit card?" Koa asked.

"Cash. A fuckin' hundred-dollar bill. Can you believe it?"

Again Koa recognized he could be onto something vital. "You have the bill?"

"Yeah. I got the bill. Haven't bin to the bank."

"Where is this hundred-dollar bill?" Koa asked.

"In the sack on the table." Moses pointed to a little table near the front door. "I always bring the night's takings home after I close the bar. Not gonna have some druggie rip me off. Then I drop it at the bank on my way to work."

Slipping on gloves, Koa stepped over to the table, opened the bag, and checked the contents. He removed the only hundred-dollar bill and slipped it into a plastic evidence envelope. "This the bill the dude with Nihoa gave you?"

"Yeah."

"And he handed it directly to you?"

"Yeah. You gonna give me a hundred for it?"

"Sure," Koa responded. "And this dude wasn't wearing gloves?"

"Hell, no."

"This scarface dude, he left through the back?"

"That's what I said."

"Didn't you think that odd? Them going out to the alley."

"Not really. I figured they had some business together."

"Like a drug deal?" Koa asked. The dark alley was tailor-made for drug transactions.

"I don't allow that shit in the bar."

"But it's okay in the alley."

"None of my business out there."

Koa wanted to minimize the chance that Moses would try to wea-
sel out of his admissions and asked, "What you've told me is the
truth, and you'd so testify if called?"

"Sure thing, boss."

CHAPTER NINE

KOA NEEDED TO talk to Ikaika, but he and Maria were on their weeklong camping trip. Koa had dropped them off at the trailhead that morning and would pick them up at the end of their hiking vacation. By now, he knew they'd already be up on the eastern slopes of Mauna Loa. Their trip was both a blessing and a problem. A blessing because the police would not know Ikaika's whereabouts and would thus be unable to arrest him until he resurfaced at the end of the trip. His absence was a problem because there was little or no cellphone service in the remote lava fields they would traverse before reaching the summit, one of the most off-the-grid locations in the whole Hawaiian Island chain.

Yet, Koa knew how to turn that problem to his advantage. Since Ikaika's last release from prison, he'd spent much of his free time hiking the most remote areas of the Big Island, a reunion with nature that Koa encouraged. Although Ikaika had recovered from his brain surgery two years ago, his doctors had warned that a hard fall could trigger internal bleeding. Koa thus worried that his brother might someday have an emergency in the backcountry and need help. The brothers covered this contingency with satellite pagers—communications devices transmitting via satellites in geosynchronous orbit and not dependent on terrestrial cell towers.

Joe Po, a cyber geek who ran a spy shop on Oʻahu and owed Koa for overlooking some mildly illegal chicanery, set up the account and furnished Koa and Ikaika with pager units. Koa knew the devices would only permit him to send and receive short messages, but they offered Koa his only hope of quickly connecting with his brother.

Koa knew the itinerary that Ikaika and Maria would follow. Heʼd driven them south on the Hawaiʻi Belt Road, past the main entrance to Hawaiʻi Volcanoes National Park, and then turned right up the narrow winding Mauna Loa strip road to the Mauna Loa Lookout. From that point, at nearly 6,700 feet above sea level, Koa watched them set out on foot along the Mauna Loa trail for the long hike to the top of the 13,678-foot mountain. Koa checked his watch. Eleven a.m. With luck, they should be no more than three miles west of where Koa had left them.

The most logical place to meet would be the Mauna Loa Lookout, but tourists and locals occasionally found their way up the scenic drive, and serious runners and cyclists often trained on the steep uphill strip road. Better to set the rendezvous point a bit west of the trailhead where they would not be observed or overheard.

Koa found his pager in the glove compartment of his police SUV and composed a short message: "URGENT. Meet ASAP 500 yards west of start point." He could only hope that Ikaika carried his pager, would see the message, and turn back to meet with Koa.

Two hours later, Koa drove onto the strip road. Heʼd heard nothing back from his brother, so he pulled to the roadside. Checking to see that no one else was close by, he repeated his previous pager message. Then, pulling back onto the asphalt, he continued up the narrow winding road.

Any other day, he would have soaked up the unique scenery as he passed through *kīpuka*, areas of old-growth forest surrounded by younger lava flows. The road was so diverse that one minute he wound through forests of tangled trees that mimicked modern dancers, but around the next bend, he'd be crossing the barren moonscape of an old lava flow. Although the woods on the eastern slope of Mauna Loa suffered from the island-wide drought, recent rain had unleashed a riot of wildflowers from the reddish-purple *'a'ali'i* to bunches of white half-flowers of *naupaka*. This time though, the dramatic and picturesque scenery passed in a blur as his mind churned over the awful news he carried and how he might best communicate it to Ikaika.

He dwelt on the conflict between his police responsibilities and family loyalties. As a cop, he knew he should escort Ikaika back to police headquarters in Hilo, but he could not bring himself to do that. Though the bloody knife with Ikaika's fingerprints was powerful evidence, Koa's instincts told him something wasn't right. The crime seemed out of character with Ikaika's post-surgery persona. And given his brother's relationship with Maria, he had trouble seeing Ikaika carousing with a lowlife like Nihoa. Aspects of the scene in the alley also seemed staged. Ikaika was no stranger to criminal prosecution and, even if guilty, would never have left a knife with his fingerprints less than a dozen feet from his victim. He was too smart to leave such a calling card. Koa needed time either to confirm the worst or to disprove the story told by the fingerprints on the bloody knife.

As he neared the lookout, he became increasingly concerned that Ikaika had yet to answer his page. Maybe he never got it. Perhaps, he'd ignored it. Koa worried that his efforts might be in vain.

A bit after 2:00 p.m., Koa reached the end of the road, parked, and grabbed two bottles of water and his binoculars from the back of his vehicle. Now on foot, he passed the small trailhead shelter built by the Civilian Conservation Corp in 1937 and headed west on the trail that ultimately led to Puʻu ʻUlaʻula Cabin and then continued through miles of hard climbing to the summit.

The tall trees soon grew sparse before giving way to drought-ravaged *pūkiawe, ʻaliʻi, pāwale,* and other low-lying shrubs on an old broken, rock-strewn lava flow. Koa followed the rough-hewn trail over the uneven ground for about 500 yards until he came to the top of a slightly elevated ridgeline. The spot where he expected to meet Ikaika offered an expansive view east over smoke and gases rising from the Kīlauea caldera. Yet he could see only about a hundred yards to the west up the trail from which Ikaika and Maria would come. He searched for any sign of them but saw no one. He thought about hiking out to the next high point but decided to wait. His brother would either show or not.

The sun bore down relentlessly on the mile-high lava mountain-side with no tall trees to provide shade, and the heat had become oppressive by the time he checked the trail about a half hour later. Finally, two figures cresting the rise eased Koa's fear that the trip had been for naught. Looking through his field glasses, he recognized Ikaika and Maria. Then, his pager began to vibrate. Digging it out of his pocket, he read the text: "On my way." Then he saw that Ikaika had sent it three hours earlier. Satellite communications were some-times like that.

Koa waved and waited for Ikaika and Maria to close the gap. The two brothers grabbed each other in a bear hug. "What's this all about, brah? It's not about Māmā, is it?" Ikaika asked anxiously.

"No, she's fine, brah. It's broiling hot out here. Let's walk back to the shade." Koa pointed to the tree line behind them, and they walked back a couple of hundred yards and off the trail into the shade of several *māmane* and *ʻōhiʻa* trees. Ikaika repeated his question.

Koa did not know how Maria would react and did not want a witness to this sensitive conversation with Ikaika. Whether Ikaika admitted or denied guilt, Koa knew it would be better if it stayed between the brothers. That created an awkward moment with Maria. Koa turned to her. "I know this may seem strange, but I need to speak to Ikaika alone. Can you give us a few minutes?"

Maria looked to Ikaika for guidance.

He nodded his consent, and the two men moved off to a shady spot some distance away from where Maria rested against a tree.

Koa had agonized over how to approach this critical conversation. He considered tackling it as a routine police interrogation where the investigator conceals what he knows while drawing out the perp's story. He rejected going down that path because Ikaika, having had extensive experience with the criminal justice system, would immediately understand that Koa suspected him of wrongdoing. That would make him distrustful. Better to be up front and build on the relationship Koa had cultivated in helping Ikaika win back his freedom.

When they had settled themselves in the shade of a drought-ravaged *māmane* tree, Koa began, "I've got some terrible news." Koa told his brother about finding Nihoa dead in the alley behind the Surfboard bar.

Ikaika appeared puzzled. "So, what's all this have to do with me? I haven't seen that guy in five or six years."

Koa read Ikaika's suntanned face for any hint of deceit but saw none. Instead, his brother seemed genuinely confused about being called back from his camping trip to be told about the death of a man he barely knew. So far, so good, Koa thought. Now for the hard part.

"We found a bloody knife in the alley not far from Nihoa's body."

Ikaika's expression didn't change. "So?" he responded.

Over the years, Koa had caught many subjects off guard in interviews and interrogation rooms. He'd studied the science of micro expressions and knew the facial signs of genuine surprise. Genuine surprise was fleeting. One could never be surprised by what one anticipated. The reaction was thus devilishly hard to fake.

Watching Ikaika's face, he added, "And your fingerprints were all over the knife."

Ikaika's eyes popped wide open, and his jaw dropped. The expression lasted only momentarily. He sat in stunned silence before finally saying, "That can't be. I haven't been anywhere near the Surfboard in years."

Koa felt a surge of relief. He had been sure Ikaika could not have killed Nihoa but now had confirmation. Not evidence, but confirmation. Now he had to find the evidence.

Ikaika must have sensed Koa's relief because he asked, "Did you think I'd gone back to my old ways? That I might even have killed Nihoa?"

"No, my *kaikaina*, I knew it couldn't be you, but the knife is damning evidence, and we have to figure out how your fingerprints turned up on it."

"Could it be a mistake in the police lab?"

"No. I've already ruled that out," Koa responded.

"Then how?" Ikaika asked.

Koa needed to be careful in questioning his brother. The police would inevitably interrogate Ikaika, and the less he knew about the actual crime scene, the better. Koa did not want to feed him information that the police might later use against him.

"Tell me about the knives you own. Not table or kitchen knives, but any others."

Ikaika thought for a moment. "I always carry this one when camping." He pulled a hunting knife from a scabbard on his belt.

That obviously wasn't the murder knife and looked nothing like the one found in the alley. "Okay. What else?"

"A Swiss Army knife."

"Others?"

"Not that I can think of, but there could be a couple of old knives and maybe a machete in the shed out back of my cabin."

"What kind of knives, Ikaika? You need to be more specific." Koa began to push a bit, knowing how critical it might be to account for all of his brother's knives.

"Gee, I don't know. I haven't been in there in ages."

"Have you handled anyone else's knives recently?"

"I use fish knives on my job, cleaning and cutting up the catch."

The ballistic knife found at the crime scene bore no relationship to the narrow, often curved profile of a fish knife. "It looks like somehow somebody got hold of a knife with your prints on it."

"How can that be?" Ikaika implored.

"That's what we need to find out." Then, changing topics, Koa asked, "Where were you the night before last?"

"At home with Maria," Ikaika answered without hesitation.

"Just Maria, no one else?" Koa asked.

"Just me and Maria." Ikaika glanced off toward the distant summit of Mauna Loa before turning back and locking eyes with his brother. "I can't go back inside. What am I going to do?" Ikaika's words bore a hint of panic.

Koa had known Ikaika would ask and had agonized over the advice he would give. As a cop, he should escort Ikaika back to police headquarters in Hilo, where his brother would be arrested and almost certainly denied bail. But, as a brother who believed Ikaika to be innocent, he'd rejected doing so. "There's something rotten going on here. Someone is trying to frame you. I need time to figure out how your fingerprints got on that knife."

"How?"

"Māmā, Nālani, and I know about your camping trip. Anyone else?"

"No. My boss knows I'm on vacation this week but not where I'll be."

"Good," Koa responded. "Stick to your plan. Hike up to the summit, stay in one of the Mauna Loa cabins, and spend some time viewing the Moku'āweoweo crater. Take the full week. No one will find you in that moonscape, and that will give me a chance to see what I can find out."

Ikaika stared silently at Koa before nodding. "Okay. If that's what you think I should do."

As they started back to rejoin Maria, Koa felt his brother's hand gently press his shoulder. Stopping momentarily, Ikaika said, "Thanks for believing me, my *kaikua'ana*."

CHAPTER TEN

PĪPILI NO KA pīlali i ke kumu kukui. Hawaiians used the expression—translated literally as "the *pīlali* gum sticks to the *kukui* tree"—to describe those who are especially close to their loved ones. It captured the special relationship Koa and Nālani shared over the six years they'd lived together.

Koa found their bond to be remarkable, in part because they were so different. A former college football fullback and Special Forces soldier, he topped six-two and weighed 190 pounds. She was as light in spirit and fluid in movement as an ethereal presence in Koa's life. Trim with the smooth, sun-kissed classic Hawaiian features, she possessed sparkling black eyes and long black hair. She was Koa's angel. They pursued vastly different professions with equal intensity; he a hard-boiled cop and she a National Park Ranger. He entered shooting competitions and raced outrigger canoes for sport. She rode horseback. Yet, despite their many differences, they had become inseparable, often anticipating each other's needs and thoughts.

* * *

Arriving home that evening, Koa barely made it through the front door of their Volcano Village cottage before Nālani sensed the burden he brought with him. She held him close, pressing herself tightly against his chest while looking up with an impish smile, inviting a lighthearted kiss. Their lips touched, and the kiss grew more sensual until she slipped away to get him a beer and lead him out the back door to the chairs in the garden she'd created.

Her garden was one of the many gifts Nālani brought to their relationship. Divided into sections for ornamentals, medicinal plants, and herbs, it surrounded a little patio with a firepit to ward off the evening chill at their 4000-foot elevation. Quiet and peaceful, it had become their favorite end-of-the-day respite. Nālani hoped the setting would relax Koa, but the taut lines across his forehead and the rigid set of his jaw seemed intractable.

"Talk to me," she whispered so softly he almost didn't hear.

"It's about Ikaika," he said with a sigh. He told her the whole story, starting with Nihoa's body in the alley and ending with his meeting with Ikaika on the slope of Mauna Loa.

"I know in my heart he's not guilty, but I have no idea why someone would try to frame him. You know, the chief is going to take me off the case and put another detective in charge, someone who won't care about an ex-con and won't look beyond the fingerprints on the knife."

Koa dropped his fist down hard on the arm of the chair in exasperation. "My brother was doing so well. Holding down a job. Finding Maria. Now, it's all turning to shit."

Despite his frustrated outburst, Nālani knew Koa needed a sounding board, not sympathy. "Could the knife have been stolen from Ikaika?" she asked.

"That was my first thought, but I questioned Ikaika about his knives, and it doesn't seem like he ever had a blade like the one I found in the alley."

Nālani tried a different tack. "Wasn't Ikaika with Maria all night? Doesn't she give him an alibi?"

"Yes, but because she's his girlfriend, the police won't place much weight on her word," Koa responded.

"Don't the police need a motive? What reason would Ikaika have for killing Nihoa?"

"That'll be a weakness in the prosecution's case," Koa conceded, "but it won't overcome the undeniable fact of Ikaika's fingerprints on the knife."

"Can fingerprints be faked or maybe transferred from something else?" Nālani asked. "Or is that in the realm of science fiction?"

The questions intrigued Koa and gave him pause. "You know, I don't know. We've always treated fingerprints as definitive, at least where there's a solid match. Besides, defendants rarely challenge a solid match. After dinner, I'll see what I can find on the internet, and tomorrow morning I'll check with a friend in the FBI. See if there's ever been a case."

Hoping to give her *ipo*—her lover—some comfort, Nālani said, "Go check it out while I fix us something to eat."

An hour later, Koa was still at his laptop when Nālani brought him a plate of white flaky *ono*—a fish sometimes known as wahoo outside of Hawai'i—rice, and salad, along with another brew. He'd found an academic article about fingerprinting and was making notes. "You may be onto something." Koa looked up at his *ipo*. "I don't understand the details—something about the oils on human fingers—but there appear to be ways to transfer fingerprints."

"You should talk to Alexia," Nālani suggested. "She must know people who understand this technical stuff." She referred to Alexia Sheppard, a local lawyer who'd represented Ikaika through all his troubles.

"That's a good idea," he responded with a hint of relief in his voice.

While fixing dinner, Nālani had been thinking of the next steps. One of the most difficult would be telling Māpuana, Koa's mother, that Ikaika was in danger of going to jail again, possibly for the rest of his life. Anticipating that difficult conversation, Nālani knew, would weigh heavily on Koa.

Standing behind him, she wrapped her arms around his shoulders. "I want to go with you up to Laupāhoehoe," she said softly, referring to his hometown village on a spit of land extending from the Hāmākua coast, where Koa grew up and Māpuana still lived.

He turned, pulled her into his lap, and kissed her softly.

CHAPTER ELEVEN

DETECTIVE MAKANUI ROSE as usual at 5:30 a.m., showered, dressed, and nearly inhaled her regular banana-papaya smoothie. Then, after a quick check of her email and a cursory scan of the local news headlines, she headed for her police SUV and the thirty-minute drive from Volcano Village to police headquarters in Hilo. Opening her front door at precisely 6:30 a.m., she stepped into the cool crisp morning air.

In an instant, the bullet from the Dragunov sniper rifle, traveling at over 2,600 feet per second, hit the left side of her chest just below her heart. The impact knocked her over, and she fell backward into the house, hitting her head on the floor. Searing pain shot through her chest, and she struggled to breathe. Her vision narrowed, the world turned gray, and she passed out. Because she fell backward, the second shot missed her.

Mrs. Goya, a neighbor, heard the gunshots and called 911. The emergency call center quickly dispatched police. When the computer system flagged Makanui's address as belonging to a police detective, Chief Detective Koa Kāne got the call.

Since he lived only a couple of miles away on the other side of Route 11, Koa was the first officer on the scene. He found his colleague Makanui unconscious just inside the front door to her house.

At first, he thought she was dead, but the rise and fall of her breathing dispelled that initial fear. Kneeling beside her, he felt for a pulse. Relieved to find her still alive, he called for EMTs and began to check for wounds. Strangely, he saw what appeared to be a bullet hole in her blouse but no blood. He ripped the garment open and discovered a badly mangled bullet embedded in her protective vest just below her heart. He opened the vest. Beneath it, she was severely bruised and had probably suffered broken ribs, but no bullet had penetrated her flesh. He couldn't tell whether the shock to her chest had knocked her out or she'd suffered a concussion from her fall.

She was alive and would survive. That knowledge triggered an intense sense of relief. He had recruited Makanui and worked closely with her. She had proven herself over and over on the job, and they had become close professional friends. Her death would have devastated him.

It was only then that he recalled a conversation in which she had credited a bulletproof vest with saving her life in an earlier incident. That's when she'd sworn she'd never be on duty without one. That pledge and her vest had saved her a second time.

She began to regain consciousness just as the EMTs arrived and groaned in pain when they put her in the back of their ambulance. Koa tried to ask her what she'd seen, but she was too groggy to respond. He wanted to ride with her to the hospital but knew he had to take command of the scene and oversee the investigation. A cop shot was a law enforcement nightmare that required his immediate and undivided attention.

Standing in the doorway of Makanui's house, Koa surveyed the area and tried to reconstruct the shooting. The A-frame was set back about thirty yards from a gravel roadway. Across the road, the forested ground sloped upward to a distant hill about a third of a mile away.

Had the shooter been in the yard or hidden in the woods across the street? The latter seemed more likely. Makanui, he knew from experience, was particularly vigilant and quick to react. So, he doubted someone in plain sight had caught her off guard.

Detective Piki was among the wave of officers who descended on the scene, and Koa sent the young detective to interview the neighbors. "Ask what they saw or heard this morning and if they've seen any unusual activity in the past couple of weeks."

Judging that the bullet most likely came from the woods across the street from Makanui's house, he instructed three other officers to form a line and search the woods. "You know the drill. Walk five or six feet apart. Go in fifty yards. Then come back on a parallel track. You're looking for the shooter's hide, for spent brass, or any other sign of an assailant. Search and photograph with your cellphones, but don't touch or disturb anything you find."

While his team went about their assignments, Koa continued to reconstruct the attack in his mind. It had taken place at approximately 6:30 a.m. Her attacker had been lying in wait and caught her the moment she opened the door. The gunman must have known Makanui's schedule, perhaps having watched her movements over time.

Who, he wondered, had a motive to kill Makanui? She'd been a cop for several years and put away countless perps. Remembering their recent conversation, he wondered if Reyes, the escaped Oʻahu bomber, had caught up with Makanui. Or maybe another of the felons she'd nailed had escaped or made parole and sought revenge. Makanui, he knew, had also worked in the Honolulu Police Department's anti-terror unit. So maybe a terrorist had sought revenge. And after leaving the Honolulu department, she'd tracked down and killed the Abu Sayyaf bandits who had kidnapped and ransomed her parents. Those insurgents certainly had motive enough to come after her.

Koa was running through the possibilities when his cell rang. He answered to hear Piki's excited voice. "Hey, boss, according to one of the neighbors, there were two gunshots in quick succession this morning. Was Makanui hit more than once?"

Koa hadn't checked Makanui's body for a second injury but had seen no evidence of more than one hit. That meant a shot must have missed and might be buried somewhere in the house. Hanging up on Piki, he searched the area around the front door. Koa checked the frame. Nothing. Retreating inside the house, he explored the floor and lower walls. Again, he found no trace of another bullet. Only when he turned back toward the front door did he see the hole in the lintel. A shot had gone high and passed through the exterior and interior panels above the front door.

Koa moved, so the holes lined up, and he could see blue sky. Then, the realization hit him like a thunderbolt. The bullet had come through the lintel on a downward angle. That could only happen if the shooter had been above the house or firing from a significant distance allowing the bullet to arc downward.

Standing in the front doorframe, Koa eyed the forest across the road. He saw no tree tall and sturdy enough to give the gunman a downward shot. Makanui, he realized, had been hit by a sniper's round fired from a considerable distance far beyond the nearby trees, probably the hilltop visible about a third of a mile away.

Koa considered the implications of his discovery. A sniper shooting from a third of a mile out had nailed Makanui on the first shot. It had to be the first shot because, otherwise, she would have reacted, jumping to the side or diving to the ground upon hearing the first discharge. Instead, the gunman must have seen her fall back into the house—maybe out of sight—and fired high in hopes the second round would catch her inside. The shooter was no amateur, and he'd cased the setup, choosing the perfect time to nail Makanui when she'd least expect it. He also picked a firing point to the east of the house, knowing that the rising sun would light his target. The perp was an experienced pro.

Koa considered his next steps—search for the shooter's hilltop hide, find the bullet lodged someplace in the house, check on Makanui in the hospital. The hilltop was the most time sensitive. The crime scene team could find the bullet, and as desperate as he was to see Makanui and get her story, he knew that could wait.

Koa was familiar with the hilltop area and knew it was inaccessible by road. Aware that it would take him an hour to climb through the rough, lava-strewn terrain and heavy brush, he called the police helicopter pilot on standby. He thought about taking Piki with him, but the young detective hadn't finished canvassing the neighbors, and Koa thought it better to let him complete that essential task. So, he decided to go it alone, and the chopper picked him up twenty minutes later at a grassy pasture less than three blocks from Makanui's house.

Koa had the pilot circle the hilltop several times so he could examine the ground before landing in one of the two clearings large enough to accommodate the chopper. Although not fully qualified as a sniper, Koa had trained on various sniper weapons while in the Special Forces and knew how professional sharpshooters worked. Exiting the aircraft and instructing the pilot to wait, he walked back and forth along the western edge of the hilltop formation, where he discovered two places he would have chosen had he been the shooter. Both offered clear views of Makanui's front door. One of the two showed some recent disturbance, and he guessed it had been the shooter's location, but the hard, black, *pāhoehoe* lava gave up few clues, and he couldn't be sure. Given his assessment of the would-be assassin's professionalism, he neither expected nor found any spent brass.

Turning to look for the shooter's possible escape routes, Koa doubted that the shooter had cut through the thick brush to the west, so he examined the back or eastern side of the hill. There, he noticed a jeep trail some two hundred yards away. Making his way down, he walked along the trail. Only a thin oil spot gave any indication that a vehicle had been present. He photographed the oil and geo-located the exact point so that the crime scene techs could collect samples. An hour later, the chopper transported him back to the pasture.

Back at Makanui's house, he found Georgina Pau and her crime scene team. He told her about the shooter's likely hilltop hide, the old fire trail on the far side, and gave her the coordinates of the oil spot he'd found. "According to a neighbor, there were two shots," he explained, gesturing to the holes in the lintel, "so there should be a bullet someplace around here."

"I know," Georgina responded, pointing. "I've already dug it out of the wall." She pulled out a small evidence bag holding a mangled bullet. "Take a look," she said, extending it in a gloved hand. "Looks like a 7.62 mm military round, but there's something odd about it."

"Odd how?" Koa asked.

"I won't be sure until I get it back to the lab and run some tests, but I think it's heavier than the standard NATO round."

"Analysis is a top priority," Koa directed.

"You think I didn't know that," she shot back.

"Sorry. I don't react well to assholes who shoot at cops."

CHAPTER TWELVE

ON THE WAY to Hilo Memorial Hospital, Koa called ahead and learned that Makanui had been x-rayed and was in the emergency room with a mild concussion, three broken ribs, and extensive bruising. He had to wait in the hall while nurses covered her chest with bandages, making sure they would not restrict her breathing. Pain etched her face when he finally got in to see her.

Makanui held a special place in Koa's esteem. At five feet eleven, tall for a native Hawaiian woman, she was physically strong and astoundingly quick. Intelligent, experienced, and observant, she had superb instincts for handling tough situations. But most critically to Koa, she shared his tenacious drive to find justice for those abused by society's many and varied predators.

He'd searched for an additional detective for over a year when she'd applied with a powerful résumé and top-notch references. At their first meeting over breakfast at Hilo's Café Pesto, she filled the one hole in her résumé—where she'd been for a year after leaving the Honolulu police force. She'd explained that she and a police colleague had successfully trapped a cell of Philippine terrorists who'd kidnapped and ransomed her parents. He remembered her words— "I think of all the people in the world who have no one to stand up for them, to right the wrongs inflicted on them. I can't help them all, but maybe I can even the score for some. That's what I want to do with my life." In this, Koa recognized her as a kindred spirit and hired her on the spot. In the year that followed, she proved herself repeatedly, and they had become close professional colleagues.

"You okay?" he asked.

"I hurt like a son of a bitch, but the docs say I'll live," she responded with a grimace.

"Can you tell me what happened?"

"There's not much to tell. I opened . . ." her voice fluttered as she took a breath before continuing . . . "opened the door, stepped out, felt this blinding pain, went over backward, and blacked out. I might have heard a second shot, but I'm not sure. Could have just been the report from the shot that hit me. I really don't know." She forced a half-smile. "Body armor came through."

"You're right about a second shot. The gunman got off at least one more round that went high, apparently hoping to hit you after you fell back into the house. The backward fall and the steel panels you were wearing saved your life. If you'd crumpled in the doorway, he'd have finished you."

She winced as she attempted to control her pain. "That's the odd thing. Those steel body panels are supposed to dissipate the kinetic force of a bullet strike. I wasn't supposed to get banged up this bad."

"I'm guessing a sniper hit you with a specially designed high-velocity round fired from maybe a third of a mile out."

She looked up abruptly and paid the price in fresh pain. "A sniper?"

"Yes, a pro. The trajectory points to a sniper in an elevated position. I think I found the point of origin on that hill east of your house. Georgina is checking, but she thinks the shooter used specialized ammunition."

Makanui was quiet for a moment, absorbing Koa's words. "This sniper knew my routine and caught me at my most vulnerable. Had to have been watching me for a while."

"Agreed. You recall any evidence of that?"

She shook her head. "No, and I'm usually pretty alert. I've got exterior video surveillance around my house. I'll check it when I get home."

"You can't go home. It's a crime scene, and that's where whoever shot at you will expect you to be. I can have the crime scene team retrieve the video. The doctors tell me they will discharge you this evening with orders to take a week of rest. Besides, we need to keep you out of sight for a few days. Maybe even let the shooter think he scored."

"Where?" she asked.

"Nālani's got a friend with an empty guesthouse. It's just on the outskirts of Volcano. Nice place. You can hole up there for a week or two. That way, only her friend and the three of us will know where you are. And Nālani will stock the fridge for you."

Makanui frowned, obviously not happy at the prospect of being out of her home. "Okay," she conceded, "but I'll need my go-bag out of my car. It's got protective gear I don't want to be without. And the laptop from my house. I'll need that, too."

"I'll make sure you get both."

She gave him the passwords for her computer and security system. "You check with the neighbors?"

"Piki's got a team interviewing everyone on the street." Koa paused. "Think it could be your nemesis, Reyes?"

"I suppose, but the MO and the timing seem wrong. He was a bomb maker. Nothing in his background suggests he's also a sniper, and it's been only a few days since he escaped. How could he arrange to get phony identification, fly to the Big Island, scope out my movements, and get in place for the hit? And where would he get a sniper rifle and specialized ammo?"

"Suggests a group effort?" Koa guessed.

"Maybe, but the guy was a loner with no family or gang connections when he was planting bombs on O'ahu. That's why it took us a year to hunt him down."

"Sure would be a weird coincidence if someone else came after you just days after Reyes escaped," Koa mused.

"Yeah, it would, but it's possible."

"You have anyone in mind?"

"No, but I put a lot of badasses away over the years with the HPD and more since I've been here."

"I've already asked Piki to pull the files on all your felony arrests."

CHAPTER THIRTEEN

WHEN KOA RETURNED to police headquarters that afternoon, he wasn't surprised that Chief Lannua wanted to see him and pronto. Bracing himself, he made his way to the chief's office. Lannua came from an old Big Island family with considerable land holdings and was more politician than law enforcement officer. His political stature benefited the department, but he often curtailed or derailed investigations in his coziness with the Island's political and business elite. He needed Koa to pursue significant cases and make solid arrests but resented Koa's tenacious pursuit of every crime, often upsetting the upper crust of Island society. As a result, they repeatedly butted heads but also grudgingly regarded each other with a kind of respect.

As he entered the chief's inner sanctum, his boss asked, "How's Makanui?"

"She's banged up and has a mild concussion, but that won't keep her down for long," Koa responded.

"We're lucky she was wearing a vest," Lannua said.

"Right, Chief."

"Where are we on identifying the shooter?"

"We're looking for a sniper, most likely a pro, who must have scoped out her routine," Koa responded.

"Well, keep me posted. But that's not the only reason why I wanted to see you."

Koa knew what was coming. Historically, the chief had frequently complained about the negative publicity associated with Ikaika's criminality, which the chief viewed as reflecting poorly on the police department. Koa resented getting tarred with the past sins of his brother. Koa expected hostility, but this time the chief was surprisingly sympathetic.

"Georgina Pau came to see me last night with news about your brother," Lannua began. "You know, I've got to take you off the case. We can't have a detective investigating a family member."

Koa knew he had no option and conceded. "I understand."

"I've asked Detective Moreau to take charge," the chief continued.

Koa suddenly understood why the chief wanted to deliver this news in person and groaned inwardly. The chief might feign sympathy, but his animus toward Ikaika motivated him to assign the case to Koa's least favorite colleague, Deputy Chief Detective Moreau. Four months earlier, Bobbie Satō, Hawai'i Island's freshly elected mayor, had pressured Police Chief Lannua to hire Moreau for the newly created number two slot in the detective bureau. Koa felt sure the appointment was in retaliation for Koa's arrest of Ronnie Satō, the mayor's son, during the mayor's upset election campaign. Worse still, Koa feared that Moreau's appointment was only the first step in Mayor Satō's plan of retribution to oust Koa as chief detective in favor of Moreau.

The affair with candidate Satō's son had been messy. The eighteen-year-old had stalked a former high school girlfriend who'd rejected his further advances. It began with Ronnie making harassing phone calls and social media posts. When the girl continued to rebuff him, things had escalated. Ronnie entered her house, scrawled threatening messages on her bedroom mirror, and defiled personal items in her dresser drawers. Koa arrested and charged him with harassment by stalking, a misdemeanor, and a judge sentenced him to attend a counseling program and pay a fine. Press coverage of the arrest and conviction became a major embarrassment for his father during the height of the mayor's campaign, and the older Satō had made his displeasure with Koa unmistakably clear.

When he'd learned of the mayor's proposal to make Moreau Deputy Chief Detective, Koa had objected. He appealed to Chief Lannua to reject the mayor's request. He argued that, as an outsider, Moreau's lack of contacts in the community would hamper his effectiveness, particularly with native Hawaiians. Besides, he added, the Hilo force had many better-qualified people who could fill the new position.

The chief nodded, signifying that he appreciated Koa's concerns but highlighted Moreau's qualifications. "He has the résumé for the job, and I've checked his references. He gets glowing reviews from Ralph Banks, the Redwood City police chief." Chief Lannua paused before directing, "Interview him, and then we'll talk again."

Unfortunately for Koa, the chief was right about Moreau's formal record. Born in Los Angeles in 1979, Moreau graduated from UC Davis in California in 2001. After graduating, he worked for a consulting firm in Washington, D.C., until 2012 and then as a temporary staffer for the U.S. Senate Foreign Relations Committee through 2013. Moreau then returned to California and worked his way up to Chief Detective in Redwood City, a northern California town about twice Hilo's size. In that capacity, he completed advanced schooling at the Federal Law Enforcement Training Center, the nation's premier police training facility. In 2020, Moreau relocated to Hawai'i to work as a special assistant to Mayor Satō in his first term.

As with all candidates for detective positions, Koa interviewed Moreau but came away unimpressed. Moreau explained that he'd left the chief detective position in Redwood City because he didn't want to live in the same community as his former wife. When Koa probed his reasons for leaving law enforcement to become Mayor Satō's aide, Moreau said the move satisfied his lifelong desire to work in politics. In asking Moreau how he would handle various hypothetical situations, Koa found his answers weak and contradictory and his knowledge of police procedures oddly lacking given his previous positions and training. Against that background, Koa had trouble understanding Moreau's renewed interest in police work.

After the interview, Koa made a second attempt to dissuade the chief from hiring Moreau, but Lannua had already made up his mind, and Koa's pleas fell on deaf ears. After that, the Chief cut Koa out of the hiring process. Koa guessed that given Moreau's paper qualifications and glowing recommendations and the department's dependence upon the mayor for the police budget, Lannua had little choice but to acquiesce to Satō's demands.

As Koa predicted based on his interview, Moreau's on-the-job performance failed to live up to his paper qualifications and references. Koa repeatedly found gaps in his adherence to proper police procedures. In addition, his lack of knowledge of Hawaiian culture and tendency to use excessive force led to unfortunate incidents. And while Chief Lannua occasionally leaked sensitive information to the mayor, Moreau was all too conspicuous in catering to the mayor's wishes.

Moreau's close ties to the mayor quickly became a growing annoyance to Koa, who believed community support for the department required policing to be apolitical. His experience told him that the "political elite" committed just as many crimes as ordinary citizens, and Koa gave no special favor to those with wealth or power. In this respect, Koa especially distrusted Satō. In his short tenure as mayor, Satō had pushed his nose more forcefully into police business than any of his predecessors, always with some political agenda. And it soon became apparent to Koa that Moreau was facilitating Satō's efforts to micromanage the police department.

For his part, Moreau knew the chief had hired him over Koa's objection and relied upon his relationship with the mayor to resist Koa's supervision. Although Koa complained to his chief, he got sympathy but no relief. It seemed the chief's hands were tied. Aware that Moreau was angling for his job, Koa knew Moreau would see prosecuting Ikaika as the way to embarrass and undermine Koa. If Koa wasn't careful, the case against Ikaika might end his career.

Koa left the chief's office disheartened but more determined than ever to exonerate his brother. But he couldn't do it alone. Nālani had been prescient when she suggested Koa consult with Alexia Sheppard, but he would have sought her out even without Nālani's encouragement. He made a quick phone call to ensure she was available and headed for Alexia's office.

Alexia had grown up in Hilo as the only daughter of the Island's go-to lawyer, negotiator, sage, and backstage advisor to its wealthiest families. Joseph Sheppard had accumulated a fortune in his lifetime, most of which he'd donated to create public facilities, fund hospitals, and feed the poor. The great man had only one child, whom he educated well, passing along his gift for the law. In time, she took over his law practice and, with her captivating voice and near-photographic memory, became the best criminal defense attorney on the Island.

Koa first met Alexia years before when she'd been a witness with vital information for the police. Later, Koa hired her to represent Ikaika, then a teenager facing his first arrest. Time and time again, she'd successfully defended Koa's brother at Koa's expense until his crimes became so egregious that she could only plead for leniency. Later, she helped Ikaika win release from prison after his medical problems, so Koa turned to her again.

Ordinarily, Koa looked forward to visiting Alexia's sun-drenched, plant-filled office on the second story above one of Hilo's historic, covered sidewalks. In her forties with brilliant green eyes and lustrous black hair frequently pulled back in a ponytail, Alexia always delivered her incisive advice in the lyrical cadence she used to charm juries. Yet today, Koa was too fixated on Ikaika's peril to appreciate either the sights or sounds.

While Alibi, Alexia's giant, green-eyed, black cat, slept atop a pile of law books, Koa described the discovery of Nihoa's body. He then told Alexia about the knife and showed her the cellphone picture he'd taken. He related his two conversations with Moses, the bartender, and the heads-up he got from Georgina about the fingerprints on the knife.

"You think someone is trying to frame him," Alexia said when he finished.

Koa wasn't sure whether it was a statement or a question but answered with an emphatic, "Yes."

"Please don't take offense, but why are you so sure?" Alexia asked.

"Several reasons. My brother has been clean for the past two years. He's got a steady job and a girlfriend. I've seen none of the evasiveness, hostility, or drug use that marked the old Ikaika. He's sworn off alcohol and so wouldn't have been in the Surfboard drinking. Then, there's the knife covered with fingerprints right there in the alley, not ten feet from Nihoa's body. Like the killer left his name and address. That's weird for almost any killer but also stupid. And Ikaika's not stupid. He wouldn't have left a trail virtually begging for a murder rap. And sure, Ikaika knows how to use a knife. He's been in knife fights, but Nihoa's body had at least a dozen punctures. The killing reflected uncontrolled rage or an execution designed to send a message. I've seen no evidence—none— of rage in Ikaika since his release, and he wouldn't kill Nihoa to send a message. Nothing about the scene is consistent with Ikaika's recent behavior."

"All good points, but you know the police won't see it that way," Alexia responded.

"There's more. Moses, the bartender at the Surfboard, says Nihoa was with a big Hawaiian who had a scar on his right cheek. That sounds like Ikaika, except my brother's scar is on his left cheek. So, the man who was with Nihoa and followed him into the alley couldn't have been Ikaika."

Alexia shook her head. "Pretty easy to confuse one side for the other in a dark bar."

"Except Moses didn't make a mistake. Listen to this." Koa pulled out his phone and played the recording he'd made of his second interview with Moses.

"Not a bad cross-examination," she responded with a smile. "I don't suppose Ikaika has an alibi."

"Only his girlfriend."

"You've talked to him?"

"Yes." Koa described his meeting with Ikaika on the Mauna Loa trail. "I saw all the qualities of genuine surprise in a way that, in my experience, nobody can fake. He didn't kill Nihoa. I'm sure of it."

"Then explain to me why someone would frame him," Alexia asked.

"He's been in numerous fights in and out of prison over the years. He's also testified against others. So, he's got lots of enemies."

She rose from behind her giant desk piled with law books and papers and walked across the room to stroke Alibi. The big cat immediately began purring rhythmically. It was something he'd seen her do as she digested and organized facts. Then, turning to face him, she said, "Have you considered that it might be a tangential attack on you?"

Her question surprised him; he hadn't thought of that possibility. "Why would you think that?"

"Attacking a police officer creates a major incident with a big police backlash. Framing a cop's ex-con brother hardly causes a ripple and might even please some in law enforcement."

She had a point. Having put away scores of criminals, he had more enemies than his brother. Yet, it was all speculation. "Interesting theory," Koa said, "but no matter who's behind the frame, we need to expose them. One way is to find evidence that Ikaika couldn't have done it. The other way is to prove that someone else did. We need to pursue both angles."

"Agreed," she replied. "Tell me what you've done, and then let's figure out how I can help."

"I'm already trying to identify this big Hawaiian guy who was with Nihoa, but I didn't have time to interview the customers before the chief took me off the case."

"Okay," Alexia responded. "I'll send my investigator around to hang out at the Surfboard. He can listen to the chatter and talk to some of the patrons in the joint that night."

"Great," Koa replied. "We need to create a detailed timeline of Ikaika's activities on the night of the murder. Did he use his phone or credit cards? Did anyone see him? Did he order a pizza or Chinese? Anything that would help show his whereabouts."

Alexia returned to her desk and started making notes on her computer. "I'll get Miura, my investigator, to talk to Ikaika's boss and find out what time he left work. Can you get Ikaika's phone and credit card records?"

"I can't go to the providers. That would get back to the chief."

"What about paper records or his online accounts?"

"I'll see what I can do," Koa responded.

Alexia made another note. "What about his car? Does it have a GPS tracker?"

"He doesn't own a car. He gets around on a secondhand motorcycle. I doubt it has GPS, but I'll check." Koa started making a list of tasks in a small notebook he carried.

"Too bad that Hilo doesn't have traffic cameras," Alexia said.

"True, but some businesses have cameras that capture street views. I'll see what I can find."

"Good," Alexia said. "That's the easy part. The knife is the hard part. I need to round up a couple of experts, and they're going to need access to the knife."

"Georgina Pau has already verified and then double-checked the print match. She didn't make a mistake, but I did some internet research last night, looking into the possibility that Ikaika's prints could have been transferred or faked. It's pretty technical stuff. You have any experience in that area?" Koa asked.

"Some," she replied. "Despite the general reliability of fingerprints, it's possible to transfer them. Experts can usually spot evidence of such a switch by testing the oils and DNA in the prints, but they will need access to the knife."

"That's going to be a problem," Koa responded. "The police aren't going to allow access before Ikaika's charged and maybe not until close to trial."

Alexia continued typing on her computer. "I know the policy, but we're going to have to find a way. How much time do we have before the police arrest Ikaika?"

"A week."

Alexia looked up from her monitor. "How do you know that?"

Koa explained that Ikaika's hike to the Mokuʻāweoweo caldera atop Mauna Loa would keep him out of circulation for at least a week.

"That doesn't give us much time."

CHAPTER FOURTEEN

KOA RETURNED TO his office, poured himself a cup of Kona coffee from the thermos on his desk, and had barely settled into his chair when Detective Moreau barged in without knocking. He was a big man at five-foot-eleven with a slight paunch and an unappealing, sharp-featured face. Sporting a deep scowl, Moreau came to an abrupt stop in front of Koa's desk. Planting both hands on his hips, he glared at Koa.

"You know the chief put me in charge of the Nihoa case, and your brother is the prime suspect. He's not at his job, and he's not at home. I need you to tell me where he is," he demanded.

Koa had anticipated this visit. Moreau, unable to locate Ikaika, would see Koa as his shortcut to finding his suspect, and Moreau was all about shortcuts. Anything to avoid the complex and sometimes tedious investigative work that solved cases. He'd also have the ulterior motive of getting back at Koa, who had reprimanded the overly aggressive detective on more than one occasion. Koa, though, had no intention of helping. He and Alexia needed as much time as possible to establish Ikaika's innocence. He wouldn't outright lie to Moreau; instead, he'd simply equivocate.

Koa returned Moreau's bulldog-like stare for a long moment before saying, "You're asking me? I'm off the case. You know that," Koa responded with a touch of irritation.

"The chief expects you to cooperate so we can arrest your brother for Nihoa's murder."

Koa knew that he shouldn't engage with Moreau, but he couldn't resist. "So, you've decided to charge him without even talking to him. Is that good police work?"

"It's an open and shut case," Moreau said, raising his voice. "Your brother has a mile-long rap sheet and left his fingerprints at the murder scene. He's not going to get off this time."

"So now you're prosecutor, jury, and judge," Koa said with an air of confidence he didn't feel.

"Don't feed me that bullshit." Moreau snarled in a deep voice. "Just tell me where he's hiding."

"I'm not my brother's keeper."

"Ikaika's boss says he's on vacation," Moreau explained. "Out for a week. He wouldn't go away without sharing his plans with you. So don't play games. Tell me where!"

Koa gestured, his hands spread outward with palms up. "You're the detective, and like I said, I'm not my brother's keeper."

Moreau was livid. "I'll find him, alright, with or without your help. And you'd better hope he doesn't resist." With that, he spun around and stormed out of the office.

Koa's deflection may have bought him valuable time, but Moreau's words were not an idle threat. The detective might not find Ikaika right away, but it was only a matter of days before he'd return from his Mauna Loa hike. Once back, he'd have to turn himself in. Otherwise, Ikaika could wind up in a nasty confrontation with Moreau or his team.

Moreau was working harder than Koa had anticipated, and Koa knew he had to act fast. He left police headquarters, heading for Ikaika's two-room cabin to search for the passwords for his online phone and credit card accounts. Koa had driven less than a mile when he identified a black SUV in the line of cars behind him as an under-cover police vehicle. He pulled into the parking lot outside a paint store, and the SUV continued past but pulled to the curb a half-block ahead. Moreau, he realized, had put a tail on him in the hope that he would lead the police to his brother.

Koa would go nowhere near his brother but still did not want Moreau's people knowing his movements. Although Hilo was no urban metropolis where one could quickly lose a tail in traffic, Koa knew how to escape scrutiny.

Working out of police headquarters in Hilo and living thirty miles away in Volcano Village, Koa regularly traveled the Hawai'i Belt Road through Kurtistown at the center of the Big Island's banana farming community. Over the years, he'd often gassed up his car there at the Phillips 76 station pumps, managed by Kawai, one of his mother's cousins.

He called Kawai on his cell, and the station manager readily agreed to lend Koa one of the station's jeeps for the afternoon. "I'll be there in a few minutes. Park the jeep behind the café with the keys under the floor mat," Koa requested.

Fifteen minutes later, Koa pulled into the Kurtistown Café parking lot next to the Phillips 76 station. He entered the café, where Kawai's sister worked behind the counter, slipped out the back door, and climbed into the jeep parked next to the trash bins. Five minutes later, he was on his way to Ikaika's cabin while his tail sat waiting for him to exit the café.

Koa figured that having not found Ikaika at home, Moreau would maintain surveillance on the place to await Ikaika's return. With police resources stretched, Koa guessed a single cop would be assigned to watch the house. No problem. Koa would park on a nearby forest fire road and hike the half-mile through the woods to the backside of his brother's remote cabin.

The irony of sneaking through the trees to the cottage was not lost on Koa. He'd done it years ago before Ikaika's surgery when he'd suspected his brother of running with a criminal gang. *Déjà vu*, all over again. He moved cautiously as he neared the house, relying on his Special Forces training to avoid detection. Checking for Moreau's stakeout, he spotted an officer sitting in an unmarked car about half-way up the long unpaved drive. The officer, obviously expecting Ikaika to approach by car, faced away from the house toward the street. As Koa anticipated, the police did not expect anyone on foot to come through the forest.

Keeping the cabin between himself and the police lookout, he crept up to the back door. After peeking through the rear window into the empty two-room log structure, Koa used the key Ikaika had given him years ago to let himself in the back door. Enough daylight filtered through the forest canopy and the cabin's dusty glass windows for Koa to see the disarray inside.

Though he didn't expect the officer posted outside to look back toward the house, he still left the lights off. The police had searched the place and left a mess with drawers pulled out, cabinets open, and paper strewn across the floor. They had even torn the bed apart. Ikaika's laptop was gone from its usual place on a small computer table. Koa assumed the police had taken it in hopes of finding an electronic trail to his whereabouts.

Koa had not asked Ikaika where he kept his passwords, but on one of his visits, he'd seen his brother referring to a list of passwords on the inside cover of a softcover book. Ikaika didn't have many books, but the search team had dumped the contents of a small bookcase into a haphazard pile on the floor. Koa knelt, sorting and thumbing through the books until he found Pratt's *Field Guide to the Birds of Hawaii and the Tropical Pacific*. He found a list of Ikaika's computer passwords inside the front cover. Scanning the list, he saw credentials for both Ikaika's wireless account and his only credit card, a Visa account.

Having found what he came for, Koa stood and started toward the back door. Some sixth sense stopped him. He looked around the small space with the feeling that he'd missed something. But what? Nothing in the clutter stood out. Years of experience had taught him to trust his instincts. Unable to determine what had triggered his unease, he retrieved his cellphone, set it to video, and quickly recorded the interior of the small cabin.

He then made his way back through the forest to the borrowed jeep. As he approached the Phillips 76 station in Kurtistown to retrieve his SUV, Koa wondered whether the man Moreau had sent to tail him was still outside the café waiting for Koa to return.

CHAPTER FIFTEEN

BACK IN HIS office, Koa watched clips from the surveillance video at Makanui's house twice without finding the slightest evidence that anyone had cased the property before the shooting. Still, he remained unconvinced. The setup for the attack was too perfect for the shooter not to have scoped out the site. Given Makanui's experience and exceptional situational awareness, the absence of detectable surveillance activity meant that the perp was a real pro who most likely used sophisticated remote technology to observe his target.

He was still considering all the angles when Georgina popped into his office.

"Guess what?" she asked with a mischievous grin.

Koa preferred straight-up answers and didn't care for guessing games, but Georgina enjoyed teasing him with her discoveries, and so he humored her. Thinking back to their earlier conversation about the bullet she found at Makanui's house, he guessed, "You found something odd about the bullet you dug out of the wall."

"Good guess," she responded.

"So tell me more," Koa insisted.

"The bullet is from a 7N14 cartridge. The Russians designed it in 1999 as a sniper round for their Snayperskaya Vintovka Dragunova rifle with a hardened core designed for greater accuracy and to penetrate plated body armor."

"You check the specs?" Koa asked.

"What do you think?" Georgina asked, playfully offended that he would doubt her thoroughness. "Muzzle velocity of 2,723 feet per second with a maximum effective range of about a half-a-mile."

Koa immediately understood the significance. "That's why Makanui got banged up with broken ribs and bruises."

"And," Georgina nodded, "she's lucky she's not dead. With the right load, it should have penetrated steel-plated body armor."

"A Dragunov?" Koa voiced his surprise. "Who has a Dragunov in Hawai'i? And where would they get Russian sniper rounds?"

"Dragunov imports have been banned in the U.S. since the late 1980s or early '90s. There are some in the hands of collectors, but they're pricey. The Russians exported the rifles to the Eastern Block and their foreign allies. So, it wouldn't be all that hard to acquire a Dragunov, but the ammo, that's a different story. I have no idea where one could get genuine 7N14 rounds in the U.S."

Koa, who had fired numerous weapons, including a Russian SVD during his Special Forces days, wondered aloud. "Why would a pro choose a Dragunov for a long-range sniper shot? The Russians designed it as a medium-range weapon carried by squad marksmen to support ground troops. There are much better modern sniper rifles on the U.S. market."

"Got me," Georgina responded. "I can't answer the why, but I'll guarantee that the bullet came from a genuine 7N14 cartridge."

Weird, Koa mused as his thoughts veered in another direction. If Reyes, the O'ahu bomber, had tried to take out Makanui, why would he use a Russian rifle? It seemed like a strange choice, but Koa nevertheless resolved to learn more about the man's history.

Shortly after Georgina left, Piki bounced into Koa's office like an overcharged toy and began talking like a sprinter. The two occasionally jogged together, and Koa knew that Piki ran and talked at warp speed.

"I've checked all the felony cases that Makanui handled in her four years with the HPD and since she's been here. Well, I limited the search to violent felonies. In addition to Reyes, the bomber guy who just escaped, she had a hand in putting away twenty-seven violent felons. Not a bad record. Six are dead. Twelve are still locked up. Of the other nine, three have left the Islands, three have regularly reported to their parole officers and seem to be adjusting to life outside. One was released four years ago and is no longer in the parole system. Two got released in the past six months."

"Names of the last two?" Koa demanded.

"Kula Kukua, charged with rape, pled to a lesser charge, incarcerated 2015, and paroled months ago. No other history of violence. Makanui arrested him before getting reassigned to the anti-terror unit."

"Doesn't sound likely," Koa said.

"I agree," Piki responded, "but the next guy is a serious possibility. Henry Nāhale, charged with resisting arrest, assaulting a police officer, possession of a prohibited firearm . . ."

"Previous felony record?" Koa interrupted to slow Piki down.

"Yeah. A long rap sheet. Mostly burglary and assault."

"Weapons?" Koa asked.

"All handguns, including one modified for rapid-fire with a large magazine."

"Go on," Koa instructed.

"Nāhale was incarcerated in 2013 and paroled last month. Makanui testified at his trial."

"You talk to his parole officer?" Koa asked.

"Yeah. The asshole's already violated his parole by missing three appointments, and the court issued a bench warrant for his arrest last week."

"Any indication he's on the Big Island?" Koa pressed.

"No, but he's got relatives down south in Nāʻālehu."

"Get an ABP out for him and alert the substation in Nāʻālehu. Make sure they know he could be armed and dangerous. And check with the TSA and the airlines. Find out if he's flown in under his own name. You get anything further on Reyes?"

"The Honolulu cops think he may have had help escaping from Hālawa prison and may be holed up someplace on Oʻahu, but they've got nothing concrete."

"What makes them think he had help?" Koa asked.

"A traffic camera caught an image that might be Reyes in a car with an accomplice."

"Sounds pretty thin."

"Maybe, except the car was stolen and later abandoned up in the hills. Seems Reyes operated out of the hill country before Makanui got her hands on him, so he knows that country. Makes it a logical place for him to hide."

"But he could have switched to another vehicle and could be anywhere?"

"I suppose," Piki said.

"Reyes is supposed to be intelligent," Koa said. "If you'd escaped from a maximum-security facility, would you go where the police would expect you to go?"

"Probably not," Piki conceded grudgingly. Then, leaving Koa's office, he paused, turning back to face Koa. "Can I say something off the record? You know, just between us."

"Sure," Koa replied.

"I heard about your brother and know the chief turned the investigation over to Moreau. I'm guessing you'll be watching Moreau and maybe doing your own digging. I just want to offer my help any way that I can."

"Thanks. I really appreciate the offer and will certainly keep it in mind, but don't do anything that puts you crosswise with Moreau or the chief."

"Yeah," Piki responded. "He's a jerk. Moreau, I mean."

* * *

That evening, Koa stopped by the Burger Joint in Hilo for two takeout grass-fed burgers, a basket of fries, and a couple of beers. He took them to the Volcano Village guesthouse Nālani arranged for Makanui. She looked more relaxed but still moved slowly. Although she tried to hide it, she was still in a lot of pain.

"Figured you'd be hungry," Koa said as they settled at a small table in a kitchen alcove, toasted to her good fortune in wearing a vest, and dug in. "You comfortable here?"

"I'd rather be at home, but it'll do for a week."

"You got your go-bag and laptop?"

"Yeah, thanks," she acknowledged.

While they ate, he told her about the 7N14 round. "Georgia thinks the shooter most likely used a Dragunov—"

"A Dragunov? Like from Russia?" she interrupted, making no effort to conceal her surprise.

"Sure looks that way," he replied. "Any connection between this Reyes guy and the Russians or their allies?"

"Not the Russians, but maybe one of their Mideast proxies," she responded. "The HPD figured he got his bomb-making training off the internet, but I found evidence that he'd traveled to

Syria for training. So, he could have been in contact with Russians there."

"So, it's not crazy to think he'd use a Dragunov to shoot you?" Koa asked, still skeptical that a professional sniper would use a Dragunov.

"He was resourceful and given enough time and money could get his hands on almost any weapon he wanted. But remember," Makanui cautioned, "he was into explosives. He wasn't a firearms guy and didn't even have a gun when we arrested him. I have real trouble seeing him with a sniper rifle, let alone handling it like a pro."

"Who else could it be?" Koa asked.

Makanui shifted in her chair to get more comfortable. "I don't know. I put away a lot of bad guys over the years. Did you identify anyone recently released from prison?"

"I had Piki review all your felony convictions. Well, at least all the violent ones. He found only one possible besides Reyes. A Hawaiian with a long rap sheet named Henry Nāhale."

"Impossible. Couldn't be crazy Henry," Makanui said definitively.

"Why not?"

"He is more than violent enough and stupid enough to go after a police officer, but it would only be in a fit of rage. He defines the word *disorganized* and has the attention span of a hopped-up two-year-old. There's no way he could have scouted my place, let alone had the patience to wait for me to open my front door."

Koa considered other possibilities. "What about Abu Sayyaf? An act of revenge for your Sulu Sea ordeal? When we first met, you were concerned about reprisals."

"I suppose it's possible. Like I told you when you hired me, I didn't go back to the Honolulu department to minimize the chances of some ISIS terrorist group retaliating for what I did in the Philippines."

Makanui referred to the reason she'd left the Honolulu police force eventually to come to the Big Island. Her parents, both avid sailors, had been aboard their fifty-three-foot sailboat in the Sulu Sea west of Mindanao when Philippine terrorists boarded their boat, kidnapped them, and held them for ransom. Their captors brutalized and nearly starved them to death in captivity.

After arranging the ransom to free her parents, Makanui, who'd spent four years with the HPD anti-terrorist squad, resigned from the Honolulu force. Then, together with Anders, a young Philippine military officer she'd met in training, she went after the kidnappers.

Makanui and Anders purchased a secondhand sailboat and sailed the Sulu Sea, hoping to attract the terrorists. They were ready when the attack came in the wee hours of a foggy, moonless night. One of the terrorists died, and Makanui captured two others.

Makanui and Anders repeatedly Tasered the captives until they revealed the location of their base camp. Makanui passed that information to the Philippine military, and the Army raided the terrorists' hideout, killing most of them and capturing a few survivors. Although the military did not permit Makanui to participate in the raid, she'd joined the medical team that rescued several hostages, some of whom were in terrible shape and subsequently died.

"It's true," Makanui continued. "I was concerned that one of the fanatics on the HPD terrorist watch list might come after my parents or me. That's why I didn't return to the HPD and am reluctant to talk about that period. Still, that was three years ago, and most of the terrorists died in the Philippine Army raid. Seems a stretch to think that one of the bad guys lived, figured out my whereabouts, and decided to come after me now."

"Maybe," Koa acknowledged, "but terrorists would have access to weapons and specialized ammo. Some probably had sniper training in Iraq or Afghanistan. And it could explain why the shooter had access to and skill with a Dragunov rifle."

Makanui tilted her head. "That's interesting. I'll talk to Anders. See if he's had any indication that Abu Sayyaf operatives are after us."

"Let me know what he says."

"Changing the subject, I hear there's a problem with your brother."

"Yeah, I think somebody's trying to frame him." Koa described the scene of the Nihoa killing in the alley behind the Surfboard, the knife, and Ikaika's fingerprints. "So, the chief has assigned the case to Moreau."

"Oh, shit! That's bad news," Makanui exclaimed. "Moreau is a serious problem. I've seen him throwing his weight around, intimidating witnesses, yelling at other officers, acting like he's some big shot. And, I've heard rumors—credible rumors—that he solicits free food, drinks, and other stuff. I'm not talking cups of coffee, but whole meals with alcohol."

"Christ. Thanks for letting me know. I'll have to wait 'til Moreau finishes the Ikaika investigation, then I'll put a stop to that."

"Coming back to your brother's problem," Makanui said, "who'd want to frame him?"

"I figured it must be one of the many enemies he's made over the years, but Alexia Sheppard—I've hired her to represent Ikaika— thinks it might be an indirect attack on me."

"Suppose," Makanui said after considering the idea, "Alexia is right, then maybe we are looking at coordinated attacks. Attacks on two separate Hilo police officers in the same week would be one hell of a coincidence."

"Who'd have the balls to do that?" Koa asked.

"I don't know, but there have been some 60,000 felonious assaults on U.S. law enforcement officers, with nearly sixty killed already this year. More than a third of those attacks were unprovoked."

"Jesus," Koa swore. "Makes you want to find another line of work." He paused. "Still, let's not get ahead of ourselves. We can't be sure that I'm the real target of this Ikaika mess, and we have no evidence that the two incidents are related."

"Agreed," Makanui said, "but we need to keep the possibility in mind as we go forward. And I mean *we*. I know you. You're going to find a way to clear your brother, and I want to help."

"Thanks. Your support means a lot. But I don't want you to have a problem with the chief."

"Screw the chief. I joined this department because of you, and I'm not going to stand by while Moreau railroads your brother."

CHAPTER SIXTEEN

THAT EVENING, KOA and Nālani joined Māpuana, Koa's mother, and Kahuna Atarau, an old and dear friend of Koa's family, at Koa's ancestral home in Laupāhoehoe on the northern coast of the Big Island. They sat on the *lānai*, bathed in cool breezes off the nearby ocean. Māpuana, a short plumpish woman with a round face and an infectious smile, had spent sixty-eight years in Laupāhoehoe, a tiny settlement of less than 500 best known for the 1946 April Fool's Day tsunami that killed twenty local students and four teachers. Although never one to complain, she'd led a hard life, raising four children by herself after losing her husband in a sugar mill accident. Her only trip off the Big Island was to be with Ikaika in Honolulu during his medical emergency. Known throughout the northern part of the island as a native healer and spiritual advisor, she treated the sick and dispirited with traditional herbal remedies.

Māpuana served her guests traditional *māmaki* tea and set out a plate of *haupia*, an old Hawaiian flan-like dessert made from coconut milk and ground arrowroot. Despite the balmy evening and the sweets, it was a somber gathering. No one touched the food. Koa had called the group together to tell Māpuana that her youngest son was again in trouble with the law. He brought Nālani, whom his mother adored, and invited Kahuna Atarau, one of Māpuana's closest friends and advisors, to help soften the blow from the awful news.

That wasn't Koa's only reason for inviting the *kahuna*. A tall, heavyset man with a heavily tattooed face, he came from a New Zealand tribal heritage. He'd arrived in Hawai'i as a teen and felt at home with the Hawaiian culture since his native Māori language, culture, and history are very similar. He'd won widespread recognition for establishing a food bank and homeless shelter in Hilo. Native Hawaiians held him in the highest esteem and often sought his counsel.

Koa knew that Nihoa, the murder victim, and many other patrons of the Surfboard bar lived off and on at the *kahuna's* homeless shelter or visited his food bank. With his deep connections in that down-trodden element of Hilo society, Koa hoped that the *kahuna* might provide insight and ferret out clues as to what had happened the night of the murder.

During his criminal years, many people described Ikaika as *he 'apu 'auhuhu kōheohoe,* a person of poisonous nature. Even his middle brother and sister turned against him, but not Māpuana. She supported Ikaika throughout his twenty-plus-year criminal career, never once wavering in her belief that, deep down, he was a good person possessed by demons. As a native healer and master at tending to a person's *mana,* or divine spirit, many regarded Māpuana as a *kahuna* in her own right. Over the years, she and her mentor and friend Kahuna Atarau had prayed incessantly for Ikaika.

In the end, events justified Māpuana's faith. After Ikaika collapsed in jail, doctors discovered two slow-growing tumors undetected since childhood that had affected his behavior. After surgery to remove the growths, Ikaika had emerged a new person, and Māpuana had rejoiced. She described the day that Ikaika became a free man as the happiest day of her life.

"It cannot be," Māpuana insisted with tears in her eyes. "Ikaika would not kill."

"I know," Koa responded, "but the police won't have your faith in him."

"Who's the victim?" Kahuna Atarau asked.

"A young hood named Johnnie Nihoa. You know him?"

"Nihoa. That's odd."

The *kahuna*'s comment piqued Koa's interest. "What's odd?"

"Nihoa was living in the shelter until a couple of weeks ago," the *kahuna* began. "But then he left. I saw him a couple of days later and asked him why he'd left. He told me he'd met a guy and come into some money."

"What guy?" Koa asked.

"He didn't say, but only an evil soul would feed Nihoa's drinking binges. That's where 'is money goes. I figured he'd be back when he dried out."

"He say anything more, anything at all, about this mysterious benefactor?" Koa asked.

"Nope."

"And you never saw him with this guy?"

"Afraid not."

"Did Nihoa have a regular drinking buddy?"

"No. Why do you ask?"

"You ever see Nihoa with Ikaika?"

"No. Never. What are you getting at?"

Koa related the bartender's description of a big Hawaiian man with a scar sitting in the Surfboard with Nihoa. "His description matched Ikaika, except he had the scar on the wrong side of the face."

"Doesn't that rule out Ikaika?"

"It might, except for the other evidence."

"What evidence?" Kahuna Atarau asked.

"Ikaika's fingerprints on a knife found not far from the body."

"His fingerprints?" Kahuna Atarau repeated. "That's powerful *mea hōʻike*, powerful evidence. How do you explain that away?"

"I believe somebody planted his fingerprints," Koa responded.

"Like someone stole a knife Ikaika handled, maybe while cutting up fish?"

"Perhaps," Koa responded, "but more likely someone transposed his fingerprints onto the knife found at the scene."

"How can that be?" Kahuna Atarau asked.

"There are ways. It's technically possible."

"Would Ikaika be stupid enough to kill someone with a knife and leave it at the scene?" Māpuana asked incredulously.

"No. That's the point," Koa conceded. "I believe somebody's framing him."

"Why would anyone frame your brother?" Māpuana asked.

"He has many ghosts from his past, Māmā," Koa said, "but it's also possible someone is trying to get at me. I've put a lot of people in jail over the years."

"You have to help him. Your ancestors would want no less," Māpuana said.

"Yes, Māmā. I am doing everything I can."

Māpuana turned to look at Kahuna Atarau.

He nodded. "I'd love to help, but I'm not sure what I can do."

"You could help identify the guy with Nihoa," Koa said.

"I don't usually help the police," he responded with a grin.

"Ahh, but you wouldn't be helping the police. Instead, you'd be trying to save Ikaika from the police," Koa replied, returning the *kahuna*'s grin.

"Okay," the *kahuna* agreed.

"And some of your residents hang out at the Surfboard bar, don't they?" Koa asked.

"You want me to talk to them? See what they remember about the night Nihoa died?"

"They're more likely to talk to you than me," Koa replied.

"What do you want to know?"

"There's something fishy about Moses's story. He's the bartender. He knows more than he's saying."

CHAPTER SEVENTEEN

THE FOLLOWING MORNING, Moreau was back in Koa's office, once again having barged his way in. Koa knew from the man's grin that he wasn't bringing good news. Koa initially thought Moreau had somehow discovered Ikaika's whereabouts and arrested him, but Moreau quickly dispelled that worry. "We've got new evidence of your brother's guilt. He's going down," Moreau said with a smirk.

Koa wanted to throw the man out of his office but restrained himself. If there had been a development, he needed to know what it was and understand its significance. "What new evidence?"

"That paper you found in Nihoa's pocket. All the blood made it a little hard to read, but we deciphered it. And guess what? It's your convict brother's cell number. Proves he and Nihoa had something going. And with those two, it had to be criminal." Moreau paused for a moment, then added, sarcastically, "Just thought you'd want to know."

Koa sensed that Moreau was baiting him, but he still felt his stomach tighten into a knot. Despite his absurd logical leaps, Moreau had found troubling evidence. Unlike Moreau, Koa tried to put the evidence in context. A person might have another's phone number for lots of reasons. Someone could even have planted it. Proof of an actual conversation would be more significant. He wondered if

Moreau had checked phone records. It was a logical investigative step, but Moreau would have gloated about it if he had phone records to show that Nihoa and Ikaika had actually talked. Still, Koa wasn't about to point out that possible weakness and send Moreau scurrying after the phone company.

"Anything else?" Koa asked in a flat, unemotional tone.

"Not today," Moreau responded as he left, taking his attitude with him.

After Moreau left, Koa sat thinking. Why would Nihoa have Ikaika's phone number? Then, he saw the anomaly. Picking up his cell, he called Kahuna Atarau. When the *kahuna* answered, Koa identified himself and asked, "Did Nihoa by any chance have a cellphone?"

The *kahuna* chuckled. "Not a chance. No provider would open an account for him, and he wouldn't waste drinking money on a prepaid. You need to volunteer down here at the shelter. If you saw how these people live, you wouldn't have to ask that question." After a moment of silence, Atarau said, "Why are you asking?"

"Nihoa had a piece of paper in his pocket when he died. Blood obscured the writing, so I couldn't read it at the time, but the lab reconstructed it. It's Ikaika's cell number. I was trying to see if there might be any record of an actual call."

"I doubt that Nihoa called Ikaika," Atarau responded, "but even if he did, it would have been from a pay phone, or maybe a phone borrowed from someone he knew."

"Thanks," Koa responded before ending the call.

Moreau, Koa realized, took way too much delight in pursuing Ikaika. Maybe Moreau was just an overly aggressive, ambition-driven personality already promoted beyond his level of competence. Somehow, though, there was more to it. But what?

That question made Koa think of Mayor Satō. The mayor still harbored a grievance against Koa for arresting his son, Ronnie. Koa suspected Satō pushed the chief to appoint Moreau out of revenge and feared that Satō and Moreau would ultimately remove him as chief detective, if not run him out of the force. But what if there were more to the mayor's vindictiveness. Could Satō have had a hand in framing Ikaika? You go after my son, and I'll come after your brother with tenfold vengeance. Moreau would then be the perfect instrument. He'd worked closely with the mayor and now served as the mayor's eyes and ears within the police department. Devoid of scruples, Moreau could use his position as Koa's peer to set up the frame, taunting Koa as the plot played out.

It seemed far-fetched, even paranoid, but Koa had long ago learned to trust his instincts. He reminded himself that even paranoids have enemies, and Moreau certainly qualified. He had to learn more about Moreau's connection with His Honor, the mayor.

Zeke Brown, the county prosecutor, was Koa's go-to source for the inside scoop on everything related to Hawai'i County politics. Repeatedly reelected by the voters, Zeke was not beholden to the mayor and had long-standing contacts throughout the Hilo government. If anyone had a line on Satō, it was Zeke.

* * *

An hour later, Koa stopped by Zeke's office where he found the prosecutor hunched over his desk with his sleeves rolled up, holding a red pen, which slashed and burned its way across some legal document that flunked Zeke's high standards. "Got a minute?" Koa asked, interrupting Zeke's editorial choreography.

"Sure," Zeke responded, dropping the pen onto the desk and leaning back into his chair. "What's on your mind?" Handsome, self-assured, and gregarious, Zeke was a big man with a big personality. A presence who dominated almost any setting. Typically outfitted in jeans and a long-sleeve dress shirt, embroidered with his initials, he sported expensive, black Lucchese cowboy boots and a fine black belt with a fancy handmade, silver buckle. At ease "talking story," sometimes profanely, with the voters who repeatedly reelected him, he often hid his first-rate intellect. Yet, anyone taken in by the good-old-boy front or who missed the intelligence behind his inquisitive hazel eyes usually lived to regret it.

"Detective Moreau and the mayor. You know that Satō forced him on the department?"

Zeke nodded. "Yeah. I've heard something like that."

"And you know that Chief Lannua put Moreau in charge of investigating Ikaika and the Nihoa murder?"

"Yeah. I know. Moreau has been in here asking for search and arrest warrants," Zeke responded.

"What you don't know—" Koa paused before continuing—"is that Moreau is relishing all this and taunting me about Ikaika's plight."

"Doesn't surprise me. Moreau thinks he's some kind of Apana Chang." Zeke referred to Honolulu's legendary Chinese detective of the 1870s, who inspired the Charlie Chan character, the fictional detective protagonist who appeared in dozens of books and movies from the 1920s to the '40s.

Koa smiled at the historical reference. "He's no Apana Chang. He's not that smart. He just intimidates witnesses who won't tell him what he wants to hear."

Again, Zeke nodded. "I've heard complaints, particularly from the native community."

Koa phrased his next statement with care. He knew Zeke would be involved in the prosecution of Ikaika if it came to that, and he didn't yet have the evidence to accuse Moreau or anyone else of trying to frame his brother. Parsing his words carefully, he said, "I've been wondering if Mayor Satō isn't exploiting the situation, encouraging Moreau to taunt me. Maybe even force me out."

"I've never known a detective with a better nose for what stinks. And that's a compliment, my friend," Zeke responded.

"Taken as such," Koa replied. "So, tell me what stinks about our mayor?"

"First off, I don't know how he got elected. Like many Japanese in Hawai'i, his grandfather fought in WWII to prove his loyalty. He came back from the war determined to discard the mantle of discrimination against the Japanese and carve a proper place in society. Satō's father benefited from his old man's efforts and became part of the Japanese political movement that took over the Hawai'i legislature and, ultimately, the governor's office in the mid-1980s.

"Satō, the old man's grandson, couldn't make it in his father's footsteps and never achieved the prominence he thought he deserved. Then, along came this last election, and Satō's out hunting for the radical vote. You witnessed his campaign. Defund the police. Sovereignty treaties for native Hawaiians. Restrict tourism. Lower taxes for the locals. Tax the hell out of the snowbirds.

"I wasn't alone in thinking he had no chance, but that was the problem. Low turnout. Less than twenty percent of the voters turned up at the polls, and the son of a bitch got elected. I've heard rumors that he bought the election, literally paying his supporters a hundred bucks to vote for him. I've had investigators out trying to find evidence, but so far, I haven't got enough to go to a grand jury. So, yeah, there's more than a bit irregular about our mayor.

"Then there's Satō's conduct in office. He's slowly dismantling the county government and putting his unqualified but loyal disciples into key positions. Moreau isn't the only example. Still, I haven't yet found proof of payoffs. And not for lack of trying."

CHAPTER EIGHTEEN

THE FEELING GNAWED at Koa. He'd missed something, something of vital importance at Ikaika's home. Sitting at his desk, Koa played the video he shot before leaving the cabin. Nothing jumped out at him, so he broke the recording down into distinct clips. He began with Ikaika's bed, now torn up by the police during their search, reviewing that section repeatedly. Nothing struck him. Switching to video clips of the books and empty bookcase, he still saw nothing out of the ordinary. Moving on to the images of the table by the front door, nothing stood out, and after reviewing it twice, he played the section showing the kitchen.

Running clips of the tiny cooking space, he noted open cabinets and drawers as the police had left them, a few dirty dishes atop the counter, and a sizeable overflowing trash container to one side of the sink. Next, he viewed video of the small dining table, one of its four chairs turned on its side. And lastly, the overstuffed armchairs facing a small TV in the rear corner of the room. Nothing triggered his special attention.

Damn it. Koa knew that something had escaped his notice. Determined to find what he'd overlooked, he viewed the videos again section by section. His eureka moment came when he reran the kitchen clips. A corner of a pizza box in the trash, near the overflowing top. Perhaps Ikaika and Maria ate pizza the night before their camping trip, the night of Nihoa's murder. Ikaika had sworn to Koa that he and Maria were home all night, so they may have used a delivery service. But who delivered pizza to a rural location outside Mountain View? In the video, he tried to make out a logo, but only the corner of the box showed above the lip of the trash basket.

Logging onto Ikaika's wireless account, Koa saw no calls on the night of the murder. So, if Ikaika hadn't ordered pizza, Maria may have phoned in the order, but he had no way of accessing her phone records. Koa checked Ikaika's Visa account and found no charge for a pizza, but that, too, was inconclusive. Ikaika could have paid cash, or Maria could have used her credit card.

Koa considered the only possible shops that might have delivered this far out of town—Domino's, Pizza Hut, and Frankie's. Domino's in Hilo was too far away for delivery, and Koa could not recall whether Frankie's even offered delivery. So, he headed off to Pizza Hut in Kea'au, about halfway between Hilo and Mountain View. Jimmy Hsu, the daytime manager, walked him through the delivery orders for the night of the murder. No luck.

Koa drove south to Frankie's on the Hawai'i Belt Road next to an Aloha gas station in Mountain View. He'd sometimes stopped there for coffee in the morning or takeout meals on his way home. He was especially fond of the pineapple pizza and Korean fries.

He pulled into one of five parking spaces in front of a nondescript building, identified by the single word "Frankies" in bright red letters on top of the word "Pizza," which had faded to the point of being barely visible. When he entered the ramshackle building, Betty Kim greeted him as usual—"Coffee, Detective?"

"Not today. I was wondering, though. Do you ever deliver?"

"Not usually, but for you, we might be able to arrange something," she replied. "We don't have the staff for deliveries, but sometimes we get Jimmy at the Aloha station to deliver for special customers."

"It's not for me, but for my brother Ikaika," Koa responded.

"Oh, he's a regular. Gets deliveries all the time."

"What about last Wednesday night?" Koa asked.

Betty disappeared into the kitchen and returned a moment later with a stack of order tickets. Riffling through the pile, she pulled out a single ticket. "Here it is. Ordered at 7:35 and sent out for delivery at 8:05. His place is only about a half-mile up the road, so Jimmy must have delivered the pizza about 8:20 or 8:25."

Koa ran the timeline in his head. He arrived at the murder scene in the alley at 10:20 p.m. The call had come into the emergency operations center at 10:05. The coroner had not established an exact time of death, but it must have happened before 10:00 p.m.

If Ikaika had been at home to accept the pizza delivery at 8:20, he could not have been in downtown Hilo at the Surfboard before 8:50. Yet, according to Moses, Nihoa and the scar-faced Hawaiian were inside the bar for more than an hour before they exited the back door. Koa's heart raced. If Jimmy could verify that Ikaika had been home at 8:20, they might be able to substantiate Ikaika's alibi. It would come down to a matter of minutes.

Koa went looking for Jimmy. He found the kid in a shed behind the Aloha gas pumps bent over the engine of an old Buick. Koa watched him for a moment before Jimmy became aware of Koa's presence. Pulling his head from the engine compartment, Jimmy asked, "Who are you?"

Koa studied the young man, dressed in greasy shorts, a stained tee shirt, and well-worn athletic shoes, before introducing himself and asking, "You do some deliveries for Frankie's?"

"Yeah, sometimes," Jimmy answered hesitantly.

"You deliver a pizza to Ikaika Kāne's place last Wednesday night?"

"Yeah, Ikaika's a regular, but I'm not sure about last Wednesday."

"You keep a log of your deliveries?"

Jimmy shook his head. "Afraid not."

"And you don't remember the last time you delivered to Ikaika?"

"I made a recent delivery, but I'm not sure of the date," Jimmy answered.

Koa thought for a moment. "What do you drive when you make deliveries?"

"The old Kia Soul parked out front." Jimmy pointed toward the area on the north side of the Aloha station.

"It have GPS?" Koa asked.

"Yeah, a handheld unit mounted on the dash," Jimmy responded. "I use it for deliveries when I'm not sure of the address."

"Let's have a look," Koa directed. If he was lucky, the GPS unit recorded Jimmy's delivery routes along with the time.

The two of them walked out to the Kia. Jimmy opened the door, accessed the GPS unit, and handed it to Koa. Sure enough, the device had logged a Wednesday trip west from Frankie's to a GPS location outside Mountain View that matched Ikaika's address ending at 8:27 p.m., followed by a return trip. Koa used his phone to photograph Jimmy, the car, the GPS device, and the relevant entry. Then, looking Jimmy in the eye, he asked, "Who answered the door and took the pizza?"

"Ikaika," Jimmy answered without hesitation. "That I remember because he asked why the delivery had taken so long."

"And why was that?" Koa asked.

"Well, I had to gas up."

* * *

Koa was back in Alexia's office that evening, but they weren't alone. He had asked Kahuna Atarau and Bobbie Miura, Alexia's investigator, to join them. "Let's hear what you've got," Koa suggested, nodding toward Atarau. "You want to go first?"

"I talked to a couple of the men in the shelter, ones who've been with me a long time, ones you can half trust. Seems like Johnnie Nihoa was boozing with some fella. A dude somewhat like Ikaika. But that's not the only time this fella's been in the Surfboard."

Koa felt a surge of hope. "Do we have dates? Something that might conflict with Ikaika's known whereabouts?"

"Nothing that specific," the *kahuna* responded. "Just the night of the killing and then a week or two before."

Koa sighed. "You get his name?"

Atarau shook his head no. "But I did hear that this dude, he was having serious words with Moses a week or two before the murder."

Koa recalled Moses's words—"I nevah seen 'im in maybe four or five years." So, Moses had lied.

"That's useful," Koa replied. "Anything else?"

Atarau shook his head. "Sorry, Koa. That's all I know."

Alexia turned to Miura, her investigator. "Tell 'em," Alexia directed. Alexia had become the best criminal lawyer on the Big Island in no small measure because of her notoriously thorough preparation. In trials, she had an encyclopedic knowledge of every witness statement and document. As good as Alexia was, Koa knew that some of the credit belonged to Miura. The thin, balding Japanese man had an extensive network of contacts and an instinct for the jugular that he kept hidden behind his nondescript features and his ability to switch to deliberately broken English or Hawaiian pidgin as circumstances might dictate.

"Alexia, she briefed me on your talk with Moses at the Surfboard," Miura began. "I figured if he were hiding something, there'd be a reason. So, I talked to a source I know at his bank. He deposited twenty-five grand just ten days before the killing. That's $25,000 in cash supposedly from a sleepy dive bar that grosses a tenth that amount in a bang-up month. The bank filed a currency transaction report with the Treasury."

"Where'd he get the money?" Koa asked.

"Don't know," Miura responded, "but it's the largest deposit since Moses opened the account. The bank officers asked about the source, and Moses mumbled something about accumulated profits. The bank didn't find that credible and is considering whether it needs to file a suspicious activity report."

"What do you make of it?" Koa asked.

"Smells like a payoff," Miura said.

"Anything else?" Alexia asked.

Miura shook his head.

"Alexia?" Koa asked.

"You go first, Koa," she responded. "Let's get all the facts on the table before we talk tactics."

"Okay," he agreed as he began to describe finding Ikaika's passwords, spotting the pizza box, and his inquiries at Pizza Hut and Frankie's. "That gives us solid proof that Ikaika was home at 8:27 p.m., and even later if you allow time for eating the pizza. Thus, he couldn't have been in the Surfboard before 8:55 at the earliest. According to Moses, Ikaika—or the look-alike—was inside the Surfboard for over an hour before leaving sometime before 10:00 p.m."

Koa let the group absorb the significance of that timing before continuing. "This fellow who supposedly looks like Ikaika paid for four rounds of drinks with a one-hundred-dollar bill. I got that bill from Moses and ran it past a fingerprint examiner. It's got prints, but not Ikaika's."

"Seems like we have enough to get the police to clear Ikaika," Miura said.

"No chance," Koa responded. "The chief has it out for Ikaika and has appointed a suck-up detective to go after him. This cop thinks Ikaika's fingerprints on the bloody knife at the scene make for an ironclad case and won't give us the time of day. Besides, as I told you on the phone, the cops have Ikaika's phone number on a scrap of bloody paper found in Nihoa's pocket."

Koa turned to Alexia, and she explained that she'd lined up two experts to check the authenticity of the fingerprints on the knife.

"How does that work?" Atarau asked.

"Everyone's fingers have ridges, called friction ridges, formed in the womb before birth. Those ridges are unique to every person and don't change over a lifetime. When someone touches something, sweat, moisture, grease from their fingers, frequently some of their DNA, gets transferred, creating unique fingerprints. A forger with the right skills can create a fingerprint mold but re-creating the right mixture of sweat, moisture, grease, and DNA is a whole different ball game. So, the forger typically substitutes oil as the transfer substance."

"Sounds pretty technical and difficult," Atarau said.

"Actually, it's not hard," Alexia explained. "There are recipes for creating false fingerprints on the internet, and recently researchers using 3-D printing created phony prints that fooled computerized fingerprint comparison systems 80 percent of the time."

"Wow. I had no idea," Atarau responded, not hiding his surprise. "And experts can detect these forgeries?"

"Yes. Experts test for the artificial oils used in forgeries and frequently find DNA that confirms their analysis."

"So, if your experts discredit the fingerprint evidence, then the case disappears," Kahuna Atarau concluded.

"That's true," Koa explained, "but the police won't give Alexia's experts access to the knife, not until after the prosecutor indicts Ikaika and we're getting ready for trial."

"Koa's unfortunately right," Alexia agreed.

"Then what do we do?" Kahuna Atarau asked.

"We gather more evidence," Alexia said, "and then we make an end run around the police."

CHAPTER NINETEEN

ALTHOUGH THE DOCTORS had ordered a week of rest, by the third day, Makanui was restless. She wasn't used to inactivity and worried that her ribs and concussion would keep her out of the upcoming Big Island World Championship Ironman for the first time in several years. Being away from her home in this unfamiliar guesthouse also heightened her anxiety.

Working on the HPD anti-terror unit, she'd learned to be obsessively self-protective. She guarded her home with both exterior cameras and motion detectors. She even stashed weapons—a gun, two knives, and a club—in various locations throughout her home. When first arriving at the guesthouse, she quickly scoped out the place, checking the living room and the kitchen's rear door. She searched for places where she might conceal herself and located a variety of potential weapons—fireplace tools, kitchen knives, and a walking stick in one of the closets—if she needed to defend herself.

Her go-bag provided her with additional means to enhance her security. In it, she carried two portable, battery-powered, wireless motion detectors. She used them in hotel rooms and whenever she traveled. She stuck one on the exterior front of the guesthouse and the other outside on the back. When triggered by movement on the grounds outside the property, they would send an alarm to a base station near her bed. Then, she laid out the rest of her gear—her Glock with an extra magazine, a Taser, her protective vest, and a handheld digital night vision monocle. She'd long ago preprogrammed her cellphone with numbers for Koa, the police dispatcher, and various emergency services.

Given the secrecy surrounding her location, she should have felt safe, but she couldn't shake a sense of unease. Her injuries only added to her feeling of vulnerability. Her mind kept returning to the possibility that an Abu Sayyaf operative had come after her. When Koa had raised the idea, she was doubtful but couldn't conjure a more likely alternative. Her thoughts returned again and again to the Dragunov.

The kidnapping of her parents, their rescue, and her subsequent trap for the pirates were traumatic events that even she, a hard-nosed cop, tried to put behind her. But, given the recent attack, she knew she needed to recall every detail of those events to help tease out any connection between then and now.

If there was a link, her instincts told her that the Dragunov was the key. The pirates who'd boarded her boat had carried AKs. After killing one of the terrorists, she and Anders had turned the two survivors over to the Philippine military. The military had then attacked the Abu Sayyaf base camp, but the brass refused to allow her to accompany the raiding party. She'd only gotten into the terrorist camp after the raid as part of the medical team that cared for the hostages.

At the time, she'd focused on the hostages but remembered seeing a pile of captured weapons at the camp. Had there been a Dragunov in the stack? She knew of the infamous Russian weapon but had never handled one and wasn't familiar with its characteristics. On the laptop Koa had retrieved from her home, she searched the web for pictures and found several showing a Dragunov with its thin barrel, flash suppressor, distinctive front sight, and signature thumb-hole stock. The images did the trick, sparking her memory. There had been several Dragunovs among the captured weapons. The thought made her shiver. If an Abu Sayyaf terrorist had recently shot her, the bastard would try again. Of that, she was sure.

She spent the rest of the day wading through her backlog of official reports and paperwork, reading an unrealistic, over-the-top crime novel, and watching TV until she could no longer bear the relentless talking heads. She found a pair of binoculars on a bookcase. Taking them out to the backyard patio, she sat, watching birds flit from tree to tree while drinking in the sounds of the forest.

That evening she feasted on the goodies Nālani had provided before crawling into bed. Try as she might to sleep, her bruised and broken ribs prevented her from getting comfortable. She got up and paced, ultimately settling into an easy chair in the corner of the bedroom. She dozed until the soft alarm from the motion detector at the front of the house woke her. The digital clock on the bedside table read 3:00 a.m.—the ideal hour for a nighttime ambush.

Instantly alert, she moved silently to the front room of the house. Ignoring the pain from her injuries, she crouched next to a window and used her night vision monocle to scan the outside area. The electronics in the little device multiplied the moonlight captured by the CMOS sensor, giving her a remarkably sharp view of the exterior surroundings.

She spotted the bearded man almost immediately. He stood at the edge of the forest with a rifle slung over his shoulder, watching the house. Without taking her eye off the man, she speed-dialed Koa. His cell rang several times before he answered. "It's Makanui. I've got an armed intruder outside. I need backup."

She assumed the man had come to kill her and considered where best to confront him. Not outside where his rifle would give him the advantage over her Glock. Not in the front room, where she'd be visible from the moment he entered the house. Instead, she chose the bedroom, where she could direct his attention to the bed and then blindside him.

She wanted to know when the man entered the house and wished she'd brought another motion detector. Improvising, she grabbed a coffee cup from the kitchen and placed it on the floor where the front door, when opened, would bang into it. Returning to the bedroom, she quickly arranged pillows on the bed, covering them with a sheet to resemble a sleeping person. She then rolled a black sweatshirt into a ball and jammed it half under a pillow. It could easily be mistaken for her black hair in the dark bedroom. Finally, she pushed the bedroom door almost all the way closed.

Satisfied she'd created an effective deception, she donned her protective vest, chambered a round in her Glock, and crouched in the corner of the bedroom partially concealed by the overstuffed chair where she'd slept. The man would have to come into the bedroom and look to his left for him to see her, and by then, she'd have him in her gunsights.

She listened intently. Crack. A sharp but soft sound. The kind of noise made from forcing a door. She waited. Then, a faint scraping sound. The coffee cup sliding across the floor pushed by the door. She felt the airflow through the room increase. Her nighttime intruder had entered the living room.

Silence. She figured he must be standing just inside the door, listening, and getting a feel of the place. A floorboard creaked. Then another. He was moving. Holding the Glock in a two-handed firing stance, she aimed toward the door right where she expected his center mass to appear.

The bedroom door began to swing open, pushed by a rifle with a narrow barrel, flash suppressor, and distinctive front sight—a

Dragunov. Wider. Wider. The door swung fully open. A bearded man stepped silently forward into the room. He pointed the rifle at the bed and fired. Hot gases mushroomed from the weapon's suppressor, the slide ejected a cartridge casing, and a deafening sound reverberated in the small room. Again. Again. And again. Bullets tore into the sheet, pillows, and the rolled-up sweatshirt on the bed. Then, he seemed to sense something amiss and stopped firing.

"Police!" Makanui yelled. "Drop the weapon."

He froze without making a sound. Then, the barrel of the Dragunov swung rapidly toward her.

CHAPTER TWENTY

KOA'S MEETING WITH Alexia, her investigator, and Kahuna Atarau ran late, and the clock struck midnight before he made it to bed. He was deep in sleep beside Nālani at 3:00 a.m. when his cell rang. Somewhat disoriented, Koa answered on the fourth ring. A couple of seconds passed before he recognized Makanui's whisper. "It's Makanui. I've got an armed intruder outside. I need backup."

The crisp urgency in her voice brought him instantly awake. He threw on clothes, called for backup, and was out of the house so quickly and quietly that Nālani never stirred. Jumping into his vehicle, he raced toward the guesthouse. He debated using his lights and siren, but not knowing Makanui's situation, opted for a silent approach. He slowed just before reaching the long winding drive to the property. A dark-colored Toyota Tacoma pickup sat just off the road. Probably the assailant's vehicle.

Stopping three-quarters of the way up the drive, Koa jumped from his SUV and nearly made it to the house before gunshots erupted. One ... two ... three ... four rounds. Rapid but evenly spaced. Fired from a semiautomatic rifle, not a handgun. He feared the intruder had shot Makanui, leaving him to face an armed assassin alone in the house. He thought about waiting for backup but only for an instant. Makanui was inside and surely needed help.

He drew his service weapon, flattened himself against the wall of the building, and sidestepped rapidly toward the open front door. Peeking around the doorframe, he found the front room empty. Stepping inside, he saw a man armed with a rifle just inside the bedroom door. The man, facing the bed, didn't see Koa. Holding his Glock two-handed, Koa aimed at the center of the man's back.

"Police! Drop the weapon!" Koa yelled. He heard Makanui's voice issuing the same command at the same instant. He felt an instantaneous surge of relief. She was alive.

Ignoring the police commands, the intruder spun rapidly to his left, raising the Dragunov. Koa fired and simultaneously heard a second pistol shot. Both his and Makanui's bullets hit the gunman who pitched over. The Dragunov thumped to the floor.

With his Glock still covering the intruder, Koa secured the Dragunov and checked the man for other weapons. "You okay?" he asked Makanui.

"I'm okay, but I wouldn't have been if I'd been in bed." She turned a light on, and he saw that bullets had ripped into the sheet and pillows, scattering feathers everywhere. Her ruse had worked, and the gunman, thinking Makanui was in bed, had aimed his firepower in that direction. That accounted for the four rifle shots Koa had heard.

He checked the gunman's pulse. "He's still alive. Call—"

"I'm already dialing," she responded.

"You recognize him?" Koa asked while working to staunch the man's bleeding.

"No, but by the looks of him, he might be Yakan or Tausug, ethnic Filipino groups active in Abu Sayyaf."

CHAPTER TWENTY-ONE

THE FOLLOWING MORNING, Koa was once again at the top of the Mauna Loa Strip Road. Foggy mist shrouded the mountainside, condensed on the leaves of the *māmame* trees, and dripped onto the parched ground. The fog and the quiet, broken only by the occasional warble of a *'akiapōlā'au* or Hawaiian honeycreeper bird, made the remote location seem like the end of the world.

Koa fretted over the coming rendezvous as he scanned the trail to the west, looking for Ikaika and Maria. Ikaika, he knew, would resist surrendering to the authorities. Koa understood that reluctance. His brother had been in jail so many times that going back behind bars would be unbearable. Yet, his defense would lack credibility if he continued to be on the lam. Worse, he risked being injured or killed by an overzealous cop. Koa had to find a way to talk sense to him.

A noise broke his concentration, and he checked the trail to the west, but the shifting fog limited his view to no more than twenty yards. He saw no one. Yet, the noise repeated itself until the curtain of mist parted, and two shapes materialized from the fog. Moments later, he saw Ikaika in the lead, followed by Maria. He waved, and his brother returned the greeting. When they drew near, Koa hugged the pair.

"You made it to the Moku'āweoweo caldera?" Koa asked.

"Yes, and it was awesome, really awesome," Maria responded enthusiastically. "We camped beside the 'Pendulum Peak' inscription left by the Wilkes expedition. It was, like, cool." She referred to the campsite on the edge of the caldera built by the United States Exploring Expedition led by Lieutenant Charles Wilkes in 1840–41, who had used a pendulum device in an unsuccessful attempt to measure slight changes in gravity at different elevations. "I couldn't believe how big the caldera is. And those wisps of steam coming off the floor. It was just awesome."

Ikaika said nothing as Maria described their trek, and Koa, feeling the weight of his brother's silence, knew he was brooding on the murder charge. Finally, Ikaika blurted out, "Am I still wanted for murdering Nihoa?"

"I'm afraid so. A team of us—"

"Then I'm out of here. I'll lay low. I'm not going back to the icehouse. No fuckin' way," Ikaika interrupted angrily.

Koa wasn't surprised at this reaction. He'd feared as much. After his surgery and recovery, Ikaika had enjoyed an everyday life free of the fear of being sent back to jail. Now that semblance of normality had been yanked away, and memories of his previous incarcerations undoubtedly made the thought of going back more horrific.

"Listen, Ikaika," Koa responded, "a team of us have been digging into this mess. We know somebody framed you, and we think we can prove it."

"Great," Ikaika responded. "I'll come back when they dismiss the charges."

"Ikaika, please just listen to our plan. It's the only way to avoid charges or get them dismissed."

Maria put her hand on Ikaika's arm. "Listen to what your brother has to say."

Ikaika said nothing, and Koa's inability to tell what his brother was thinking left Koa unnerved. Then, after a long silence, Ikaika yielded just a little. "I'm listening," he said tentatively.

"Four of us, Alexia, her investigator, Kahuna Atarau, and I have been gathering facts, but we need your help. We want to meet in a secure place and work out the best next steps."

"Where?" Ikaika asked.

"Alexia's farm. You'll be safe there while we work things out."

"I'm not going back to jail," Ikaika said defiantly.

Having persuaded his brother to take the first step, Koa didn't respond. He'd have a better chance of getting Ikaika to surrender after his brother understood Alexia's strategy for exonerating him.

Koa drove Ikaika and Maria to Alexia's nineteenth-century farmhouse on the outskirts of Hilo north of the Wailuku River. The fields of sugarcane that once surrounded the old house had long since given way to macadamia nut and avocado trees under Alexia's watchful eye. Still, despite her modernization, the long tree-lined drive, steps to the home's gracious *lānai*, formal foyer, and parlor with its early American federal-style furnishings felt like stepping back in time.

Koa introduced Ikaika and Maria to Bobbie Miura and Maria to Alexia and Kahuna Atarau, whom Ikaika already knew. Alexia welcomed Ikaika, whom she'd represented many times, and embraced Maria. Alexia explained that no attorney-client privilege would shield their discussions because not everyone present was a client. "Thus," she said, "it would be better if Ikaika mostly listened rather than said anything that might affect his defense."

He agreed.

Koa led the discussion as he, Atarau, and Miura explained their findings. Ikaika, who'd remained silent and appeared to be brooding, leaned forward attentively when Miura described the $25,000 deposit to Moses's bank account. Koa hoped that his brother was beginning to understand the possible strength of the evidence the group had collected. Then, when Koa mentioned the pizza box, Ikaika couldn't restrain himself. "That's right. We ordered a pizza, and Jimmy delivered it. That proves that Maria and I were home that night."

"It's helpful," Koa responded, "but the timing is tight. If Moses, the bartender, is to be believed, and this fellow who looks like you was in the bar for more than an hour with Nihoa, it refutes Moses's identification of you. Unfortunately, that doesn't prove you weren't in the alley a little before ten p.m."

When the group had exhausted their review of the evidence they'd gathered, Alexia asked Koa and Ikaika to accompany her to another room. When Ikaika insisted that Maria join them, Alexia started to object, but Koa signaled her to acquiesce, and she did.

In what had once been a library but was now her home office, Alexia introduced Ken Hirokawa, a former police officer. He had substantial experience in administering and reading polygraph tests. "We have," Alexia began—turning to face Ikaika— "collected a lot of evidence establishing your innocence, but we'd need to add a polygraph test. You okay with that?"

Koa and Alexia had debated whether to employ Hirokawa to administer a lie detector test to Ikaika. While widely used in law enforcement circles, scientific research established that the results are inaccurate 15 to 20 percent of the time. Although Koa recognized the possibility of a false result, he was convinced of Ikaika's innocence and figured that a test administered by an expert regularly used by the police might make a difference in obtaining access to the murder weapon.

Ikaika looked first at Koa, who nodded, and then at Maria, who said, "Makes sense." Turning back to Alexia, Ikaika reluctantly nodded affirmatively. Hirokawa explained the polygraph procedure to

Ikaika and hooked him up to the machine. Koa, Maria, and Alexia left while the ex-cop took Ikaika through background questions before asking the critical inquiries about Ikaika's whereabouts on the night of the murder. An hour passed before Hirokawa and Ikaika came out to the *lānai* to which the others had retreated. "His answers are consistent with truth-telling," Hirokawa announced.

When they regrouped, Koa summed up. "We have a lot of circumstantial evidence that Ikaika didn't kill Johnnie Nihoa, but with Ikaika's fingerprints on the murder weapon, it's not enough to get the charges dropped." He paused. "If we could neutralize the fingerprint evidence, the police would have no case. Alexia's got experts lined up to analyze the prints, but we need access to the knife. Unfortunately, the police won't cooperate at this stage, so we want to enlist the prosecutor. If Zeke Brown hears what we have, there's a good chance he will allow Alexia's experts to test the prints on the knife."

"To convince him of your good faith—" Koa turned to Ikaika—"you're going to have to turn yourself in . . ."

"I'm not going back to jail," Ikaika blurted out forcefully.

"What's the alternative?" Koa asked. "You could hide out for a while, but the police would ultimately find you, and as a fugitive from justice, the police might use force to arrest you. That would mess up your chances of avoiding an indictment and a trial."

"I can't. I can't go back inside. I'll die," Ikaika protested more in sadness than anger.

"Ikaika." Maria's soft voice surprised Koa. "Remember what you told me about listening to your brother? How he saved you after your surgery? Why you were right to listen to his advice? I think you need to listen to him now."

In that instant, Maria grew in Koa's esteem. She'd been quiet throughout the meeting but had grasped the severity of the situation and the wisdom of Koa's plan to clear Ikaika's name. She also picked the right moment to speak and chose her words for maximum impact on Ikaika. Koa held his breath, waiting for Ikaika's reaction.

Koa could almost see the battle raging in Ikaika's mind. His rational side understood the logic of Koa's proposal while raw fear of returning to jail propelled his resistance. Koa guessed his brother could feel the walls closing in on him. Watching Ikaika's face, Koa worried that Ikaika's fear would cloud his judgment.

Koa had a plan for that eventuality. He wasn't going to let Ikaika go into hiding. That would destroy any chance of averting a trial and carry an unacceptable risk that an abusive cop like Moreau might harm Ikaika. If Ikaika refused to cooperate, Koa would arrest him. God, he hoped it would not come to that, but if it did, he would not hesitate to act.

As they waited expectantly, Ikaika looked from Alexia to Maria and finally to Koa. "Okay," he said slowly, drawing out the words, "we'll do it your way."

CHAPTER TWENTY-TWO

A POLICE FORENSICS team led by Georgina found ample evidence to confirm what had happened at the guesthouse. Four bullet holes in the bedding, four spent cartridges from the Dragunov, gunpowder residue on the bearded man's hands, and the trajectory of the two police bullets that hit him all supported the officers' reports. That made it easy for Chief Lannua to clear Koa and Makanui to return to duty the day after the shooting.

The two of them stood in the hospital corridor looking through the glass window at the gunman who lay motionless in bed. A tangle of tubes and wires connected him to oxygen, heart rate, blood pressure, and other assorted monitors. His coarse features, beard, and unshaven face gave him a distinctly unfriendly look.

"He looks Yakan or Tausug," Makanui said, referring to ethnic groups that populated the Sulu archipelago. "Kind of reinforces the possible Abu Sayyaf connection."

A police guard stood next to the door, and another occupied a chair in the corner of the hospital room. The two officers had a list of medical personnel authorized to enter and instructions to keep all others out.

Koa, who had arranged to meet the attending physician, looked at his watch. "We're a bit early. The doctor should be here shortly."

"Who is this guy?" Makanui asked rhetorically. They'd found no identification, no registration for the Tacoma pickup, and no indication of how her assailant had arrived on the Big Island or where he might have been staying. His fingerprints were not in the Hawai'i state database or the FBI's automated fingerprint identification system. Koa had sent the man's picture and prints to the FBI's Joint Terrorism Task Force and the Philippine National Counter-Terror Action Group. So far, he'd received no response.

They did recover the man's cellphone, a cheap prepaid model with several calls from the same number in its call history. That number turned out to be another prepaid cell, the last call from which had come just hours before the second attack on Makanui. That phone was now off the air and thus untraceable, but when last used had connected through a downtown Hilo cell tower.

"What I want to know is how this dude—" Koa tilted his head toward the man in the hospital bed—"learned your whereabouts. Few people outside the police department and the hospital knew that you'd survived the first assassination attempt, and even fewer knew you were staying in the Volcano Village guesthouse."

"I doubt he found out on his own," Makanui responded. "Someone must have leaked the information to him. That would explain the timing of the last call."

"Maybe," Koa acknowledged, "but as far as I know, only you and I, Nālani, the chief, and the owner of the guesthouse knew where you were, and I can't see any of them leaking it."

"Could someone have followed you or me?" Makanui asked.

"It's possible, or someone might have put a tracker on my car," Koa speculated.

While Koa and Makanui talked, a woman in hospital scrubs approached and held out her hand. "I'm doctor Bautista."

Koa introduced himself and Makanui. "Thanks for meeting with us. What can you tell us about your patient?"

"His condition is serious. He's got two gunshot wounds and suffered substantial blood loss. The shock put him in what we call a minimally conscious state, meaning that he does have some awareness of his environment, responds to stimuli, and in his case, is capable of only disorganized speech."

"Has he given you his name?" Makanui asked.

"No, I haven't heard a name. In periods of apparent agitation, he speaks in some foreign language."

"You remember anything he said . . . any of his words?" Makanui asked.

The doctor paused as she tried to remember. "*Jolo*, I think. He said *jolo* or something like that."

Makanui turned to Koa. "Jolo Island. It's in the Sulu Archipelago. Where Abu Sayyaf has one of its primary bases."

"Is he likely to recover?" Koa asked.

"Physically, yes, but it's too early to tell whether he's suffered brain damage as a result of the loss of blood."

When the doctor left, Koa speculated, "If it was an Abu Sayyaf attack, how could he have gotten his hands on the intelligence and money to pull it off?"

"I'm not sure about the intelligence," Makanui responded, "but before we went hunting for pirates in the Sula Sea, Anders and I did some research on Abu Sayyaf funding. In those days, the group got most of its money from criminal activities and kidnappings in the Philippines. Government raids stopped most of that, so I'd guess these terrorists are hurting for money. Still, there's something off about all of this."

"In what way?" Koa asked.

"So far as I know, Abu Sayyaf has never conducted an op outside the Philippines and maybe Malaysia or Indonesia. Seems odd that they'd reach across the Pacific just to target me."

"Revenge can be a powerful motive."

"I get that, but there are lots of targets for revenge—the soldiers who invaded the pirate base camp and killed many of the terrorists, the army commanders, and my partner, Anders. I talked to Anders. So far as he knows, those guys haven't gone after any of the other people involved in the raid we enabled. What makes me stand out?"

"Good question." Koa pointed to the hospital bed. "Hopefully, the doctors will unscramble his brains, and he'll tell us when he wakes up."

CHAPTER TWENTY-THREE

THAT AFTERNOON, KOA called Zeke Brown. Koa hoped that their long relationship would lend credibility to the request he was about to make. "I need to talk to you about my brother's problem. Okay?" Koa asked.

"I thought your buddy Moreau was running that investigation," Zeke responded.

Koa let the "your buddy" tweak slide. Zeke knew the scuttlebutt on Moreau, but Koa wanted to stay focused on his objective. "Ikaika's innocent, and I think we can prove it."

Zeke, who often hid his prowess behind a laid-back façade, was one of the sharpest listeners Koa had ever encountered, and he picked up on the "we" in Koa's statement. "You already hired your lady lawyer to represent him?"

"Yes," Koa responded, "and we want to meet to explain his defense. But first, Alexia and I want to bring Ikaika into your office to surrender."

"Why my office and not the police department?" Zeke asked.

"A lot of cops have it in for Ikaika. Especially Moreau, whom the chief has put in charge of the Ikaika investigation. You know about his history of using excessive force. I'm worried about Ikaika's safety and thought you might have a word with the police."

"Okay," Zeke responded. "When?"

"This afternoon," Koa replied, "and then Alexia and I want to talk to you about the case. You free?"

"I'll put you on my calendar—say for about two p.m.—and get one of my assistants to join us," Zeke responded.

Zeke's desire to have an assistant present didn't surprise Koa. They'd pursued a lot of cases together and were close socially as well as professionally. Koa and Nālani had been frequent visitors at Zeke's house for parties and barbeques. Nālani had reciprocated by inviting Zeke and his wife, Amanda, to their Volcano cottage for her signature seared 'ahi. Koa's friend Hook Hao had taken all four of them fishing for broad-billed sailfish on his commercial fishing vessel, the Ka'upu. Given their close relationship, Zeke would want a colleague present to assure that he remained above reproach.

An hour later, Koa and Alexia walked Ikaika into the prosecutor's office, and Zeke then called the police. Putting the phone down, Zeke turned to Koa. "Moreau is on his way with a posse."

"He needs a posse for a voluntary surrender?" Koa asked.

"You know Moreau. He needs an audience but might not like this show."

In no time, Moreau showed up with three officers in tow.

Zeke addressed them in no uncertain terms. "Ikaika has surrendered voluntarily, and I have guaranteed his safety in custody." Zeke looked Moreau in the eye. "I'm going to hold you personally responsible for his safety. You understand?"

Koa thought he detected a hint of disappointment in Moreau's face, but the man got the message. His job would be in jeopardy if anything happened to Ikaika.

"I understand," Moreau responded. He put the cuffs on Ikaika and led him out of the prosecutor's office.

After Moreau left with Ikaika, Zeke called Sarah Van Dyke, his principal assistant, into his office. Koa suppressed a smile upon seeing Sarah. He wondered if Zeke knew his history with Sarah. She was a descendant of one of Hawai'i's early missionary families who arrived in the Islands from Boston in 1820. Her father now owned a large cattle ranch on the slopes of the Kohala mountains in northwest Hawai'i.

Growing up on the Big Island, Sarah attended Hawai'i Preparatory Academy in Kamuela, ranked as one of the best private schools in the state. Years ago, Koa caught her and several classmates smoking pot in an abandoned cabin on the outskirts of the rural, cattle-country town. Rather than arresting them and ruining their records, Koa had given them a stern talking-to and put them on informal probation for a year. In this present meeting, neither Koa nor Sarah gave any indication of their past interaction.

"This is your dime. What's on your mind?" Zeke began, leaning back in his chair and swinging his boots up onto his long-suffering desk.

"We believe Ikaika is innocent," Koa began, "and we've got a lot of evidence to prove it. Both he and Maria, his girlfriend, will testify that he was home all night when someone murdered Nihoa. It so happens that they ordered pizza, and the delivery man will verify that Ikaika was home at the time when Moses, the Surfboard bartender, says Ikaika was inside the bar. As for Moses's identification of Ikaika, we can establish that it's faulty. He puts Ikaika's scar on the wrong cheek. Moses also claims the man he identified as Ikaika paid for four rounds of drinks with a hundred-dollar bill. We have that bill, and Ikaika's fingerprints are not on it. Moses also lied to me. Contrary to other witnesses, he stated that he had only one recent contact with this man he says was Ikaika. Then there is an unexplained $25,000 deposit in Moses's bank account ten days before Nihoa's murder. That suggests that someone may have paid Moses to frame Ikaika. Finally, Ken Hirokawa, a former police expert—your office has used him in the past—administered a lie detector test, which Ikaika passed."

"Why would anyone frame Ikaika?" Sarah asked.

"I can suggest two possible reasons," Alexia interjected. "First, Ikaika has enemies, including in the police and parole department—people who were unhappy with his pardon and want him back in jail. Second, someone might be using Ikaika to get at Koa."

"You have evidence of the latter?" Zeke asked skeptically, his interest piqued.

"No," Alexia responded, "but I do find the proximity of the attacks on Makanui and the charges against Ikaika suspicious."

"You don't usually share your client's defenses before trial. So, why are you telling us this?" Sarah asked.

"I'm sharing this information because it leaves the knife with Ikaika's fingerprints as the only substantial evidence against him. We believe our experts could establish that someone fabricated Ikaika's fingerprints."

"Fabricate fingerprints?" Sarah asked in disbelief.

"I know it's unusual," Alexia responded, "but not unprecedented. There are instructions for fabricating fingerprints on the internet, including by experts who had 80 percent success in beating print comparison systems. I have employed two fingerprint experts who will testify as to past instances of fingerprint fabrication and are prepared to test the prints on the knife."

"So, you want us to give your experts pretrial access to the knife?" Zeke asked.

"Yes, under the supervision of your experts to vet the findings," Alexia responded.

"Why on earth would we do that?" Sarah asked.

"We would have the right to examine the evidence after you file charges, so you're not giving anything away. Neither of us wants to try an innocent man," Alexia responded.

"It's an unusual request," Zeke said. "Give us a moment alone to discuss it."

Alexia and Koa left the room, waiting fifteen minutes before Zeke summoned them back. When they returned, Zeke nodded to Sarah, indicating that she should take the lead.

"Your arguments appear to have some merit, but we need some time to check out what you've told us. So give us a couple of days, and we'll get back to you."

CHAPTER TWENTY-FOUR

NĀLANI, ON HORSEBACK in her park ranger's uniform and high black leather boots, rode slowly along Hilina Pali Road. Beside her, ʻOlina Crow, a fellow park ranger, rode a quarter horse born and bred on the 130,000-acre Parker Ranch, the largest of the many cattle ranches on the Big Island. They followed the inland-facing ridge of Koaʻe fault zone along the northwestern edge of the southern flank of the Kīlauea volcano, a giant landmass sliding a few centimeters per year to the southeast into the ocean.

Fleecy white clouds skittered across the blue sky, chased across the volcanic landscape by their shadows. A *nēnē*, a goose endemic to the Islands, darted across the trail and into the underbrush. As they rode, the two park rangers searched for changes wrought by a large earthquake recorded the previous day by the volcano observatory seismographs. Stopping frequently, Nālani photographed rockfalls and other places where the quake had changed the landscape. She was in her element—the part of her job she liked best—communing with the magnificent wilderness of the national park. It changed with each outing, whether from a new eruption, an earthquake, a burst of new plant life, or just weathering from the wind and rain.

The two rangers made their way slowly, sometimes doubling back to observe from a different angle. Their experienced eyes spotted even the most subtle changes in the primordial landscape. A riot of new flowers, a freshly fallen tree, the yellow flash of an 'amakihi bird, or the circling of a hunting 'io, a Hawaiian hawk. Knowing they would be rewarded with breathtaking views when they reached the end of the road charged their sense of anticipation.

The Hilina Pali Road ended at a lookout on the pali, a cliff rising some 1,400 feet above a lava plain that extended to the ocean's edge. Four small campgrounds—Ka'aha, Halapē, Keauhou, and 'Āpua Point—gave the only hint of human presence in the vast expanse. The stunning views amidst brisk breezes from the ocean made the overlook one of Nālani's favorite places in the park. She and Koa had often picnicked here, and its association with the love of her life only added to its allure.

With the horses tethered to a post, the two rangers sat on the cliff's edge with their backs to the afternoon sun, reveling in the cool ocean air and unparalleled views. Both of Hawaiian ancestry, Nālani was thin and lithe with long flowing black hair, while 'Olina wore a few extra pounds and sported an infectious smile under short-cropped hair. As they chatted, Nālani spotted a couple hiking across the plain below toward the Ka'aha campground and pulled binoculars from her pack.

"Recognize them?" 'Olina asked.

"Yeah," Nālani responded. "They were in the backcountry office yesterday for permits." Although the requirement was often honored in the breach, the park required all hikers in more remote areas to obtain permits. While Nālani tracked the hikers' progress, 'Olina pulled a package from her pack and unwrapped several squares of kūlolo, a traditional fudge-like treat made of taro and coconut. She held a piece out to Nālani as she helped herself.

"I knew there was a reason I asked you to come along," Nālani teased, savoring the sweet Hawaiian candy.

"Sure," 'Olina chuckled, "so you wouldn't get lost out here in this paradise."

"Yeah, right," Nālani shot back.

Two more squares of *kulolo* and the women were back on their feet. While they untied the horses, 'Olina said, "Don't forget dinner tonight."

The dinner was, in fact, foremost in Nālani's mind. Upset about the likely murder charges against his brother, Koa wanted to cancel. But, after Nālani reminded him that 'Olina was her best friend and that reservations at Takenoko Sushi were nearly impossible to get, he relented and agreed to go. Nālani shared none of that background with 'Olina, instead saying, "Not a chance. Koa and I have been looking forward to it for weeks."

* * *

At six that evening, Koa and Nālani met 'Olina and Fred Crow at Takenoko Sushi in a strip mall in Hilo. Takenoko's was an intimate spot so popular that it typically took months to secure a reservation, although Pam Takenoko almost always found a place for Koa when he called. When they arrived, Pam escorted them to four of the ten seats at the sushi bar, where sushi master chef Kobayashi greeted them warmly with a respectful bow. Having dined at Takenoko before, the party knew they were in for a treat.

The evening began with sake, moved on to seaweed salad, crab and avocado, *ebi*, *unagi*, *maguro*, *toro*, and *tamago* before the meal ended with *yuzu* sorbet. The cold sake, top-notch sashimi, and intimate company made for a lighthearted evening. When only sake remained, Fred, a parole officer, asked about Ikaika, and the mood shifted.

"I hear the police are looking at your brother for the Johnnie Nihoa thing."

Although Fred might have seen something on the news, Koa guessed that Moyan, Ikaika's former parole officer, who hated Ikaika and wanted him locked up for the rest of his life, had gleefully related Ikaika's troubles to his colleague. "That's true," Koa responded, "but I'm convinced he didn't do it. You've been with Ikaika at our place a couple of times since his surgery. You've seen the changes in him."

"I know, and I also have my doubts about who stuck the knife in Nihoa. There's something odd about the whole thing."

"In what way?" Koa asked, suddenly earnest.

Nālani pushed her stool back from the counter. "While you guys talk shop, 'Olina and I are going for a stroll. Maybe walk off some of this fabulous food."

Koa recognized and appreciated Nālani's savvy. She'd intuited that Fred would be more forthcoming mano-a-mano, especially if it related to his parole work.

Fred watched the two women walk out of earshot before responding. "I've got this parolee who's a snitch. He keeps his ear to the ground, and I buy him lunch or give him a few bucks from time to time."

Koa knew how that worked. He signaled for another round of sake.

"This guy," Fred continued, "he hangs around with the Surfboard crowd. Says he sees Johnnie Nihoa every so often. Then, about ten days back, he tells me Nihoa's all excited because he's coming into a big score. That makes me curious because nobody with a brain is going to hire Nihoa. Even if he were sober, which would be as likely as a thousand-year flood, he'd need help pickin' his teeth." Fred took a sip of sake.

Koa hadn't made the connection before but wasn't surprised that Fred knew Nihoa. The kid had been in jail and would have been through the parole system. Fred would know of him even if Nihoa had a different parole officer. "So, you asked your parolee follow-up questions?" Koa asked.

"Right. He says Nihoa was bragging that some big dude had hired him for a job. My guy quotes Nihoa as saying it'll be the biggest payday of his life."

"More like his last payday," Koa said.

"That's what I started thinking after Nihoa turned up dead. That someone set him up."

"Any idea about who would do that?" Koa asked.

"Nope. Just some big dude, and that describes a sizable chunk of the population."

Koa took a sip of his sake before saying, "If you don't have a problem with it, I'd like to talk to your parolee."

"Fine by me. He's due in my office at noon tomorrow."

CHAPTER TWENTY-FIVE

SPEEDBOAT MAN, WHOSE real name was 'Aukai, earned his money running drugs and serving as an enforcer for drug lords. At sixteen, he'd made his first kill, a Hawaiian kid who'd gotten crosswise of a *batu*—methamphetamine—gang. 'Aukai hadn't felt a thing when he put the barrel of the Saturday night special against the kid's head and pulled the trigger. The Army had taught him to use more refined guns, and Iraq had educated him in the art of killing.

Now, he had a new gig, an extremely lucrative job worth a hundred grand. Opportunities like that didn't come along every day or even every year. The gig had come from some guy whom 'Aukai had met only on the phone. He went by an odd name—Kōkua—and was fast becoming 'Aukai's most significant financial angel. He'd paid surprisingly large amounts for collecting intelligence, transporting people and explosives, and setting up safe houses. 'Aukai had secretly transported two of his people and some supplies ashore from freighters preparing to dock in Hilo.

Now Kōkua wanted some Filipino dude in a bed at Hilo Medical Center put to sleep—permanently. Shouldn't be hard. The only wrinkle was timing. Kōkua wanted it to happen today before "the guy wakes up" but left the specifics up to 'Aukai. "Do it quietly if you can but use explosives if that's what it takes. I don't care how. Just get it done." Those were Kōkua's words. 'Aukai wondered if Kōkua meant that literally. He'd blown up lots of things but never a patient in a hospital.

He had little time for recon and needed to prepare for various alternatives depending on the lay of the land. Still, it was nothing he hadn't done before. He packed his gear—lethal drugs, a knife, hand-guns, rifles, a small explosive charge, and several changes of clothes—into his pickup. He then added his dream weapon, an M79 grenade launcher—essentially a 40mm, single-shot, break-action, sawed-off shotgun. What the GIs in Vietnam called a "thumper." He didn't have a license, so it wasn't legal, but it hadn't been hard to get. The Army shipped thousands to Vietnam, and civilian agencies used them with non-lethal cartridges for crowd control. He'd purchased it from the son of a GI who'd acquired it during the Vietnam War.

Buying the gun had been a snap. Getting the ammo was another thing altogether. HE—high explosive—rounds were strictly illegal outside the military, but he could legally obtain chalk, flashbang, and tear gas rounds. So, he bought some non-lethal ammo, disassembled it, and repacked the shells with explosives. After test-firing the weapon in a remote ravine on Mauna Loa, he'd practiced until he could nail his target every time. He didn't expect to use it on this gig, but in his warped world, more firepower was always a good thing.

His pickup was his favorite set of wheels, and he wouldn't risk driving it to the hospital even with false plates. So instead, he parked it in the block-long-block-wide Walmart shopping center lot and went searching for a car he could steal. He chose a five-year-old Prius, unlocked it with an electronic device that emulated a keyless entry fob, transferred his gear, and was on the road in less than ten minutes.

He knew exactly where to go. A text message from Kōkua had provided the target's room number—214—on the second floor at the back of the hospital. Thirty minutes later, he parked the stolen Prius in the Hilo Medical Center parking lot and strolled into the building dressed in a medical orderly's blue scrubs with a nurse's cap and surgical face mask. A tiny lens behind a pinhole in his name tag worked like a GoPro sending video to his phone. He blended perfectly with the surroundings, and no one paid him much notice as he took the elevator to the second floor and followed the signs to the 200 block of rooms at the rear of the building. Security cameras were everywhere, but the cap and blue surgical face mask he and many hospital personnel wore made him nearly impossible to identify.

Turning a corner onto a second-floor hallway, he spotted the policewoman standing outside one of the patient rooms. He walked casually down the corridor and, passing the guard, glanced through the open door into room 214. Shit. A second police officer sat on a chair inside the room where a deeply tanned man with Asian features lay in bed connected by wires and tubes to various medical devices. Continuing down the hallway, 'Aukai found a stairwell and left the building.

Back in his stolen wheels, he considered his options. He could pose as an orderly checking vitals and get into the hospital room without a problem. He could probably take out the two police officers before shooting the patient with his silenced handgun, but that was risky. Lots could and probably would go wrong. One of the officers might get off a shot. Even if he weren't hit, the sound of a gunshot in the hospital would bring people running. If he was lucky and the hit went down like clockwork, there would still be hundreds of pictures of him. They might not have his face, but they'd have his exact biometrics, and alerted by the gunshots, bystanders might see and remember him. They might even catch him making his getaway in his stolen car.

Retrieving his phone, he keyed the video he'd captured through the pinhole camera behind his name tag and replayed the section showing the patient's hallway several times. Nothing he saw diminished the problems he'd foreseen. The more he thought about the direct approach, the less he liked it. Still, he had to find a way. He wasn't going to let anything stand between him and a hundred-grand payday.

What had Kōkua said—"Do it quietly if you can but use explosives if that's what it takes. I don't care how. Just get it done." Then it dawned on him. He could blow the man and his guards up. He could even do it remotely without exposing himself, eliminating the risk of being recognized.

Hunkering down in the back seat, he changed out of his scrubs and into jeans, a muted, nondescript tee shirt, and workman's boots, like the clothes worn by contractors at a nearby construction site. Moving his stolen vehicle and parking it to facilitate a quick getaway, he grabbed the black nylon bag containing his M79 grenade launcher and ambled into the woods behind the hospital.

He picked a spot in the woods behind the building with a clear view of the second-floor windows. Room 214 was in the middle of the corridor, so it had to be behind one of the three center windows. Again, keying the covert video he'd taken inside the hospital, he counted the rooms. The window in room 214 had to be in the middle, but he waited to be sure. Five minutes later, when a man appeared in the window—a policeman—'Aukai had his confirmation.

'Aukai checked the distance with a laser range finder. He then broke the grenade launcher open like a break-action shotgun, slipped one of his modified high explosive cartridges into the chamber, and locked the barrel into position. The M79 was well known for its accuracy, and an experienced shooter with a precise distance measurement could easily hit a window-sized target. Having spent hours practicing with chalk-filled target practice rounds, 'Aukai qualified.

He flipped up the graduated sight, adjusted it for the range, put the stock to his shoulder, aimed, and squeezed the trigger. The gun made a thumping sound, but the nearest person was far away and would likely not have noticed. The projectile sailed through the air, smashed the middle, second-floor window, and exploded inside the room with a tremendous bang. Flames erupted, jetting twenty feet out of the window, followed by a plume of black smoke. Fire alarms sounded inside the hospital and generator-powered emergency lights illuminated.

Smoke rose high above the hospital as ʻAukai drove away. He'd earned a hundred grand. He was smiling when he parked the Prius close to where he'd stolen it and transferred his gear to his pickup.

CHAPTER TWENTY-SIX

THE MORNING AFTER his dinner with Nālani, Fred, and 'Olina, Koa and Alexia went to see Ikaika in jail. As they entered the jail facility, they met Maria coming from visiting Ikaika. They stopped to talk, and Koa asked how his brother was holding up.

"He feels confined and claustrophobic but puts on a good face for me. I hope you can get him out on bail."

"We're going to try," Alexia responded, "but it's going to be a long shot. So please don't get your hopes up. Try to stay focused on the big picture. Our goal is to get charges dropped."

"I was afraid you'd say that." Maria paused nervously before changing topics. "An investigator from the prosecutor's office visited me late yesterday afternoon. Asked me questions about Ikaika. I told him we were together all night, that I ordered pizza, and paid for it with my credit card. I showed him the call on my phone and told him that Jimmy delivered the pizza sometime between eight and nine o'clock. I think he believed me."

"That's great," Alexia said.

"Do your best, please," Maria implored them before leaving.

Although Ikaika had just been in the jail's visiting area, Koa and Alexia had to wait for guards to bring Ikaika to a small conference room reserved for attorney meetings with inmates. When he finally arrived wearing an orange jumpsuit, he looked tired and depressed.

"How you holding up, brah?" Koa asked.

"I hate being locked up. I thought I'd put all this behind me, and I don't like Maria seeing me like this. It's not fair. I wasn't anywhere near the Surfboard Bar, and I didn't kill Nihoa."

"I know," Koa said. "It isn't fair, and hopefully, you'll only be in here a few more days."

"That's easy for you to say, but I'm the one in here. This is hell for me," Ikaika said, letting the emotion show in his voice.

"I get it. Believe me, I do," Koa responded. "Alexia has always had your back, and I worked my ass off to get you a pardon after your surgery. We're doing everything we can to get you out of here."

Ikaika let out a long sigh. "I know this isn't your fault, and you're only trying to help. I'm just scared . . . scared I'll get locked away forever . . . scared of losing Maria. I got my life back and now . . . now it's falling apart."

"I hear you, Ikaika," Alexia said before she went on to describe the meeting with the prosecutors and their promise to respond in a day or two. "They need to verify what we told them before they decide on giving us pretrial access to the murder weapon."

"What are the odds?" Ikaika asked. "And don't con me."

"They didn't reject our request, and they'll be able to verify everything we told them. Zeke seemed particularly interested in the mysterious $25,000 deposit to Moses's bank account. So, I think the chances are good."

He nodded. "God, I hope you're right."

Alexia then explained what would likely happen at the bail hearing scheduled for later that morning and warned that he was unlikely to be granted bail.

"You think I don't know that?" Ikaika said.

CHAPTER TWENTY-SEVEN

KOA AND ALEXIA were on their way out of the jail when Koa's cell rang. He answered to hear Makanui calling with uncharacteristic urgency in her voice. "Somebody just bombed the Hilo Medical Center."

"Christ. What happened? Are there injuries?"

"I don't have details. I'm on my way there now."

Turning to Alexia, Koa said, "Sorry. We can talk later." Then, he took off running for his SUV. He made it to the hospital in twelve minutes. His was one of dozens of emergency vehicles—police cars, ambulances, fire trucks, and fire department command vehicles—surrounding the building. Parking half a block away, he forced his way through the emergency personnel until he spotted Derrell Ohira, the fire chief.

"What's happening?" Koa asked.

"Somebody bombed one of the hospital rooms on the second floor at the back of the building. Fire personnel have cleared that wing, and the bomb squad is up there now checking for other devices."

"Injuries?" Koa asked.

"So far, it's two dead, both in the same room, and some bruises and broken bones in the panic that followed the explosion."

The moment he heard "two dead, both in the same room," Koa figured that the bomber had killed the man who'd attacked Makanui and one of the police officers guarding him. "Which room?"

"Dunno. Just second floor, back side."

Flashing his credentials, Koa made it into the building and up a flight of stairs to the second floor. As he entered the back hall, smoke damage and a burnt, twisted doorframe in the middle of the corridor seemed to confirm his fears about their prisoner. Yet, as he moved closer, he sensed something out of kilter. When he reached the damaged door, he saw that the room was 212. Room 214, where Makanui's attacker had been, was empty but largely undamaged.

He called Makanui. "Where are you?"

"In the veteran's home next door to the hospital where they've moved some of the patients. The guy who attacked me is here, still semi-conscious, but otherwise unhurt."

"That's good news. What about the cops guarding the prisoner?"

"Shook up. Maybe some hearing loss, but still on two feet."

"Even better news. Then who got killed?" Koa asked.

"You remember the grocery store robbery last week?"

"Where some hopped-up kid pulled a gun and got shot by an off-duty cop?"

"Yeah. Well, the cop, an old-timer named Hali'a —you probably knew him—was interviewing the perp in room 212. Unfortunately, he and the juvie didn't make it."

"Jesus. That's awful. Hali'a gets a medal one day, and he's dead the next."

"Makes you wonder when your number will be up," she responded.

"The cops tell you what happened?"

"Not much. Walters, the policewoman on duty in the hallway, thinks she heard glass shatter before the blast, but here's the strange thing. Neither cop saw anybody in the corridor before the bomb went off. Sounds like the device was radio-controlled or on a timer."

"You think our prisoner was the intended target?"

"Had to be," Makanui replied. "Who the hell would kill an aging cop and a drugged-out juvie in custody for a measly robbery? And with a bomb, no less. Had to be a hit on our guy gone south."

"I need to be at my brother's bail hearing and then interview one of Fred Crow's parolees. Get Piki to find a secure place to hide our Dragunov shooter, maybe a private clinic. Tell Piki to pick a handful of reliable officers to guard the man. Then, you come over here to supervise this investigation until I can get free. Okay?"

"You got it."

CHAPTER TWENTY-EIGHT

KOA WASN'T SURPRISED to see Hardy Moyan at Ikaika's bail hearing. Koa had a long history with Moyan, Ikaika's former hard-ass parole officer. In Moyan's view, Ikaika was an incorrigible repeat offender who deserved life in prison. The parole officer had repeatedly urged the courts to impose the longest possible sentences on him and had strenuously opposed parole at every opportunity. He'd even objected to allowing Ikaika a compassionate visit when Māmā had been seriously ill.

Detective Moreau entered the court and took a seat next to Moyan. No doubt, Koa thought, the pair of them had come to gloat over Ikaika's predicament. Koa found their coziness annoying but had no doubt that's what Moreau intended. The overwhelming likelihood that the court would deny bail increased Koa's irritation.

The police brought Ikaika, dressed in prison overalls and shackles, into the courtroom. If Moyan and Moreau expected a beaten-down and depressed Ikaika, they were disappointed. Although Koa knew how hard it had been for Ikaika to surrender and how much he hated incarceration, he stood erect with his head held high. Ikaika might feel defeated, but he'd never give Moyan the satisfaction of showing it.

Judge Hitachi took the bench, and the clerk called the case. Koa had expected to see Zeke at the prosecution table, but Sarah Van

Dyke, Zeke's principal assistant, represented the State. Zeke typically handled murder cases, and Koa wondered if Zeke's absence was significant.

When prompted, Ikaika pleaded not guilty in a loud but respectful voice.

The judge then asked the prosecutor for the State's position on bail.

Sarah stood to respond. "Your Honor, the State requests that the defendant be remanded to custody pending trial. This case involves the murder of a young man in a back alley here in Hilo. The State expects to present substantial evidence of the defendant's guilt."

Koa waited for more, but Sarah stopped. Koa, who'd attended countless bail hearings, could hardly believe Sarah's plain vanilla argument. She hadn't recited Ikaika's lengthy criminal history nor described the bloody crime scene with multiple stab wounds. She hadn't mentioned that a witness had seen Ikaika or someone who looked like him with the victim moments before the killing. Most surprisingly, she had not mentioned the knife with Ikaika's fingerprints. The omissions left Koa scratching his head and wondering how Alexia would respond. She had come prepared to address each aspect of the prosecution's evidence but now had little to attack.

The judge turned to Alexia.

"Your Honor," she began, "there is substantial evidence that someone other than the defendant committed this crime. There are no witnesses to the killing, the defendant has a verifiable alibi, and many unexplained circumstances surround the victim's death. The defendant has lived in Hawai'i his entire life, voluntarily surrendered to the police, and is not a flight risk. He will agree to surrender travel documents and wear an electronic bracelet or meet such other conditions as the court may direct."

Judge Hitachi, a dignified man of Japanese descent in his fifties, had been on the bench for two decades. Koa had been in his courtroom many times and had often sought search and arrest warrants from him in his chambers and occasionally at the judge's home. As a result, he'd learned to read the judge's expressions and body language. Like Koa, the judge seemed mystified by the course of the proceedings. The prosecutor sought the denial of bail but was not making much of a case. That fact appeared to disturb Moreau and Moyan, who were whispering and shaking their heads. Judge Hitachi had presided over at least one of Ikaika's previous guilty pleas and had to know that the prosecutor was pulling punches. That alone told the judge the prosecutor didn't feel strongly about the denial of bail.

Turning to the prosecutor, Judge Hatachi asked, "Wasn't the defendant previously convicted of a crime involving violence against a person within the past ten years, and under our law doesn't that create a rebuttable presumption against bail?"

The question, Koa thought, was a bad sign, suggesting the court would not grant bail.

"That's correct, Your Honor," Sarah responded, again without emphasizing the point or reciting either the number or details of Ikaika's convictions.

"Miss Sheppard," the judge asked, "are you prepared to rebut the presumption against bail?"

"Yes, Your Honor. The defendant was previously convicted but subsequently pardoned by the governor based on extensive medical testimony that his previous conduct had been affected by frontal lobe brain tumors. The experts also testified that the defendant would be unlikely to commit further crimes following the removal of the tumors. In short, the governor's pardon wipes out the previous convictions."

Judge Hitachi had heard enough. "Well, that does rebut the presumption, leaving in place the legislative preference for bail before trial. I will set bail at $100,000. In addition, the defendant is ordered to surrender travel documents, remain in Hawai'i County, wear an electronic monitor, and report weekly to a parole officer."

Koa could hardly believe his ears. He had come to the courtroom virtually sure that Ikaika would not get bail. Now Ikaika would not have to spend another night in jail. The judge had set a high bail, but Koa could help his brother pull together ten percent of that amount to secure a bail bond. Their mother would be overjoyed.

As the jailers took Ikaika away to begin processing his release, Koa joined Alexia on the way out of the courtroom. "What happened in there?" he asked.

"I talked to Sarah just before the hearing," Alexia began. "Zeke's investigators checked some of the things we told them. They interviewed Maria, who vouched for Ikaika's alibi. They also verified Moses's $25,000 bank deposit. They agree that the timing shortly before the murder, the abnormally large amount in relation to Moses's regular deposits, its all-cash nature, and his flaky explanation make his credibility suspect. Bottom line, while they're not ready to drop the case, they have significant doubts about Ikaika's guilt. I'm guessing they wanted to say they opposed bail but wouldn't stake their credibility on it."

"Does that mean they'll submit the knife to our experts?" Koa asked.

"That, I'm afraid, remains to be seen."

CHAPTER TWENTY-NINE

AFTER THE BAIL hearing, Koa met Fred Crow's parolee, twenty-six-year-old Ahe Mahiʻai, in Fred's office. On parole after serving time for theft, Ahe reacted nervously to Koa's presence. "Hey, man, you trying to hook dis poor Hawaiian up for da kine bad thing?" he asked.

Koa smiled. "No. I'm not here to hassle you. You did a good thing in telling your parole officer about Johnnie Nihoa, and I just want to follow up with a few questions. You okay with that?"

Ahe looked at Fred for reassurance. When his parole officer nodded, Ahe said, "I guess."

"Tell me about Nihoa."

"*He ipu pala ʻole.*

Koa chuckled softly at the expression. Translated literally, it meant a calabash without *poi*, the starchy Polynesian food paste made from *taro*, but the idiom was universally understood to refer to a dimwit. "And you heard him say something about a big score?"

"Yeah, but who know if dat be true."

"Why do you say that?" Koa asked.

"*Pulu i ka wai naoa a ke kēhau.*"

Wet with dew, Koa translated. "So, he was drunk?"

"Da man, he bin drunk 'fore he gits out of bed in da morning," Ahe said dismissively.

"So, what did he say?" Koa asked.

"He says he hook up dis big dude wid a scar on 'is right cheek, 'nd da guy was gonna make 'im rich like a *kukui* tree oozing gum," Ahe responded, reciting a Hawaiian expression for prosperity.

"He said right cheek?" Koa asked.

"Yeah, dat's what he said. I 'member 'cause he drew a line down 'is cheek wid 'is finger like he were makin' a scar." Ahe mimicked the gesture on his right cheek.

"But you didn't believe him?" Koa asked.

"Nihoa, da man, he had a wad money in 'is pocket. More dan five hundred. No way he earn da kine dollar so must be some truth in 'is talk."

Ahe's story, Koa thought, explained the hundred dollars he'd found in Nihoa's pocket. Yet, nothing explained why a stranger would hire a habitual drunk, let alone pay him a substantial sum in advance.

"You ever see this big dude?"

Ahe chuckled. "I wish. Could be I gets 'is money."

"He have a name?"

"Never hear no name," Ahe answered.

"Where'd they meet?"

"Nihoa say he come to da shelter where Nihoa, he hangs," Ahe said.

"You know anything about this dude other than the scar on his face?"

Ahe pondered the question before shaking his head negatively. "Ya cops ask 'bout da kine strange stuff."

CHAPTER THIRTY

LATER THAT AFTERNOON, Koa was in Zeke's office on another
case—the prosecution of a rapist who'd attacked a fifteen-year-old
girl. Koa had arrested the man in possession of a piece of the girl's
clothing, and Zeke was preparing him for testimony when the prosecutor's cellphone rang. Zeke answered and identified himself. Then
his face went pale. "When?" he snapped, followed by "where?" Then,
"Oh my God."

Zeke rose from his chair and summoned Koa to follow as he
moved quickly toward the door.

"What's happening?" Koa demanded as the two men ran through
the building toward Zeke's car.

"Stay calm 'til we know more. It's Nālani. She's been in an
accident."

"Oh my God. An accident? Where? Is she okay?" Koa pleaded,
but Zeke had no answers.

When they reached Zeke's red Ford 150 pickup truck, Zeke
climbed behind the wheel and slapped a police light on the dash. Koa
rode shotgun, and they roared out of the parking lot with the emergency light flashing. Zeke wove in and out of the traffic like a
NASCAR driver practicing for the Daytona 500.

"Tell me what you know," Koa demanded, unable to mask the dread in his voice.

"Only that Nālani has been in a bad accident. Just hang on. We'll be there in a few minutes."

"Where?"

Once they hit Route 11, Zeke pushed the pickup to 75 mph. "Just outside the park."

As they approached Volcano Village, the traffic backed up, and Zeke drove forward on the shoulder to get around the gridlock to the accident scene. When a civilian pulled onto the shoulder to get a few car lengths ahead, blocking their way, Zeke hit the horn, and the flashing light on the dashboard drove the interloper aside.

They were still half a mile away when Koa saw a column of black smoke rising in the distance. His heart sank. The image came out of nowhere. He saw Nālani's face and recalled being captivated by her smile when they first met at a fundraiser. He replayed in his mind their outings in the national park and on the slopes of Mauna Loa. Their first kiss. Her patience in teaching him about orchids and indigenous songbirds. That delicious night camping under the stars when they had first made love. She had become the epicenter of his existence and the root of his happiest moments. Fear knotted his stomach. The thought of losing her was more than he could bear.

His dread turned to anguish and became nearly paralyzing when the still burning car, surrounded at a distance by ambulances, police cruisers, and firetrucks, first came into his view. Firefighters shot geysers of water on the burning vehicle. Koa prayed that there'd been a mistake and it wasn't Nālani's car, but hope vanished when he spotted the RANGER vanity plate on the heavily damaged front section of the vehicle. Although the fire had blackened its blue paint, it was Nālani's car.

Koa instantly saw that it was no ordinary automobile accident but instead looked more like the scene of a terrorist bombing in some foreign country. An explosion had torn the roof off and blown the doors outward at impossible angles. The force of the blast had displaced the engine block, and fire had charred the entire vehicle. It was not unlike the military vehicles destroyed by rocket-propelled grenades Koa had seen in Mogadishu. No one could have survived such a catastrophe. His heart sank.

Zeke stopped, and Koa sprang from the pickup and raced toward the still flaming vehicle. He was within fifty feet and felt the blinding heat of the flames when two firemen grabbed him, dragging him back to one of their trucks.

"That's my girlfriend. I've got to save her," he screamed, struggling to get free from the firemen's hold.

"Sorry, man. I'm sorry, but she's gone. There's nothing you can do for her now," one of them said in an empathetic voice.

CHAPTER THIRTY-ONE

USUALLY, ONE OF the most assertive first responders in any emergency, Koa sat on the back bumper of an ambulance with his head in his hands. In an instant, his life had blown apart. Nālani, his miracle, was now gone.

Zeke came to sit beside him at the rear of the ambulance. "I'm so sorry, Koa. She was such a flower—an orchid, a beautiful orchid." Zeke, Koa knew, meant well, but his words only made the heartbreak more intense. Near tears, he stood and walked to the edge of the roadway, staring into the forest without really seeing. He had never imagined a love so sweet, so deep, so magical. And once experienced, he couldn't imagine life without her.

Where, he asked himself, had Nālani been going at 2:30 p.m.? Then he remembered. She'd planned to teach a grade school class from Mountain View Elementary about native birds. The *ʻapapane*, *ʻākepa*, *palila*, *ʻelepaio*, and others. It was a tribute to Nālani that he could name and even recognize them. The school was going to bus the kids to the national park. He looked at his watch, 3:10 p.m. So why had she been on the road? Had that class been canceled? He suddenly sensed something amiss, something he intuited but couldn't explain.

The firefighters finally snuffed out the blazing fire. Koa turned and moved toward the wreck. Zeke tried to stop him. "Don't, Koa. This is not the way you want to remember her."

He pushed past, and Zeke stopped trying to restrain him. The car had exploded. Not a gas tank explosion, but a bomb. He saw it in the twisted metal, and despite the water from the fire hoses, he smelled the caustic residue in the air, still fed by curls of smoke. He knew the smell from his Special Forces days. Once you inhaled that stench—a smoky mixture of burnt rubber, seared metal, corrosive chemicals, and human flesh—you never forgot it.

He forced himself to examine the scene, focusing on the driver's side. It was awful. The force of the detonation had torn the driver apart. His mind flashed back again to the nightmares he'd experienced as an Army Special Forces officer in Mogadishu. This scene made him physically sick, but he fought the urge to turn away. He felt compelled to look. His eyes searched the blackened mess for something recognizable. A piece of red cloth. It wasn't Nālani's favorite color. He tried to remember what she had worn that morning but drew a blank.

He saw a burned leg, missing its foot, then the bony fingers of a heavily scorched hand, and continued searching until something clicked in his mind. It was like finding a discordant note, something odd or out of place at a crime scene. He refocused on the charred hand—a hand with engagement and wedding rings. But he and Nālani weren't married. They'd talked about it but hadn't finally decided. She didn't have engagement or wedding rings.

He reached for his cellphone, but it rang before he extracted it. The caller ID said Nālani. He couldn't believe his eyes. Could it be? He answered, "Nalāni?" his hoarse voice barely recognizable.

She replied, "Koa?"

"Where are you?" He could barely get the words out.

"Park headquarters. I just finished with my grade school class. They were fun. Lots of interest and some great questions," she said enthusiastically. Then she recognized the anguish in his voice and caught herself. "You sound awful. What's wrong?"

Ignoring her questions, he asked, "Where's your car?"

"I let 'Olina borrow it. She had a dental appointment in Hilo. Why? What's going on?" Now it was Nālani who spoke with urgency in her voice.

He couldn't tell her over the phone that her best friend and coworker—one with whom she'd just dined—had been blown up and burned to bits. So instead, he said, "There's been an accident. I'll be there in a few minutes to fill you in."

CHAPTER THIRTY-TWO

KOA FOUND NĀLANI in the park visitor's center and greeted her with a long and intense embrace, holding on to her as if they were in a mighty storm.

She saw his look of grave concern. "What's wrong?" she asked insistently.

Knowing how she'd likely take the horrible news and not wanting to embarrass her in front of her colleagues, he led her outside to a nearby picnic table. "You'd better sit down. I do have some terrible news. It's about 'Olina."

She sat down. "What about her? Was she in an accident?"

"More than an accident, *ipo*. There was an explosion. The bomb squad boys are going over it now, but it sure looks like a bomb. 'Olina didn't make it."

Nālani inhaled sharply, her face drained of color, and tears filled her eyes. "Oh my God, no. Not 'Olina. She was like a sister."

"I know, and I'm so sorry."

After a long silence filled with tears, she asked, "Does Fred know?" barely getting the words out between sobs.

"Not yet. I need to tell him in person, and I'm going there next as soon as I know you're all right."

Her sobbing slowly stopped, and she began to compose herself. Koa knew she was trying to process the news. "A bomb? It was for me. Oh my God. It had to be. 'Olina only asked to borrow the car a couple of hours ago after Fred got tied up."

"It looks that way. Whoever's behind this couldn't have anticipated 'Olina would be driving your car instead of you."

"But why? Why me? What have I done?"

"We don't know yet," Koa said, "but I'm guessing this is about me and not you. Maybe somebody I put away."

Suddenly, there were no more tears, and she was all business. As a park ranger, she'd attended the federal law enforcement officer's training program and was no stranger to potential threats. His job as a detective had put them both in danger before, and they'd agreed on specific protocols to keep them safe. "So, they may try again."

"It's possible. I've assigned a cop to be with you today, and I'll arrange with Hank to send several of his best people to guard you and my family." Koa referred to Hank Silvers, a former Army ranger buddy who'd left the service to build a first-class international executive protection service based in Seattle.

"You think it's that serious?" she asked.

"I do. Something's not right. First, the attempt to frame Ikaika, then the attacks on Makanui, the bombing of the hospital, and now this explosion. The timing is awfully suspicious."

"You think they're all related?"

"If not, it's one hell of a coincidence."

CHAPTER THIRTY-THREE

TWO DAYS LATER, Koa and Alexia were back in the prosecutor's office with Zeke and Sarah. Before they got down to business, Zeke asked how Fred Crow was dealing with the death of his wife.

"It's tough," Koa responded. "They were childhood sweethearts, married for twenty years, and were devoted to each other. It's worse, I think, because it was so unexpected. Fred never had a chance to say goodbye. I feel for him. There is a memorial for 'Olina planned for next week. I know Fred would appreciate seeing you there."

"Definitely. I'll be there."

"Turning to business," Koa began, "there's a new urgency to our request to allow Alexia's experts access to test the authenticity of Ikaika's fingerprints on the purported murder weapon in the Nihoa case. We now suspect links between the twin attacks on Makanui, the case against Ikaika, the hospital bombing, and the attempted murder of Nālani, which resulted in the actual murder of 'Olina Crow."

"Hold on," Zeke interrupted. "What makes you think the events are related."

"The timing and the fact that all the events involve the people closest to Koa," Alexia answered.

"Let me break things down for you," Koa began. "As you know, there are less than a dozen murders on the Big Island in the average year. So, it's way out of the ordinary to have four murders—Nihoa, 'Olina, Officer Hali'a, and his teen offender—and several additional attempts all happen in the same week. And here in Hawai'i, killing police officers in the line of duty is even rarer—three here on the Big Island in the past twenty years. Now we have a cop killed at the hospital, two recent attempts on a police detective, and a third on a police officer's significant other. What are the chances it's all a coincidence? Pretty damn small."

"The common denominator," Alexia interjected, "appears to be Koa. He recruited Makanui; they've worked extensively together and are close colleagues. Ikaika is his brother, and any harm to Nālani would devastate him."

"Isn't there evidence that a Philippine terrorist carried out the attacks on Makanui?" Sarah asked.

"Well," Koa responded, "we have an unidentified man in custody, but his background is unclear. He might be a Philippine radical, but that's supported only by the weapon he used—a Russian-made Dragunov rifle available in many countries, including the U.S.—and the man's largely incoherent mutterings. According to doctors, he's in a minimally cognitive state."

"You got anything else you want to say?" Zeke asked.

"Yes, three things," Koa responded. "First, testing the knife will go a long way toward proving—or disproving—that the events are related. If the prints are real, it undercuts the likelihood of a relationship, but if they're fake, then it will be pretty clear that someone's out to get me."

"Fair point," Zeke conceded.

"Second, there's a new fact you should know. Maria told us that your investigator talked to her, and I assume you've checked out other facts, such as the $25,000 deposit to the bartender's bank account. You might also want to talk to one of Fred Crow's parolees, a guy named Ahe Mahi'ai. He says that just before his death, Nihoa met a big dude with a scar on his right cheek, who was going to 'make him rich like a *kukui* tree oozing gum.' I think those were his exact words. It couldn't have been Ikaika, whose scar is on his left cheek, and it explains where Nihoa got the hundred bucks I found in his pocket. It's also more than a little odd that anyone would hire an unreliable drunk like Nihoa and downright weird to pay him in advance. Unless, of course, it's a setup to get him in the right place at the right time to wind up dead in the alley behind the Surfboard.

"Lastly, as you know, the chief has removed me from the police team investigating Nihoa's death. If the events are related as we believe, it limits me to investigating only parts of one of the most serious criminal cases in Big Island history. If Ikaika's fingerprints on the knife are genuine, I'll have to live with that restriction. If someone framed Ikaika, as I believe, then the case against Ikaika goes away, and I will have full scope to investigate whatever the hell is going on."

Zeke looked first to Koa and then Alexia to see if either one wanted to say more. Hearing nothing, he said, "Sarah and I need to confer. Give us a few minutes."

Koa and Alexia waited outside the prosecutor's office a mere five minutes before Zeke called them back. "We will agree to let your experts examine the knife under the supervision of a government expert," Zeke said, "on one condition. You have to agree in advance that if the experts agree that the prints are Ikaika's, they will be allowed to testify to their findings without objection."

Koa hid his concern. The condition meant that if Alexia's experts failed to find a flaw in the prints, Ikaika would almost certainly be convicted. Koa didn't like putting Ikaika's freedom directly on the line, but he had little choice. If they didn't challenge the fingerprints, a jury would likely find Ikaika guilty beyond a reasonable doubt. Better to do it now rather than at trial.

Koa looked to Alexia, who nodded affirmatively, accepting Zeke's condition.

"When and where do you want to do the analysis?" Zeke asked.

"As soon as possible in a lab at UH Hilo," Alexia responded.

"Text me the names of your experts so we can check them out," Zeke responded. "I'll talk to our expert from the Honolulu crime lab. Maybe the experts can agree on a date and time."

"Great," Alexia said.

CHAPTER THIRTY-FOUR

"YOU WANTED TO see me?" Makanui asked, poking her head into the door of Koa's office.

"Yes. C'mon in and close the door."

Makanui obliged and sat opposite Koa. "You're up to something," she said with a smile.

"You offered to help with Ikaika's problem?"

"Absolutely."

"I think Moses, the Surfboard bartender, holds the key to the whole Ikaika fiasco, but given the chief's instructions, I can't lean on him."

"You want me to do that?" Makanui asked.

"Only if you are comfortable. It might tick off the chief."

"Screw that. Fill me in and tell me what you want."

"Bring him in. Use the Kea'au police station. That way, the chief is less likely to hear about it. Put the squeeze on him. There's an unexplained $25,000 deposit to his bank account a couple of weeks before Nihoa's murder. I'm guessing it's a payoff and maybe the key to breaking this thing wide open." Koa then handed her a thick file. "Alexia's investigator got Moses's prints, and I ran them through the bureau. His real name is Edwards, and he's got an interesting rap sheet. That file has everything I could find on Moses. There's enough there so you should be able to crack him like a *kukui* nut."

"Tonight?" Makanui asked.

"If you're sure you're okay with this," Koa responded.

"Don't worry about me. If the chief fires me, I can always go back to the Honolulu Police Department," she said with a grin.

*   *   *

Koa watched through the one-way mirror of the interrogation room. Moses, in full Surfboard dress—shorts, a grubby tee shirt, and ratty sneakers without socks—seemed even larger than Koa remembered. He was over six feet tall and had to be pushing 280 pounds with heavily muscled arms but a good deal of flab around the waist. The ordinarily cocky bartender appeared distinctly nervous, drumming his fingers on the table and shifting every which way on his chair. Koa hoped Makanui would play on the man's evident unease.

"What's this all about, Detective?" Moses demanded when Makanui stepped into the room and took a seat opposite him.

She ignored the question, carefully laying out papers from the folder Koa had given her. Then she stared silently at the man.

When Moses could no longer tolerate the tense silence, he repeated his question.

Again, ignoring his inquiry, Makanui spoke. "You lied to the police before, Moses. You do that again, and I'll put your ass behind bars." She proceeded to read Moses his *Miranda* rights.

Unnerved, Moses talked over her recitation of his rights. "Am I in trouble? Do I need an attorney?"

"That's entirely up to you," she responded curtly after completing the warning. "You understand your rights?"

He hesitated and then nodded. "Yep."

Again, Makanui said nothing, and when Moses could no longer bear the quiet, he asked, "What'd ya want to know?"

"Who was the big Hawaiian in the bar with Nihoa that night?"

"What night?" Moses, momentarily reverting to his cheeky self, asked with a smirk.

"Cut the shit, Moses. You know what night."

"Ikaika," Moses responded snidely, raising his voice as though that might add credibility to his answer. "I recognized him from the scar on his cheek."

Makanui said nothing for several moments before dropping her fist onto the table so hard that the heavy wooden furniture seemed to jump off the floor. "Bullshit," she roared.

Moses jerked away from the table, nearly falling backward, before steadying himself.

Makanui stuck a finger in his face. "I know who you are, Mister Edwards. I have your rap sheet, and I know why you changed your name. One more lie, you sorry son of a bitch, and I'll put you back in the slammer. Maybe back with your same cellmates. Is that what you want?"

All color drained from the man's face, and he began to tremble. "Please, I can't go back. I can't. You don't know what they did to me," he pleaded, his voice suddenly an octave higher.

Makanui understood the man's fear of returning to prison, where he'd almost certainly suffered at the hands of other inmates. She might even have felt sorry for him, but she had no sympathy for pedophiles.

"Okay, Moses." She now spoke in calmer tones, deliberately reverting to his assumed name. She didn't want him shutting down on her or requesting a lawyer. Instead, she wanted him to see a way out, even though it might be an illusion. "Let's start over. Maybe there is still a way for you to get out of the mess you're in. So, again, who was the big Hawaiian in the bar with Nihoa that night?"

He said nothing and remained quiet for so long that she thought she'd lost him. Then, finally, he came to some sort of internal decision. "He knew about my past. I didn't have a choice."

"Okay," she encouraged him. "I understand, but we still need to go through what happened. Who was he, this man who knew about your past?"

"Yeah . . . okay . . . 'is name were Keola. That's what he said."

"Keola what?" she asked.

"I never knowed 'is last name."

"Then how do you know him?"

"He came into the bar a couple of weeks ago."

"And?" Makanui prompted.

"He said he wanted a favor."

"Just a favor?" she prodded.

Moses hesitated and looked down at the table. "Yeah, just a favor, except he said he'd tell everybody about my past if I didn't agree."

"Like a $25,000 favor?" Makanui asked with a knowing edge in her voice.

Moses looked up, unable to suppress his surprise. "How? . . . How'd ya knowed about that?" he blurted.

Makanui ignored the question. "And what did you agree to do for $25,000?"

Moses's hands began to shake. "It were this carrot and stick thing. I agree, I git paid. I don't agree, and everybody, they would knowed what I did."

"And what was the favor?" Makanui asked.

Again, he looked down. "I was supposed to put the frame on Ikaika."

Still watching through the one-way glass, Koa wanted to grab the scumbag by the neck and put him down like a rabid dog.

"So, what really happened?" Makanui asked.

"Dis Keola dude, he asks me to hook 'im up wid a drunk. One who wouldn't knowed what hit 'im. So, I put 'im together with Johnnie Nihoa. Keola spends a couple of nights drinkin' with the dumb shit, tellin' 'im he's gonna be rich as some Hawaiian king." Moses paused.

"Go on," Makanui ordered. "What else?"

"Keola gets the stupid fuck too drunk to stand. So, after Keola pays the tab, I gotta help 'im carry Nihoa out to the alley, where Keola sticks 'im. An' sticks 'im again and again. Bled like a fuckin' pig. Den Keola pulls this black knife out of 'is pocket, rubs it around in Nihoa's blood, and tosses it against the wall."

Koa felt a wave of relief. He realized he'd been holding his breath and slowly exhaled. He now had solid testimony that Ikaika had not killed Nihoa. They might still have to solve the mystery of Ikaika's fingerprints on the knife, but Moses's confession put his brother out of danger.

Turning back to the one-way mirror, he heard Makanui ask, "You just stood there while this Keola murdered the kid?"

"Yeah. I had nothin' to do with da killin'."

Koa recalled the condition of Nihoa's body in the alley behind the bar. No defensive wounds. No blood on his hands. Koa had wondered at the time why Nihoa made no effort to fight back or at least staunch his bleeding. Now he had the answer.

In the interrogation room, Makanui followed up with a sucker punch. "You did nothing except hold the kid up so Keola could stab him to death."

Both she and Koa saw the look of guilt register across Moses's face before the man looked down at the table.

"Admit it," Makanui demanded, raising her voice. "Tell me you held Nihoa up while Keola stabbed him."

Silence.

"I can see it in your face, Moses. Tell me you did it," she prodded.

Silence.

"You want to go back inside . . . back with your former cellmates?"

Coming to terms with the reality of his position, Moses whispered so softly Koa almost missed it, "Yeah, I did."

"Say it," Makanui demanded.

"I held him up while . . ."

"While what?"

"While Keola . . . Keola . . . stab . . . stabbed 'im."

"Then what happened?"

"Then Keola turns to me an' says, 'You know what you got to do.' I knowed and went back in the bar to call 911."

"We're going to take a short break," Makanui said, stepping out of the interrogation room to confer with Koa.

"Well done," Koa said. "You've exonerated Ikaika."

"And now I've got to book this moron. He's confessed to conspiracy to murder or at least to being an accessory to murder. Anything more I should ask him before dropping the hammer?" Makanui asked.

"Let's get a police artist in here and see if we can get a picture of this Keola figure."

"Good idea."

Responding to Makanui's call, Kelly Galanis, a police sketch artist, arrived with her laptop and photo books. She had Moses describe Keola and then pick out similar facial characteristics from photographs. Once she had a rough sketch on her laptop screen, Moses suggested refinements, including the shape of his facial scar, until she had created what Moses judged to be a good likeness. At one point, Moses described the side of Keola's face as "rubbery," and Koa worried that Keola might have been wearing a mask or other disguise that would make the whole sketch concept irrelevant.

Once Kelly finished her rendition, she left Moses in the interrogation room and stepped outside to share her work with Koa and Makanui. One look at the sketch told Koa just how radically Moses had lied. The face in the drawing looked more Asian than Hawaiian and bore little resemblance to Ikaika.

When Makanui returned to the interrogation room, Moses asked, "Kin I go back to the bar now?"

The two officers could barely contain their incredulity. Did this idiot who'd just confessed to being an accessory to murder think he could just go home? Makanui ended that fantasy by arresting Moses, handcuffing him, and having him transported back to police headquarters in Hilo.

CHAPTER THIRTY-FIVE

KOA, MAKANUI, AND Alexia reconvened with Sarah and Zeke in Zeke's office the following morning. After summarizing Makanui's interrogation of Moses and his subsequent confession, Koa played the videotape for Zeke. "So," Koa concluded, "we now know that this Keola fellow paid Moses to frame Ikaika for Nihoa's murder, and having identified the killers, we know Ikaika is not guilty."

Zeke nodded. "It sure looks that way."

"Forgive me if I have a couple of questions," Sarah interjected. "How reliable is that confession? Moses is not very bright, he's previously lied, and Makanui leaned hard on him. So, it wouldn't be surprising if he decided to recant, especially after he lawyers up."

"But—" Koa started to interrupt.

"Let me finish," Sarah said with her fierce blue eyes fixed on Koa. "His lawyer's going to argue that the interrogation was irregular. The chief assigned the case to Moreau, and it's no secret he's been in here seeking subpoenas and arrest warrants. I'm betting he didn't know about that interrogation. I'm also guessing that despite the chief's order, you"—she tilted her head toward Koa—"put Makanui up to it and were watching through the one-way mirror."

"What are you saying?" Koa demanded, struggling to keep the irritation out of his voice. "That you don't believe his confession? You still think Ikaika's guilty?"

"Not at all," Sarah responded. "But before we take Moses's confession to the bank, we ought to get the experts' opinion on the fingerprints. If they're fake, that makes the confession more credible. If they're Ikaika's, then we still have a problem."

Koa, who expected immediate vindication for Ikaika, hid his disappointment. He knew Sarah had a point, and he had little choice but to agree. Still, he worried that Ikaika might still be in danger.

Zeke closed the door on any rebuttal. "Sarah makes some good points."

"Okay," Koa agreed, "we'll hear what the experts have to say this afternoon."

"That's settled," Zeke said. "Now let's turn to the broader issue. In less than a week, a sniper goes after Makanui, someone most likely set out to frame Ikaika, and a bomber tries to kill Nālani. Then somebody bombs a hospital room trying to kill a potential witness. So, what do we think is going on?"

"Could be an attack on the police force," Makanui suggested.

"That fits with the shots at you," Zeke said, "but framing Ikaika and the bombing of Nālani's car seem more personal and aimed at Koa."

"I'm afraid that's right," Koa acknowledged. "I didn't see the shots at Makanui as aimed at me. I thought it might be someone like Reyes who she put away or maybe revenge for her success in battling Abu Sayyaf insurgents after they kidnapped her parents. But unless you believe in coincidences, the effort to frame Ikaika and the bombing of Nālani's car make it look like I'm the real target."

"I have trouble chalking up these four extreme acts in less than ten days to coincidence. So, I think you guys are on to something," Zeke responded.

"I agree it's a real possibility," Makanui added. "And if that's right, it's not your typical felon seeking revenge. Someone or some group has gone to a lot of trouble and expense to launch a series of assaults."

"So, what do we do?" Zeke asked.

"Defense first," Koa responded. "If someone is coming after me by attacking my police colleagues and my family, then others around me might be in danger. I've arranged for an old Army buddy who runs an executive protection service out of Seattle to protect Nālani and my family. As part of the law enforcement community, Zeke, you could also be a target. So I've assigned police officers to guard you." He pointed to Zeke. "As well as Makanui. She and I are mixing up our normal routines, and, Zeke, you need to do the same, too."

"Okay, we've got our backs pretty well covered. What about offense?" Zeke asked. "I want to catch these bastards."

"We have several leads," Koa explained. "We've got a team following up on the Makanui shooting, trying to trace the Dragunov and the ammunition, and we have feelers out to the U.S. Joint Task Force and the Philippine authorities to identify the man someone tried to kill at the Hilo Medical Center.

"Cap Roberts in tech support is working with explosives experts from Honolulu, the FBI, and the ATF analyzing the bomb residue and trigger mechanism on Nālani's car and whatever destroyed the hospital room and killed Officer Hali'a.

"Then there's running down the source of the $25,000 deposit to Moses's bank account." Looking directly at Sarah, Koa said, "Given the chief's order, I can't do that until you clear Ikaika, and I guarantee you Moreau isn't working that angle."

Zeke looked at Makanui. "Can you pursue that? Tell the chief it's at my request if he asks."

"Sure," she agreed.

"You going to start with Keola?" Zeke asked.

"Yes," Koa responded. Then locking eyes with Sarah, he added, "As soon as you clear Ikaika so I can work on the case."

"Oh, screw that." Zeke waved a hand as though dismissing the matter. "Get on it now. Find this Keola character. I'll square it with the chief if he gets his back up."

"Good," Koa responded. "Makanui got a police artist to work with Moses and create a drawing of Keola. She already got that out to the force. With luck, an officer will spot him."

"Let's hope," Zeke said, concluding the meting.

CHAPTER THIRTY-SIX

GIANT DROPLETS OF rain fell in Hilo, but a vibrant double rainbow graced the sky over Mauna Kea. Koa regarded the natural phenomenon as a good omen when he and Alexia arrived at the UH Hilo campus. They met Zeke on the way to the evolutionary genomics facility. "Where's Sarah?" Koa asked.

"She's in court, handling another case," Zeke responded.

They entered a conference room next to a DNA testing facility where Doctors Reingold, Matthews, and Pelika introduced themselves. Simon Reingold was tall and thin with a narrow, sharply contoured face. By contrast, Billy Matthews, a short, plump man with round reddish features, had an ever-present smile. Martha Pelika, an intense young woman with a no-nonsense demeanor, had her hair pulled back into a tight bun. Koa had often seen her name on reports from the Honolulu Police Crime Laboratory, which she headed.

Alexia had hired Drs. Reingold and Matthews to analyze the fingerprints on the knife found at the Nihoa murder site, and Zeke had arranged for Dr. Pelika to supervise their analysis for the State. Koa had pestered Alexia for any information about the results, but she had insisted they await the final findings. Her reticence only ratcheted up Koa's apprehension.

With introductions concluded and everyone seated, Dr. Pelika explained the process. "The Hawai'i police have provided us with a black ballistic knife found at the scene of the homicide of a man named Johnnie Nihoa. The police and the attorney for a suspect requested tests to determine whether the fingerprints on the knife match those of Ikaika Kāne and, more importantly, whether he made them.

"As you know, fingerprint examiners have concluded with a high degree of confidence that the prints match those of Ikaika Kāne. We, too, have confirmed that finding. Usually, that would be the end of the matter, but in this case, the suspect's attorney asserted that Ikaika's prints were not placed on the knife by him.

"Under my supervision, Drs. Reingold and Matthews extracted both liquids and traces of DNA from the fingerprints on the knife. The liquids, mostly oils, were subjected to several tests to determine their composition and origin. Finally, we sequenced fragments of extracted DNA and compared them with Ikaika Kāne's DNA. Drs. Reingold and Matthews can walk you through the science, but I'll give you the bottom line."

Koa leaned forward in his chair, taking in long, slow breaths as he struggled to control his racing heart. The doctor's next words would help determine whether Ikaika went home a free man or spent the rest of his life in prison.

"In short," Dr. Pelika summarized, "the oils extracted from the fingerprints are synthetic and not of human origin. Their artificial nature means that the prints were most likely molded from their original source and transferred to the knife. While the DNA fragments are not sufficient to identify their source, we did recover enough genetic material to make certain negative comparisons—that is, to rule out certain sources. A comparison with Ikaika Kāne's DNA rules him out as the source. In summary, although the prints on the knife match the friction ridges on Ikaika's fingertips, they are not genuine fingerprints. He did not place them on the knife."

Koa was ecstatic. Against seemingly insurmountable odds, they'd convinced the prosecutor to permit an extraordinary pre-indictment test of fingerprints, and they'd established that somebody had framed Ikaika. And, with Ikaika fully exonerated, Koa could assume full command of the investigation.

*   *   *

That evening, Koa hosted a celebratory dinner for Ikaika at the Volcano Village Kīlauea Lodge, formerly a YMCA camp built in 1938. Nālani and Maria attended along with Alexia, Makanui, Māpuana, and Kahuna Atarau. Wine and beer flowed freely. Between the appetizer and the entrée, Ikaika rose and clanked a spoon against his glass.

"After living a third of my life in jail, I hit bottom. But my mother, she always believed in me. Only the gods know where she got the patience. Koa and I've been through some tough times, but he never gave up on me. I owe a lot of people—Alexia, who fought my legal battles, the docs who took the evil thing out of my head, and the very special doc who went to bat for me with the parole board and our former governor. Then I found a miracle, my love."

He blew Maria a kiss.

Ikaika then went on, "You guys can't know what it felt like to be caged up again—maybe for the rest of my life. I was afraid. I'm not ashamed to say that. I was scared I'd let you all down and terrified I'd lose Maria. I owe you all my life and freedom. *Hoʻomaikaʻi ʻia au i kou kōkua mai*—I am grateful for your help. *Mahalo nui.*"

CHAPTER THIRTY-SEVEN

THE FOLLOWING MORNING, Koa returned to headquarters. Swallowing his anger at Chief Lannua's handling of the case, he sent a polite note to the chief, stating that with Ikaika cleared, he would resume responsibility for the investigation of Johnnie Nihoa's murder. He then called Moreau to his office.

Koa got no reply from the chief, but Moreau appeared at Koa's door half an hour later. "You wanted to see me?" he asked, making little effort to hide the snide tone in his voice.

"Take a seat, Moreau." Koa pointed to the chair opposite his desk. "It's time we got a few things straight about how we operate around here."

"There's nothing wrong with how I'm doing my job. The chief ordered me to take command of the case, and I followed the strongest, and I might add, the most obvious lead."

"I've got no problem with your taking command. That's what we do," Koa responded. "But I do have a problem with your methods."

"What are you talking about?" Moreau asserted, now raising his voice in anger. "Your brother's fingerprints on the knife made the case a no-brainer."

Koa hated that expression and thought it perfectly described Moreau's mental acuity. "Except they were phony," Koa shot back.

"Yeah," Moreau said, "and how often does that happen?"

"You might have asked yourself why a smart guy like Ikaika—who has a fair amount of experience with the law—would leave the murder weapon with his fingerprints at the crime scene. Sort of like a calling card. That didn't seem odd?"

"Criminals do stupid things all the time," Moreau snapped back, refusing to acknowledge Koa's point.

"You never gave it a thought 'cause it was a no-brainer." Koa threw the phrase back at Moreau. "And you failed to consider the surrounding circumstances. For example," Koa said, "it never dawned on you that the big Hawaiian in the bar with the scar on his right cheek could not have been Ikaika."

"And how would I have known that?" Moreau challenged.

"Well, it would have been pretty obvious to anyone paying attention to the details. Like, comparing Moses's description with one of Ikaika's old mug shots."

"What good would that have done?"

"You still don't get it, do you? If you had done so . . . if you'd focused on the details instead of what seemed obvious . . . you'd have noticed that Ikaika's scar is on his left cheek, not his right."

"Maybe," Moreau shot back defensively, "but witnesses confuse things like that all the time, especially in a dark bar."

"And I don't suppose you found out that a pizza delivery guy saw Ikaika at home at the time when Moses put him inside the Surfboard," Koa continued.

"Well, no," Moreau admitted, "but it wouldn't have mattered. Ikaika might still have been in the alley when Nihoa got knifed."

"And you never discovered that Moses made a highly unusual and suspicious $25,000 deposit to his bank account shortly before the murder."

"No. Why is that relevant?"

"A $25,000 deposit in cash with a flaky explanation, triggering the bank to consider a suspicious activity report. Doesn't it suggest that Moses might have an incentive to lie?" Koa asked.

Moreau shrugged. "Could be lots of reasons for something like that."

Koa pointed a finger at the detective. "There are always lots of reasons why people do things, but you considered none of them, preferring an easy answer. You didn't think the case through and instead let your bias drive the investigation. You wanted Ikaika to be the killer from the start, so you didn't bother to test the evidence. That's the essence of bad police work." *That and your hope of embarrassing me and aspiring to take my job*, Koa thought but didn't say. As he spoke, Koa saw anger in Moreau's eyes and sensed he'd touched a raw nerve.

"Save me the lecture, Detective," Moreau snarled. "If you're going to fire me, just do it."

Koa sat dead still, controlling his emotions. He'd dearly love nothing more than to rid himself of this incompetent detective but knew it would be a mistake. The chief and the mayor would be furious. And working with Zeke, he'd learned enough about the law to know that firing Moreau would only draw a lawsuit. Litigation would expose the details of an ongoing investigation and distort Koa's family interest in the case. Better to keep your problem children in the tent rather than let them run loose.

"I'm not going to fire you. On the contrary, my job is to make you a better detective. You need to approach every investigation with an open mind and be suspicious of the obvious."

"Yeah, right," Moreau responded, letting his resentment show.

Leaning back in his chair, Koa gestured for Moreau to leave. He needed to refocus on his most urgent priority, discovering who was behind the attacks on Makanui, Ikaika, Nālani, and the hospital.

CHAPTER THIRTY-EIGHT

MAKANUI RAN VARIATIONS of Keola's name through the DMV database, comparing the hits against Moses's sketch. No luck. Koa, she knew, suspected that Keola might not be the murderer's real name and that the scar on his cheek might have been artificial. They'd distributed Keola's picture, both with and without the scar, to police officers with instructions to find the man but not apprehend or alert the suspect. The flyers instructed officers to call at any hour if they spotted their quarry. If they could find Keola—whatever his real name might be—Koa wanted to establish surveillance and try to identify his associates.

Koa went back to the Surfboard with the sketch in hand that evening. A young woman wearing a sequined tee shirt over bare breasts tended the bar. The tee shirt proclaimed her name to be Suzy. She denied ever having seen Keola but pointed to two regulars. "One of them might have seen him," she suggested. Each recognized Keola but added nothing to what Koa already knew, except confirmation that the sketch was reasonably accurate.

It took time, but Koa's cell rang at 4:00 p.m. on the second day. An officer canvassing local businesses with copies of Keola's picture had located a gas station attendant in Nāʻālehu who recalled seeing a man resembling Keola.

Hoping he'd found a promising lead, Koa interviewed the attendant. The cashier had seen Keola late that morning when he came into the station's convenience store to buy snacks and beer. The attendant, busy with a line of customers, had not noticed the make, model, or license number of Keola's car.

Video from the camera above the cashier gave Koa his first photo of Keola. The man bore a striking resemblance to the artist's sketch but with a slightly thinner face and no scar. He'd been right, Koa thought, in guessing that the man had worn a prosthetic and had somehow managed to get the scar on the wrong cheek.

Koa took stills from the gas station video to the jail, where Moses identified Keola. The footage from the camera over the gas pumps included pictures of Keola's car, a black Kia. Koa saw nothing distinctive about the nondescript vehicle except a white *shaka* sticker on the rear. The *shaka* gesture—a hand with thumb and little finger extended while the three middle fingers remained curled—common in Hawai'i, signified hang loose, take it easy, right on, and other friendly messages.

A check on the license plates proved them to have been stolen off a vehicle in Pāhala, preventing the police from obtaining Keola's address, but Koa figured there might be another way to locate him. Both Pāhala, the site of the license plate theft, and Nā'ālehu were small towns in the sparsely populated southeastern part of the Big Island. Since people usually gassed up locally, Koa guessed that Keola lived nearby.

The Hawai'i Belt Road carried most of the traffic between the two towns, but an old, narrow asphalt roadway once used by trucks hauling freshly cut sugarcane from the nearby fields also linked the two towns. Koa assigned officers to patrol both roads, watching for a black Kia with a white *shaka* sticker on the left rear.

Cathy Tang, an ambitious young police academy graduate from the Kea'au police substation, was one of several officers assigned to the traffic search. Knowing that there were many black Kias on the road, she brought her own technique to the task. She set up a video-equipped Lidar speed detection unit on the old cane road. Starting her shift at noon, Cathy aimed her equipment at every black car coming toward her. At 3:47 p.m., she captured an image of a black Kia. The driver, visible through the windshield, looked a lot like the police sketch of Keola. Then as the car whizzed by, she spotted the white *shaka* emblem on the left rear. Following at a distance through Pahala, she saw it turn south on the Hawai'i Belt Road and then left onto Alahaki Road. About halfway up the dead-end street, the Kia pulled into the driveway of a white clapboard house. Following the instructions printed at the bottom of the photo flyer, Cathy called Koa and texted him her photo of the driver and the Alahaki Road address.

Pretty sure that Cathy had nailed it, Koa instructed her to maintain surveillance on the junction of Alahaki Road and the Belt Road, well out of sight of the house where Keola had parked. Racing to Cathy's location, he assessed the situation but found no suitable spot for direct surveillance of the property where Keola apparently resided. Still, since Alahaki Road dead-ended at a circle around a water tank a quarter mile beyond the house, the police established an observation post near where Alahaki Road intersected with the Hawai'i Belt Road. From that location, the police could observe Keola's comings and goings. Koa also equipped the stakeout team with a drone, enabling officers to determine whether cars turning on to Alahaki Road stopped at the Keola property.

After learning that the property had no landline, Koa obtained a warrant, permitting the police to employ an IMSI catcher or Stingray device. It created a fake cell tower between a subject's cellphone and the carrier's actual tower. With it, the police could identify any mobile phone at Keola's location and intercept calls to or from that phone. It didn't take long to pick up a signal from a cellphone at Keola's location and determine that it had an anonymously purchased SIM card—i.e., a burner.

With physical and electronic surveillance in place, the police played a waiting game, hoping that Keola would contact his associates.

CHAPTER THIRTY-NINE

Cᴀᴘ Rᴏʙᴇʀᴛs, ᴛʜᴇ head of Hilo police technical services, came to Koa's office with Glen Corey from the Honolulu office of the Bureau of Alcohol, Tobacco, and Firearms. In compliance with federal requirements, the Hilo police had notified the bureau of the bombing of Nālani's car and, subsequently, the explosion at the hospital. Cap explained that Corey, a slender, middle-aged man with a receding hairline, had analyzed the debris from the bombing of Nālani's car and the residue from the explosion at the medical center. "We've got reports on both incidents. Let's start with the car. Tell 'im what you've got," Cap suggested.

"Although the car was a mess, we were able to reconstruct the trigger and identify the explosive," Corey began. "It looks like the trigger connected to the speedometer and set off a bomb when the car reached roughly forty miles per hour. That allowed the driver to leave the national park where the speed limit is twenty-five and reach the highway. As soon as the driver accelerated, the bomb exploded."

"And the explosive?" Koa asked.

"Semtex, the old military explosive originally developed in the 1950s in Czechoslovakia. It's the same stuff used to bring down Pan Am Flight 103 over Lockerbie, Scotland, in December 1988. And it doesn't take much—twelve ounces in the case of Pan Am 103. The chemical composition of this bomb tells us the explosive was part of 700 tons that we previously identified as having been shipped to Libya in the late 1970s. Since then, Libya has supplied parts of that shipment to dozens of terrorist groups around the world."

"Jesus!" Koa exclaimed. "So, there must be a terrorist connection to the car bombing?" he asked.

"Yes, sir," Corey responded. "There's no way to trace the Semtex's exact path from Libya in the '70s to Hawai'i in 2021, but I can guarantee that it passed through one or more terrorist networks."

"So, there's no way to know who sent the Semtex to Hawai'i?" Koa asked.

"Not from the chemical composition of the explosive, but you know as well as anyone that every bomb maker has a signature—the use of a particular component, the way the bomb maker routes, twists, or solders the wires, or maybe the type of housing. We've even found the bomb maker's DNA on some devices. There's always something that ties the bomb to its maker."

"Did you identify a signature for this bomb?" Koa asked.

"Yes. The bureau has a vast database of bombs and bomb makers, including signatures, with inputs from Interpol, international police, and foreign military sources. Based on the comparisons we've found, there's a strong possibility that an Iraqi-trained Abu Sayyaf explosives expert named Muhammad Khalili assembled the critical components of this bomb. He created the bombs used in terror attacks at a night market in Davao City in 2016 and a Roman Catholic cathedral in the southern Philippines in 2019. He's a pro."

"That tells us something," Koa responded. "It's not the only possible link to Abu Sayyaf." He explained that one of his officers who'd had a run-in with Abu Sayyaf had recently escaped two assassination attempts in which the would-be assassin used a Dragunov rifle like those supplied to Abu Sayyaf.

"I see the connection," Corey agreed, "but it would be surprising if Abu Sayyaf were operating in Hawai'i. According to intelligence reports, Abu Sayyaf is a small terrorist group operating mostly in the Mindanao area of the Philippines, Malaysia, and maybe Indonesia. They get only limited support from ISIS and other radical groups in Iraq and Afghanistan. Despite their Islamic connections, the group is not well funded. They'd have to have a powerful motive to attempt assassinations in Hawai'i."

"I'm not sure about the funding or logistics," Koa responded, "but they were plenty motivated to come after Makanui." He paused, thinking. "Still, it doesn't explain the attack on Nālani. Neither she nor I have any connection to Abu Sayyaf."

"Can't help you there," Corey said.

"What about the hospital bombing? Same signature?" Koa asked.

"Different deal altogether," Corey responded.

"How so?"

"Best we can tell from what we found in the debris, it was some kind of grenade. The residue points to gunpowder, most likely home brewed. And fragments found at the scene suggest the explosive was packaged in a commercially available shell, maybe a practice round or a CS gas canister. Could have been fired from a starter or flare gun, but more likely a military grenade launcher. The lab is still tracing the components."

"That's surprising," Koa said. Then, after thinking about it, he added, "Maybe not. Whoever is behind this didn't expect us to arrest the Dragunov shooter. The attempt to kill him suggests his co-conspirators are afraid he'll talk and want him silenced before he regains full consciousness. Could be they acted hurriedly and improvised."

"Sounds reasonable," Cap Roberts agreed.

"And," Koa said, "it means our concussed friend might have something interesting to say if he wakes up."

CHAPTER FORTY

DURING THE FIRST twenty-four hours of surveillance, Keola received no visitors and no calls. Then, at 8:05 p.m., his burner phone rang. Alerted by an alarm, the surveillance team listened intently while simultaneously recording the call.

Keola answered, "*Oo.*"

Speaking in what sounded like a deliberately distorted voice, the caller said, "*Sigurado ka handa na para sa susunod na atake?*"

Once again, Keola repeated, "*Oo.*"

The caller then said, "*Gawin ito. Ang boss ay galit. Mas mabuting huwag kang mabigo sa pagkakataong ito,*" and hung up.

The watchers texted the recording to Koa, who forwarded it to a language expert at UH Hilo. He quickly got a chilling response. The language was Filipino, and the transcript read:

"*Yeah.*"

"*Are you ready for the next attack?*"

"*Yeah.*"

"*Do it. The boss is angry. You'd better not fail this time.*"

The brief conversation gave Koa several insights. The "next attack" language pretty much confirmed that the previous attacks on Makanui, Ikaika, and Nālani were all part of a coordinated strategy. It said to Koa that Keola was a foot soldier taking orders from others.

The reference to "the boss" meant that there were at least two levels of the organization above Keola. The Filipino language provided the third possible link—in addition to the Dragunov and the maker of the Semtex bomb—to the Abu Sayyaf terrorist group in the Philippines.

The apparent Abu Sayyaf connection puzzled Koa. The Philippine terrorist group had every reason to seek revenge against Makanui, who had killed one of their number, captured two others, and led Philippine forces to their base camp. Yet, they had no beef against Koa, his brother, or Nālani. None of them had played any role in Makanui's assault on the group, and so far as Koa knew, he'd never arrested anyone with a connection to the terrorist organization. So why attack him or those close to him? He was missing something—something vital.

Most critically, the call indicated that another attack was imminent. That created a dilemma for Koa. He wanted to continue surveillance to gather more intel but had to stop Keola from further violence. He alerted the surveillance team that Keola might be on the move and instructed them not to lose sight of their quarry under any circumstances. Concerned that Keola might somehow slip away undetected, he ordered the surveillance team to fly the drone over Keola's house every fifteen minutes. He then warned the Seattle security group watching over his family and Nālani, as well as the police officers protecting Makanui and Zeke, that an attack might be imminent.

Koa's directive to maintain drone surveillance turned out to be prescient. Shortly after the call ended, the drone's infrared camera recorded Keola leaving the house, getting into his Kia, and backing out of the drive. To the surprise of the drone operator, Keola headed away from the main road toward the water tank at the end of Alahaki Road. Once there, Keola parked and walked into the woods. "What's he doing?" Maru, one of the surveillance team members, asked.

Despite the tree canopy, the infrared sensors tracked Keola as he walked about a hundred yards into the forest before disappearing. "We've lost infrared coverage. He must be in a cave or a lava tube," Maru said.

Then, five minutes later, Keola reappeared headed back toward his car, carrying an object. The drone operator zoomed in. "He's got a bag or a case. It's hard to see the detail in infrared," Maru announced. Keola placed the bag or case in the trunk of his car and drove back past his house to the Hawai'i Belt Road, where he turned toward Hilo.

Koa had anticipated that Keola would leave the house and had prepared for that eventuality by asking Zeke to get search warrants. Minutes after Keola turned onto the highway, Koa sent a team to search Keola's house. He also instructed the team to check the spot in the forest a hundred yards west of the water tank where Keola had retrieved the object he'd placed in the trunk of his car.

While the search team went to work, Koa activated the Hilo SWAT team already on standby. He faced a difficult decision—arrest Keola immediately or wait until his intentions became apparent. He had a solid case against Keola for Nihoa's murder. An immediate arrest provided maximum public safety but wouldn't give Koa evidence linking Keola to the Makanui shootings or the bombings of Nālani's car and the hospital. Nor was it likely to identify Keola's associates. Koa also wanted to determine Keola's current target, catching him in the act, if possible, without risking another life. The time of day—now after 9:30 p.m. and dark—also complicated the situation, making it harder to surveil Keola and increasing the risk that he could evade them. After weighing the alternatives, Koa opted to let the drama play out, at least for a time.

Multiple police and SWAT operatives took turns following Keola's car into Hilo, keeping in constant radio contact with Koa, who commanded the operation from his SUV in downtown Hilo. Keola parked in an industrial area at the edge of town, retrieved the case from the trunk, and entered a dilapidated warehouse building. Members of the SWAT team in different vehicles surrounded the building and waited. Minutes passed before the officer at the back of the building reported. "One of the bay doors is rolling up. There's a cable service van pulling out."

"Who's driving?" Koa demanded.

"Can't tell. It's too dark."

Koa immediately sensed something amiss. There was no cable company office nearby and no reason for the van to be in the warehouse. "Follow the van," Koa ordered, sending two units after the vehicle while the remaining unit continued to monitor the warehouse.

All remained quiet at the warehouse while the van headed further downtown, turning onto Kamehameha Avenue and then following the Hawai'i Belt Road north. The van might be headed anywhere on the northeastern coast of the Big Island, but the proximity of Zeke's oceanfront home made it the most likely destination. The prosecutor lived just a couple of blocks off the Hawai'i Belt Road near Pauka'a Point north of Hilo.

Koa headed for Zeke's place, driving fast, using only his blue bubble light to warn other drivers. He thought about instructing the police officer guarding Zeke to move the prosecutor and his wife to a safe location, but there wasn't enough time. So he settled for warning the officer. Getting the cop on his cell, Koa identified himself. "There's a possible assassin coming for Zeke. Warn him, get him and his wife in a protected place, and stay alert for an intruder. Backup is less than ten minutes away."

Five minutes later, one of the SWAT officers reported, "Subject van turned on to Ku'ikahi Street." Then seconds later, "Subject van turning onto Poko Place. Stopping."

Koa had guessed right. Less than a block long, Poko Place ended in a cul-de-sac and provided access to a handful of oceanfront homes, including Zeke's place. The prosecutor appeared to be the next target. Less than a minute away, Koa radioed back, "Maintain surveillance. Move in and arrest at the first hostile act."

When Koa pulled up behind the two SWAT cars, officers had binoculars pointed at the van about fifty yards away. A soft breeze brought a light mist—what the Hawaiians call *noe kolo*—creeping inland from the nearby ocean. Only waves lapping along the rocky shoreline and the incessant chirping of invasive coqui frogs broke the silence. A crescent moon provided minimal illumination. "What's he doing?" Koa asked.

"Just sitting there," the officer replied, handing the field glasses to Koa.

"You're sure he's still in the van?" Koa asked apprehensively.

"Yes, sir," the officer responded.

Koa watched the van for another half minute before its back doors opened, and Keola climbed out, holding a double-magnum-sized bottle in each hand. Koa instantly identified the threat. He'd seen enough Molotov cocktails in his military service to recognize an arsonist's tool. And Keola held big double magnums, three-liter bottles, probably filled with an especially volatile fluid like acetone. "Christ," Koa swore, "he's going to torch Zeke's house. Get 'im."

Koa and two other officers raced toward the subject. They were still twenty-five yards away when Keola heard them coming, turned, and hurled one of the bottles toward them. It hit the ground ten yards in front of Koa and, triggered by some mechanism, exploded, sending glass flying and a wall of flames blocking their path forward. One of the officers screamed and turned back, his bloodied hands covering his face.

Zeke had entertained Koa and Nālani at his home, so Koa knew its location and layout. Yelling at the remaining officer to follow, he cut left, down a driveway to avoid the flames, and kept going around a neighboring building toward Zeke's place. Turning another corner, Koa saw movement ahead and caught a glimpse of Keola. "Police. Stop!" Koa yelled.

Keola stopped but not to surrender. The instant Koa saw the gun, he dropped to the ground. A loud popping sounded, followed by a whoosh, as an incendiary flare passed above him and barely missed the other officers. Koa, focused on stopping Keola before he reached Zeke's house, had his Glock out and pointed at Keola before the flare exploded against a palm tree, setting it alight. Still, Koa couldn't fire, not with an occupied dwelling behind his target. Too much risk of hitting a civilian.

Keola turned and ran with Koa, back on his feet, closing the distance. He knew that flare guns, like single-barrel, break-action shotguns, fired only single rounds, making it unlikely that Keola would take time to reload, but the man probably had another weapon. And Keola was still carrying a second firebomb, which could be just as deadly as a bullet.

Approaching his target, Keola stopped, faced Zeke's home, raised the Molotov cocktail, and cocked his arm, ready to hurl the bottle at his target. Koa, now with a clean shot, brought his Glock up and sighted on the man's center mass. "Don't do it, Keola," he yelled.

His arm still cocked, ready to throw, Keola slowly turned his head to look at Koa. Koa held his gun steady on the man's chest, ready to squeeze the trigger the instant that Keola's arm began to move forward. They stood like statues, eyes locked, for what seemed like an eternity before Keola seemed to understand that he would pay with his life if he threw the firebomb.

"Put it down and step back," Koa ordered.

Keola hesitated and then slowly lowered his arm, stooped, and placed the double magnum gently on the ground. "Move away to the left and get on the ground. Face down, hands behind your back," Koa ordered. Keola complied, and Koa, giving the incendiary a wide berth, handcuffed the man and secured the Sig Sauer P226 pistol Keola carried at the small of his back. He also recovered the flare gun and three more incendiary shells.

Koa turned Keola over to SWAT officers to be transported back to headquarters, called the bomb squad, verified that Zeke was okay, and went to check on the injured officer. The man suffered facial cuts and minor burns to his hands when the firebomb exploded but would recover. By the time he was ready to inspect the van, fire engines had arrived and extinguished the burning palm, and the bomb squad had neutralized the second incendiary device. A search of the van turned up four more similar devices. Keola had come prepared to do severe damage. Of that, Koa had no doubt. Koa had the bomb boys take photographs and left them to defuse the devices.

Those Molotov cocktails were only the first of the evidence against Keola. Officers executing the search warrant on his house found over $250,000 in cash, a burner phone, and a laptop computer. They found a small cave hollowed out below a ledge at the forest site west of the water tower. Inside, officers recovered a bomb like the one used to blow up Nālani's car, plus two dozen handguns, rifles, flare pistols, and boxes of ammo. Koa guessed that Keola had obtained the Sig Sauer pistol, flare gun, and incendiary cartridges from this hidden arsenal. He and Zeke had all the evidence they needed to charge and convict Keola. At the same time, they'd secured a terrifying glimpse into the size and financing of the group attacking the Hilo law enforcement community.

That was only the first shocker. When computer technicians accessed the laptop, they found a string of text messages from a single untraceable cellphone with a prepaid SIM card. Attachments included multiple photographs of the cottage Koa shared with Nālani, their vehicles, driver's licenses, law enforcement credentials, unlisted cell numbers, biographical details, Social Security numbers, daily calendars, and schedules. Other messages contained similar information for Zeke.

Much of the information was readily obtainable, but some, like Social Security numbers, law enforcement credentials, daily calendars, and schedules, was available only to law enforcement personnel. Koa wondered whether a hacker had accessed protected records or someone in the county government, most likely in the police department, had fed information to Keola. An insider aiding criminals attacking the Hilo law enforcement community would complicate what was already a nightmare situation.

CHAPTER FORTY-ONE

THE FOLLOWING MORNING, Koa stood in the door to Zeke's office watching his friend, who appeared to be engrossed in some legal document with his black boots planted firmly atop his desk. When Zeke looked up and saw Koa at the door, he grinned and said, "Thanks for saving my bacon."

Returning Zeke's greeting, Koa said, "Hope you're going to make it worth my while."

Zeke dropped his feet to the floor and spread his arms wide. "Okay, what do you want?"

"I want you to tell me what the hell is going on. There's some madman behind these attacks, and I can't make the pieces fit."

"Fill me in on what the searches turned up," Zeke requested.

"The forest search"—Koa explained the small cave near the water tank at the end of Alahaki Road—"turned up another bomb like the one used on Nālani's car and enough guns and ammo to equip a national guard unit. In addition, we recovered a burner phone with a single preprogrammed number and a computer from Keola's residence. The computer files include pictures of Nālani's Lexus, your pickup, and a ton of personal information about you, me, and Nālani, some of it quite confidential. Stuff you wouldn't easily discover without access, either directly or through hacking. And get this—two hundred fifty thousand dollars in currency."

Zeke whistled. "That's serious money."

"You bet. And our friend was well organized. Kept a spreadsheet on his laptop showing he paid out at least one hundred fifty thousand dollars. I'm guessing he was coordinating all or part of the recent attacks. We know that twenty-five thousand went to Moses, but the spreadsheet uses codes, so we haven't figured out who got the other one hundred twenty-five grand."

"What else?"

"The ATF explosive guys say the bombs used on Nālani's car and the one we found in Keola's woodland stash all have the signature of an Abu Sayyaf bomb maker named Muhammad Khalili."

"You interrogated this Keola character yet?" Zeke asked.

"No. He's got himself a lawyer and isn't talking," Koa responded.

Zeke shifted in his chair. "Too bad. He could tell us what's going on."

"I have a little surprise that might get him to change his mind."

"You want to share?" Zeke asked.

"I've been talking to the ATF guys, and here's what I have in mind, but I'll need your help." Koa explained what he planned to do.

"Clever," Zeke acknowledged. "Success, I'd guess, depends on who represents this Keola fellow."

"In the meantime," Koa said, "tell me who has a motive to attack the Hilo police and the county prosecutor, the money to commit almost a half-million dollars to the effort, and access to Libyan Semtex assembled by an Abu Sayyaf bomb maker. There can't be many people who fit that description."

Zeke swung his feet back up onto his desk and leaned back in his chair. "Seems most likely someone we prosecuted. Who else has a motive to go after the police?"

"I agree," Koa said, "but most of the criminals we lock up don't have $250,000, and other than Makanui, nobody in the department or among those we've arrested or convicted has any connection to Abu Sayyaf."

"Okay. Let's try the brainstorming thing. What about activists in the sovereignty movement? We know they're unhappy with the new Japanese mayor who hasn't delivered on his promises of more special privileges for native Hawaiians. On top of that, we had two unfortunate police overreactions drawing protests, including radicals from O'ahu and the mainland."

"I suppose it's possible," Koa responded, "but it seems unlikely, especially with Makanui and me, both Hawaiian, as principal targets."

"Some of the activists regard you as traitors to the cause," Zeke responded.

"Yeah, I hear that all the time. I'll check it out with some of my sovereignty friends." Koa paused. "Can you think of any other possibilities?"

"What about the senator's aide. What was his name?"

"Keahi?" Koa responded. He referred to one of his Hawaiian contemporaries. He and Koa had grown up as friends, but unknown to Koa, his friend felt slighted in life and envious of Koa's successes. This discontent had radicalized young Keahi and made him vulnerable. The Chinese Ministry of State Security had successfully recruited Keahi in college, eventually turning him into a spy. Obtaining an internship on Capitol Hill, he'd advanced to become the principal aide to a senior U.S. senator and ultimately provided a gold mine of information to his Chinese handlers. Koa, working with the feds, had uncloaked him. Before being taken back to the mainland for debriefing and a life sentence in a federal penitentiary, he'd threatened Koa.

"That's him," Zeke said. "He had money stashed away in offshore accounts and plenty of reason to hate you, me, and Makanui. I never believed that he would come completely clean or that the feds would find all his hidden assets."

Koa shook his head in disagreement. "I've thought about him, but I don't see how it's possible. Sure, he has a motive and has made threats, but the feds took his money and locked him up in some maximum-security prison. From what I've heard, the inmates have little or no communication with the outside world. Besides, he had nothing to do with Abu Sayyaf."

"Could you check with your federal friends, just to be sure?" Zeke asked.

"Will do," Koa responded. "Can't hurt to check."

"Could it be someone with a perceived police brutality complaint or something like that?" Zeke asked.

Koa again shook his head at the notion. "Seems far-fetched. We haven't had many brutality complaints, and the few we've had got resolved. A couple cost the county some money, but no big settlements."

"You have any secret enemies I don't know about?" Zeke asked.

Koa grasped the rhetorical nature of Zeke's question, but it still sparked a wave of guilt. In his introspective moments, he tormented himself with the thought that the recent attacks were somehow retribution for his accidental killing thirty-plus years ago of Anthony Hazzard, the man who'd tormented his father. He knew he was being paranoid, but guilt was his ever-present burden—a weight he could never share with Zeke or anyone else.

*   *   *

After leaving Zeke's office, Koa called Rachael Goodling in the National Security Division of the U.S. Department of Justice. Koa and Makanui had worked with Goodling and her DOJ and FBI team in uncovering a Chinese espionage ring led by Keahi. After exchanging pleasantries, Koa explained that someone had attacked the Big Island law enforcement community.

"I know," Rachael responded. "I got an alert from the ATF about the involvement of an Abu Sayyaf bomb maker who's been on our terror radar for years. I'm sorry—"

"That's not the only Abu Sayyaf connection," Koa interrupted and described the Dragunov attacks on Makanui and the instructions Keola had received in Filipino.

"That's interesting. I want one of my people to take a deeper dive. I'll have them contact you. What can I do in the meantime?"

Koa hesitated, choosing his words. "This may seem like an odd question, but is there any chance that our old nemesis, Kāwika Keahi, could be involved in these attacks?"

"Not a chance," she responded. "The FBI counter-espionage boys spent months debriefing him, tearing apart every moment of his life from the day he was born. Intelligence agencies, some with classified names, reconstructed every communication he ever had. They found and confiscated every last dollar of his onshore and offshore funds. He's locked up in a cell twenty-three hours a day. He can't go to the bathroom except on camera and can't communicate with anyone outside, let alone run an op from incarceration. You're chasing ghosts on that one."

"Thanks, Rachael. That's what I expected, but we're trying to run down every possibility."

"Give my best to Zeke and Makanui," she said before hanging up.

With that avenue of inquiry buttoned up, Koa waited until early evening to look for Makaiao. The tall, well-educated activist was a distant relative on his mother's side where there were so many "uncles" that Koa couldn't remember the exact relationship. Since Koa knew of no ongoing demonstrations on the Island, he figured he'd find Makaiao at his place, a specialty vegetable farm on the Mauna Kea slopes above the Hāmākua coast. Koa didn't bother to call ahead. Makaiao had a cellphone, but the sovereignty advocate refused to be a slave to any form of *haole* technology and seldom answered.

Koa drove up Chin Chuck Road to Makaiao's small farm along the Hakalau Stream on the northern slope of Mauna Kea a couple of miles inland from Hakalau Bay. With fertile soils, abundant sunshine, and plentiful water, sugarcane had once covered the fields. The Hakalau Sugar Mill had processed the crop and loaded the sugar on ships in Hakalau Bay. The mill, closed in the early 1960s, was now a ruin. The sugarcane had long ago disappeared, except for isolated wild clumps along highways. Now, the area along the stream hosted dozens of small farms, growing vegetables, fruits, herbs, avocados, papayas, and other crops.

Koa let himself through the gate, drove down the rutted gravel drive, and found Makaiao working with exotic orchids in his greenhouse. Looking up when Koa entered, Makaiao said, "This can't be good news."

The less-than-friendly greeting didn't faze Koa. The two men had a turbulent relationship. A savvy, college-educated student of Hawaiian culture and history, Makaiao deeply resented the Western exploitation of the Islands and its indigenous people. Not unlike African Americans and Native American Indians, he understood the continuing effects of past discrimination. Because *haoles* had expropriated the richest land, native Hawaiians often got only the most arid, volcanic places for their homes and farms. Laws forbidding the use of the Hawaiian language in government and schools had starved much traditional Hawaiian culture to the point of near extinction. Only in recent years had Hawaiian art begun a resurgence and native nautical techniques enjoyed a revival. Makaiao's discontent, bordering on bitterness, extended to the police and the justice system that arrested, prosecuted, and incarcerated native Hawaiians at disproportional rates.

Makaiao frequently disparaged Koa's Hawaiian heritage, describing him as *hapa haole,* part white, *ho'ohaole 'ia,* having Western ways, or *māka'ikui,* a spying detective. Still, the two men shared a fragile mutual respect on a personal level. In private, Makaiao begrudgingly acknowledged Koa's contributions, coaching *heihei wa'a,* canoe racing, to native teens, and counseling Hawaiian *'ōpio lawehala,* juvenile delinquents. They also helped each other out when it suited their mutual interests. Koa protected the activists' right to gather for lawful protests, and Makaiao occasionally helped the police when it served the native rights cause.

At six-two, Koa rarely looked up to anyone, but Makaiao, who stood nearly a head taller, was an exception. With dark lava-colored hair and gleaming white teeth, he was a classic Hawaiian. "*Aloha.* It's good to see you, too," Koa responded with a smile. Then, recognizing the rare orchid in Makaiao's hand, he added, "I see you finally scored a gold Kinabalu orchid."

Makaiao's jaw dropped in astonishment, but he quickly recovered. "So, Nālani has created an orchidologist. Maybe now you'll change jobs and stop hassling us poor Hawaiians."

Koa laughed. "Someday, but for the moment, I need your help."

"As a beggar? Or do you offer something in return?"

"I've got a six-pack of Bikini Blonde in the car," Koa said.

"*Haole* beer," Makaiao protested. "Is that the best you could do?"

"The store didn't have *'awa,*" Koa quipped, referring to the traditional and ceremonial narcotic drink also known as kava.

"Use more foresight next time, but okay for now. Get the beer. I'll meet you on the *lānai*."

They sat on the *lānai* at the front of Makaiao's modest ranch house overlooking the coast and the ocean. The sky glowed in soft pastel colors. A tug, headed for Honolulu, pulled a barge piled high with Matson line containers on a long tow cable. Closer to shore, a pair of outrigger canoes raced back toward Hilo, and just barely visible, Koa thought he could see the spouts of humpback whales.

Makaiao popped a tab and took a long swallow of beer. "So, your *haole* friends let you down, and you need this poor Hawaiian to bail you out."

"Something like that," Koa responded. "First, I wanted you to know that the department is upset about the way officers handled the demonstrations a week ago." He referred to a local protest against the Navy's pollution of groundwater on Oʻahu. "They were out of line, and the chief reprimanded them."

"Jesus, man. You must be desperate if you're starting with an apology."

"Just want to set the record straight," Koa responded.

"For the record, that kind of police abuse only helps our cause by creating more supporters and sympathizers."

"I'm sure that's true, but it's not the reason we don't tolerate misconduct." Koa told Makaiao about the attempt to frame Ikaika and attacks on Makanui and Zeke. Then he added, "We've kept it quiet, so it hasn't been in the news."

"Any relation to that car bombing or that hospital thing that have been in the news?" Makaiao asked.

The man, Koa thought, was quick and surprisingly well informed. He didn't particularly want to confirm Makaiao's guesses but needed to secure the man's cooperation. "Yes, there are connections," Koa conceded.

"So, what's this got to do with me?"

Koa had prepared for this moment. Asking if sovereignty activists were involved would only come across as casting aspersions, so Koa chose a different tack. "There is evidence that Philippine terrorists from a group calling itself Abu Sayyaf centered in the Mindanao area carried out some of the attacks."

"You mean real terrorists, not like us activists?" Makaiao said sarcastically.

The taunt got under Koa's skin, but he restrained himself. "Yes, I mean criminals who blow up cars and hospitals, killing innocent folks."

Makaiao sat silent for several moments before saying, "Okay. But what's all this got to do with me?"

"You heard of any Filipino strangers wandering about, maybe looking for guns or other local support?" Koa asked.

"No, but I'll ask around."

Koa pushed into more volatile territory. "Or any radicals from the mainland groups fighting wars with the authorities?"

Makaiao paused, and Koa wasn't sure he was going to answer. Finally, he said, "You know that off-island activists, including some whose tactics I don't like, participated in recent protests against the construction of the Thirty Meter Telescope on Mauna Kea. Most of them went back home, and I doubt any who haven't left are involved in local violence, but I'll check. If I get the slightest whiff of involvement in attacks on the police, I'll tell you. I don't tolerate that shit any more than you do."

"Thanks," Koa responded. "I owe you."

"A big one," Makaiao responded with a chuckle. "And next time, bring 'awa."

CHAPTER FORTY-TWO

IN THE HOURS since arresting Keola for attempting to firebomb Zeke's home, Koa had learned quite a lot about the man. His name wasn't Keola, and he wasn't Hawaiian. The FBI matched his fingerprints to one Ismael Hafeez, born in Zamboanga on the southwest corner of Mindanao Island in the Philippines. The U.S. and Filipino governments listed him as an Abu Sayyaf terrorist, and his file said he'd attended Islamic training camps in Libya and Afghanistan. Customs and Immigration had no record of his entry into the United States, so Koa did not know when or how he'd arrived in Hawai'i.

After Koa arrested him, federal authorities sought to detain Ismael on federal charges. The U.S. Attorney in Honolulu sent Assistant U.S. Attorney Greta Jones and two FBI agents to take custody of the suspect for trial on federal terror charges in Honolulu. Koa and Zeke resisted, citing their critical need for information to prevent further attacks on the Hilo Police Department. Zeke threatened to involve the governor and Hawai'i's senior U.S. senator. A standoff ensued before the two agencies reached a compromise. If Koa could get Ismael to talk, the feds would let Hawai'i prosecute him for murder. Otherwise, Jones and the FBI would take custody of him.

Zeke and Koa feared that Ismael's co-conspirators would engage a high-powered lawyer, more interested in protecting them than serving Ismael's best interests. Instead, Ismael hired Howard Kim, a local known to represent drug dealers and burglary suspects. Koa found Ismael's choice of legal counsel encouraging.

Koa, Zeke, and AUSA Jones took Kim aside. Koa outlined the overwhelming case against Ismael, including possessing a bomb identical to the one that killed 'Olina in Nālani's car. Jones then explained that since Ismael was a foreigner who'd used a weapon of mass destruction, namely a bomb, to kill 'Olina, a U.S. citizen, in a public place, the federal government could prosecute him as a terrorist and seek the death penalty.

Howard Kim's eyes went wide at the mention of the death penalty. He'd never tried a death penalty case. Since life in prison was the maximum punishment for any crime under state law, few Hawai'i lawyers had experience in capital cases. "The death penalty?" Kim repeated as though it couldn't be true.

"Yes," Jones assured him and helpfully provided copies of the relevant statutes.

Zeke and Koa let the threat of dying from a lethal injection sink in before Koa offered his alternative. "If your client cooperates fully and tells us who put him up to killing 'Olina Crow as well as everything he knows about the attacks on Makanui, Ikaika, and the county prosecutor, the feds will agree not to seek the death penalty and defer to the state to prosecute. That way, your client can avoid the death penalty."

"I'll have to think about your offer and discuss it with my client," Howard responded.

"That's fine," Koa replied. "You and your client have two hours to decide."

"What!" Howard exclaimed. "That's unacceptable."

"Maybe, but that's the deal. Two FBI agents are waiting outside to take Ismael back to Honolulu, where the U.S. Attorney will indict him on federal terrorism charges. He's on a plane out of here unless he agrees to cooperate."

Howard stiffened. "I said I need to consult my client."

Koa escorted Kim to the interrogation room and returned to the conference room where Zeke and Jones waited.

"Think he'll deal?" Zeke asked.

"I have no idea," Koa responded, "but it's sure worth a try."

Forty-five minutes later, Howard was back in the conference room. "My client says he'll cooperate if you release him in a foreign country of his choice."

Koa didn't need to check with the others to answer that question. "No deal. I'll let the FBI agents know we're ready to let them have him." Koa stood and moved toward the door.

"Wait a minute," Howard said. "He's worried about his safety if he cooperates. He doesn't want to die in jail."

"We can arrange segregated custody," Koa shot back.

"For the duration of his sentence?" Kim asked.

"If that's what he wants," Koa said.

"He wants the deal in writing," Kim demanded.

"I'll have to talk to the U.S. Attorney about that," Jones responded before stepping out of the room. Forty-five minutes later, she was back with a faxed copy of a letter agreement signed by the U.S. Attorney. The agreement provided that if Ismael pled guilty to murdering 'Olina and cooperated fully and truthfully, the United States would not seek to invoke the death penalty. Howard countersigned and arranged for his client to do likewise. They were ready to hear what the man had to say.

* * *

When Koa entered the interrogation room with Jones and Ismael's lawyer, the prisoner sat in a chair bolted to the floor. His jailers had cuffed his hands to a post in the center of the table in front of him. Chains linked his leg irons.

Koa studied him, detecting a conscious nonchalance in the man's posture. That, in Koa's experience, did not bode well. He started the video recorder and asked those present to identify themselves. He then acknowledged that he and Assistant U.S. Attorney Jones intended to interview Ismael under the agreement he and his counsel had signed.

Koa set the tone with a warning. "Do you understand that you must answer our questions fully and truthfully? Otherwise, the federal charges and death penalty will be back on the table."

"Yeah, I get it," Ismael acknowledged.

"How did you arrive in Hawai'i?" Koa asked.

"Boat."

"From where?"

"From my country you call Mindanao."

"On what vessel?" Koa asked.

"*Davao*. Nasty ship. From Filipino Cebu town."

Koa knew because there was no customs record of legal entry that Ismael had done so illegally. To test the man's credibility, he asked, "So you cleared customs in Hilo?"

The corners of Ismael's mouth turned up slightly. Koa read it as a tell. The man had recognized the question as a potential trap.

"I leave ship 'fore it go dock."

"How?" Koa asked.

"Over the side. To boat 'fore harbor."

"Anyone go over the side with you?"

"No. I alone."

"Who else was aboard this boat?"

"Only pilot."

"The pilot's name?"

"Dunno," Ismael replied. "He wear balaclava. No name. Just password."

"Where did you land?"

Ismael seemed to struggle. "Down coast at black sand place."

"Punalu'u?" Koa asked.

"Yes. Punalu'u." But the word came out mangled.

That, Koa thought, made sense. Punalu'u, the site of one of Hawai'i's most famous black sand beaches, was only a short distance from Ismael's Alahaki Road hideout. "What time did you land?"

"Sun just up," Ismael answered.

"That would be on the same date that the *Davao* docked in Hilo?" Koa asked.

"Yeah."

Wondering if there might be a way to identify the pilot, Koa asked, "Anyone see you?"

"Maybe. Few campers by place."

"What happened then?" Koa asked.

"The pilot, he give keys to car. Map on seat. I follow map to a house on Alahaki Road." Again, Ismael mispronounced the name.

Quickly switching topics to throw Ismael off, Koa asked, "Where did you get the bomb?" He deliberately used the singular, creating another potential trap for Ismael.

"It," Ismael answered hesitantly, "already there."

"Just one?" Koa demanded.

Again, Ismael paused, and Koa guessed he was considering whether he could get away with a lie. Opting for the truth, he said, "Two."

"Where?"

"In the forest ninety meter from water tank."

"Who were the targets?" Koa demanded.

"Your woman friend. Only target I have," Ismael responded and then paused before adding, "then him." He pointed to Zeke.

"Why target my girlfriend?"

"Dunno. I follow order."

"What about the other bomb?"

"I maybe get more names," Ismael acknowledged.

"How?"

"Burner."

"From whom?"

"I never know. Only code name."

"What code name?"

"Kōkua." The name came out mangled. Koa asked him to repeat it, and he complied.

Koa puzzled over the Hawaiian name—Kōkua. Translated literally, it meant help or helper but had a deeper significance, meaning loving support to others without expecting personal gain or anything in return. The concept, like *aloha*, was deeply embedded in Hawaiian culture and taught to children from an early age. In the current context, it seemed an odd code name. None of Koa's adversaries in this ordeal offered sincere or loving help, and he doubted that any of them acted without expectation of personal gain. It was more like *Kōkua hewa*—partners in crime.

"What do you know about this Kōkua?"

"Him local bossman."

"Who is his boss?"

"Rich man. Very powerful. Very dangerous."

"Who is he?"

"Dunno."

"Where is he?"

"Dunno."

"How do you know he's rich and powerful?"

"How else I get many guns and two bombs?" Ismael responded.

"Why did you try to burn Zeke Brown's home?"

"Kōkua tell me."

"Why?"

"Dunno."

"Who sent you to Hawai'i?"

"Abu Sayyaf bossman."

"Who is that?"

"Muhammad Khalili."

"The bomb maker?"

Ismael looked surprised that Koa knew the name. "Yeah."

"Why is Abu Sayyaf trying to kill officials and others here in Hawai'i?"

"Money. My bossman in Mindanao. He get millions U.S. dolla. And guns for Abu Sayyaf."

"From whom?"

"Dunno. Man came to camp. Talk bossman."

"What man?"

"White man, infidel."

"When?"

With his hands fastened to the post in the middle of the table, Ismael counted something on his fingers. "Maybe five months past."

The questioning went on for hours. They covered Ismael's efforts to frame Ikaika, but learned little more than what Moses had told them. The laptop computer containing personal details of the targets had been in the Alahaki Road house when Ismael arrived. He had no idea who had provided it. He knew nothing about the attacks on Makanui or the Dragunov rifle the sniper had used.

"You believe him?" Zeke asked when they wrapped up for the day.

"He passed all the tests I threw at him, but cooperators almost always hold something back. So, I don't think we got everything."

"Was it worth it?" Zeke asked.

"We didn't get the grand slam I'd hoped for, but we learned a couple of things. Abu Sayyaf is selling terrorist services. That explains why these Filipinos are attacking people with no relation to that group. We also learned that some infidel *haole*—not part of Abu Sayyaf—negotiated to purchase the services of hired killers and arranged a big payment. He or one of his co-conspirators using the code name Kōkua is their local commander. And the phone call we recorded giving orders to Ismael already told us that the local commander is not at the top of the food chain. According to Ismael, someone rich, powerful, and dangerous is calling the shots. So, we got some critical parts of the puzzle. Besides, we didn't give up much. The feds haven't executed anyone since the Trump administration."

CHAPTER FORTY-THREE

KOA PUT ASIDE his disappointments from the Ismael interview to focus on the next steps. He knew his priorities—track down the sailor who transported Ismael from the ship to the black sand beach and identify the leaker inside the Hilo government feeding confidential information to those attacking the police. He wasn't without potential leads. He could track the ownership of the house Ismael had used, dig deeper into the computer the police had recovered from the Alahaki Road house, and try to tease information out of Ismael's cellphone. It was the kind of detailed, tedious police work that had propelled Koa's career from the outset.

Koa asked an assistant to check on the ownership of the house. He assigned Cap Roberts to work his magic on the computer. Then, he selected Piki, his most technically savvy detective, to tackle the cellphones. With three of the most immediate tasks assigned to others, Koa hit the road. He was going to see if there was anything to learn from a visit to Punalu'u.

He drove south on the Hawai'i Belt Road past Volcano Village and the National Park before turning left onto the Ninole Loop Road. Pulling up to the Punalu'u campground near the beach, he figured he was probably wasting his time. There was what—a one in fifty chance—that anyone would have seen, let alone remembered, a man emerging from a powerboat shortly after dawn a couple of weeks ago. Yet, he knew from experience that diligence in following up every lead often yielded surprising results. Besides, he knew something unknown to most others.

In modern times, tourists flocked to Punaluʻu to see the black sand and the *honu*, green sea turtles, that fed on red seaweed and other marine plants in the protected bay and napped on the black sand or nearby rocky outcroppings. Some visitors even became enthralled with the legend of Kauila, a giant *honu*, a large green sea turtle, that morphed into a young woman who protected the *keiki*, the children, swimming in the cove.

But most visitors knew neither the meaning nor the history of Punaluʻu. Koa knew the name meant "spring waters" and came from the freshwater aquifer that emptied into the sea near the beach. Three nearby *heiau*, or temple platforms, offered evidence of the significance of Punaluʻu to ancient Hawaiians. The remnants of a concrete pier and other nearby decaying facilities stood testament to its importance as a commercial port during the height of Hawaiʻi's sugar plantation days. More recently, in 1975, a tsunami triggered by a 7.2 magnitude earthquake on the eastern side of Kīlauea hit the Punaluʻu area, causing severe damage.

Koa parked next to a large RV and knocked on the door. Koa thought a response unlikely, and none was forthcoming. At this midafternoon hour, Samantha Carpo and Kathy Worth, the RV owners, would be out checking their traps. Kathy had been a classmate of Nālani's in the environmental sciences program at Cal Poly in San Luis Obispo. Though their careers developed in different directions, they remained in touch.

Kathy and her partner, Samantha, both biologists, recently secured a permit from the Hawaiʻi Department of Natural Resources to study the endangered species in and around Punaluʻu. The *honu*, green sea turtles, and *honu ʻea*, rare hawkbill turtles, thrived along the isolated coast, along with the *ʻio*, the Hawaiian hawk, the *opeʻapeʻa*, the hoary Hawaiian bat, and the orange-black damselfly. In addition to these regular inhabitants, rare Hawaiian monk seals also occasionally visited.

Three weeks back, Nālani and Koa had spent a weekend helping Kathy and Samantha set up their equipment on the rocky shores, inlets, and brackish ponds around Punaluʻu. While the researchers took countless photographs and made contemporaneous notes, their principal tool was the camera trap. These small battery-powered cameras used a variety of triggering methods. Some snapped pictures periodically, often as frequently as every three minutes. Motion sensors activated others. A few rode the ocean waves tethered in place by anchors on the seafloor. Others used infrared flash, while different models relied on super sensitive electronics to capture images in near darkness.

Koa hoped to benefit from their setup. With a bit of luck, one of their cameras had captured an image of a boat arriving around sunrise and discharging a passenger near one of the area's parking lots on the same date the freighter *Davao* docked in Hilo. With fantastic luck, he might even be able to identify the small craft and its pilot.

After asking around the campground, Koa found the two researchers near a tiny inlet about a quarter mile north of the black sand beach. "Hey there! Koa, what brings you out here?" Kathy asked with a welcoming smile. Kathy was tall and lanky in her late thirties with honey brown hair and intense hazel eyes.

Not wanting to alarm them, Koa explained that he hoped one of their cameras caught a picture of a boat used by a smuggler. Kathy looked at Samantha. "You've done all the initial photo reviews. Seen any boats?"

"Sure," Samantha responded. "Several, though I wouldn't know if any is the one you're looking for." Samantha was the shorter of the two, sporting a tangled mop of blonde curls.

"Can I see what you've got?" Koa asked.

"Sure," Samantha said, pushing her hair away from her face, "but it'll take a while. We've collected over 60,000 photos."

Koa whistled. "Wow. That many?"

"Afraid so. We have thirty cameras that take pictures on average every fifteen minutes, and we've been here for three weeks. Do the math."

Daunted by the prospect of checking 60,000 pictures, Koa searched for a faster way. "How are they organized?"

"By date, time, camera number, and species, if present."

Koa, who'd checked the date the Philippine freighter *Davao* had docked in Hilo, responded, "I have the date and general time of day."

"In that case, checking should be a piece of cake," Samantha responded.

Koa waited while the two women finished transferring pictures from the two cameras at the inlet and accompanied them back to their RV. Samantha led him to a workspace with a computer, several storage drives, and a giant thirty-inch monitor. Pulling up a database program, she input the date the *Davao* docked.

"What time parameters should I use?" Samantha asked.

"Sunrise would have been a bit before six a.m. Can you designate a window, let's say, an hour before and an hour after?"

Samantha entered the times and pressed RETURN. "Done. I assume you want images from cameras north of and in Punaluʻu bay?"

"Sure," Koa responded, knowing that the speedboat would have picked up its passenger near Hilo and thus arrived at Punaluʻu from the north.

Samantha referred to a chart and then entered camera numbers. Moments later, postage-stamp-sized thumbnail images began to pop up on the monitor in rows that ultimately filled the screen and scrolled off the bottom. Reading a number off the header, Samantha said, "That's 147 pictures."

"Can you go through them one by one?" Koa asked.

"Sure," Samantha replied, and with a few clicks of her mouse, individual images filled the entire thirty-inch screen one after another.

"Stop," Koa said when one of the pictures, shot from the rocky shore, included a dark-colored boat in the distance. That one picture made his trip to Punalu'u worthwhile. In Hawaiian mythology, a sighting of the *honu* foretold good luck. Koa didn't put much stock in the old folklore but was happy to give the Punalu'u turtles their due. "Can you zoom in on the boat?"

Samantha manipulated the mouse, and the boat grew larger but, unfortunately, also fuzzier. "These little research cameras aren't good for long-distance shots," she said apologetically.

"That's okay. If you can text the original to me, I may be able to have the police lab work on it."

Samantha obliged. They resumed their review and found five more images with the boat or some part of it in the background. Koa was not sufficiently familiar with local watercraft to identify the vessel, but he had Samantha forward all five photos. He was pretty sure that with appropriate enhancement, his fisherman friend, Hook Hao, would know the boat and maybe even its owner.

CHAPTER FORTY-FOUR

Koa stood at the entrance to the police lab. Cap Roberts, working on a computer set atop an electronics bench with multiple monitors, looked up. "Jesus, Koa, I know you're in an all-fired hurry to get results, but these things take time." He was a big man with huge hands, and Koa was always amazed at the intricate work he did with such large fingers. Like a concert pianist with five thumbs.

"Believe it or not, I'm not here to bug you about Ismael's computer. Instead, I've got more work for you. Wouldn't want you to get bored."

"Fat chance of that," Cap snapped. "So, what do you want now?"

"I've got some fuzzy pictures of the boat that I think may have hauled our terrorist friend from Hilo down to Punalu'u. I was hoping you could enlarge and enhance them."

"I suppose you want them now?"

"Maybe for a six-pack of Paniolo Pale Ale," Koa suggested.

"Gimme the fucking pictures."

Koa forwarded the files he'd received from Samantha to Cap's work computer. Cap loaded the first image on his giant monitor and studied it for a moment. "You take this with an old iPhone 4?" Cap asked, referring to the earliest iPhone with a camera. "You need to get yourself a better camera. A broken Go Pro would do a better job." Cap clicked to the following picture before Koa could answer, revealing a poorly focused image of the back half of a boat at the top-right edge of the frame. Turning toward Koa, he said, "You're supposed to point the camera at the subject. Didn't they teach you that in detective school?"

Koa finally managed to respond, explaining the limitations of his source. Cap then went to work, starting with the best images using various tools to increase the resolution, clarify, and sharpen each of the six images. After several minutes, he selected the three best pictures on his monitor. "That's the best I can do with the equipment I have here. The lab in Honolulu might be able to do a bit more, but nobody is going to turn these sorry gems into fine art."

Koa examined the images. They weren't perfect, but still significantly clearer and sharper than the originals. Looking at Cap, he said, "You're a magician, my friend."

"Flattery won't get you out of buying beer," Cap responded. "I assume you want prints?"

Koa nodded, and Cap sent the three images to a printer.

"Thanks," Koa said as he took the 8 x 10 prints and headed for the door.

"Make sure the beer is well iced," Cap said.

Koa turned back at the door. "I'll come by around six. We can share a brew while you fill me in on Ismael's computer."

"You're impossible," Cap retorted, insisting, as usual, on the last word.

*　　*　　*

With a quick call, Koa learned that Hook Hao, piloting his commercial fishing trawler, the *Kaʻupu*, or *Albatross*, had just cleared the Hilo breakwater headed for its mooring along the quay near the mouth of the Wailoa River. Koa had just enough time to reach the dock and watch Hook ease the *Ka'upu* into its home with the skill of a fighter pilot executing a perfect landing on a carrier deck. Koa caught one of the mooring lines and secured it around a bollard before stepping onto the deck. He waited while Hook and a deckhand carried four large coolers to the nearby Suisan fish market, where they transferred the day's catch to walk-in refrigerators.

With the deckhand on his way home, Hook returned to the *Ka'upu*, where he and Koa settled into deck chairs under the cloudless evening sky. Even seated, the big seven-foot fisherman looked bigger than life. "Good outing?" Koa asked.

"Not bad," Hook responded, his bald head gleaming in the final glow of the setting sun. He pulled two bottles of Bikini Blonde Lager from a nearby ice chest and handed one to Koa. "The wind was blowing hard, and the sea was choppy, but the catch was better than average."

Koa nodded. "And how's Reggie?"

Reggie was Hook's son and the reason Hook had become a police informant more than a decade earlier. The recollection was as fresh in Koa's mind as if it had happened yesterday. He'd arrested Reggie, along with several other teens, for growing marijuana. Hook had shown up at the police station and, making his point by telling a Hawaiian fable, offered to help the police if Koa released Reggie. Hook had proved himself an invaluable source in the intervening years, and their relationship gradually deepened into a cherished friendship. It was, Koa thought, one of the best deals he'd ever made.

"So, what brings you to the waterfront?" Hook asked, sipping his lager.

Koa handed Hook the three pictures that Cap had enhanced and printed. "I'm looking for a line on this boat."

Hook studied the prints carefully one at a time before flipping back to the one with the sharpest image of the boat. "You're keeping your day job, I hope. You don't have a future as a photographer."

Koa smiled. "Rest assured, my friend, you're not alone in that view. Actually, they're not mine, and I was lucky to get them off a couple of environmentalists using cameras to track endangered species around Punaluʻu."

"Thought I recognized the inlet." To Koa, the broken lava rocks could have been anywhere on the Island or even on the other Hawaiian Islands. Yet, after a lifetime of navigating the local waters, Hook knew every nook and cranny of the Big Island's coastline.

"The boat's an ACB Extreme Sport model. It's hard to tell from this picture, but I'd guess twenty-nine to thirty feet from stem to stern. It's a good solid ride for a sport fisherman, but it's unusual to see one painted black like this. Makes me think the owner wants to be invisible at night."

"You mean for smuggling?"

"Yeah, that's exactly what I'm thinking."

"You seen it?"

"Yeah, I've seen it a couple of times down south, past Nāʻālehu closer to South Point." Hook referred to the southernmost point of the Big Island, also the southernmost spot in the United States.

"Know who owns it or where I can find it?"

"No idea. It's not docked anywhere on this side of the Island. I'd guess the owner's got it on a trailer and launches from a boat ramp."

"Any idea where?" Koa asked.

"Maybe Kaulana. That's the only ramp on the southeast coast."

Koa pictured the tiny, isolated cove at Kaulana, south of Punaluʻu. Dropping Ismael at Punaluʻu and heading south to pull the boat out of the water made sense. In a flash, it hit Koa. If the vessel had gone south from Punaluʻu, one of Samantha's cameras south of the black sand beach might also have photographed it.

Excusing himself for a moment, Koa called Samantha and, catching her at her computer, asked her to check the southern cameras

using the same day and time parameters. Before he and Hook finished their beers, Samantha called back. Koa had guessed right. Her
cameras had captured images of the black boat headed south.

Koa stopped for a moment to consider priorities, weighing
whether he should devote a day or two to a time-consuming search
for the dark-colored boat. His instincts told him the speedboat pilot
was a critical figure in the plot against the police. The smuggler could
have ferried other co-conspirators or their supplies. If Koa could find
him, he might lead the police to others involved in the scheme. He'd
likely have been in contact with the higher-ups in the conspiracy who
would have given him the information he needed to meet the *Davao*.

Koa resolved to go to Kaulana.

*   *   *

Before he could make the trip south to Kaulana, Koa and Nālani
needed to pay their respects and extend their sympathies to Fred
Crow. As they drove to the church, Nālani voiced the guilt that had
nagged at her since learning of 'Olina's death. "It should have been
me," she confided to Koa.

Taking one hand off the steering wheel, he gently cupped it over
hers. "Although I understand why you might say that, there's no reason for you to feel that way. No one could have anticipated that your
lending 'Olina your car would result in her death. She was simply in
the wrong place at the wrong time. It's terrible, but you're not to
blame."

"I'm not sure Fred will feel that way," Nālani said, trying to hold
back tears.

"Fred knew that you and 'Olina were as close as sisters. I'm betting
he will want to comfort you as much as you want to give him solace.
I suspect that's one of the reasons he asked you to speak."

"I hope so."

It was a beautiful service in a church overflowing with mourners and flowers. Nālani offered the first of the eulogies, remembering ʻOlina as "my dearest friend and colleague. She was a bright light who illuminated every moment for those around her. I will miss her always, but never more so than when I stand on the *pali* at the Hilina lookout, where we often sat together enjoying the magnificent solitude of the national park."

Fred, showing a fortitude that few bereaved spouses possess, delivered a heartfelt eulogy for the love of his life and soulmate of twenty years. At the end of the service when they extended their condolences, Fred embraced Nālani in a long hug. "She loved you like a sister, and I know this is hard for you, too. We will both miss her terribly."

CHAPTER FORTY-FIVE

SOUTH POINT HELD a special place in Koa's pantheon. Nothing but 2,500 miles of open ocean separated Tahiti and South Point, where fishing shrines and other artifacts led archeologists to believe Polynesian seafarers first landed in Hawai'i about 1,500 years ago. The length of that voyage and the number of previous failures are lost in the mists of history. So, too, are many of the original chants that guided Polynesian navigators across such long distances. What Koa did know was that in 1975 the *Hōkūle'a*, a replica of a traditional Polynesian voyaging canoe, made the journey from Hawai'i to Tahiti in thirty-four days.

Thirty-four days. He'd often tried to imagine the daunting uncertainty of a month on the hostile open waters with no lifeline or other means of communication with the outside world. It gave him an abiding appreciation for the fortitude of his forebears who, as intrepid adventurers upon a mysterious sea, had no clue what lay in wait for them beyond the horizon. The courage and quest to conquer the unknown reminded him of the banner he kept on his office wall—*I ulu nō ka lālā i ke kumu.* Without our ancestors, we would not be.

On the geologically active Big Island, where earthquakes and lava flows had reshaped much of the landscape, most of the terrain around

South Point was tens of thousands of years old. Koa imagined that it looked a lot like what his remote seafaring ancestors had discovered.

Koa had been to South Point many times. As a teen, he, like many other young Hawaiians, dove from the high cliffs into the crystal-clear waters far below. The big dive was a rite of passage, a challenge to overcome, a proof of courage. He'd returned many times to swim at the nearby Green Sand Beach, long before it had become a perennial tourist attraction.

If, as seemed likely, the pilot who'd carried Ismael to Punalu'u had pulled his boat from the ocean at the Kaulana boat ramp, he'd probably stored it somewhere in the extreme southern part of the island, most likely in one of the nearby Hawaiian homeland developments. Koa might find a witness at Kaulana who knew of the boat and its owner, but that was a long shot. He could drive through the various subdivisions looking for the vessel, but there were hundreds of homes within an easy drive of the Kaulana inlet. He needed a more systematic approach.

With no easy solution, Koa resigned himself to spending a lot of time asking businesses and residents if they had seen the boat. The only saving grace was that a dark-colored or black boat was a rarity. Light-colored craft reflected the sun's heat; they were also more visible, especially at night or in foggy weather, and therefore less likely to collide with other watercraft.

Two days after his visit with Hook Hao aboard the *Ka'upu*, Koa gathered detective Piki and three street cops in separate cars. Knowing that many native Hawaiian residents in the rural south part of the Island sympathized with the sovereignty movement and would be suspicious of police, he chose officers from that area who were fluent in Hawaiian. After briefing them, he led the little convoy on the seventy-five-mile drive from Hilo toward South Point. When they arrived at Nā'ālehu, the southernmost town on the Island, he sent

Piki and the three cops, equipped with pictures of the boat, in different directions to make inquiries about a dark-colored ACB Extreme Sport watercraft.

He continued toward the turnoff to South Point and the Kaulana boat ramp. Once on South Point Road, the only paved highway to the southernmost tip of the U.S., Koa drove past the aging Pakini Nu wind farm. Where South Point Road forked, he went left past the crumbling, graffiti-encrusted remnants of the Ka Lae Military Reservation, also known as Morse Field. It had been an Army airfield at the beginning of WWII. Equipped with fuel tanks and a 6,000-foot runway, protected by gun emplacements, it had been a vital refueling stop on the trans-Pacific air ferry route from the U.S. to Australia and the Philippines. After Pearl Harbor, the Army, fearing that the Japanese might invade the airfield, destroyed the runway and plowed up the adjacent open ground.

Reaching the end of the poorly paved asphalt road, he followed a rutted dirt trail about 400 yards to the Kaulana boat ramp sloping down into a sheltered inlet. A couple of locals were putting a small fishing boat into the ocean. Koa chatted with them, asking about the dark-colored craft in question, but got nothing useful.

Koa then went to see what he could find in landlocked Discovery Harbor, the nearest community to Kaulana, periodically checking in with Piki and the other officers by cellphone. He struck out at Discovery Harbor, and the reports from his team were equally discouraging.

Then, around noon, he answered his cell to hear Piki's uber-excited voice. The young detective had searched the large community of Hawaiian Ocean View just northwest of South Point. "I think I've found the boat. Meet me in the parking lot of the Thai restaurant on Route 11 at the first turnoff into Ocean View."

Koa found Piki sitting in his car in the restaurant parking lot with a Matrice RTX drone resting on the hood. When Koa joined the young cop inside the vehicle, Piki explained. "I figured that flying a drone over the Ocean View properties would be faster and allow me to see into backyards and other places that might not be visible from the street." Then, holding up the drone controller, he pointed to the screen. "Look at this."

Watching a previously captured video, Koa saw a bird's-eye view of a run-down house with a rusted, green tin roof. A boat covered with gray canvas on a trailer sat next to the dwelling. "It's the right size," Koa acknowledged, "but what makes you so sure it's our boat?"

Piki took the controller and started another video before handing it back to Koa. In this video, the drone descended to a lower altitude to photograph the vessel's side. From this angle, canvas covered only the wheelhouse, leaving a matte-black fiberglass hull exposed.

"It's a real possibility," Koa said. "Have you driven by and checked it out?"

"I thought about it," Piki said, "but figured I might spook the owner. So, I decided to wait for you."

Koa looked at his young colleague with renewed esteem. Piki had always been impetuous and too quick to jump to conclusions. Maybe, he was maturing. He'd not only come up with an ingenious and efficient search strategy but also exercised restraint and good judgment. "Good work," Koa complimented him. "You made the right call."

"Thanks," Piki responded, clearly pleased with his accomplishment.

"So, where is this place?"

Piki pulled out a map. "It's here." He pointed to a spot in the north-eastern corner of the subdivision. "It's pretty isolated. Well up the Mauna Loa slope. There's no other building close. I'd never have seen the boat without the drone."

Koa studied the map. It was an ideal place to stay off the radar. Koa guessed that police rarely ventured to that remote corner of Ocean

View. At first, he thought the only exit was back through the subdivision. Then, he noticed a rough track behind the property, giving the resident a backdoor way out. That made it an ideal hideout. Everything about the setup triggered his instincts. He decided to recall the three officers searching other communities.

When they reconvened, all five drove into Ocean View and up the slope toward the property, stopping short so that Koa could get a feel of the situation. The house, a ramshackle affair with an attached two-car garage, sat at the extreme northeast corner of the subdivision. Paint peeled from the walls, and rust covered most of the corroded metal roof. An old car on blocks, a broken-down trailer, discarded tires, and other junk lay scattered in the adjoining area. The nearest neighbor was at least two football fields distant behind a tangle of long-thorned *kiawe* trees and dense wild shrubbery.

A light visible through a front window even in the afternoon daylight and a late model Ford sedan in the yard suggested someone was at home. Koa spotted three security cameras under the eaves of the building. Realizing the need to proceed cautiously, he called the dispatcher to get the owner's name and asked for a criminal background check. Calling back, the dispatcher reported that the owner, thirty-five-year-old Mākaha ʻAukai, had been convicted of assault with a deadly weapon. That only heightened Koa's concern.

The man's name certainly fit with his criminal history. The name Mākaha meant fierce or savage and derived from the Mākaha Valley on Oʻahu that had once been home to a group of bandits known to rob unsuspecting travelers.

Koa figured that a show of force would overwhelm the occupant and discourage overt hostility. He followed one of the marked police cars into the driveway while the others parked, and then they gathered in front of the house. Leaving three officers in the drive, he and Piki moved around the side of the building to examine the boat. It was, in fact, an ACB Extreme Sport, painted black from the keel to the top of the wheelhouse. Koa doubted there were two such vessels in the South Point area and felt confident he'd found the craft that had ferried Ismael from Hilo to Punaluʻu.

Given the security cameras, anyone inside had to know the police had arrived. They'd also probably seen Koa and Piki inspecting the boat. Yet, oddly, no one came out to confront them. Everything about the situation made Koa uneasy.

Koa repeated his previous warning to his colleagues to use utmost caution and sent two officers around the building to cover the rear. He'd read news accounts of an FBI agent shot through a closed door while serving a warrant. He wasn't about to have any of his team suffer a similar fate. Koa approached the front door from the left while Piki moved in from the right. They took positions to either side of the door. Reaching out to his right, Koa banged on the door and yelled, "Police."

He'd barely pulled his hand back before three shots shattered the door, sending shards of wood flying in every direction. Both he and Piki dove for cover. Koa used his cell to alert the cops behind the house to block an escape to the rear. "Everyone, take cover and hold your position. We are going to contain and wait for the SWAT team. Acknowledge." The officers each responded, "Roger that."

There were no more immediate shots from inside. Koa and Piki, covering for each other, quickly retreated to protected positions— Koa near his police SUV and Piki behind a low rock wall—where they could watch the front of the house. Koa then called the dispatcher, reported shots fired, and summoned the SWAT team. Then at his request, the dispatcher connected him to Makanui. Koa asked her to collect more background on ʻAukai, alert the county prosecutor, and get subpoenas for ʻAukai's bank and phone records and search warrants for his home, boat, and property.

Koa figured that it would take the SWAT team on standby about forty minutes to assemble and helicopter south to Ocean View. Fire units and EMT personnel coming from the town of Captain Cook on the west side of the Island should arrive at about the same time. While they waited, Koa sent Piki to the only two neighboring properties within a quarter mile to gather what information he could on ʻAukai. Twenty minutes later, Piki reported that ʻAukai lived alone and rarely interacted with his neighbors. He spent most of his time fishing but seemed never to catch anything. Koa guessed that fishing was his cover for smuggling.

Shortly after that, Makanui called from police headquarters. "Be careful, Koa," she began. "According to Army records, ʻAukai was a sharpshooter in Iraq who got dishonorably discharged for killing an Iraqi civilian. And then, about a year ago, the DEA flagged him as a drug courier for one of the Island's drug kingpins." She'd also checked with the phone providers and gave Koa ʻAukai's cell number.

About forty-five minutes after Koa's summons, more police, a fire truck, and an ambulance arrived. Five minutes later, a police helicopter landed down the road out of gunfire range. The SWAT team, headed by Officer Awani, climbed out, and Koa briefed Awani. "Have your men set up a secure perimeter. We believe ʻAukai is alone inside, but we're not certain, and there could be others. I'm going to try talking him out. If that doesn't work, we'll use tear gas. Tell your men I want to take him alive."

After the SWAT team secured the perimeter, Koa called ʻAukai's cellphone. Koa could hear the phone ringing inside the house, but no one answered. He then addressed ʻAukai with a megaphone. "Mākaha ʻAukai, I'm Chief Detective Koa Kāne with the Hawaiʻi County Police. We want to end this peacefully before anyone gets hurt. Please answer your cell so we can talk this out." He got no response and tried several more times using alternative messages with the same result. Silence.

After a half hour of trying to establish contact, Koa signaled Awani, and one of his men fired a tear gas canister through a front window. They watched the gas billow out and begin to fill the house, but still, nothing happened. Koa wondered if 'Aukai had a gas mask or had succeeded in sealing off some part of the dwelling. Minutes passed with no reaction.

Koa thought he heard a motor start but couldn't locate the source of the sound. He glanced around. Nothing obvious. Then, an engine roared, the double garage doors burst apart, and a green Ford 150 pickup truck barreled out of the garage, scattering splintered wood like toothpicks. Koa got the briefest glimpse of 'Aukai behind the wheel. Police cars blocked the driveway, so the truck turned to the left, cutting through shrubs and kicking up a cloud of red dust. Koa expected the vehicle to turn toward the dirt track behind the house, but instead, it plowed through the brush, dodging an obstacle course of trees, headed toward the street.

Awani, who carried a Colt M4 carbine, opened fire, puncturing both near-side front and rear tires. The truck swerved, careening off a tree, and nearly flipped over before 'Aukai regained momentary control. 'Aukai jerked the wheel to avoid another large tree but over-corrected. The vehicle lurched to the left, spun 180 degrees, bounced off another tree, and stopped dead, throwing 'Aukai into the dash.

A perfect stillness descended on the scene for a long moment before 'Aukai pushed the driver's door open and stumbled out holding a handgun. He looked around wildly for an instant before raising his gun. Koa wasn't sure whether he intended to take his own life or shoot one of the police officers. Before 'Aukai could pull the trigger, one of the SWAT team fired. The bullet hit 'Aukai's shoulder and twirled the man around, slamming him back against the truck. He lost his grip on his gun and dropped it.

Two SWAT team officers charged and wrestled the man to the ground. Koa placed 'Aukai under arrest and had the paramedics tend to his wound before sending him off to Hilo Memorial Hospital under heavy guard.

CHAPTER FORTY-SIX

KOA SOON LEARNED why 'Aukai had resisted the police. His home proved to be a gold mine for drug investigators. On his first walk-through, Koa found over a hundred pounds of Puna Gold marijuana, several kilos of cocaine, and an assortment of pills. The discovery triggered mixed feelings. He relished taking a big-time drug courier off the streets. Still, the commercial quantities ensured that the DEA would insist on interrogating and prosecuting 'Aukai. In Koa's experience, no agency was more difficult than the federal drug cowboys. DEA involvement would complicate, if not impede, Koa from getting information from the man. If Koa had his way, he'd proceed without even informing the DEA, but Chief Lannua, never one to antagonize the feds, would insist on notification.

Still, notice and prompt notice were different. Koa decided to extract every bit of intelligence he could before involving the DEA. Makanui, working with Zeke, obtained warrants, and given the quantity of evidence, Koa asked Georgina to bring an extra-large crime scene team. While that team was en route, Koa went looking for evidence tying 'Aukai to the attacks on the police. He found little—a cellphone, a calendar posted on a kitchen wall with two dates circled, and a single key on a peg in the kitchen. He photographed the calendar and bagged the cellphone for Piki to add to his analysis. The dearth of proof puzzled Koa. Could he have pursued 'Aukai by mistake? Maybe the man was nothing more than a drug courier.

Koa walked outside and around to the boat. With Piki's help, he stripped off the cover. Standing back, he compared the enhanced versions of Samantha's pictures with the actual boat. Same hull. Roughly the same length. Same raised forecastle. Same wheelhouse. Same deck railings. All painted a dull black. It had to be the right boat.

Climbing onto the trailer and hoisting himself over the stern, he conducted a thorough search of the watercraft. Standard nautical charts, various fishing gear, a cooler full of Maui Pale Ale, and a cabinet full of snack food. No locked cabinets. In a cubbyhole on the bridge, he found a black ski mask. Ismael had described the boat's pilot as wearing a balaclava. Further confirmation that they'd found the right vessel. Nothing else incriminating.

Back inside, he studied the calendar. Someone, most likely 'Aukai, had circled two dates with a black marker—the date the Philippine freighter *Davao* had docked in Hilo and another six days earlier. Maybe the earlier date involved another pickup from Hilo. Koa called the Hilo port harbormaster, provided the date, and asked whether any foreign ship had docked that day. It was a good guess. After checking, the harbormaster reported that another cargo carrier, the *Bimi*, had entered the port at 6:30 a.m. that morning. Koa guessed that 'Aukai had smuggled another co-conspirator onto the island, perhaps the shooter with the Dragunov who'd tried to take out Makanui.

Koa thought about the logistics. 'Aukai would have needed the ship's description and schedule to pluck Ismael off the *Davao*. He would have had to come alongside in the dark, signal to Ismael on the deck, hold the boat in position while the crew offloaded Ismael's belongings, and the man descended a rope or ladder. All the while, both the ship and the boat would have been moving, perhaps dramatically, with the ocean waves. Maybe they'd had some electronic signaling device to facilitate the process, but it was still not a simple task. In addition, 'Aukai or an accomplice must have prepositioned a car for Ismael at Punalu'u. Someone had located and secured the house on Alahaki Road and stocked the forest drop with the bombs, guns, and ammo the police had discovered there. Koa supposed one man alone could have pulled it off, but 'Aukai more likely had accomplices.

They found no evidence of the planning or execution for any of those steps. Koa knew he was missing something. Maybe the key he'd seen in 'Aukai's kitchen held the answer. After photographing it for the crime scene team, he and Piki looked for the matching lock. They found nothing in the house, the boat, or 'Aukai's vehicles. Unwilling to give up, Koa searched for alternatives. Someone aiding Ismael had stored arms and bombs in a remote drop away from his Alahaki Road house. Maybe 'Aukai had used the same strategy. But where?

Koa tried to put himself in 'Aukai's place. Where would the man hide his secrets? Looking out the window at the treeless scrubland behind the house, Koa suddenly focused on the dirt road behind the property. When 'Aukai broke out of the garage, Koa expected him to avoid the significant police presence in front and turn toward the dirt trail at the back of the property. It would have provided a faster and less treacherous escape route with no trees to dodge. Yet, 'Aukai had chosen a much tougher path and headed into the greatest concentration of police. Why? Maybe a diversion to lead the police away from the back of the property.

"C'mon," Koa said, leading Piki out the back door. They spread out, searching back and forth in a rough grid pattern. About twenty-five yards behind the house, near the back of the property, Piki found a small patch of recently disturbed reddish earth. Scraping with his foot, he uncovered something metal. "Koa, come look at this," he yelled.

Koa joined him, and together they pushed the loose dirt aside to reveal two steel panels secured with a padlock. Wearing gloves to preserve prints on the lock, Koa tried the key. It slid easily into the locking mechanism, and the lock popped open. Piki, also wearing gloves, knelt and lifted the steel panels, folding them back on their hinges.

The two detectives found themselves staring into a hole more than a dozen feet deep with a ladder positioned against one side. Using his Maglite to illuminate the way, Koa ventured down the ladder and into an adjoining cavern.

Koa found himself in a room-sized cave, part of a lava tube formed at the end of an eruption when molten rock flowing in covered channels drained away, leaving an empty cave. There were lava tubes all over the island, some closet-sized and others large enough to hold a freight train. Only this one wasn't vacant.

Shining his light around the cave, he noticed an electrical box with a switch handle. Realizing that 'Aukai must have run a buried electrical cable from the house, he pushed the switch handle into the "on" position, and light flooded the little cavern. Before venturing further, Koa used his cellphone camera to record the scene.

What he saw stunned him. A small table with two chairs sat in the center. A cellphone, almost certainly a burner, lay on the table. A workbench ran along one wall. A corkboard plastered with maps, photos, and drawings filled the back wall. An array of firearms, including an M79 grenade launcher, hung from racks on the other sidewall. He had found 'Aukai's war room, command center, workshop, and arsenal. 'Aukai, fearing that the police would find this place, had deliberately tried to lead the police away by going in the opposite direction.

It took him only a moment, though, to realize that 'Aukai was far more than a foot soldier in this war against the police. Focusing on the corkboard, Koa saw seven columns of photographs and documents. Images of Makanui, Ikaika, Nālani, Zeke, and Alexia Sheppard, arrayed from left to right, headed each of the first five columns. They appeared to be surveillance pictures taken with a telephoto lens. The last two columns were blank.

Koa stepped closer to the board and began to process what he saw. The column under Makanui's picture held several aerial views of her house and a topographic map of the surrounding area. Koa recognized the large black "X" on the map as the hilltop from which the Dragunov gunman had fired.

'Aukai had pinned photos of Johnnie Nihoa, the Surfboard bar, Moses, the bar's back door, and the alley under Ikaika's picture. The last image in that column caught Koa's attention—a photo of a black ballistic knife like the one found near Nihoa's body.

The column beneath Nālani's picture showed her car parked in front of the cottage she shared with Koa and again in the National Park headquarters parking lot. An illustration of a bomb and a schematic of her car's underside showed attachment points for the bomb. A satellite map in the column beneath Zeke's picture depicted the neighborhood around his oceanfront home with possible approaches marked in red.

Koa guessed that 'Aukai had planned the attacks on Makanui, Nālani, and Zeke, together with the trumped-up charge against Ikaika, and had done so in this underground cave. The M79 grenade launcher on the armament wall suggested that 'Aukai attacked the Hilo Medical Center. Turning to the workbench, Koa found boxes of chalk spotting rounds for the M79 and the equipment for disassembling and repacking those non-lethal projectiles with gunpowder.

That discovery confirmed that 'Aukai had engineered the hospital attack, most likely as the shooter.

The fifth column explained why 'Aukai had been so desperate to lead the police away from this hideaway and the information it contained. That column revealed the details of an attack that had yet to occur. Studying the fifth column, Koa felt a shiver of dread. 'Aukai had planned to kill Alexia Sheppard, and soon.

The corkboard held several pictures of Alexia's car, a red BMW, but no plans for a bomb. Multiple photos detailed the engine compartment, the electronic fuel injection system, the brake system master cylinder, hydraulic fluid lines, and emergency brakes. A copy of Alexia's schedule detailing a trip from Hilo across the Island to Kona and a map of her route across the Saddle Road alerted Koa to the immediate danger. Koa couldn't imagine how 'Aukai had gotten her schedule but assumed it was accurate.

According to that schedule, she was already on the road, planning to spend the night in Kona in preparation for a court appearance first thing in the morning. He stared at a red "X" on the map where the road left the saddle plateau and descended a steep miles-long grade. The drawings showed some sort of attachment to the brake master cylinder and a schematic for rewiring the electronics controlling the injection system. He couldn't be sure but, based on the images before him, guessed that 'Aukai had tampered with Alexia's car, setting her up for a serious if not fatal accident. If, as depicted on the drawings, he had set the car to accelerate and disabled the brakes, Alexia would be going downhill at over 100 mph with no way to stop.

Koa had to warn her and fast. He'd known her for more than a decade, repeatedly turning to her to aid his brother and more recently to help Koa himself out of a jam. He respected her extraordinary legal skill but even more had come to value her friendship. An image of her at the window in her office stroking Alibi, her big black cat, popped into his mind. He couldn't bear the thought of her suffering a grievous injury or death.

Climbing back to the surface, Koa thought for a moment, yelled for Piki to take charge, and raced for the SWAT team helicopter, preparing to ferry Awani and his men back to Hilo. The pilot was already powering up when Koa waved him off. Boarding the chopper, he instructed the pilot to radio the dispatcher and patch him through to Makanui. Seconds ticked by as he waited for a connection.

"Hurry up," he said to no one in particular, knowing that it wouldn't do any good. Finally, she came on the line, and he explained the situation. She put him on hold while she tried to call Alexia. Seconds passed.

"She's not picking up," Makanui reported.

Koa wracked his brain. How could he stop a runaway car on a downhill slope without causing a crash? He'd driven the highway many times and pictured the road winding down the steep slope. Signs warned truckers to use lower gears on the seven percent downgrade. The road ended at a "T" intersection with the Hawai'i Belt Road. A speeding car could never make the turn and would crash into a rugged lava field, killing or severely wounding the occupants.

He remembered a Highway Department press release about the safety features of the new highway. It triggered an idea and then a plan. He doubted he'd have enough time. Even if he could act quickly enough, he wasn't sure his strategy would save Alexia, but it was the best he could do.

He gave Makanui instructions and commandeered the helicopter, turning to Awani and asking him and his team to dismount with a hurried apology. Then he instructed the pilot to take off. Once airborne, he directed the pilot to go north along the Hawai'i Belt Road up the western side of the Island at maximum speed. While the

MD500E chopper shot north at 155 mph, Koa radioed the Kona Police Department and got patched through to the units policing traffic on the Saddle Road. One unit was already nearly in position, and another was close enough to assist. He explained the situation, instructed the officers to close the road, and create signs with their rooftop or rear-window LED message boards to warn Alexia.

The chopper gained altitude along the western slope of Mauna Loa, passed just east of the Pu'uhonau o Hōnaunau National Historical Park, and sped on toward the village of Captain Cook. At that point, it veered eastward, climbed to seven thousand feet, and crossed the gap between Hualālai mountain on the west and Mauna Loa on the east. They flew just east of the sixteenth-century *Ahu a 'Umi heiau*, which was once the seat of the Island's government before the first Westerners arrived. In the co-pilot's seat, Koa began scanning through binoculars, searching for Alexia's red BMW.

He hoped to get close and wave Alexia to a stop before she reached the point where 'Aukai, or more likely one of his co-conspirators, had programmed her car to accelerate without brakes. The sun began to set, filling the western sky with vivid reds and oranges. The fading light made it harder to see, and smoke from a wild brushfire to the north drifted over the area, intermittently obscuring his view. The wind shifted, and he caught a glimpse of the car just as it reached the intersection where the old Saddle Road branched off the new highway. She was fast closing in on the spot marked by the red X Koa had seen on the map in 'Aukai's bunker—the point at which he feared the car would begin to accelerate. He was too far away to signal and cursed his luck.

Alexia's car rolled forward, reached the downslope, and accelerated. Faster. Faster. Seventy-five miles per hour. Eighty. Ninety. Koa's reading of the materials in 'Aukai's war room had been correct. Speedboat man or his accomplices had sabotaged Alexia's car.

Following Koa's directions, the police had blocked all other traffic in both directions. Alexia had to be frantic, but at least she had the broad highway all to herself. She rocketed by the first police car with its lights flashing on the shoulder on the uphill side of the road. Koa couldn't tell from the air whether the cop had programmed his electronic sign as directed. Nor could he guess whether Alexia, obviously in distress and unable to control her vehicle, had seen, let alone absorbed, the message.

The helicopter was now nearly on top of the red BMW. Although he doubted that she could hear, he began to address her over the hailer on the chopper. Ahead, the police had erected a line of red cones channeling the speeding car toward the right side of the road. To Koa's relief, Alexia eased the speeding vehicle to the right. Then, going more than one hundred miles per hour and still accelerating, she flew past a second police car. This time Koa saw the message board flashing a warning to Alexia but doubted that she, struggling to control her speeding vehicle, would see it and understand. It was, Koa thought, her only chance. And a slim chance at best.

The car hurtled toward Alexia's only possible escape. A mile. A half-mile. Four hundred yards. One hundred yards. The vehicle veered to the right, hit the rough ground, bounced into the air, slammed back to earth, and swayed from side to side, threatening to flip over like a boat in rough water. Then, all four wheels connected with the uneven ground, and the car plowed upward, climbing the runaway truck ramp. Up . . . up, still trying to accelerate, wheels spinning, throwing up clouds of loose gravel and debris.

The car slowed, its speed bleeding away as it lost traction on the steep uphill ramp, but the engine wouldn't give up. The vehicle was still going too fast when it hit the collapsible barrier at the top of the ramp with stunning force. The bumper bent, the hood crumpled, and the radiator broke, spewing clouds of steam. The engine finally began to cough and seize up. The crash also knocked fuel lines loose, allowing gasoline to spray across the engine compartment, igniting a fire.

The pilot set the chopper down on a small open patch of ground. Koa threw open the door, jumped to the ground, and ran for the crippled car. Fire consumed the engine compartment and smoke curled around him as he wrenched the driver's door open. He pushed the airbag off Alexia, struggling for a moment with the seat belt before pulling out his pocketknife and cutting the strap. Having freed her, he dragged the dazed woman from the car. He'd moved her only a dozen yards before the vehicle exploded in a fireball.

CHAPTER FORTY-SEVEN

KOA RODE IN the ambulance with Alexia to the Kona Community Hospital. Banged up by the crash and in shock, she was admitted for observation but would recover. By the time Koa was satisfied that she'd be okay, it was well after dark. Despite the hour, Koa rushed back to ʻAukai's underground hideaway. He needed to spend time there to learn everything he could about ʻAukai's role in what had become a mysterious and insidious plot against the Big Island law enforcement community. On his way, he called Nālani to be sure she was safe and to let her know that he would be working late, possibly through the night.

The threat of future violence seemed clear from ʻAukai's corkboard. The first five of its seven columns chronicled attacks against Makanui, Ikaika, Nālani, Zeke, and Alexia that had already happened. Ominously, the last two columns—yet to be completed—seemed to foretell future targets.

With a sense of foreboding, Koa guessed the last column was for him. The past attacks—against his colleague, his brother, his precious Nālani, his friend the county prosecutor, and his legal counsel—had touched those closest to him. If they were the outer rings of the target, he was the bull's-eye. It made sense in the warped way that criminal minds worked, and he could think of no other culmination for the conspiracy.

In a sense, he felt relief that the endgame was near. He'd always prefer a personal attack to one on his family, Nālani, or his colleagues. As a cop, a soldier, and even as a teen, he'd accepted and lived with risk. Diving from the high cliffs at South Point, pursuing his father's nemesis, volunteering for Special Forces, accepting the dangers of being a cop—all invited risk. He'd become inured to it as part of his everyday life. Almost reflexively, he anticipated and prepared for sudden danger. He wasn't surprised to find himself almost wanting to bring it on and be done with it.

But he surmised from the empty sixth column that there was one more unknown target before the attackers turned to him. Who was the mysterious next target? Piki? Somehow the young detective didn't fit the pattern. Chief Lannua? He was responsible for everything the police did but mostly stayed above the fray, giving a criminal less motive to take revenge on him. Still, he had to warn the chief. Judge Hitachi? If a criminal sought revenge, Hitachi fit the profile as the most probable sentencing judge. He seemed to Koa the likely next target.

Koa checked the time on his phone—nearly midnight. It didn't matter. Tomorrow might be too late. He called Chief Lannua. "Chief," Koa began, "sorry to call so late, but it's important. I've just come from a cave behind a house where a guy named 'Aukai holed up. He played a starring role in the attacks on Makanui, Ikaika, Nālani, Zeke, and an effort to kill Alexia Sheppard this afternoon. We found evidence suggesting that 'Aukai and possibly others intended to go after at least two other people. And you know, Chief, I'm worried you may be the next target."

"Me? What makes you think that?"

Koa explained the corkboard with two blank columns. "We've arrested three criminals involved in attacks on people in law enforcement or close to me—the Dragunov shooter, Ismael, and now 'Aukai—and we know from an intercepted phone call that there are other co-conspirators still out there. We also know that Ismael had another bomb. That bomb and the blank columns on the corkboard tell me that these killers have at least two more attacks in the works. And you fit the profile of the past targets."

"Sounds pretty thin," Lannua responded. "Could be any one of your team or somebody outside the department, like Judge Hitachi, but I'll be careful."

"I think it's serious, Chief. At least vary your routine and take a guard with you."

"Okay, Koa. I'll think about it."

Koa then called Zeke, told him about 'Aukai's arrest, and explained the attack on Alexia, which profoundly shocked Zeke.

"Jesus," Zeke exclaimed. "That's awful. Luckily for her, you figured it out in time."

"Five minutes later, and she'd be dead instead of recovering in a Kona hospital bed," Koa responded, before going on to describe the two empty columns on 'Aukai's underground wall and explaining his analysis.

"I have to say, I agree you're the main target and the common thread that ties it all together. I mean, each of the previous attacks points in that direction, but why? Who's behind this and why? That's what we've got to figure out."

"I've racked my brain, and I just don't have a clue," Koa conceded.

"You checked Keahi's status with the feds?" Zeke again referred to Koa's childhood friend who'd ultimately turned Chinese spy and blamed Koa for his arrest and prosecution.

"Yeah," Koa answered. "I talked to Goodling. You remember her, the lawyer from the National Security Division of the U.S. Department of Justice? She assured me that the intelligence agencies pumped Keahi dry, confiscated every penny of his ill-gotten gains, and have him sequestered incommunicado in a federal prison. So that's a dead end."

"What about activist Hawaiian radicals here on the Island, maybe with help from Antifa anarchists from the mainland?" Zeke asked.

"I can see Antifa attacking police departments in Portland, Chicago, or Minneapolis, but the Big Island? Seems improbable. What reason would they have to stage attacks here?" Koa replied. "Besides, I hooked up with one of my activist relatives. He's well connected in the Hawaiian sovereignty community and says he knows of no anti-police goings-on around here."

"And you have no other clue?" Zeke persisted.

Once again, Koa wondered whether the descendants of Hazzard, the man whose killing he'd covered up as a teenager more than thirty years ago, had somehow discovered his crime and sought revenge. He couldn't imagine how that would be possible and had dismissed the notion as guilt-fueled paranoia. In any event, he couldn't incriminate himself by disclosing that possibility, however remote, to Zeke. So, he said simply, "I have no idea."

In the end, Zeke agreed that Judge Hitachi could well be in danger. Despite the hour, the two of them contacted the judge at home. The judge sounded sleepy when he answered the phone but quickly realized the seriousness of the situation as Zeke explained the potential risk.

"You think it's someone I sentenced?" he asked.

"We don't know, Your Honor," Zeke responded, "but you and Chief Lannua are among the most likely targets, so we'd like to assign police guards to protect you when you're not in the courthouse surrounded by deputies and marshals."

In his decades on the bench, the judge had dealt with many violent offenders, including some who attacked law enforcement personnel, and learned never to underestimate the risks inherent in dispensing justice. "Well, Zeke," he responded, "if you and Koa think it's warranted, I'll accept your judgment and whatever protection you deem necessary." Koa was not surprised that Judge Hitachi, unlike Chief Lannua, had welcomed the offer.

CHAPTER FORTY-EIGHT

WHEN KOA ARRIVED in his office the following morning, he found Piki waiting. Koa knew from the excited look on the young detective's face that Piki was hot to reveal some new information or insight.

"You remember the burner phone we found in Aukui's secret underground cave?" Piki began before Koa could even sit down.

"Sure. What about it?"

"Well, he erased the call history, but we found a single text message. It took us a while to break the lock on the phone, but Cap Roberts had some software from the FBI . . ."

Tired from his nighttime review of the materials in 'Aukai's workshop and the post-midnight calls warning the chief and Judge Hitachi, Koa had little patience for the tangentially relevant technical details. "Please get to the point?"

"Sure, boss. Just take a look at the message we found on 'Aukai's burner phone," Piki responded, handing Koa a sheet of paper. The message read:

It's Kōkua. Details for the job. Name is Faisal. Now semi-conscious. Room 214. Second floor. Backside Hilo Memorial. Execution urgent. Use any possible means. Blow him up if necessary. Do not share mission with ANYONE. Do not fail.

The message—instructions for the attack on the shooter hospital-ized after his second attack on Makanui—seemed straightforward enough. The man's name was apparently Faisal. Yet the penultimate sentence—"Do not share with ANYONE"—was odd. Given the instruction to commit murder, warning ʻAukai not to talk to the authorities or other outsiders was superfluous. The words had to com-mand secrecy from other members of the conspiracy, but why would Kōkua want ʻAukai to keep the hit from his co-conspirators, espe-cially since the murder itself would not have been secret?

"What do you make of it?" Koa asked.

"The message didn't come from the same number as the call we intercepted at the Alahaki Road place that Keola occupied, but it did come through the same cell tower in Hilo," Piki reported. "So I'm guessing that this Kōkua guy, whoever he is, called the shots for both the hit on Zeke and this Faisal guy."

"That would mean that Kōkua is bilingual, using Filipino with Keola and English for ʻAukai."

"That wouldn't be surprising," Piki responded. "More than 20 per-cent of the Island's population is all or part Filipino, including a lot of police officers."

"Right," Koa acknowledged, "but it also gives us one more thing to use in figuring out who this Kōkua is. What do you make of the do-not-share part of the text?"

"Looks like Kōkua might be ordering the hit on the down-low."

"Okay," Koa continued thinking out loud, "but is it the murder or just the shooter's identity he's trying to hide?"

"Oh," Piki exclaimed, "I see where you are going. There'd be no way to keep the hit secret, so he must have been trying to hide something else."

"Maybe," Koa mused, "their failure to nail their targets is causing some discontent among the conspirators."

"Wouldn't be a bad thing," Piki said. "Could even work in our favor."

CHAPTER FORTY-NINE

THE FOLLOWING AFTERNOON, detectives, street cops, and administrative personnel crowded into the police training facility that doubled as a conference center. Mock champagne flowed like water as they raised their glasses to Chief Lannua on his sixtieth birthday. The chief was in a fine mood, accepting congratulations and sharing jokes with his staff. The department press officer snapped pictures while an assistant shot video.

For Koa, these events afforded an intriguing window into departmental relationships and personalities. Most of the senior people, who interacted with the chief daily, were at ease, if not nonchalant. They offered congratulations and never fawned, instead preferring to work the crowd. Many more junior people, though, hung back, often intimidated by the higher-ups around them. A few seized the moment, making themselves known or currying favor. True to form, Moreau, the biggest suck-up of all, openly pandered to the chief.

Unlike purely departmental affairs, this gathering offered Koa a rare chance to observe Bobbie Satō, the county's relatively new mayor. Satō had run on a defund-the-police, tax-reduction platform, which had backfired, resulting in increased crime. Business and homeowners weren't happy with Satō. Against this background, the bombing of Nālani's car and the attack on Hilo Medical Center generated a political firestorm. Satō responded by blaming the police, leading to clashes with Chief Lannua and the county council.

The press also openly criticized the mayor for placing his friends and relatives in county jobs. The practice wasn't new, but it had gotten out of hand under Satō. Moreau was far from the only example.

At first, Koa wondered if Satō's attendance at the birthday party might be an attempt to mend fences, but he quickly abandoned that hope. Instead of mingling with the department's senior staff to establish rapport, Satō stood apart, surrounded by his political aides. Moreau was the only officer to join that circle, once again causing Koa to wonder about the connection between him and the mayor.

As soon as the room filled with well-wishers, Satō stepped up to the microphone set up for birthday tributes. The room fell silent.

Without even a nod to the celebratory nature of the occasion, Satō began: "The current public safety situation is unacceptable. Burglaries have tripled. Street robberies are out of control. The police department is not doing the job. You need to get out on the street and step up to the plate. You need to make Hilo the safest town in America."

Koa heard grumbling from the assembled crowd about budget cuts and unpaid overtime, and several officers turned their backs.

The mayor continued: "We need a better, stronger, and more efficient police force. If you cannot overcome your failure and control crime in this city, then we need new leadership."

Perhaps sensing the hostile mood, Satō quickly ended his speech and walked out of the room, followed by his sycophants. Koa couldn't imagine a less politic message or more inappropriate timing.

For the first time since he'd joined the force, Koa worried about the department's future. Defunding the police could only lead to more crime, as in every mainland jurisdiction that bought into the slogan. Exhorting an overworked and underpaid police department to step up to the plate fostered frustration, stress, and officer retirements, exacerbating the problem. Worst of all, inserting people like Moreau with his tendency to use excessive force alienated the public, undercutting support for the police.

The chief looked distinctly unhappy and motioned for the head of the patrol division to take the microphone. After several moments of stunned silence, that officer stepped to the podium. "Now that the mayor has scolded us all," he began, "let's join ranks and congratulate our chief. It's not only his sixtieth birthday but also his fifteenth year as leader of the Hilo Police Department." Trying to lighten the mood after the mayor's downer speech, he alluded to the "little HPD" as smaller but responsible for much more territory than the "big HPD" in Honolulu. "And despite what our mayor thinks, Chief Lannua is a great leader devoted to serving the people of this county." That drew a round of applause and put a tiny bit of spirit back into the party.

Koa then took the podium to present the chief with a giant birthday card propped against a tall easel. Over 400 of the department's sworn officers and dozens of civilian staffers had signed the card. He then yielded the microphone to the head of the intelligence division, who awed the crowd by having his staff unveil a six-foot-wide birthday cake in the shape of the Big Island.

After cheers and shouts of "speech, speech," the chief took the microphone.

"*Mahalo*, to you all for this surprise party. As you all know, I generally don't like surprises, but this one is special and most welcome. While I have the microphone and this captive audience, I want to extend my heartfelt appreciation for your hard work and dedication day in and day out. No organization is better than the people who are part of it, and you are the ones who have made the Hilo Police Department outstanding. Again, *mahalo nui* . . . and eat up."

Not surprisingly, not a morsel of cake remained when the party broke up forty minutes later.

Koa had just settled back in his office, hoping to ferret out more clues from the evidence they'd gathered, when an explosion rocked the building, shattering windows. Smoke began to pour from the ventilation system, filling offices and corridors. Fire alarms screeched. People screamed and ran for the exits. Having sensed that the blast came from above, Koa entered the nearest stairwell and forced his way upward against the press of people headed for the exits.

When he emerged on the top floor, the damage exceeded his worst fears. Chaos ruled with senior people stumbling out of their offices, some disoriented and others suffering from smoke inhalation, hearing loss, or other injuries. The chief's assistant sat on the floor in shock with blood on her face. Smoke billowed from the chief's office.

Wetting a handkerchief in a water fountain, Koa covered his face and headed into the chief's smoldering office. Even through the veil of sooty air, the scene horrified him. Some titanic force had split Lannua's massive desk, throwing the chief backward out of his chair and onto the credenza behind him. His unrecognizable charred head hung from his torso by a few ligaments. His right arm was missing, and his left arm ended in a ragged stub above the elbow. Pieces of his clothing hung in singed tatters, and burns covered most of his upper body. He'd died from an explosion in his office on his sixtieth birthday. Death had come instantaneously. That was the only saving grace.

Using his cell, Koa called for fire and rescue personnel. He then got through to the chief of patrol, filled him in on what had happened, and asked him to gather enough officers to protect the building and keep everyone out of the crime scene in the chief's office. Reaching Makanui and Piki, who had evacuated the building, Koa directed them to canvass the top floor to check for injuries. Running down a mental checklist, he instructed Georgina Pau to assemble her crime scene team to process the bomb site. As required by federal regulations, he notified the feds of the bombing. He then located Deputy Police Chief Kama, who was on vacation, to inform him that according to the emergency management plan, he had just become acting police chief. Finally, Koa called Zeke and the mayor. Then, he called Nālani to let her know what had happened and that he was okay.

Only after briefing Zeke and the mayor did Koa's emotions well up within him. Anger surged foremost, directed toward the demented criminals who'd invaded police headquarters to kill its chief. Guilt followed at his failure to persuade the chief to take more extraordinary precautions, although he wasn't sure what the chief might have done differently. Koa had worried about an attack on the chief at home or while in transit; it had never occurred to him that Lannua would be in danger inside the police department, let alone at his desk. Sadness followed at losing a friend and colleague with whom he'd often disagreed but also respected. Lastly, determination to root out those responsible overwhelmed all other feelings.

The tragedy should have filled him with fear. The chief's death filled one of the two blank columns on the right side of 'Aukai's corkboard. He had little doubt he was next. They—whoever they were— had warned him through attacks on his family and colleagues. He needed to protect himself, and to do that, he had to suppress his fear and concentrate all his energies on catching those responsible.

If Koa had been driven before, he was now possessed. While the forensics team worked to recover evidence from the chief's office, Koa started checking to determine who might have had access. Long before the bombing, guards and security doors controlled access to the internal parts of police headquarters. Key card access made security even tighter on the executive floor, although more than one person often entered after one of a group swiped a pass through the reader. Camera surveillance also protected the top floor, but it had been disabled. Given those factors, Koa felt confident that an insider had planted the bomb that killed the chief.

As soon as paramedics gave the okay, Koa interviewed Alice Moffet, the chief's longtime assistant. Struggling to control her tears, she described returning from the birthday gathering to find a beautifully wrapped birthday gift on the chief's desk. It had arrived while she attended the festivities. Thinking that someone had simply left a birthday present for the chief, she hadn't given the package a second thought.

As soon as he heard about the beautifully wrapped birthday gift on the chief's desk, Koa figured that it had contained the explosive that killed the chief. He immediately shared his hunch with Georgina, who confirmed that initial forensics indicated that the explosion had originated on the chief's desk and blown tiny particles of gift wrapping throughout the room. With that confirmation in hand, he continued to interview Alice.

Considering the time she spent preparing for and attending the party, she guessed she'd been away from the chief's office suite for about seventy-five minutes. She had no idea who had left the gift and had been at her desk outside the chief's office when the bomb exploded. It blew the door to the chief's office off its hinges, showering her with debris, but fortunately, her injuries were not life-threatening. She'd kept a file of threatening letters and notes sent to the chief over the years but recalled nothing recent and had no idea who might have wished the chief harm.

Koa also interviewed the other officers and assistants who'd been on the floor during the relevant time. Most had attended the birthday party, and none noticed anyone in the vicinity of the chief's office carrying a birthday present. Nor had they seen anything remotely suspicious.

He assigned Piki and several administrative staff to sort through the photos and video taken at the party to eliminate people who'd been continuously present in the training center during the seventy-five minutes when someone had placed the gift on the chief's desk. The same team reviewed the security logs to identify everyone who'd been on the chief's floor during that critical time frame.

In the end, they came up with a list of twenty-three possible names—senior staff, detectives, and administrators—who could have had access to the chief's office in his absence. Koa went over the list again and again. Almost all were longtime police department employees, and Koa had a hard time envisioning any of them planting the bomb that killed their chief. He wondered if someone had somehow circumvented the security systems.

As he reviewed the list yet again, Koa noticed that Moreau's name was not among those who'd been on the executive floor. Although he disliked Moreau, Koa didn't believe he'd killed the chief. Indeed, Moreau had always sought to curry favor with the man who'd hired him over Koa's objection. Still, Koa asked Piki whether there was any reason to suspect Moreau. "There's nothing to suggest that he was on the chief's floor," Piki responded. "He didn't swipe his pass through any of the readers. Besides, he's all over the photos and videos of the party posing with the mayor, the chief, and other detectives, or in the background of other shots. I think he was in the party room the whole time." That seemed to rule Moreau out as the bomber.

Cap Roberts and federal explosive experts examined the wreckage and residue in the chief's office. Based on their preliminary review, they guessed that the bomb had contained Semtex and seemed consistent with the one used on Nālani's car.

Koa kicked himself. Once again, he had underestimated the power and reach of the cabal in pursuit of the Hilo Police. He called the head of the intelligence division to ask him to review security protocols in and around police headquarters and substations and make recommendations for improvement, where necessary. Both vowed never again to leave the department vulnerable to an attack from within.

CHAPTER FIFTY

Two days after the chief's death, a large crowd of mourners gathered for his funeral at the Haili Church, the oldest house of worship in Hilo. Originally a grass hut, called Waiākea Mission Station, one of Hawai'i's early missionaries dedicated it in 1824. More grass buildings and one constructed of timber followed the initial structure before the Reverend Titus Coan dedicated the present Greek Revival sanctuary in 1859. Built of 'ōhi'a wood from the slopes of Mauna Loa and fitted with pews of *koa*, it had survived earthquakes that damaged stone buildings nearby.

When the service began, mourners packed the sanctuary, leaving an overflow crowd to gather outside. The chief's wife and adult daughter took their places in the front pew. Koa served as a pallbearer with police commissioners and other department heads. The somber entourage carried the chief's coffin, draped in a Hawaiian flag, into the church before setting the closed casket before the altar.

Koa sat in the second row with other senior police officers. Through the reading of scripture, the homily, and prayers, he recalled his long association with Chief Lannua. They'd often disagreed, especially when Lannua tried to protect the Island's elite, but even more frequently fought together for justice and shared a mutual respect. Together, they had caught the Pōhakuloa murderer, found justice for loners who lived and died off the grid, uncloaked those responsible for the deaths of innocent schoolchildren, and exposed a Chinese spy. Koa knew he and the community would miss the chief.

After a perfunctory eulogy by Mayor Satō, it was Koa's turn. At the podium, he shared his recollections of working with the chief throughout his tenure as a detective before concluding: "No man has served this Island and its people with more dedication and compassion than Chief Lannua. I, like all our officers and citizens, will miss him dearly."

When Koa returned to his pew, Moreau surprised him by ascending to the podium to deliver his own tribute. Koa couldn't imagine who asked the deputy chief detective to speak. The man had only been with the department a few short months, and Koa doubted he knew, much less interacted, with the chief's family. The oddity of Moreau's role in the funeral rites left Koa feeling uneasy. Something he did not understand was afoot.

Koa's concerns only deepened as the day's events wore on. Under heavy gray skies and drizzle, accentuating the solemnity of the Chief's internment at Homelani Memorial Cemetery, Koa spotted Moreau huddled with the police commission chairman under a large black umbrella. Later, as the proceedings broke up, Moreau and Mayor Satō lingered, engaging intensely with each other.

Observing these interludes, Koa thought about his recent conversation with Zeke. The prosecutor had warned that Mayor Satō was "slowly dismantling the county government and putting his unqualified but loyal disciples into key positions." Zeke's instincts now seemed prophetic since Satō had subsequently replaced both the directors of Finance and Human Resources with cronies of dubious qualifications.

Koa's apprehension deepened as he considered the prospect that Satō might also be seeking direct control of the police department with Moreau as chief. The idea was so absurd that Koa almost dismissed it. He couldn't think of a less qualified successor to Chief Lannua. Moreau was less than competent in his present capacity and lacked the skills to manage a police department with more than 1000 employees, serving 186,000 residents and five million annual visitors scattered over more than 4000 square miles.

Yet, Koa had no illusions. Mayor Satō might well succeed, and Moreau as chief could end Koa's career as well as severely damage the department. Koa already knew of several instances in which Moreau had used excessive force, angering community leaders. Koa had also witnessed Moreau in action during the Ikaika episode and its aftermath. Even in those limited interactions, Koa recognized something peculiar, and maybe dangerous, about the man.

Koa felt a sense of urgency to know all there was to know about the deputy chief detective installed over his objections. Surely there were skeletons in Moreau's background—something that would disqualify him, or at least raise questions. Koa would talk to Zeke again. The two of them needed to develop a strategy to head off any such travesty. The key, though, would be the Police Commission, for while Satō wielded considerable influence over the selection process, he lacked the power to appoint a new police chief. That authority resided with the commission.

Koa wasn't the only police officer who noticed the confab between Moreau and the mayor. Later that afternoon, back at headquarters, David Thurston, the patrol division commander, popped into Koa's office. "I saw your guy Moreau kissin' the mayor's ass at the funeral. So, what's that all about? How come they're new best friends?"

"You tell me. It's weird," Koa responded.

"What I heard," Thurston said, "is that Satō wants Moreau as his puppet running the department. God help us if that happens."

"Unbelievable!" Koa exclaimed, implicitly seeking further information rather than disclosing his own suspicions. "Where'd you hear that?"

"One of the commissioners."

"Moreau is in way over his head," Koa responded. "I cannot imagine the commission appointing someone with zero leadership experience."

"Stranger things have happened," Thurston responded. "And my source tells me Satō is putting serious pressure on the commissioners."

Although he had a pretty good sense of Satō's motivation, Koa still asked, "Why's the mayor so hot on this guy?"

"Politics, my friend. Plain old Hilo politics," Thurston said. "With crime out of control and his failure to deliver on election promises, Satō knows he's going to have trouble getting reelected, and he's trying to buy votes from key constituencies. You've seen what his guy in Finance is doing. Cutting tax assessments for favored voters. And the hack he put in charge of Human Resources is passing out jobs like election candy. Just imagine what Satō will do with the police department. We won't just be fixing parkin' tickets."

CHAPTER FIFTY-ONE

KOA WAS STILL pondering his exchange with Thurston when Makanui popped her head in Koa's door. "We got some intel from the Philippine authorities."

"Tell me what you've got."

She opened a folder, spreading the contents across Koa's desk. "According to this report from the Philippine anti-terror agency, Faisal, the shooter who attacked me, is a commander in the Abu Sayyaf brigade. I think he is the brother of the guy I killed the night they boarded our sailboat in the Sula Sea. But that's not the most interesting part."

"How so?" Koa said.

Makanui pointed to a paragraph she'd highlighted in yellow. "Read that."

Koa read:

"*Reliable informant [name blacked out] provided intel that he recognized a former American AID officer meeting with top Abu Sayyaf Group (ASG) commanders on Jolo Island in early 2021. He offered weapons and a large sum of money, believed to be more than five million U.S. dollars if ASG would carry out certain operations on U.S. soil. The informant says ASG commanders assigned senior operatives, including Faisal Yasir, to this U.S. operation.*"

Koa looked up. "Interesting. It fits with what we heard from Ismael. Do you have a line on this former AID officer?"

"Nothing on that yet, but I'm digging. I'm assuming the informant recognized this AID dude because he once worked in the Mindanao area. That narrows the search. There can't be that many possibles."

"How are you going about it?" Koa asked.

"Three ways," Makanui responded. "I have requested data on all AID officers assigned to the Philippines in the past fifteen years. I'm getting passport info on such officers from the State Department to cross-check the AID data. I've also gone back to the Philippine authorities to ask for a description and, if possible, pictures of the AID officer their informer ID'd."

"Sounds like you have the bases covered," Koa said. "Keep me posted."

As Makanui turned toward the door, her cellphone buzzed. She answered, listened for a moment, and said, "We'll be there in ten."

Waving for Koa to join her, she said, "Faisal just awakened from his minimally cognitive state."

A nurse prepped them at the private clinic where Piki had Faisal under guard. "He says his name is Faisal. Says he's a political prisoner and wants asylum."

"I'll bet he does," Makanui said.

The two officers found Faisal sitting in bed, still attached to various medical monitors. He looked pale and weak. He stared searingly at Makanui with hostile black eyes, ignoring Koa, who began to read him his *Miranda* rights.

"I kill ya like ya kill my . . . my brother." He spat the words in angry, broken English.

"You didn't count on my protective vest," she responded.

"Bitch! I no talk ya."

"That's too bad," she replied, "because I'm the only one who can help you."

"No. I politic prisoner. I want asylum."

Makanui chuckled. "You're just a common criminal. And you won't be getting asylum. But you could help yourself if you tell us what you know."

"I no talk."

She looked him straight in the eye and spoke slowly in clipped sentences to make sure he got the message. "That's your right. But let me explain things. We know you are Faisal Yasir. We know you are a senior Abu Sayyaf commander. We know the Philippine military . . ."

His eyes went wide in shock. "No . . . no . . . ya mistake."

"There's no mistake, Faisal. The Philippine military wants to get their hands on you. They've been after you since you escaped after the raid on your camp. I hear you killed a soldier during your escape. I think you know what the Philippine military will do to you. I'm sure you know what's happened to some of your comrades."

He started to protest, but she cut him off. "Here's what we are going to do, Faisal. You're going to tell us everything you know. If you don't or you lie to us, we're going to call Colonel Ramos. You know Colonel Ramos. He's head of *Pambansang Lupon ng Pagsa-sagawa Laban sa Terorismo*. I think they call him *demonyo*, the devil."

Her message delivered fluently, partly in his language, triggered raw terror. It showed in his face and a visible tremor.

"Do you understand?"

"Oo." Reluctantly, he answered "yes" in Filipino.

"Good. Now, who sent you to Hawai'i?"

"You no send me back Mindanao?" he asked, his voice unsteady.

She had no intention of sending him back to the Philippines under any circumstances, but he didn't need to know that. "Not if you answer our questions and tell us the truth."

Faisal hesitated, apparently weighing his options. "No *demonyo?*"

"Not if you are truthful," she repeated.

"Abu Sayyaf send me."

"Why?"

"Ya kill my brother."

"We know that's not the only reason."

At that, Faisal appeared confused. Koa guessed that despite Makanui's threats, the man planned to lie in answering their questions. Koa had seen the strategy pursued many times by many suspects. He called it pseudo cooperation. Faisal would soon realize that it wouldn't work with Makanui.

"We know about the money," Makanui asserted. "Tell us about the man who came to your camp on Jolo Island."

That struck a nerve. Faisal's expression changed to one of bewilderment. "What?"

Koa smiled inwardly. Makanui was doing a great job intimidating Faisal on one hand while keeping him off balance by demonstrating her knowledge of his activities. It was Interrogation 101, but he'd rarely seen it done so well.

"The former AID officer. Tell us about him," Makanui pushed.

"From 2006. After Zamboanga bombs. Talks fail," Faisal said.

"You are saying this man was involved in the MILF negotiations in 2006?" Makanui turned to Koa. "The Philippine government attempted unsuccessfully to negotiate a peace agreement with the Moro Islamic Liberation Front in 2006."

"Yes," Faisal said, "2006."

"And now, fifteen years later, this same man promised money?" Makanui asked.

"Yes."

"And what else? Guns?" she suggested.

"Yes. Much guns."

"And my location?"

"Yes."

Koa and Makanui weren't sure how many operatives Abu Sayyaf had sent to Hawai'i, so Makanui tried to trick Faisal into revealing that information. "This man, he paid for three Abu Sayyaf men?"

Faisal appeared confused and said nothing.

"You and Ismael, and who else?"

Faisal seemed surprised at the mention of Ismael but still said nothing.

"You need to give us the name of the third operative if you want our help," she prodded.

"Dunno," Faisal responded.

His response was ambiguous. It could be that he didn't know, but it might also mean that Abu Sayyaf had sent only two operatives. Makanui apparently had the same thought and asked, "Did Abu Sayyaf send more than two operatives?"

"Only two I know."

"Who helped you here in Hawai'i?" Makanui asked.

Silence.

"We know someone in Hawai'i gave you instructions by burner phone. Who?"

Once again, Makanui surprised Faisal, and it showed on his face, but he didn't answer.

"You want to see *demonyo*?" she asked.

Silence.

"Did you get instructions from 'Aukai?"

A look of puzzlement crossed his face. He appeared not to recognize the name.

Makanui sensed that he wouldn't answer but tried one more time. "Who is Kōkua?"

He appeared stunned for just a moment before recovering and saying nothing. His reaction told them they'd identified Faisal's handler, but Koa realized that Faisal feared that handler more than he feared *demonyo*. Faisal had reached the limit of his cooperation.

CHAPTER FIFTY-TWO

THE TELEPHONE CALL surprised Koa. He hadn't expected to appear before the Hawai'i County Police Commission, but the invitation might as well have been a subpoena. Compliance wasn't voluntary. And like a subpoena for testimony, it provided no clue to its purpose. He was, in any event, happy to be of service.

The meeting turned out to be informal but not altogether friendly. The nine commission members, one from each of the Island's districts, met him in a large conference room in the Hilo City Hall. Koa had briefed the group on several previous occasions but always with Chief Lannua by his side. This time he was flying solo.

The chairman opened the proceedings by acknowledging the chief's death before welcoming Koa. "Our purpose in inviting you here this morning is to get your impressions and opinion on a candidate for our new chief of police."

The agenda surprised Koa. It had been less than five days since the bombing killed Chief Lannua. So far as Koa knew, there had been no job posting for a new police chief, nor had the commission had time to search for suitable candidates.

"Who's the candidate?" Koa asked.

"Amado Moreau," the chairman responded.

Koa nearly bit his lip, suppressing the urge to say, "You're kidding."

He restrained himself and paused for a moment to formulate his thoughts. The Commission, he knew, focused a lot of its attention on police–community relations and the adverse effects of police misconduct. He wanted to ask about the lack of public notice and a proper search but decided to get a better sense of the meeting first. "I guess I'm surprised that he's under consideration," Koa began, speaking respectfully.

"The mayor has proposed him as a candidate, and we'd like to get your views," the chairman responded.

Ordinarily, Koa would have tried to be politic, but he regarded the proposal as potentially damaging to the department and the community. Moreau had provoked nasty confrontations with the local populace, and his appointment as chief would not be well received. "First, he has no experience leading an organization of any size, let alone a large police force. Second, he lacks expertise with and respect for proper police procedures. Third, he's only been on the force for a few months and has few, if any, relationships in the community. The few contacts he had didn't turn out well. Fourth, he's had hostile encounters with several officers and does not enjoy the respect of the bulk of the force. And finally, I've reprimanded him multiple times for the use of excessive force."

As he spoke, Koa watched the commissioners' expressions. The strength of his criticism seemed to surprise three or four members and annoy others. Koa paused, waiting for questions, which then came flying across the table. "Can you give us some specifics on his excessive use of force?" Commissioner Southland asked. Southland's words came at Koa from the opposite end of the conference table. As he spoke, Koa saw the chairman's closely spaced eyes blink quickly, and his hands fidget ever so slightly. He wondered if the man was ill.

"Certainly, Commissioner. Two months ago, I reprimanded him for slapping a fourteen-year-old Hawaiian child across the face and threatening to punch him."

"You didn't personally witness that event, did you, Detective?" Commissioner Mitchell, the representative of the Hilo district and a close confidant of Mayor Satō, asked. Mitchell had the sagging, blotchy face and rounded middle of a lifetime of heavy drinking.

"No, Commissioner, but two other officers did, and their body cameras recorded the encounter. Unfortunately, there were also other civilians present. I questioned the two officers and reviewed the video before reprimanding Detective Moreau."

"I can see why the community might be upset," Commissioner Southard acknowledged.

Displeased with Koa's assessment, Mitchell asked pointedly, "What are Detective Moreau's shortcomings concerning police procedures?"

"Two come immediately to mind. Moreau interrogated a suspect and elicited a confession without giving a *Miranda* warning orally or in writing. As a result, the county prosecutor declined prosecution, and a guilty man went free. On another occasion, he failed to wear gloves or protective clothing and contaminated a crime scene."

As Koa's case against Moreau grew more substantial and specific, Koa could see Commissioner Mitchell appear increasingly upset. "Isn't it true, Detective Kāne, that your own ambition to become police chief colors your unflattering evaluation of Detective Moreau?"

Koa resented the personal attack and could see that Commissioner Mitchell's hostile question did not sit well with the other commissioners. After a pause, Koa responded, "No, sir, that is not true. I have not applied to be chief and have no intention of doing so. I'm happy with my role in leading the detective division. I do, however, care about the department's public image, understand the importance of public support in carrying out our mission, and value the high morale within the department under Chief Lannua. I strongly recommend against appointing Officer Moreau as police chief because it would severely damage the department's public image, undermine public support for our mission, and adversely affect officer morale."

Commissioner Mitchell appeared unmoved, but Koa saw several of the other commissioners nodding in agreement with Koa's points. Still, Mitchell persisted. "Isn't it true that you opposed Mr. Moreau's selection as deputy chief detective?"

Although Mitchell must have thought the question would help his candidate, he'd miscalculated. Koa responded, "Yes, Commissioner Mitchell, I did oppose his appointment, and his conduct since then has only reaffirmed my judgment in that respect."

Mitchell had grown progressively angrier, and his face was now bright red, but Koa could see several of his associates suppress a smile.

*　　*　　*

Koa barely made it back to police headquarters before an assistant summoned him to the mayor's office. The call told Koa that his performance before the police commissioners had pissed off the mayor. He did not doubt that he was in for one of the mayor's infamous tongue lashings. So be it. He'd answered the police commission's questions honestly and without exaggeration. If anything, he'd understated his concerns about Moreau.

As Koa anticipated, Mayor Satō, small of stature but possessed of an enormous ego, was hopping mad. When Koa entered his office, Mayor Satō was pacing around while Police Commissioner Mitchell sat stony-faced at his conference table. Koa guessed that Mitchell had gone straight from the police commission meeting to the mayor's office.

"What the hell are you up to, Detective? Sabotaging my choice for chief of police," Satō began in an imperious voice.

Koa started to respond, but the mayor cut him off.

"Don't give me excuses. You are going to meet with the police commission again tomorrow morning, apologize for your slander, and admit that you pursued a personal vendetta against Detective Moreau."

Koa had heard stories about Mayor Satō's bullying tactics but hadn't previously experienced them firsthand. Still, he remained undeterred. "I'm sorry, Mister Mayor, but I gave the police commission my honest and truthful opinion, motivated only by what is best for the police department."

Satō raised his voice. "I decide what is best for the police department. You will do as I say."

"I'm sorry, sir," Koa said. "Respectfully, sir, I told the police commission the truth, and I stand by that truth."

Satō was now livid, and his eyes flashed with anger. With unrestrained hostility in his voice, the mayor snapped back, "You're making a mistake, Detective. I will have your job if you don't get in line." Satō paused for a moment, assuming Koa would back down. When Koa said nothing, Satō shouted, "Get out of here."

The mayor's over-the-top performance stunned Koa. It had been heavy-handed and tactless. More overbearing than any of the many rumors he'd heard about Satō. It made him question what he thought he knew about Satō's motivation. Was it all about the politics of reelection? Or was there something else going on? Maybe Moreau had some hold over the mayor. Of more immediate concern, Koa wondered if the mayor would get him fired.

He needed to talk to his friend Zeke. If anyone could put the mayor's conduct in context, it would be Zeke. Leaving City Hall, Koa walked across the parking lot to the prosecutor's office, where he found Zeke leaning back in his chair, talking on the phone.

Ending the call, Zeke greeted him. "I hear you been fighting with our prickly mayor."

"If words could kill, I'd be dead," Koa responded. Then, amazed as always by Zeke's extraordinary grasp of everything happening on the Big Island, Koa asked, "How'd you hear about it?"

"The chairman of the police commission told me about your performance at the meeting this morning. Heard you ripped Mitchell a new asshole in front of his colleagues."

"Served him right for questioning my integrity," Koa responded. "But tell me, what's Moreau got on the mayor? An illegitimate child? An illicit affair? Dirty pictures? I mean, what? Why else would the mayor go out of his way to put an unqualified guy like Moreau in the chief's chair? And why no public notice and no search for a truly qualified replacement?"

"Good questions, and I don't have answers," Zeke responded. "I don't even have a handle on Moreau. So, who is he anyway? I'm as much in the dark as you on this one."

"I don't know much about his background. He appeared out of nowhere a few months ago working for Satō. The mayor leaned on the chief who hired him as deputy chief detective over my objection. He's been a problem ever since."

"So, you didn't vet him before he joined the force?" Zeke asked.

"Hell no. Chief Lannua handled the vetting."

"Well, we need to check him out, don't we?" Zeke said.

"Agreed," Koa responded, "before the mayor fires me."

"That's not going to happen," Zeke assured Koa with a knowing look.

"How can you be so sure?"

"Satō makes lots of idle threats trying to get his way. It's his MO. Besides, he's going to be in a brutal fight in the next election and doesn't need a wrongful termination suit for firing his top Hawaiian detective. Not for giving truthful statements to the police commission."

*   *   *

Koa wasn't sure how, but word of his run-ins with Commissioner Mitchell and the mayor filtered back to Moreau. The man came charging into Koa's office like an angry hornet. Slamming the door behind him, he demanded an explanation. "Why are you sabotaging my appointment as chief?"

Koa smiled at the confrontational approach. "I didn't realize the police commission had posted the position or was even actively looking at this time."

"That's all bullshit." Moreau raised his voice. "Deputy Chief Kama, now acting chief, is too old and already half-retired. The force needs a new chief to stabilize things, and the mayor submitted my name to the police commission." Moreau pointed at Koa. "Then, you fucked it up."

"Really?" Koa asked. "You've only been on the force for a few months. You don't have any command experience. You don't think before you act, and you alienate important groups in the local community. Bottom line, you don't have the skill, temperament, or judgment to lead the department. So why should the mayor appoint you?"

"You're full of shit. I'm the best man for the job, and if you want to remain with the force, you'd better fix it with the police commission."

"You threatening me?"

"I'm telling you. If you don't take back what you said, the mayor's going to fire you."

"We'll see about that."

"I'm warning you," Moreau responded, raising his voice.

If it had been up to Koa, he would have fired Moreau on the spot, but again, he restrained himself. Koa didn't need a lawsuit from Moreau any more than the mayor needed a lawsuit from Koa. Moreau's aggressiveness and bid to become chief would be comical if they weren't serious. Koa needed to dig into the man's background. Who was he, what made him tick, and what were his ties to the mayor? Blackmail or extortion seemed the most likely, but he couldn't rule out bribery or some other explanation. Whatever the relationship, it had an unpleasant odor and deserved scrutiny.

Looking Moreau in the eye, Koa said, "Look, Moreau, you're not qualified, and I'm not going to support you. That's the bottom line."

"You're a bastard, and you won't be so high and mighty when Satō cans you," Moreau said as he turned and left.

CHAPTER FIFTY-THREE

No ONE IN the detective bureau could beat Piki in perseverance, especially on technology issues. That explained why Koa had assigned him to learn everything possible about the burner phones used by the assailants. Piki initially focused on three untraceable phones—two that the police had recovered from Ismael, Faisal, and an additional one, located in downtown Hilo, that Kōkua had used to communicate with Ismael. Later he'd added 'Aukai's burner phone and the second Hilo burner used to direct 'Aukai.

Koa figured that the Hilo burners belonged to someone in the police department, an outsider with access to police information, or a hacker, but a police insider seemed most likely. He based that conclusion on the leak of Makanui's location in the Volcano Village guesthouse leading to the second attempt on her life. He was sure that leak had come from within the department, where just a handful of police insiders knew or could have learned of Makanui's location. The personal identification and scheduling data found in the Alahaki Road house only reinforced his assessment that a police source provided information to 'Aukai and the two Abu Sayyaf operatives.

The chief's murder increased Koa's sense of urgency in identifying the leaker. Someone with unfettered access and intimate knowledge of departmental security had disabled cameras, evaded security protocols, and killed Lannua. Since it seemed unlikely that there were two internal traitors, Koa guessed that the leaker who used the Hilo burners had killed the chief.

Piki's task involved identifying the telephone carrier associated with each of the three burners the police had recovered and subpoenaing phone records for those phones. He would then analyze the calls and obtain the logs for any other phones called from the three burners. Koa also hoped Piki could determine how the users acquired their burners and their respective SIM cards. Koa knew the time-consuming nature of obtaining phone records and tracing acquisition history through subpoenas. Still, he was eager for a report on Piki's progress.

Koa summoned Piki to his office. When the young detective arrived, Koa asked, "Identified our leaker yet?"

"Afraid not," Piki said, "but I found something weird."

"Explain."

"The Hilo burner phones—the one that called the Dragunov shooter, Ismael, and the different one that called 'Aukai—and several other burners were purchased by a known criminal named Billy Maroni."

"How did you figure that out?" Koa asked.

"From the numbers. I got the SIM card IDs and traced them through the wholesaler to the store," Piki replied.

"Okay, go on," Koa urged.

"We traced the phones to Kelepona, a local phone store, and found video of Maroni buying several prepaid phones. He was a mid-level distributor of opioids and other illicit drugs before we took him off the street in a raid on his drug den about six weeks ago. Maroni copped a plea and is currently in jail. So, he couldn't be the Hilo caller."

"Somehow, his phones got into someone else's hands." Koa stated the obvious.

"Right."

"Have you talked to Maroni?" Koa asked.

"I tried, but he clammed up. I thought maybe you might be more persuasive," Piki said with a grin.

"Get me all the files on this Maroni guy."

Twenty-four hours later, Koa and Piki sat across the table from Maroni in an interrogation room at the Hālawa Correctional Facility on Oʻahu. Having learned that Maroni smoked unfiltered Camel Turkish Gold cigarettes, Koa pushed a full pack across the table to Maroni. The drug dealer looked suspiciously at the offering for only a moment before tearing it open and lighting up. Koa let him savor the cancer stick before saying, "We want to ask you some questions about the police raid on your place."

"What's in it for me?" Maroni responded predictably as he blew smoke their way. Maroni was stocky with a swarthy look reinforced by the deep circles under his unfriendly black eyes.

"How'd you like to be up for parole in six months?"

Maroni scoffed. "Don't con me. Nobody gets parole the first time around."

"Those with support from prosecutors do," Koa replied.

"I want it in writing," Maroni snapped back, his interest piqued.

Having anticipated this reaction, Koa produced a letter from Zeke's office stating that he would support parole if Maroni's cooperation proved "significant."

Maroni shook his head. "Don't mean nothing 'cause you get to decide what's significant."

"You got a better offer from somebody else?" Koa asked.

Maroni took another long drag on his cigarette. "What ya want to know."

"Tell us about the police raid on your place."

"Ya ain't gonna increase my sentence 'cause of the shit I tell ya?" Maroni asked suspiciously.

"We're not here about you," Koa assured him.

"Fuckin' cops took my stash and still burned me."

"How?" Koa asked.

"There was three times more drugs than they charged. Them cops was bandits."

"What else did they take?" Koa pressed.

"Cash, jewelry, and my electronic shit."

"What electronics?"

"A couple of computers with monitors, speakers, and printers, a Sony PlayStation, and some phones."

"Tell me about the phones," Koa asked.

"They was burners. You know the type."

"How many?" Piki asked.

"I don't know exactly. A half dozen, maybe?"

"And you bought them at Kelepona?" Piki followed up.

Maroni appeared surprised. "How'd you know that?"

Undeterred, Piki repeated the question.

"Yeah. At Kelepona."

"And you bought them all—all half dozen—at the same time?"

"Yeah."

"And the cops took all of them?"

"Yeah."

* * *

According to police reports on the Maroni raid, several officers had secured the crime scene. Only three—patrolmen Wakano and Henry and Sergeant Hirako—had processed the scene. Hirako, as the senior officer, signed off on the property inventory and checked the seized goods into the police evidence room. After going over the reports with Koa, Piki said, "Hirako must have known the police confiscated more stuff. Let's bring him in and sweat him."

Koa shook his head. "Hirako and Wakano are old-timers. They've worked together for years. Henry is the new kid on that block. We'll start with him."

Piki, eager to learn, asked, "Why?"

"He's more likely to talk, especially if he thinks Hirako ratted him out."

A couple of hours later, Koa and Piki had patrolman Henry across the table in an interrogation room at police headquarters in Hilo. In his mid-twenties, his baby face made him look as though he might still be in high school. He blanched when Koa read him his *Miranda* rights.

"I ain't . . . ain't done nothing wrong, sir," he stuttered.

"We'll see about that," Koa said. "Tell us about the inventory of property seized from the raid on Maroni's drug crib. You remember that raid, don't you?"

"I don't have nothing to say about that," Henry responded off the bat.

"Is that because maybe you failed to report all the seized goods? Made off with two-thirds of the drugs and some other stuff?"

Henry looked stricken. "Not me. It wasn't me," he blurted out.

"Then who was it?" Koa demanded, continuing his aggressive approach.

"Nobody . . . nobody faked the inventory." Henry's voice quivered with the apparent lie.

In what Koa recognized as one of the oddities of the American justice system, the law permitted police officers conducting interrogations to make deceptive statements and outright lies to secure confessions. "That's not what Sergeant Hirako says," Koa shot back even though he hadn't spoken to Hirako.

"No . . . no," Henry stuttered, "he can't pin his shit on me. I had nothing to do with it."

"Then, I think you'd better come clean," Koa said, now speaking softly.

"It was Sergeant Hirako's deal, he and Wakano. They submitted just enough evidence to assure a conviction and skimmed the rest. I told them I wanted no part of it."

"And what did they do with the rest?" Piki asked.

"I'm not sure about the drugs. I think Hirako sold them to a street dealer, based on things he said. They pawned the electronics. They'd done it before."

"How do you know that?" Piki followed up.

"They talked and laughed about doubling their salaries. Said it was the best thing about being police officers."

Scared out of his wits, Henry had become a font of information, and Koa judged that it was time to raise what he cared about. "What about burner phones seized in the raid?"

"Hirako kept them. He was always looking for burners. Asked me and Wakano to keep an eye out for 'em."

"Why?" Piki asked.

"Not sure, but I can guess. Probably to contact street dealers when he had drugs or maybe other shit to unload."

As he often did when he flipped a co-conspirator during an active investigation, Koa warned Henry not to alert his partners in crime. "We appreciate your cooperation," Koa said, bringing the interview to a close. "If you want to stay out of jail, you'll keep your mouth shut about this meeting. Got it?"

Now thoroughly chastened, Henry readily agreed, "Yes, sir. I got it."

When they'd left the interrogation room, Piki turned to Koa. "You're not going to charge him?"

"All in good time, my friend."

* * *

After Henry left, Piki wanted to confront Hirako and Wakano, but Koa vetoed the idea. "Hirako's a tough bastard. It'll be his word again Henry's. We're not going to get squat out of him without more than we've got."

"You think he's the guy behind the Hilo burner?" Piki asked.

Always inclined to make his subordinates think for themselves, Koa asked, "What do *you* think?"

"I think he's our guy," Piki responded.

"It's a big step to go from knocking off drug cribs to murdering police officers," Koa said.

"So, what do we do next?" Piki asked.

"We're going to set a trap," Koa responded before explaining what he planned.

* * *

Two nights later, Koa arranged for Makanui to send Hirako and Wakano to raid a supposed drug den at a dilapidated house on the outskirts of Hilo. The two officers had no idea that the raid was a setup where drugs, cash, and electronics borrowed from the police evidence room had been carefully inventoried and tagged with trackers. The officers conducted the raid unaware of surveillance inside and outside the residence recording their movements. Nor did they know that Koa had arranged with Zeke to secure Judge Hitachi's approval for wiretaps on the three burner phones the officers recovered in the raid.

* * *

Koa had a basket full of evidence by the end of the following day. Hirako submitted a false inventory accounting for less than half of the drugs and property seized. He'd contacted a street-level drug dealer on one of the recorded burner phones and agreed to sell the drugs he'd failed to include in the inventory. A team of police officers staked out the agreed point of sale and arrested both Hirako and his buyer. Wakano pawned over $500 in electronics seized in the raid. Police arrested him coming out of the pawnshop.

Within minutes of the arrests, Koa gave the go-ahead to teams with warrants, also approved by Judge Hitachi, to search the three rogue officers' homes, cars, and police lockers. They found a total of four burner phones—one in Hirako's police locker and three more at his home. Yet, none operated on the numbers associated with the Hilo burners used to communicate with the Dragunov shooter, Ismael, or 'Aukai.

Piki, excited about the success of the operation, told Koa, "I'll bet the police commission will be happy we got these corrupt bastards."

Koa smiled at his naïveté. "Don't count on it. That group is never happy about anything that reflects badly on the police."

"You mean they'd rather leave crooked cops on the force?" Piki asked.

"I didn't say that."

*   *   *

Koa spent an hour with Zeke working out the best strategy for pressuring Sergeant Hirako to talk. They had him on a dozen or more possible charges ranging from submitting false reports to the theft of police property to drug dealing. Consecutive sentences would put him away for a long time. Koa figured he was smart enough to know he was going down and would want to cut his losses. They decided on a take-it-or-leave-it offer—plead to a single class C felony for theft with a maximum sentence of five years in exchange for full cooperation. It was a tough deal but far better than the corrupt cop would get if he went to trial.

They met Hirako and his attorney in an interrogation room, and Zeke outlined a dozen charges he could include in an indictment. Koa then offered Hirako the single felony count deal. "There's no negotiation. Take it or leave it and understand that the deal requires your complete cooperation. Anything less, and Zeke drops the hammer."

They gave the man a chance to confer with his attorney, but he had no choice. Within fifteen minutes, Hirako agreed.

Despite his decision to cooperate, he acted surprised when Koa asked him, "Tell us about the cellphones you took during the Maroni raid."

"The cellphones?"

"Yes, the burner phones from the Maroni raid."

"I stashed them," he responded hesitantly as he adjusted to his new role on an unfamiliar side of the interrogation table.

"Where?"

"In my police locker. I wanted 'em handy in case I needed one while I was on duty."

"All of them?"

"Yeah."

"Where are they now?"

"Gone. Some bastard broke into my locker and made off with six burners. The ones from the Maroni raid."

"When? When were they stolen?"

"About a month ago."

"Who stole them?" Koa asked.

"Hell if I know."

"Who knew you had those burners in your locker?" Zeke asked.

"I don't know. There was guys in and out of the locker room all the time. Someone probably saw me with one of the phones."

Koa felt a keen sense of disappointment. It had been a promising lead, and he and Piki had worked it well. Still, it had petered out, leaving them with nothing. Well, almost nothing. He guessed a cop had stolen Hirako's stuff from the police locker room, but that didn't mean the cop had used the burners. The thief might have sold or pawned them. All Koa's work hadn't gotten him much closer to the elusive Hilo burners. Koa ordered a fingerprint check on Hirako's locker but harbored no expectation that it would amount to much of anything.

He could see that Piki was disappointed at the failure of their efforts. Turning to him, Koa said, "It didn't work out, but that's not your fault. You did a great job to get us as far as we got." Koa forced a smile. "And remember, we got three bad cops off the street, including Henry, who resigned from the force in a plea deal to avoid prosecution."

"Thanks, boss," Piki acknowledged. "There's one more thing I'd like to try."

"What's that?"

"The owner of Kelepona isn't positive, but she said she thought the six phones that Maroni bought have sequential telephone numbers. Our Hilo caller appears to be smart enough to switch burners, but he might use one of the other phones from that same sequence. I'd like to put wiretaps on all those numbers. Maybe our guy will use one of those phones."

"Worth a try. Talk to Zeke about a warrant."

*   *   *

Discouraged, Koa decided to call it a day. Before leaving police head-quarters, he checked with the security people guarding Nālani and his family. He guessed the next attack would be aimed directly at him, but was still relieved to find his loved ones safe. He'd tried to convince Nālani to take some time off to visit her sister on Maui or go shopping in San Francisco, but she wouldn't hear of it. "I'm not going any-where," she'd insisted. "I'm going to stand with you in this fight, and we'll get through it together." He could only hope she was right.

CHAPTER FIFTY-FOUR

THE FOLLOWING MORNING, Koa, Makanui, Zeke, and Sarah met in the prosecutor's office to discuss the 'Aukai case. Over steaming cups of Kona coffee, Koa began, "I asked Makanui to come along to brief you on the information she obtained from Philippine authorities before we decide what to do with 'Aukai."

"Okay," Zeke said, "what have you learned?"

Makanui shared the intelligence she'd received from the Philippine authorities. "It's pretty specific, and it corroborates what Ismael told us, namely that somebody paid Abu Sayyaf big bucks for hired guns to attack the Hawai'i police."

"There are lots of cases," Koa explained, "where a perp engages a hired killer. But I'll admit this is the first time I've heard of someone hiring a terrorist group to carry out what seem to be personal attacks. To make it work, the mastermind behind these attacks picked a small, poorly financed group, one that could be motivated by a big payoff and, in this case, also one with a connection to one of the targets, namely Makanui."

"So, whoever is behind Ismael, Faisal, and 'Aukai must have known about my Sulu Sea activities," Makanui added. "Koa and I have run down all the likely candidates and come up empty."

"Maybe this ʻAukai fellow can shed some light on who's behind this nightmare," Zeke said. "I've reached an agreement with federal drug enforcement authorities on the ʻAukai case. After hours of negotiation, they agreed to allow Hawaiʻi to take precedence in prosecuting ʻAukai. But, in exchange, they insisted that the State not give ʻAukai a favorable plea deal unless he gives up the names of his drug suppliers and customers.

"I've formulated the criminal charges the State intends to pursue against ʻAukai, including the murder of Officer Haliʻa, conspiracy to murder ʻOlina Crow, attempted murders of Nālani, Alexia, Piki, and Koa, resisting arrest, and other miscellaneous charges."

"You're going after him for shooting at us through the door?" Koa asked.

"Damn straight. He's lucky you jumped out of the way, or I'd be charging him with your murder," Zeke said with a wry smile.

"I'm the one who's lucky, and I'll happily settle for attempted murder," Koa said, remembering how close he and Piki came to taking multiple bullets. "Think he'll deal?"

"He's facing multiple life sentences without parole, so he might be willing to bargain," Zeke explained.

"He's also got a long rap sheet," Koa reminded Zeke, "which won't help him at sentencing. So, what's your bottom line?"

"If he tells us who is behind the attacks on the police force and cooperates with the feds, I could see going to twenty-five years, maybe with an opportunity for parole after twenty."

"That's a pretty good deal for a guy who'd otherwise spend the rest of his life wearing an orange jumpsuit with a number on it," Koa said.

"We'll see," Zeke responded. "I've given up predicting the workings of the criminal mind."

Koa chuckled. "C'mon, Zeke. That won't happen 'til you pull those boots off for the last time."

* * *

Back at the police headquarters, they waited for the jailers to deliver ʻAukai. He got banged up when he wrapped his truck around a tree and took a bullet in the shoulder trying to evade the Hilo SWAT team. The medics had fitted his arm with a sling and stitched and bandaged his face, but he still wore a defiant air. With his rap sheet and time spent behind bars, he had developed the shell of a hardened criminal. He'd be a hard nut to crack, and the involvement of federal drug agents would only complicate things. They wanted the names of his drug suppliers, and ʻAukai might rightfully be afraid of brutal retaliation if he named names. Still, absent a break from the prosecutor, ʻAukai faced the near certainty of life without parole. And the drug lords could still get at him in jail if they worried that he would someday start talking. The man had a hard choice to make.

After guards secured the prisoner, fastening his free hand to the table, Koa and Zeke accompanied ʻAukai's lawyer, Carmen Diaz, into the interrogation room. Koa regarded ʻAukai's choice of lawyer as a good sign. Diaz had a solid reputation as an effective but pragmatic advocate. She wasn't one of the cartel lawyers who spent their lives representing drug dealers. Koa guessed ʻAukai had chosen her because his current problem was a whole lot more serious than the typical drug rap. She'd fight hard for her client but wouldn't con him into a costly trial he'd inevitably lose. She'd realistically lay out the risks he faced.

The two cops and the prosecutor sat across the table from the speedboat driver and his lawyer. Koa repeated the usual warnings.

"We'd like to ask you some questions," Zeke began.

"No bother 'cause I not talking," ʻAukai responded.

"You're not interested in trying to reduce your life sentence?" Zeke asked.

Diaz motioned to her client not to answer. Instead, she replied on his behalf. "What do you have in mind?"

"Depends on what he has to say," Zeke responded.

"But you're offering my client something less than life?" she asked.

"That's correct," Zeke acknowledged. "How much less depends on the completeness of his cooperation."

"I not going to rat nobody out," 'Aukai blurted out, disregarding his lawyer's guidance.

Koa had been waiting for just such an opportunity. He knew 'Aukai had ferried Ismael from the Philippine freighter to Punalu'u and figured, based on the circled dates on 'Aukai's calendar, that he had also brought Faisal ashore. "Too bad," Koa said, "because Ismael and Faisal ratted you out. They put you dead center in a murder rap."

After a moment's hesitation, 'Aukai tried to feign surprise. "Who?"

Despite the question, Koa sensed the man knew all about the two Abu Sayyaf operatives. Having cut a chink out of 'Aukai's armor, Koa drove the knife home. "They'll be getting lenient treatment while you rot in prison for the rest of your life."

'Aukai looked like he wanted to leap across the table to choke Koa but remained silent.

Zeke abruptly pushed his chair back from the table and stood to leave. "Then I guess it'll just be multiple life sentences with no parole."

"Das not fair. I nevah kill nobody," 'Aukai snapped, his words wet with spittle.

"What about 'Olina Crow?" Koa challenged.

"That weren't me," 'Aukai shot back.

"When the jury sees what we found in your underground haunt, they'll know you had a hand in killing 'Olina Crow," Zeke interjected. "Your lawyer will tell you that it doesn't matter that you intended to kill Nālani and got the wrong person. Then there's officer Hali'a and the teenager who died in Room 212 at Hilo Memorial."

"You can't pin that on me," 'Aukai asserted.

"Oh, but we can," Zeke said. "We've even got Kōkua's voicemail ordering the hit and telling you where to attack."

Although Koa knew that Zeke intended to surprise 'Aukai with the voicemail, he had not predicted the man's reaction. The hardened criminal went white as bleached whalebone and sagged in his chair.

"With your criminal record, killing a police officer and a teenager in police custody—not to mention all the other crimes—you'll get the max. You'll die an old man in a prison cell if the drug lords don't kill you first."

Koa pushed his chair back and stood up. "Think it over. The man you're protecting will be drinking beer and fishing while you're sitting in a ten-by-ten cell worrying about an attack from some other inmate."

Koa, Zeke, and Makanui stepped out of the room, but before closing the door, Zeke turned to 'Aukai. "If you change your mind, your lawyer knows where to find me."

Koa asked, "Think he'll crack?"

"I'm betting," Zeke said, "the seed you planted about the others ratting on him and the Kōkua voicemail will gnaw at him. We'll just have to see whether it makes him crack."

CHAPTER FIFTY-FIVE

CARMEN DIAZ, 'AUKAI'S lawyer, was in Zeke's office bright and early the following morning. Her client wanted to deal. "He'll talk if you cap his sentence at ten years for all offenses, state and federal," she proposed.

The offer was absurd. There was no way that either Zeke or the feds would agree to let a violent criminal like 'Aukai back on the streets after only ten years or less if he got parole. Still, Zeke regarded the offer as progress. It meant that Diaz's client understood the peril he faced and wanted to avoid life in prison.

"That's not going to cut it," Zeke responded.

"Well, make my client a counter," Diaz said.

"Before responding on the merits," Zeke said, "I need to be sure we're on the same page. Any deal would require 'Aukai to tell us everything he knows about the recent attacks and give the feds chapter and verse about his drug dealings. That means naming names. We're talking complete and truthful cooperation."

"I've explained that," Diaz responded, "and he's prepared to tell all for the right deal so long as neither you nor the feds bring new charges based on his disclosures."

"So, he's prepared to admit to additional crimes?"

"Hypothetically, that might be a possibility," she acknowledged.

"I was thinking somewhere between twenty-five and thirty years, depending on the value of his information."

"Jesus, Zeke, you're a hard man."

"Come off it, Carmen. You've been around the block enough. You didn't come in here expecting I'd sign off on ten years."

She smiled at the backhanded compliment. "Now, to quote your words, I need to be sure we're on the same page. I'm not going to oversell what he has to offer and have the deal blow up in my face. He doesn't know who's ultimately behind the attacks on you and the others here in Hawai'i, but he does have information that may—I emphasize may—help you identify that person."

"Okay," Zeke said. "Let's cut to the chase. I can sell a thirty-year cap with a possibility of parole after twenty-five if we're happy with his cooperation."

Diaz looked disappointed, but Zeke guessed her reaction was pretense. "I'll take it back to my client, but I'm not hopeful."

When she walked out of the office, Zeke smiled, pleased with the progress he'd made. He'd have bet a month's pay they'd have a deal. And he would have won.

*   *   *

'Aukai looked tired, if not defeated when the jailers escorted him back to the interrogation room to face Koa, Makanui, and Zeke. His counsel summarized the terms of 'Aukai's agreement with Zeke, and the prosecutor confirmed her recitation.

'Aukai asked to have his uninjured hand freed from the chain fastening him to a post in the middle of the table, and Zeke agreed, pointing out that Koa had an armed guard just outside the door.

"Who's behind these attacks on the police?" Koa asked.

"Somebody who hates your fuckin' guts," 'Aukai responded, pointing a ragged finger at Koa.

"Why?"

"I no got no idea, but whoever it is, he wants to hurt you bad. He wanted you to see your brother back in prison, your girlfriend's body in pieces, your lady lawyer friend twisted up in a car wreck, and your buddy here"—he pointed to Zeke—"burned up in his own house."

Koa replayed 'Aukai's words in his mind—"I no got no idea, but whoever it is"—and realized that 'Aukai wasn't talking about Kōkua, but someone higher up the chain. Maybe the bossman mentioned in the telephone call they intercepted at the Alahaki Road house. "Who is this guy who hates me? Is it Kōkua?"

"Hell, no. Not Kōkua. He's just a go-between, like a courier in a drug network. I'm talking about on top of Kōkua. Calls himself Pāna'i."

"Pāna'i," Koa repeated, recognizing the Hawaiian word for vengeance. Sensing a break in the case, Koa leaned forward. "Talk to me about this Pāna'i?"

"Nope, I nevah met the guy. Only spoke on burner phones."

"Okay, tell me about your relationship. How you first contacted him. What did you do for him?"

"About five or six years ago, a guy I did business with, drug business, gave me a burner and told me to call a number. This Pāna'i guy—only he wasn't using that name back then—wanted me to courier some stuff for him. He was payin' good money, so I made some deliveries for him. Then he goes quiet for years. About six weeks ago, he calls and tells me he wants me to work with Kōkua, and he's talking serious money, so I'm in business. He had me pulling Ismael and Faisal off of freighters and handling the logistics for the hits he wanted."

Koa and Zeke pumped ʻAukai for further information about Pānaʻi but got nothing useful and eventually turned to other topics.

"What about the attack on Makanui?" Koa asked.

"Ah, that was a freebie for the Abu Sayyaf gang. Kind of icing on top of their cash and guns," ʻAukai responded.

"How do you know that?" Zeke asked.

"From Faisal. He claimed Makanui killed his brother during some kind of operation off the Philippine coast. Faisal's been dreaming of takin' 'er down ever since. The guy who hired Ismael and Faisal told 'em where to find Makanui as a teaser to get them on board."

"What guy?" Zeke asked.

"Never met 'im, but Ismael recognized 'im from years ago when this guy worked for the U.S. government."

That jibed with what they'd learned from Ismael. Still, Koa thought about what he'd just heard. ʻAukai had referred to the attacks on Ikaika, Nālani, Alexia, and Zeke as part of a plan to make Koa suffer. They now had confirmation that the whole series of attacks was personal. ʻAukai had also described the two attempts on Makanui's life as a freebie to entice Abu Sayyaf to join the party. All that made sense. But what about the chief? ʻAukai had not mentioned Lannua. "What about the attack on Chief Lannua?"

"Ah, that came later. Not part of the plan. Least not at the beginning."

"So," Koa asked, "how did that come about?"

"Kōkua calls me and wants one of the bombs. Tells me to leave it in a Hilo warehouse. So that's what I did. Never knew the target 'til it was on the news. Couldn't believe it was the fuckin' chief of police in his own office and on his fuckin' birthday. That takes some balls."

"How many bombs did you have?" Koa asked.

"Four. Picked 'em up off some freighter east of Hilo."

"So, there are three left?" Zeke asked.

"Naw. I stashed two for Ismael and left one for Kōkua like I said. One's left."

That squared with what Koa knew. Ismael had used one on Nālani's car, and the police had recovered one from the cave near the water tank on Alahaki Road. A third bomb killed Chief Lannua. "Where's the fourth bomb?"

"In a cave 'bout two hundred yards back of my house."

Koa used his cell to alert the bomb squad and send them south to secure the explosives.

Zeke then asked, "What do you know about Kōkua?"

"I know his voice."

"Describe his voice," Zeke directed.

"I kin do one better. I didn't trust the bastard, so I taped 'is calls."

Koa and Zeke exchanged glances. Diaz had said her client had something that might help identify the person orchestrating things, but neither Koa nor Zeke had expected recordings. If 'Aukai had recordings of his conversations with Kōkua, then Koa had a decent shot of identifying him, especially if he turned out to be a police department employee, which seemed likely given his apparent access to confidential information. And if Koa could nail Kōkua, then he'd have a decent chance of identifying Pāna'i. "Where are these recordings?" Koa asked.

'Aukai looked at his counsel. "She got 'em."

Carman Diaz produced a flash drive and said, "It contains recordings of conversations between 'Aukai and a man directing his actions."

Koa, Makanui, and Zeke took the flash drive to a nearby conference room, where they began to play the recordings. Almost immediately, they discovered a problem. 'Aukai's voice came through audibly, but the other voice was faint and scratchy, either because of the phone connection or the way 'Aukai had made the recording. They spent fifteen minutes playing back a series of conversations, trying to decipher the second speaker's words before concluding that they needed expert help to identify the caller. Koa suggested using Cap Roberts, who'd already worked on the case, but Zeke wanted to use independent experts from Oʻahu.

Koa, eager as always to drive the investigation forward, felt frustrated. He believed in pushing investigations at warp speed. And nothing was more central than identifying Kōkua, who had instructed Ismael, Faisal, and ʻAukai, and who'd probably killed the chief. That Koa himself was the likely next target only increased his urgency. Still, he knew how important it was to have Zeke's buy-in and respected Zeke's desire to secure the best possible evidence.

CHAPTER FIFTY-SIX

HATRED, UNLIKE HIGH water, is loath to recede. On the contrary, nourished by time, animous becomes ever more corrosive. Three thousand–plus miles east of Hawai'i, hatred consumed Pāna'i. It filled his every waking moment. He seethed with unbridled fury and an unimaginable craving for revenge.

He had devised a plan—subtle, devious, and above all, vengeful—to inflict incalculable pain on his enemy. That enemy would die, but not before he and those closest to him suffered horribly. *Lingchi*, the Chinese called it. The lingering death of a thousand cuts. A form of torture employed in Asian areas for a thousand years before governments banned it in the early 1900s. Traditionally, the executioner made tiny cuts, starting on the chest, and continuing to the arms and legs until death. Beheading and dismemberment then perfected the punishment. *Lingchi* deprived its victims not only of life in this world but of existence in the afterlife, for in Confucian thought, that required a complete body. *Lingchi* was thus forever, its punishment eternal.

Pāna'i had watched a film of the *lingchi* death of Fou Tchou-Li, a Mongolian who killed his prince in 1905. Fascinated, he watched the gruesome execution more than a dozen times over the years. Nothing would have made revenge sweeter than to impose traditional *lingchi* on those at the center of his enmity. But, alas, such a glorious event was not to be. Failing the real thing, he would settle for emotional *lingchi*—the slow accumulation of psychological trauma—followed by a violent death. Unimaginable emotional anguish would precede physical death, yet both would come, and slowly—ever so slowly. A modern reinterpretation of the ancient torment.

Fueled by vast ill-gotten gains buried deep in the dark landscape of shell companies and numbered accounts, Pānaʻi had hired Kōkua to do his bidding with ʻAukai's assistance. He preferred a hands-on approach and hated controlling all things remotely. Too much could go wrong, but his choices were few. At his direction, Kōkua and ʻAukai had secretly constructed a small army of operatives, weapons dealers, bomb makers, and killers. They had implemented Pānaʻi's carefully choreographed plans from recruitment to transportation to reconnaissance to action.

There had been a near disaster when that she-devil Makanui had survived Faisal's first assassination attempt. Pānaʻi had been furious. He had screamed and cursed and threatened retribution on Kōkua, describing in minute detail how his executioners would perform traditional *lingchi* on Kōkua if he should fail a second time. The man had been terrified, but in Pānaʻi's view, near paralyzing fear was an excellent motivator.

After that terrible warning, Pānaʻi believed his plan had proceeded smoothly. Kōkua had described Ismael's efforts to frame Ikaika, including the anguish Koa had suffered when the court denied bail. With the forged fingerprints, Koa's brother would soon be convicted and sentenced to life in prison. Pānaʻi could still hear the excitement in Kōkua's voice when he'd reported the deaths of Makanui and Nālani, the latter causing Koa untold anguish. Soon Zeke, Alexia, and Judge Hitachi would also die. Then there would be just one target left.

Pānaʻi did not know that Kōkua had lied to him. His threat to have his executioners perform *lingchi* on Kōkua had backfired. Kōkua, fearful of dying a death of a thousand cuts, had led Pānaʻi to believe his operations were successful when, in fact, they had failed.

CHAPTER FIFTY-SEVEN

KOA HADN'T EXPECTED to learn much when he asked Georgina to check for prints on Sergeant Hirako's locker. Once again, she surprised him.

"There's not much," she reported. "Lots of Hirako's prints as you'd expect, and some useless smeared prints. Like someone did a half-assed job of wiping the locker down. Could be a janitor, or maybe someone brushed up against the locker. No way to tell."

"So, nothing we can use?"

"Well, there was one print at the edge of the smear. I put it through our local print elimination database but got no hits. That seemed odd since there shouldn't be outsiders in the police locker room. So, I forwarded the print to the bureau."

"And?" Koa prompted.

"The FBI identified the print as belonging to Angelo Cruz. That's weird because there's no Angelo Cruz in the department. I can't even find anyone by that name on the Big Island. So how could his print have wound up on Hirako's locker?"

"Could there be an error in the print matching?" Koa asked.

"No. I checked. There's no mistake."

"You check the FBI's identity history summary for Cruz?"

"Yes. There's no criminal history. Some government agency submitted the fingerprint record."

"You're right," Koa acknowledged. "It is weird. Likely won't amount to much, but I'm going to have Piki see what he can find."

"Sounds good," Georgina said.

*   *   *

The following morning, an irrepressible Piki was in Koa's office. Having planted himself in front of Koa's desk, he shifted from foot to foot, hardly able to contain himself as he waited for Koa to finish a call and put the handset back in its cradle. "What did you find out about our mysterious Mister Cruz?" Koa asked.

"Get this. Angelo Cruz was a field officer with the U.S. Agency for International Development assigned to the U.S. Embassy in the Philippines from 2005 to late 2007."

Koa sat upright. "You're serious?"

"Yes, boss. I got the info straight from the head of security at the USAID office in D.C."

"You get a bio?"

"Yeah. Cruz was born in 1980 in the Philippines to American parents. Graduated from American University in Washington, D.C., in 2002. Worked for USAID from 2003 to 2010. Fluent in Filipino and various related dialects. Left the USAID for temporary work on Capitol Hill. One of the intelligence committees. Nothing on social media."

"Was he involved in those 2006 peace negotiations with"—Koa checked a pile of yellow Post-its until he found his note about the negotiations— "with the MILF?"

"I asked, but the head of security at USAID didn't know."

"Okay," Koa began, thinking out loud, "but Cruz was in the Philippines at that time. He's fluent in Filipino dialects. Helping to broker international peace is part of the USAID mission. Let's just assume for the moment that he played a role in the 2006 negotiations. He would likely have known, and maybe even been in direct contact with, the insurgents."

"So, years later, Cruz could have been the one who promised the Abu Sayyaf guys a pot of guns and money to send killers to Hawai'i," Piki suggested.

"What's Cruz's connection to Hawai'i?" Koa asked

"None that I could find," Piki replied quickly.

"Still," Koa continued, "we know from Cruz's fingerprint on Hirako's locker that he's been here, and recently, too. Not just on the Big Island but inside police headquarters. And not just anywhere in headquarters but touching the locker where Hirako stored burner phones subsequently used by Kōkua to direct killers sent here by Abu Sayyaf."

Piki looked confused. "That's all true, boss. But we've never done anything to Cruz. We didn't even know he existed until we found his fingerprint. So what possible motive could he have to hurt you and those around you?"

"Cruz is most likely hired help," Koa responded. "'Aukai told us that Pāna'i was the mastermind behind these attacks. 'Aukai described Kōkua as just a 'go-between, like a courier in a drug network.' And don't forget the call to Ismael that we intercepted." Once again, Koa shuffled through the stickies on his desk until he found what he wanted. "When the guy using the Hilo burner ordered Ismael to execute the next hit—the one on Zeke—he said '*Do it. The boss is angry. Never fail again.*' If Cruz is Kōkua, he's not the 'boss.' He's getting paid just like the Abu Sayyaf boys."

"Sounds like we should bring him in and question him," Piki said. "Maybe put out an APB."

"Hard to do without a physical description or a picture."

"My contact is faxing me a photo."

"I want to see it the moment it arrives," Koa directed.

"You got it."

Twenty minutes later, Piki was back with a grainy black-and-white facsimile of a 2004 photo. It showed a man, probably in his twenties, with a full beard and mustache. Koa saw something vaguely familiar about the face but couldn't place it. "You ever seen him?"

"Don't think so," Piki replied.

Koa stared at the face, wondering how it might have changed in seventeen years. "Get onto one of the police sketch artists. Let's see what he'd look like seventeen years older without all the facial hair."

"You got it."

After Piki left, Koa worried about holes in his speculation. According to Georgina's research, there was no Cruz in the police department or anywhere on the Big Island. Cruz's fingerprint by itself proved only that he'd touched the locker. Still, the fingerprint of a USAID officer who spoke Filipino and who'd most likely participated in the MILF negotiations on the locker containing the burner phones couldn't be a coincidence.

It also seemed unlikely that anyone outside the department could secure access to the police locker room without arousing suspicion. Of course, Cruz could have posed as a janitor or a maintenance man, but why touch Hirako's locker except to get the burners, and how would an outsider have known about the hard-to-trace burner phones inside that particular locker?

Koa supposed that Cruz could have had an accomplice inside the department. Yet, that led to a different conundrum. If Cruz had an accomplice, why had Cruz rather than the inside accomplice accessed Hirako's locker?

Then, there was the explosion that killed the chief. Had that, too, been Cruz's handiwork? How could he have made his way undetected into the chief's office? Once again, it seemed unlikely that Cruz was acting alone. More probably, Cruz had an accomplice inside the police department, someone who'd leaked confidential personal and scheduling information, known Makanui's whereabouts, and maybe planted the bomb in the chief's office.

There remained too many unanswered questions. Deep down, Koa knew he was onto something but must be missing critical pieces of information. Like a code without the key.

*   *   *

When Koa asked the department's Human Resources head for Moreau's personnel file, she produced a thin folder. Back in his office, Koa placed the file on his desk and closed the door to review its meager contents. To his astonishment, it consisted of only three documents—a résumé, a letter from the mayor, and a certification from the deputy mayor.

Moreau's hiring had, in Koa's view, been irregular. Koa had hired every other detective, but not Moreau. Chief Lannua had vetted and hired Moreau over Koa's objection. This skimpy personal file revealed that the process had been more than irregular; it had been downright weird. The letter from Mayor Satō sang Moreau's praises and practically ordered Chief Lannua to hire Moreau for the newly created position of deputy chief detective. Koa had seen Mayor Satō's predecessors promote favored candidates, but this letter went well beyond a simple recommendation.

The deputy mayor's certification was the strangest of all. In it, the deputy mayor certified that he had performed an independent background check on Moreau, finding no criminal history. It then directed that Moreau should be exempt from the mandatory back-ground and fingerprint checks applicable to all police department job applicants. Koa had never seen a document like it and couldn't imagine why Lannua would have agreed. Or maybe it wasn't so hard to figure out. At the time, Satō and Lannua had been in a knock-down fight over the police budget. Lannua had not won his bid for increased departmental funding, but he'd avoided the drastic cuts proposed by the mayor, who ran on a platform to defund the police. Maybe Moreau had been part of the bargain. With Lannua now dead, Koa would probably never know for sure.

Koa turned to the résumé. He had seen it when he'd first interviewed Moreau but now examined it skeptically in light of the other documents indicating that the police department had not conducted its mandatory background check. He skipped over Moreau's college education and early career to focus on the man's police experience as chief of detectives in Redwood City, California. This file copy of the résumé, apparently the one the Chief had used in vetting Moreau, bore handwritten notes in Lannua's distinctive handwriting. Moreau had listed Redwood City Police Chief Ralph Banks as a reference, and the chief had circled Banks's name and phone number. In the margin, Lannua, apparently after speaking with Banks, had written "top-notch officer," "knowledgeable," and "excellent community relations."

When Koa saw the words "excellent community relations," he knew Moreau had somehow rigged the favorable reference. The man he knew as Moreau did not have the temperament for good, let alone excellent, community relations. Koa grabbed his cell and dialed the number shown for Chief Banks. After a moment, he was surprised to hear a phone company not-in-service announcement. Strange. Although only a few months had passed, maybe Banks had retired or moved. Or maybe not. Koa checked the internet for the number of the Redwood City Police Department and dialed. A desk sergeant answered, "Redwood City Police." After identifying himself, Koa asked for Ralph Banks. There was a long pause before the cop informed Koa that the force had no officer named Ralph Banks.

"You're sure," Koa asked.

"Yes, sir. I checked our computer. There's been no officer by that name in the past ten years," the Redwood City officer responded.

Shocked by what he had learned, Koa realized that Moreau's whole résumé was likely phony. He called Piki and instructed him to fax the Federal Law Enforcement Training Center registrar for a copy of Moreau's transcript before adding, "While you're at it, get his transcript from UC Davis, as well."

Koa then checked the police fingerprints and DNA databases used to identify and eliminate trace evidence left by officers at crime scenes. Once again, he found an irregularity. Moreau had neither fingerprints nor DNA on file.

Now sure that something was seriously wrong, Koa called Georgina Pau and told her that Moreau did not have fingerprints or DNA on file.

"Tell me about it," she responded. "I've been after him for months."

"You mean he refused?" Koa asked.

"He hasn't exactly refused. He just never seems to have time. Keeps putting it off."

"Think you could get a set of his prints? Maybe from his office or his car." Koa asked, knowing it was a rhetorical question.

"On your authority, you bet."

"Do it and run the prints through the FBI database," Koa directed.

Koa had once heard that 85 percent of job applicants had lied or exaggerated their qualifications on résumés. Moreau would be an outlier even by that standard. And Moreau's failure to follow departmental policy requiring officers to submit fingerprints and DNA suggested a more ominous problem.

CHAPTER FIFTY-EIGHT

WEALTH PROVIDES ACCESS to privilege. That's true even at the ADMAX federal super-max prison in Florence, Colorado, known as the Alcatraz of the Rockies. The only super-max prison in the U.S., it houses roughly 400 prisoners. Its illustrious inmates include the World Trade Center bomber, the Shoe bomber, the Boston Marathon bomber, and several notorious Russian and Chinese spies. Most recently, it welcomed the Mexican drug lord El Chapo.

Built by the Federal Bureau of Prisons, ADMAX imposes such extreme isolation that inmates never see anything of the world outside, not even the great Rocky Mountains that loom just to the west. Prisoners spend twenty-three hours a day locked down in concrete cells, without cellphones and only minimal electronic entertainment. The Bureau of Prisons had even blocked the internet throughout the facility. Legal advocates for prisoners describe it as one of the most dehumanizing places on earth.

Pānaʻi had been in this surreal hi-tech dungeon for well more than two years, and he seethed with uncontrolled fury. He bridled at his confinement but also harbored an insidious secret. Those who'd prosecuted him had made a world-class blunder. He'd spent his entire professional life planning for the possibility that the law would catch up with him. Thus, he'd built and maintained an extensive network of allies, secret bank accounts, and other hidden assets, including whole businesses owned in nominee names through impenetrable mazes of shell companies registered in foreign jurisdictions. So intricate was his labyrinth of deceit that, in confiscating his assets, the feds had missed several of his carefully concealed offshore accounts and enterprises, leaving him with access to hundreds of millions of dollars. Nor had they rooted out the staunchest and most elusive of his helpers and allies.

Prisons were notorious for their corruption, a publicly acknowledged problem that the Federal Bureau of Prisons had attempted to avoid with special safeguards at their showcase ADMAX prison. Yet, Pāna'i's secret minions and enormous hidden wealth enabled him to arrange privileges even in the most secure facilities. State-of-the-art vetting and rotation of guards, massively intrusive surveillance, and CIA-type security checks were no match for the human greed fueled by Pāna'i's millions of dollars in bribes. His payroll included guards and administrators inside the prison walls and a battalion of minions outside.

Foremost among his special privileges were rudimentary cellphones with prepaid SIM cards and periods of unsupervised privacy to conduct his affairs. Phones and privacy allowed him to transfer funds from his secret offshore financial accounts, manage his bribes, and direct an extensive external criminal network.

As the sun set over the mountains to the west, a friendly guard, who now drove a brand-new Tesla, led Pāna'i down a hallway to a small room reserved for inmates to meet with their lawyers. Divided by a glass barrier typical of high-security prison visiting rooms, it was one of the few places in the entire complex devoid of surveillance monitors because the law forbade intrusions on attorney–client communications. Alone inside the room, Pāna'i conducted business free of constraints without risk of being overheard. He once figured that he'd paid half a million in bribes for every hour of this illicit privacy. He didn't care. Fancy cars and expensive jewelry were of no use to him in prison, but privacy to direct his criminal enterprise was precious.

He checked for voicemails using one of several burner phones at his disposal. Nothing from Kōkua, but there was one from his top operative in Hawai'i, a man who'd worked for Pāna'i years ago and escaped the fallout of the disaster that had landed Pāna'i in the ADMAX prison. This agent had remained in deep cover in the Aloha State. The man was to make contact only in the direst emergency, and the unexpected message surprised Pāna'i. With some trepidation, he pressed PLAY.

"They have deceived you. Ismael, Faisal, and 'Aukai are in police custody. Ikaika is free of the murder frame. The girlfriend, the lawyer, and the prosecutor all survived. Kōkua went rogue and killed the police chief. They have double-crossed you.

Loyal as ever, I await instructions."

Pāna'i exploded with rage, pounding his fist on the table until pain shot through his hand and up his arm. Kōkua had betrayed him. Only fear of drawing the attention of some incorruptible prison authority kept him from screaming at the top of his lungs.

He dialed and left a voicemail for Kōkua, which contained instructions and a threat. Switching to a different burner phone, he called his top spy in Hawai'i. His instructions were simple—wait a week and kill the deceivers.

CHAPTER FIFTY-NINE

GEORGINA AND PIKI appeared simultaneously in Koa's office, each excited and speaking over the other.

"Whoa. Slow down," Koa said. "Piki, you're first."

"Okay, boss," Piki, near breathless, replied. "I checked with the Federal Law Enforcement Training Center. They have no record of Moreau attending any course at any of their facilities. But that's not all," Piki added, his speech accelerating, "According to the registrar at UC Davis, Moreau never attended classes there either. His résumé is phony. We're talking made up like a fairy tale."

"That's not the half of it," Georgina interrupted. "Moreau isn't his real name. I got prints from his office and his car. Those prints match the single print on Hirako's locker. The man's name is Angelo Cruz."

"He's the officer who worked for USAID out of the U.S. Philippine embassy in 2005 and 2006," Piki interjected.

"Christ!" Koa roared. "He's got to be the one who hired the Abu Sayyaf hit men." He paused, thinking. "And, I'm betting that he found some clever way to access the chief's office during the birthday celebration. We've got to find him. See if he's in the building. Alert Makanui and the SWAT team. Put out an APB. Find the bastard before he kills someone else."

At that moment, Koa's cell rang.

"Hey, Koa, it's Zeke. We got the recording back from the experts in Honolulu. They identified the voice. It's—"

"Moreau," Koa interrupted, "except his real name is Cruz. He's the man with the Hilo burner giving orders to the Abu Sayyaf killers, and I'll lay you odds that he killed the chief, too."

"Jesus," Zeke said. "Where the hell is he now?"

"Don't know, but we'll soon have half the force looking for him."

* * *

Koa took command of the search from the department's emergency operations center. Reports filtered in over the next hour. Moreau, aka Cruz, wasn't in his office. The duty sergeant reported that he'd signed in earlier but had not signed out. A search of headquarters failed to locate Moreau anywhere on police department premises. Next came word that he had checked a police vehicle out of the motor pool. Koa cursed. Something had spooked Cruz, and now they had no clue to his whereabouts. Koa had the dispatcher alert officers all over the Island to look for Moreau and report the instant they spotted him or the police vehicle he had taken.

Koa asked Zeke to get a search warrant for Moreau's apartment and sent Piki to see what he could find. Piki discovered a laptop stashed in a hidden compartment at the back of a closet. On it, he found copies of materials identical to those found in Ismael's Alahaki Road hideout. Piki also found maps of the Punalu'u area and the Kaulana boat ramp. A check on Moreau's browsing history turned up multiple searches for private aircraft charter services.

"I think Moreau planned escape routes if he needed to get out in a hurry," Piki concluded, sharing what he'd learned with Koa.

"Agreed," Koa responded. "Get some officers out to the airports. Tell 'em to watch commercial and charter operators, especially the charter guys. And post guards at Punalu'u and Kaulana."

Koa wondered if Moreau knew the police were on to him. If so, he'd likely be on the run. He'd also be more dangerous. Both Piki and Georgina had been discreet in their inquiries and claimed not to have done anything to tip Moreau off. Still, his sudden disappearance from police headquarters and the suggestion that he might have chartered an airplane suggested that he knew Koa had unmasked him. Maybe Moreau had learned that Koa had requested his personnel file or seen one of the FBI faxes related to his fingerprints. There was no way for Koa to know.

At noon, Piki dashed into the command center. "Koa, Koa, you've got to hear this." He paused to catch his breath. "Remember, I told you the burner phones that Maroni bought had sequential numbers." Piki commandeered a computer terminal as he spoke and loaded a flash drive. "I told you I was going to put wiretaps on those phones?"

"Yes, I remember."

"Well," Piki went on excitedly, "one of the taps picked up a call—" Piki looked at his watch—"about ten minutes ago." He opened a file on the flash drive and hit the AUDIO PLAY icon.

They heard a phone ringing.

"*Kōkua here,*" Moreau, aka Cruz, stated, followed by a numeric code.

Then another voice blasted over the phone in harsh tones.

"*You've been lying to me. You lied about Makanui, Koa's brother, and Nālani. I know Ismael, Faisal, and 'Aukai are in police custody. You lied. And lied. Did you think I wouldn't discover the truth? You have one last chance. Kill that bastard Koa Kāne. Kill the bastard! Or my people will hunt you down and squash you like vermin. It's his life or yours, you lying son of a bitch.*"

Koa sat stunned as the recording ended. It wasn't the message. He'd faced dangerous criminals before. It was the voice! He knew that voice! *Kāwika Keahi*, his childhood friend, turned traitor and spy for the Chinese. The feds had supposedly taken the man's last penny and locked him away incommunicado for life. How could he be the force behind the attack on the Hilo police? The feds had said it was impossible, but there was no denying that voice. Koa had heard it a thousand times since childhood.

Koa didn't know how, but Keahi had outsmarted the feds. He must have concealed some of his offshore accounts. He might be in an airtight federal penitentiary, yet he'd somehow found a hole in the security. He'd directed a criminal network, hired Moreau, aka Cruz, bought the services of terrorist killers, and planned dastardly attacks aimed at Koa, the man he hated with untold venom, along with Koa's family, friends, and colleagues.

The intercepted message told Koa that Keahi's money and threats had their limits since he had not been able to control Moreau. Keahi, the traitor, had created Moreau, a traitor to his police colleagues. Moreau must have lied to Keahi about killing Makanui and the failure of other attacks. Somehow Keahi learned of Moreau's double-cross and had now threatened him. So much for loyalty among traitors. Killing Koa was now Moreau's only hope of survival.

Koa went cold, feeling a premonition so strong he could almost touch it. He saw Keahi in his mind as sharp as the day they'd last met. Keahi had poured out his bitter hatred of Koa. Koa heard the words again as if Keahi was there shouting in his ear. "*You were the glory boy . . . babe magnet . . . dating the hottest chick on the Island . . . and what did I have . . . I was a fucking lowlife aide . . . as common as stray cats.*" That jealousy might have left Keahi ripe for the blandishments of his Chinese spymasters, but it wasn't, Koa knew, the true source of the man's unbridled contempt for his former friend. No, that corrosive force came from the simple fact that Koa had ripped away Keahi's aura of success and put him in a cage for life.

Koa suddenly knew where Moreau, aka Kōkua, aka Cruz, was going and what he intended. He could only hope he wasn't too late.

CHAPTER SIXTY

KOA'S CELL RANG as he reached for it. Answering, he heard a woman's panicked voice. "Something weird just happened. A cop just barged in here looking for Nālani. We told him she wasn't here, but he got furious, demanding to know where she is. He threatened to kill us if we didn't tell him. After I did, he smashed our radio and rushed out of here. I tried to reach Nālani on her cell, but cell service is spotty, or maybe she's in the tube. Anyway, she's not answering."

Koa recognized the voice—one of Nālani's coworkers at the national park. Koa fought for control. Now more than ever, he needed to be clearheaded and in command. Nālani's life—and his own—were on the line. He had to outthink the most devious and ruthless killer he'd ever pursued. Taking a deep breath to steady his nerves, he asked, "Who?" seeking confirmation of what in his heart he already knew.

"A cop. Named Moreau."

"Where? Where is Nālani working today?" Koa demanded.

"Thurston Lava Tube. There's a big group visiting today."

Koa thought he understood. Moreau, aka Cruz, under orders to kill Koa, was going to kidnap Nālani to get at his ultimate target. Moreau needed Nālani to draw Koa into a death trap, and then he'd use Nālani as a hostage to shield him from the police while he escaped. With Koa dead, she would be Cruz's ticket out of Hawai'i. As long as he held her hostage, he could hold off an assault by the police. Given his inquiries about Punalu'u, Kaulana, and chartered flights, Cruz most likely planned to leave by boat or chartered aircraft, maybe even creating alternative escape routes. Then, after using Nālani to secure safe passage off the Island, he'd kill her.

Koa instructed the police dispatcher to flood the national park with police and requested that park rangers clear the tourists from the area around the Thurston Lava Tube as quickly as possible. He grabbed a protective vest and tactical gear, alerted Makanui to meet him, and ran for the police helicopter he had previously put on standby. Fifteen minutes later, he and Makanui, suited up in black body armor, were airborne heading south toward the national park. When they reached the park, Koa directed the pilot toward the Kīlauea Iki crater overlook and the Thurston Lava Tube.

*   *   *

Cruz drove his police cruiser from the park's visitor center around the curving Crater Rim Drive past the first Kīlauea Iki trailhead toward the parking area for the Thurston Lava Tube. The last message from Pāna'i should have panicked him, but Cruz was strangely calm, focused on what he had to do to save his skin. Every man had a vulnerability, a crack in his shell that Cruz could exploit. Nālani was Koa's weak spot. He'd give his life to save her. She would be the bait.

She had not been at park headquarters as he'd expected. Instead, she was working near where Cruz planned to kill Koa. That could work to his advantage, but only if he could find her in the mass of tourists that typically swarmed the major attraction. Cruz slowed as he passed the sign for the Thurston Lava Tube and entered the roadside parking area jammed with cars and tourist buses. Luckily, a car was just pulling out of one of the limited parking spaces. Cruz grabbed it, flipping on his emergency lights to scare off another driver aiming for the same spot.

Once out of the car, he spotted a park ranger in uniform. Forcing himself to smile, Cruz approached the man, flashed his police credentials, and politely asked, "I'm looking for Nālani, one of your park rangers. At park headquarters, they told me she'd be around here somewhere."

"Sure," the ranger responded, "she's just down the trail. You want me to radio her for you?"

"That would be great. Ask her to meet me here in the parking area. I'll just wait over by the entrance trail."

A long five minutes later, Nālani emerged from the forest path into the parking lot. Cruz waved to her, and she approached him with a questioning look, curious why he needed to speak with her. When she was close, he brought his hand up, holding a folded tourist map from which the barrel of his Glock protruded. "Do exactly as I say, and you'll live. Try anything foolish, and I'll kill you. Understand?"

Momentarily stunned, Nālani quickly recovered her composure and nodded her compliance.

"Now walk slowly back into the forest. I'll be right behind you with my gun pointed at your spine."

CHAPTER SIXTY-ONE

IN THE EARLY 1400s, Kīlauea began a historical eruption called the Ailā'au flow that lasted sixty years and covered more than 165 square miles. As the lava flowed north from near the Kīlauea crater, it coalesced into channels that became deeper until they crusted over. The lava, then underground where it retained its extraordinary heat, flowed north in subterranean tubes. When the eruption stopped, the molten lava drained away, leaving tunnels. One such conduit, the Kazumura cave, runs twenty-five miles. Another, shorter lava tube called *Nāhuku* in Hawaiian, or Thurston for the *haole* who allegedly "discovered" it in 1913, is one of the premier tourist attractions in Hawai'i Volcanoes National Park.

The Thurston Lava Tube, roughly 1,600 feet in length, is divided into two parts, separated by a ceiling collapse that allows access to either section. The first section, approximately 450 feet long, is the only part accessible to tourists. Visitors follow a short entrance path to the loop trail. They go counterclockwise around that loop through a magical rain forest and across a short bridge into the cavern of the Thurston Lava Tube. After walking through the first 450 feet of the cave, they climb a set of stairs to emerge through the collapsed ceiling and continue along the loop through the forest back to where they started.

The public part of the cavern varies in height and width but is large enough in places to hold an eighteen-wheeler. Long thin strands of *ʻōhiʻa* roots dangle from the ceiling, and white microbial matter clings to the walls in patches. Water typically forms puddles on the floor, and the cave walls glow in vivid yellows and oranges in the indirect lighting installed by the Park Service. Blocked off behind a chain-link gate, emblazoned with a "DO NOT ENTER" warning, the lava tube extends well beyond the stairs where tourists exit. Unlike its public counterpart, the off-limits section of the cavern has an uneven floor that makes for rough going in total darkness.

As the helicopter descended toward its landing, Koa took in the scene. Park rangers had not yet cleared the area of tourists. Cars jammed the small parking area, and a dozen tourist buses lined the roadside. Streams of people headed into the forest, while others emerged and wandered toward their cars or buses. As the pilot circled lower and those on the ground realized that the chopper intended to land, they began running in every direction. Slowly, the middle of the road cleared, and the pilot dropped gingerly toward the ground.

As they touched down, Koa spotted a lone police car—it had to be the one Moreau had taken from the motor pool—in the roadside parking area near the entrance walkway to the Thurston Lava Tube. A park police vehicle—most likely the one used by Nālani—was parked nearby. That's when he saw Moreau following Nālani with a folded map pointed at her back. They were at the beginning of the entrance trail leading toward the lava tube. She appeared to be unharmed in the brief look Koa had before Moreau pushed her up the walkway, and trees blocked Koa's view.

"He's taking her into the rain forest and maybe into the tube," Makanui said into her communications headset. "What's he going to do?"

"This is where he plans to kill me," Koa responded. "He'll make me come to him to save Nālani, and after he kills me, he'll use her as a hostage to make his escape."

"Shit," Makanui exclaimed. "This is going to be a nightmare with all these tourists."

She was right, Koa thought, but the crush of people would present problems for Moreau, too. In a crowd, he'd have trouble watching his back, increasing the likelihood that an officer could surprise him. It seemed an odd choice for Moreau to make. Why, Koa asked himself, would Moreau take such a risk?

As they prepared to exit the chopper, Koa itemized the equipment they would need if Moreau took Nālani into the tube. Given the dim lighting in the cavern and the possibility that Moreau would disable what little light there was, they needed emergency lights and, if everything went dark, night vision goggles. He started to alert Makanui, but she was a step ahead of him, adding a rifle from the equipment locker in the chopper to what she fished out of her tactical gear.

They ran for the trailhead, pushing past the throng of tourists. At the tee junction, where the entrance trail went to the right and the exit trail returned from the left, Koa shouted into the crowd of tourists, "The cop with the woman. Which way did they go?"

Someone pointed toward the exit trail, while another park visitor yelled, "They went the wrong way."

In a flash, Koa understood. Moreau wasn't heading for the tourist attraction but instead toward the off-limits area of the cavern. He'd use Nālani to lure Koa into the darkness and keep her close as a shield while he shot Koa. Moreau had devised a simple but effective plan, and with Nālani in danger, Koa had little choice but to play his game.

Koa and Makanui raced down the exit trail toward the steps at the end of the public attraction. When they reached the chain-link gate that cordoned off the non-public part of the tube, they saw that

Moreau had broken the lock, leaving the gate open. Koa had guessed right about Moreau's intentions.

Koa knew the odds favored Moreau, and he had only one chance to save Nālani and himself. But he also had something Moreau didn't, something that might help him take Moreau by surprise. He had Nālani. She was a fully trained federal law enforcement officer, and given previous threats, they had worked out a series of code words to trigger various escape and evasion tactics.

Koa whispered instructions to Makanui. They agreed, and he said, "Don't focus on me. I can take care of myself. Your priority is to save Nālani."

"Wait," Makanui whispered as Koa started forward. Squatting, she scooped a handful of black mud from one of the puddles and smeared it on her face, avoiding her eyes. When she stood, she was black as coal from head to toe—black hair, face, body armor, slacks, and shoes. "Okay, let's do it," she said.

The two of them moved silently into the off-limits cave. Koa kept his thumb on the switch of a super bright emergency light, now in the off mode, but pointed straight forward. Makanui followed close behind him, so close she might have been his shadow. Step-by-step, they moved forward, waiting for Moreau to challenge Koa. They were twenty-five feet inside the cave in near-total darkness when Moreau pointed a light at Koa, who instantly flicked on the emergency light, flooding the cavern with 100,000 lumens aimed straight at Moreau.

While the blinding light obscured Moreau's vision, Makanui darted quickly to the side of the cave and flattened herself on the floor with her rifle aimed at Moreau. She became virtually invisible in her black body armor and clothing, with her face blackened. Koa saw Moreau holding Nālani in front of him with a Glock pistol pointed at her head. His eyes locked on Koa, but he gave no sign that he was aware of Makanui's presence.

"Kill that fucking light," Moreau roared.

Koa obliged, snapping the light off, dropping it, and raising his hands in a gesture of surrender. That left only Moreau's light, fastened to a hard hat, pointed directly at Koa, as the only illumination in the otherwise dark space. Still, reflecting off white microbial matter clinging to the walls, it gave off enough light for Koa to see that Moreau had his left arm around Nālani's neck with the Glock in his right hand, its barrel pressed against her temple. Despite her predicament, she appeared calm and in control of herself. Even though he was looking for a sign, Koa almost missed Nālani's blinking in the dim light. She blinked three times in rapid succession to let Koa know she'd be alert to his signals.

"It's over, Cruz," Koa said in a firm and steady voice.

The man flinched at the use of his real name. He hadn't expected Koa to know.

"We know Keahi is calling the shots," Koa continued, "from his max lockup. The feds have his phones and are wise to his secret accounts. They're tracing his payments and are freezing your accounts if they haven't done so already."

"That's bullshit!" Cruz screamed.

Koa fixed his gaze on the gun pointed at Nālani's head as he responded. He was betting that Cruz wouldn't shoot Nālani because he needed her alive as a shield to escape. Only when Cruz moved the weapon to aim at him would Koa need to act. In the meantime, Koa wanted to keep him talking in the slim hope he could de-escalate the situation. "Then, how do I know Keahi's name and the numerical code you use to identify yourself." Koa recited the code.

"How could you know that?" Cruz demanded.

"Your burner phone. We have a wiretap on your burner phone, one of those you stole from Hirako's locker."

The gun remained pressed against Nālani's head, so Koa continued, "How'd you hook up with Keahi? Was it while you were both working on Capitol Hill?"

Cruz nodded, and Koa thought he heard a faint yes. The tiny verbal response was a step in the right direction. His only hope for a nonviolent endgame required him to get the man talking. "You were with the U.S. embassy in the Philippines and involved in the 2006 MILF peace negotiations. Keahi sent you back there to contact old Abu Sayyaf acquaintances, to offer them guns and money in exchange for assassins, and to tell them where they could find Makanui."

"You think you're so smart," Cruz replied. "Keahi told me you were an arrogant bastard. Except now I've got the gun, and you've got your hands in the air. You're not so fucking smart, are you?"

In other circumstances, Koa would have smiled at Cruz's need to be superior. Instead, he asked another question. "Why, Cruz? Why go on this rampage against the police? Was it just money?"

Cruz snorted. "Just money. Yeah, it was just money. More money than you can imagine. More money than I can spend in a lifetime."

Cruz continued to press the barrel of his gun against Nālani's head, and Koa strived to keep him talking for as long as possible.

"How'd you get Abu Sayyaf to send Ismael, Faisal, and Muhammad Khalili's bombs?"

Again, Cruz seemed surprised at the extent of Koa's knowledge. "Guns and money," Cruz responded. "The Philippine military beat the shit out of that group. They were desperate for guns and money. You can buy a whole terrorist army for ten million dollars and a few crates of surplus weapons. And Faisal, he'd have come for nothing. He's dreamed of killing Makanui ever since she killed his brother. Where is that bitch, anyway? You should have brought her along so I could have finished what Faisal started."

Koa resisted the temptation to look to his left, where Makanui lay concealed on the floor. "And 'Aukai?" Koa asked. "How'd you loop him into Keahi's private war?"

"Keahi knew him from his time years ago in Hawai'i."

Keep him talking. Keep him talking. Koa recited the mantra in his head. "Chief Lannua. That wasn't part of Keahi's plan, was it? So why kill the chief?"

Cruz let out a short, humorless laugh. "It wasn't supposed to end in this godforsaken lava tube. A few days hence I'd have poisoned you like Putin does to his adversaries, and you'd have left this world in agonizing pain. With the chief dead, yours truly would have investigated your death and ruled it a heart attack. There'd have been no one left to investigate me or Satō."

Cruz's gun began to waver. Koa couldn't tell whether Cruz was tiring or getting ready to turn the weapon on Koa. "Put the gun down, Cruz. It's time to end this."

"You're right," Cruz said. "It is time to end this." Slowly, Cruz began to turn the gun toward Koa.

"BASTARD!" Koa screamed, emphasizing the code word he and Nālani had practiced many times.

Everything then happened with blinding speed. Nālani kicked Cruz's shin with bone-shattering force. Reacting reflexively, he released her neck, and she dropped to the cave floor. He tried to bring his gun to bear on Koa, but he was too slow. Makanui illuminated the laser sight on her rifle, confirmed the red dot on the bridge of Cruz's nose, and squeezed the trigger. The cave exploded with the roar of the gunshot, and the sound reverberated off the cave walls. Makanui's bullet hit its mark and exited through the back of Cruz's skull, leaving a golf-ball-sized hole and splattering Cruz's brains into the lava tube behind him. His gun and hard hat went flying, plunging the cave into blackness.

Koa shook his head to clear the ringing in his ears. From the timbre of the shot, he knew that Makanui had fired her rifle but had no idea of the result until she switched on her flashlight. Heaving a sigh of relief, Koa rushed forward to bring Nālani to her feet and into a tight embrace.

CHAPTER SIXTY-TWO

KOA HAD DECEIVED Cruz. Having prioritized Nālani's safety over everything else, he hadn't informed the feds that Keahi had outfoxed them. Despite their assurances to the contrary, Keahi had managed to conceal enormous wealth. Locked up in the super-max prison in Florence, Colorado, he had found ways to communicate with the outside world, move money, and direct his associates' criminal affairs.

It was time for Koa to alert his federal friends and put a stop to Keahi's nefarious activities. Koa once again called Rachael Goodling in the Division of National Security in the Department of Justice. "Twice in two weeks. This is getting to be a regular thing," Rachael said after he identified himself.

"And you're not going to like what I have to say," Koa said.

"Okay," she responded cautiously. "Surprise me."

"You didn't finish your job with Kāwika Keahi. You left him with untold millions in secret offshore accounts, which he used to pay a bunch of terrorists to kill me, my girlfriend, and several others in law enforcement here on the Big Island. He even tried to frame my brother for murder and caused the assassination of Police Chief Lannua."

"That's impossible," Rachael responded vehemently. "Keahi's in the most secure prison in the world with absolutely no access to outside communications."

"I think you'd better listen to this wiretap recording of a call made yesterday to a burner phone in Hawai'i." Koa then played the recording to a profoundly shocked Goodling.

"Recognize the voice?"

"Shit!" she exclaimed. "Tell me what's going on."

Koa gave her a more complete rundown, including the murders of 'Olina Crow, Officer Hilia, his teenage prisoner, and Chief Lannua. "There is a ton of evidence you're going to want to sort through, including contacts and money payments to an Abu Sayyaf terrorist cell in the Philippines. I think you or one of your people should come out here for a thorough briefing. You also need to find out what's going on at that fancy super-max prison."

* * *

Two days later, Nālani, Makanui, and Koa met for dinner at Café Pesto on Hilo's main drag. Nālani and Koa raised their glasses to toast and thank Makanui. "I'm never going to feel the same about that lava tube," Nālani said. "I'm afraid it has lost its magic, but I suppose that's a small price to pay to be done with this whole Keahi nightmare."

"It's not over," Koa said, causing both women to stare at him in surprise.

"What's not over about it?" Makanui asked.

"How did Keahi learn that his boy Cruz had lied?" Koa asked.

Koa watched the light dawn in Nālani's eyes. "Somebody . . . somebody here in Hawai'i must have told him."

"Exactly," Koa agreed, "and that means that Keahi had another set of eyes here."

"Who?" Nālani asked.

"Mayor Satō?" Makanui suggested.

"That was my first thought," Koa replied, "but the pieces don't fit. Satō sponsored Cruz and tried to make him chief of police. Why would he rat on his own guy?" Koa paused for a sip of wine before continuing. "Satō's dirty, but in a different way. I'm guessing Keahi was the kingmaker in Satō's election. He needed a way to get Cruz into the police department, and he knew he couldn't bribe Lannua. So, he gave Satō a lot of money to buy the last mayoral election. Satō won and then put Cruz in the police department."

"I see where you're going." Makanui picked up the thread. "Then Satō and Cruz decided they could outsmart Keahi by lying to him. They must have thought he wouldn't find out. They figured they'd install Cruz as police chief. That would stop the police from investigating Satō's illegal campaign tactics and give him an additional way to extort campaign contributions and pressure people into voting for him."

"Only Keahi had a spy who ratted on the pair of them," Nālani completed the picture.

"Right," Koa agreed. "It's the only way all the pieces fit."

"But who's the spy?" Nālani asked

"Honestly, I have no idea," Koa conceded. "But there's someone else involved whom we haven't yet identified."

They had finished dinner and were enjoying dessert when Koa's cell rang. He answered to hear the police dispatcher report that a car bomb had just killed Mayor Satō.

"Oh my God," Nālani gasped when Koa shared the news.

"Wow," Makanui exclaimed. "But it does confirm Koa's theory. Keahi's got another disciple here on the Big Island."

* * *

Two weeks later, Koa met Rachael Goodling in Florence, Colorado, where they had breakfast together. The DOJ national security lawyer was just as formidable as she'd been when she and Koa had first pursued Keahi. Over coffee at a small café, Goodling handed Koa a short transcript. "We got this off the voicemail on one of Keahi's phones when we shut down his prison scam. Thought you ought to see it."

The transcript read:

"They have deceived you. Ismael, Faisal, and 'Aukai are in police custody. Ikaika is free of the murder frame. The girlfriend, the lawyer, and the prosecutor survived. Kōkua went rogue and killed the police chief. They double-crossed you.

Loyal as ever, I await instructions."

Koa read it three times, focusing on the word "they," which appeared twice. In the context of everything he'd learned, "they" could only mean Cruz and Satō. Looking up, he asked Goodling, "Who left this message?"

"It must have been someone in Hawai'i, but we have no idea who. The call came from a burner and bounced through a dozen foreign proxy servers. We have no way to trace it."

Koa nodded. The transcript confirmed his suspicions. "Whoever it is killed Mayor Satō."

*   *   *

Later that morning, Goodling and Koa entered the federal super-max facility. A guard escorted them to an interview area, divided in half by a counter and an impenetrable glass wall. Kāwika Keahi sat inside that barricade while Koa and Goodling stared at him through the glass. He looked older than Koa remembered, with thinning hair turning gray. Koa supposed that isolation in a cell for twenty-three hours a day would do that to a man.

Despite having two visitors, Keahi's gaze fixed only on Koa. His expression appeared devilishly cool yet somehow radiated maniacal hatred for his boyhood friend. Koa picked up the handset that would allow them to communicate, and Keahi did likewise. Both remained silent for a long pause before Koa spoke, their eyes locked each to the other. "You sent Cruz to kill Nālani—to kill me—and others. Thank the gods, you failed. Others, though, weren't so lucky—'Olina Crow, Officer Hali'a, Chief Lannua, and Mayor Satō—they're all dead. And for what? You're never getting out of here. The feds have indicted you for 'Olina's murder and a dozen other crimes. And that's not all. They're going for the death penalty, and I'll be there every step of the way, cheering them on."

Koa started to replace the handset on its hook, but Keahi's voice gave him pause.

"You'll never be rid of me, Koa. I'll haunt you and Nālani 'til they put you in the ground."

Koa showed no outward reaction, but Keahi's words still chilled him. He wanted to brush them off as demented but idle threats. Yet, he knew better than to be dismissive of anyone so malevolent and resourceful. Certainly not with Mayor Satō's killer still loyal to Keahi and at large on the Big Island. Unwilling to show his nemesis even a hint of fear, Koa replaced the receiver in its cradle and rose, turning his back to the traitor. As he and Goodling made their way to the door, muted sounds emanated from the other side of the glass partition. Though muffled, Keahi's screams were still intelligible. "Watch your back, Koa. And Nālani's, too."

AUTHOR'S NOTE

The great English writer Samuel Johnson said, "Revenge is an act of passion; vengeance of justice. Injuries are revenged; crimes are avenged." In *Retribution*, continuing the saga of the conflict between two men who were once childhood friends, Keahi, driven by jealousy and his own inadequacies, seeks revenge. Koa responds by seeking vengeance for Keahi's crimes.

The difference between revenge and vengeance has never been more vital than in our country today. We have devolved into a state where even minor events of ordinary life—a perceived slight, a declined credit card, the discourtesy of another driver—can provoke disproportionate, even lethal, revenge. In a country with nearly 400 million guns in private hands and more than 45,000 annual gun deaths, lethal acts of revenge have become a daily occurrence.

We would do well to remember the words of Marcus Aurelius, the Roman emperor who said, "The best revenge is to be unlike him who performed the injury."

BOOK CLUB
DISCUSSION QUESTIONS

1. Describe the cross currents in Koa's life and how they have shaped his personal life. His career?

2. How does Koa navigate between the *haole* and the native Hawaiian worlds?

3. Where do you think Koa draws the line between right and wrong? Legally? Morally? Does that make him a better . . . or a flawed detective?

4. Koa has a "bonded" relationship with Zeke Brown. Upon what foundation do you think that relationship is built?

5. Why is the rate of poverty and incarceration for native Hawaiians higher than that of the *haole* population? Did you find that surprising? Disturbing?

6. If you have read earlier Koa Kāne novels, particularly *Death of a Messenger*, the first of the series, do you think Koa has changed?

7. Do you think Koa and Nālani will ever marry? Have children and start a family?

8. Will Koa ever confide his dark secret to Nālani?

9. Do you think Koa has a political future on the Big Island or the state of Hawai'i?

PUBLISHER'S NOTE

We trust that you enjoyed *Retribution*, the fifth in the Koa Kāne Hawaiian Mystery Series. While the other four novels stand on their own and can be read in any order, the publication sequence is as follows:

Death of a Messenger (Book 1)

A ritual, sadistic murder on the Army's live-fire training ground throws Hilo, Hawai'i's, Detective Koa Kāne into the throes of the Big Island's cultural conflicts.

"This book's vivid, thrilling conclusion is both unique and atmospheric in a whodunit featuring a resilient sleuth successfully defending his native tropical paradise."   —*Kirkus Reviews*

Off the Grid (Book 2)

A scrap of cloth fluttering in the wind leads Hilo Police Chief Detective Koa Kāne to the tortured remains of an unfortunate soul left to burn in the path of an advancing lava flow.

"Readers who crave watching a smart cop work in a crackerjack police procedural will find a beauty here. Want a good espionage adventure? It's here, too, with intrigue, betrayal, assassination."

—*Booklist* (Starred Review)

Fire and Vengeance (Book 3)

Never has Koa's motivation been greater than when he learns that an elementary school was placed atop a volcanic vent, which has now exploded.

"Moves with volcanic force to a heartfelt, gripping conclusion."

—Rick Mofina, *USA Today* best-selling author

Treachery Times Two (Book 4)

Secret military weapons, saboteurs, a volcanic eruption—and a probe of Chief Detective Koa Kāne's criminal past.

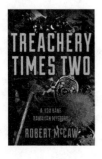

"McCaw ably blends police procedural, espionage thriller, and guilt-ridden personal saga. Readers will look forward to Koa's further adventures."

—*Publishers Weekly*

If you liked *Retribution*, we would be very appreciative if you would consider leaving a review. As you probably already know, book reviews are important to authors and they are very grateful when a reader makes the special effort to write a review, however brief.

We hope that you will read the entire Koa Kāne Hawaiian Mystery Series and will look forward to more to come.

For more information, please visit the author's website:
www.robertbmccaw.com

Happy Reading,
Oceanview Publishing
Your Home for Mystery, Thriller, and Suspense